A Channel of Your Peace

a Novel

Veronica Smallhorn

Full Quiver Publishing
Pakenham, ON

A Channel of Your Peace
Copyright 2020 Veronica Smallhorn

Published by
Full Quiver Publishing
PO Box 244
Pakenham, Ontario K0A 2X0
www.fullquiverpublishing.com

ISBN Number: 978-1-987970-14-2
Printed and bound in the USA
Cover design: James Hrkach
Cover photo: Veronica Smallhorn
Cover model: MarioGuti iStock

NATIONAL LIBRARY OF CANADA
CATALOGUING IN PUBLICATION

Published by FQ Publishing
A Division of Innate Productions

Note: Spellings are British as this novel takes place in Australia.

*For Our Lord and God Jesus Christ, truly present
in all the tabernacles of the world. May the whole world
burn with love for You!*

*For my parents Ron and Barbara Smallhorn, whose
faithfulness to the Church's teachings on marriage and
family are my first and best example.*

*And for my dear family, my husband Pablo Jiménez
Lobeira, and our wonderful children Daniel, Benjamin
and Gabriela, whose love inspires me each day to live out
God's call to know, love and serve Him — through you.*

Chapter 1

Erin Rafferty sat in her pew about a third of the way down the church, watching the nuptials unfolding before her. Without realising she was doing so, she sat up straighter and leaned forward a little. A smile began forming on her face. They were coming to her favourite part.

"Bianca, take this ring as a sign of my love and fidelity." The beaming groom grinned in a joyful but appropriately subdued manner as he placed the ring on his bride's finger.

He looks so happy, thought Erin. *Make sure you're watching, Gareth.* She stole a sideways glance at her fiancé to gauge his reaction. He was yawning and studying his fingernails. Erin shook her head.

"Ryan, take this ring as a sign of my love and fidelity." The petite bride, a friend of Erin's since high school, returned the gesture, smiling up at her new spouse.

Erin grinned from ear to ear, blinking back a few tears. She and Gareth had been to four or five weddings in the last year or so, but this bit got her every time. Somehow, she found this exchange of rings to be particularly stirring. Why was that? Perhaps it was that Bianca and Ryan were clearly such a wonderful match. The beautiful exchange momentarily removed her annoyance about being in a church, let alone the Catholic church she found herself in. What were they thinking? Most of their other friends had gotten married in vineyards or public gardens.

She drew in a deep breath and allowed herself to phase out a little as one of Ryan's groomsmen approached the ambo to read the Prayers of the Faithful. Fiddling with her bracelet, her eye caught the solitaire diamond ring on her own finger. Gareth had chosen it for her when they had become engaged five years ago. She recalled now, with some discomfort, that Bianca and Ryan didn't know each other back then. Now here they were at their wedding day.

Erin tried to shrug off the thought. *There's no rule saying you need to be married to be happy in a relationship*, she reassured herself. *So many marriages don't even last as long as we've been together*. Then she cringed. How many more times did she need to tell herself that? More and more frequently since the "wedding avalanche" started.

Stop it, Erin. Since when did others' happiness upset her? She knew her life was fantastic — terrific job, great friends and a gorgeous fiancé. And having lived together since their engagement, they were basically married, right? Erin forced herself back into the moment, reaching out for Gareth's hand. He took her hand, turning to give her a quick smile. She smiled back and squeezed his fingers.

After the signing of the register, the organ struck up and the bridal party began processing down the aisle. Erin stood, smoothing out her new blue cocktail dress and followed Gareth and the other guests out of the church. She stepped out into the lovely April afternoon. Early autumn was a beautiful time of year in Canberra. With the heat of summer now over, the golden sunlight still provided a good deal of warmth, while the intense colour of the leaves of claret ashes and red oaks began falling, carpeting the paved footpaths next to where they grew.

She breathed in the cool, fresh air and watched as the bridal party and families assembled for photos. At that moment, she heard a voice behind her and felt a finger in her side.

"Hey, missy, where've you been?"

She turned to find a very short woman with long, blonde hair, lugging a pregnant stomach around in front of her. The woman — Bianca's cousin, Joanna — grinned up at her. The last time she had seen Jo was at her wedding about six months earlier.

"Jo!" Erin cried out, reaching forward to give her a hug. "What do you mean where have I been? Where have *you* been? I didn't realise you were pregnant!" She placed her hand gingerly on her friend's enlarged tummy.

"I've been lying low," Joanna said. "I had complications the first three months. I'm five and a half months now, even though I must appear further along 'cause I'm such a shorty. We weren't planning on having a baby this soon, but we're both thrilled anyway." She stroked her tummy gently. "I'm much better now, so I was well enough to make Bianca's wedding."

Just then, Joanna's husband, John, a man a good eight inches taller than Joanna, sidled up to her and put his arm around her shoulder.

"Everything all right, Jo? Do you need to sit down?" he said, beginning to fuss over her.

"I'm fine; I was just saying hello to Erin," she said, tilting her head in Erin's direction and raising her eyebrows in disapproval.

"Sorry, Erin," he said, seeming to relax somewhat. "Nice to see you. How are you?"

"It's totally fine, Johnno," Erin replied. "I'm fine, thanks, and congratulations. How exciting for you both."

"Thank you. She's been doing a wonderful job with this baby," he said, looking tenderly down at his wife.

Erin regarded them, observing something in them, something that eluded her. That irritating sensation crept up on her again. A feeling of — what was it? *That's it — being left behind.*

"Hey, where's Gareth?" John asked, interrupting her thoughts. Erin looked around.

"He was with me a moment ago." She spied him on the steps of the church laughing with a group of their male friends. John turned and spotted them.

"Think I'll go over and say hello. I'll leave you ladies to

chat, if you're okay," he said, peering again at Joanna.

"Yes, I'm fine. I'm not made of glass," Jo laughed as she shooed John towards his friends.

Erin turned her attention back to Joanna. "So what complications are you suffering, if you don't mind my asking?"

"No, of course I don't mind," Joanna said, placing a hand at the base of her back and rubbing it. "Hyperemesis gravidarum."

Erin raised an eyebrow. "Hyper what?" she asked, wondering what torments it involved.

Joanna laughed. "Vomiting — extreme vomiting. Worse than normal for the first trimester. I got so dehydrated at one point they hospitalised me. It didn't affect the baby, though, which was what worried us most."

A pang of guilt rose up inside Erin. They had always been friends — she, Jo and Bianca. It occurred to her that perhaps she'd been avoiding her married friends, or those whose marriages were approaching.

Seeming to pick up on Erin's thoughts, Joanna spoke up. "So, you must be pretty busy. How's the copywriting job going at — where is it you're working again?"

"Roland's Advertising. Fine. Yes, it has been busy." This was true. She had been working late many nights to meet deadlines and keep up her chances for promotion at the boutique agency. "But not so busy that I couldn't have called you sometime over the last six months, though. It hasn't been so easy for you to stay in touch, but I don't have an excuse."

Joanna laughed off Erin's concern. "Nah, once I'd have been upset with you, but impending motherhood seems to be mellowing me out!"

"Wow, I can't believe it. You're going to be a beautiful mum." Erin swallowed. "Makes me kind of wish Gareth would..." she let her words trail off. Horrified, a lump began forming at the back of her throat, and tears began to sting behind her eyes. Couldn't she leave off being so daft for one afternoon? But there was little hiding from it, especially at a wedding. She was aching to be married herself. To begin that "next phase" everyone else was starting.

Joanna regarded her, without judgement or condescension, seeming to understand.

"Then tell him to get a move on — add a wedding band to that beautiful engagement ring," she said, winking. "In all seriousness, why don't you talk to Gareth about this? You can't always expect the guys to clue in."

"Yeah, but I'm not sure what to do to make things uncomfortable enough for him to change." Erin sighed. "I keep telling myself not to worry, but everyone getting married is highlighting what I *don't* have, rather than what I *do* have."

"Well, you won't lose anything by talking to him. What sort of a relationship are you in if he's not willing to listen and take on board something as serious as this? It's important to you, so it should be important to him. Just say something to him, hon. I promise you, you won't be sorry you did."

A warm rush flooded Erin's heart, and she smiled at Jo, grateful her friend had seen her and sought her out. "Thanks, Jo," she said. "I think I will." She turned in the direction of the bridal party, seeing Bianca and Ryan standing for a photo with the young priest from the wedding.

"Shouldn't you be heading over there for family photos?"

"Yes, I should or I'm going to miss out." Joanna wrapped her shawl around herself then pointed. "See the priest? He's Father Nicholas Bentley, Ryan's cousin."

"Oh, so that would explain why they got married in a church." Erin spoke before she could catch herself, remembering Joanna and John also had a church wedding. She thought about Bianca. *A priest in the family?*

How weird.

"Bianca and Ryan have been attending Mass together, actually — Father Nick prepared them for their wedding."

Erin's mouth dropped open. "Really?" She wouldn't have picked it. Bianca had hardly been in a church since their school days.

"Well, life's full of surprises," Joanna said, pointing at her stomach. "Not all of them bad!"

"No, I suppose not. Are you going to the reception?"

"Maybe not, we might head off home soon," Jo said, as she started heading towards John. "Stay in touch, though, okay? Keep me posted."

"I will." Erin waved as her friend took John's hand and led him over to the photographer. The young priest, complete with Roman collar, stepped away from the bridal party and began walking back in Erin's direction towards the church. He gave her a cordial smile and nod as he passed. Erin scrunched her face into something approximating a smile, convinced it didn't come off well. Her contact with priests in recent years was limited to the odd wedding and baptism, and all the priests she knew growing up were decades older than her. Strange, encountering a priest who was around her age.

Well, Bianca and Ryan could do the holy thing if they wanted, but she certainly didn't plan on going back inside a church anytime soon.

*****

Later in the evening, after the wedding reception, Erin climbed into the driver's seat of Gareth's Mazda, having assumed the role of designated driver after Gareth had more to drink than she was comfortable with. She started the engine and drove out of the hotel carpark. Gareth leaned over and switched on the radio.

She glanced at him as he began humming along with the song playing and reached for the volume button. "Mind if I turn that down a bit?"

"Yeah, no problem," Gareth said without looking at her. Erin adjusted the sound and put her hand back on the steering wheel.

Erin thought back over the evening. The reception had been fun; Ryan and Bianca had put on a wonderful party. The band was amazing, and Erin enjoyed dancing. Gareth seemed to enjoy himself too, though he'd spent much of the night talking with the guys, her friends' husbands and fiancés mostly. They sat in silence for a few minutes as she drove on to the main drag and picked up speed.

Talk to him. Joanna had encouraged her to talk. It was a short drive home but there were a few quiet minutes to talk. Perhaps now was the right time to bring up the issue of his inability to commit to a stable future. After a couple of minutes Erin spoke up.

"Gareth, I'm wondering," she said, making an effort to sound relaxed and laissez-faire. "How would you feel about setting a date for our wedding sometime soon?"

Despite the darkness in the car, the light from the dashboard showed Gareth scrunch up his handsome face ever so slightly and furrow his brow. "What's brought this on? Not all these weddings we've been going to?"

Erin's chest tightened a little, and she began to feel defensive. She was hoping his first response to her suggestion would be a little less...detached. "Maybe a bit, but we've been engaged for five years. We've been together for seven. If we're committed to staying with each other, why not seal it forever by getting married?"

"What's the rush, Erin?" he asked. "We're still young."

Rush? Five years is a rush? "Yes, but we're not getting younger. I'm almost twenty-seven. Yes, we have a lovely life together. But we still don't own a home, and we've never even mentioned having kids. How long do you want to put all this off? Marriage is a normal thing to want, Gareth. People get married all the time, but we never seem to get around to discussing it."

"I hear you. But I don't think it's such a priority now. How would we fit a wedding in at the moment with our work schedules? We agreed buying a home would be best when we've saved a large enough deposit for the kind of house we want. It would be crazy to consider kids until we've got a home to accommodate them." He paused as she eased off the accelerator to negotiate a turn. "Besides, we don't need to be married to enjoy the benefits. Is your Catholic upbringing suddenly getting to you?"

What? Erin froze for a moment, not knowing how to respond. Was that all he was getting out of their relationship?

"Gareth, some things are more important than money — and, and — planning. It doesn't take months of planning or millions of dollars to get married. Plenty of busy people find time to marry the one they love." Indignation rose in her and she grew flustered. "And you know that I don't see marriage as a way to legitimise sex!"

"Sorry, I didn't mean that." He turned and smiled at her. "I think it might be smarter for us to put it off a little longer. But I promise we should talk about it again sometime soon. Sound okay?"

That was it? It was like he didn't care at all about her opinion. She thought back to the hours earlier, remembering the expressions on Ryan's and John's faces as they regarded their wives.

"Gareth, this is so important to me. I don't want to go on like this forever."

"We won't," Gareth responded with a decisive tone. "But I don't think I can handle it now. Please give me a little more time."

With that, the conversation appeared over. Erin sat in silence, taking a moment to look out the side window as she drove over Commonwealth Avenue Bridge towards their inner-south home. The down lights from the National Library reflected off Lake Burley Griffin and shimmered on the dark, still water. *What more can I do?* She couldn't force him to marry her.

Minutes later she pulled into the driveway of their modern apartment and tapped a remote-control button in the console to open the garage door. She drove in and turned off the engine. A restlessness settled deep in Erin's heart.

"Gareth," she said, turning to look at him. "Do you love me?"

"What sort of a question is that?" he chided. "Come on, let's go inside."

Chapter 2

Erin couldn't sleep. She turned over in her bed and glanced at her bedside clock. 1.38 am. Sighing, she got out of bed, grabbed her dressing gown and tiptoed out of the bedroom, pulling the door shut behind her with a gentle click.

When they arrived home from the wedding earlier, she had felt tired and discouraged at Gareth's lack of enthusiasm for marrying her. But it astounded her the way his mood altered the second she got into bed. Crazily, she had gone along with it. Afterwards, she'd felt furious with herself and not a little used. Perhaps it was a lapse in her judgement; he deserved the same rejection he'd given her that night — not her open arms. But presented with the chance to be close to him, to feel his arms around her right when he was being so distant...well, at least he got what he wanted. And now that he was snoring like a pneumatic drill, she found it impossible to drop off to sleep.

Erin went downstairs to the kitchen. She took a wine glass from the cabinet, opened the fridge and poured herself a glass of white wine from a half-finished bottle sitting in the door. Glass in hand, she padded over to the window in the living room and pulled back the curtains to look into the shared courtyard in their apartment block. The immaculately pruned bushes and trees cast dark shadows over the paving stones. All was still. She listened closely for a moment for any noise outside. There was no sound, not even a solitary car arriving home late from a party or night out. No distractions. Nothing to shield her from her own introspection.

Taking a sip from her glass, she thought back to the brief conversation with Gareth in the car and his comment about her Catholic background. Her initial reaction was to dismiss it all as rubbish. But on reflection, she began wondering if he had a point.

She had long prided herself on being free of the shackles of her childhood faith but was now struggling to explain to herself why marriage was suddenly so important to her. Yes, having friends who were getting married had something to do with it. But that alone couldn't explain this new longing to belong to someone — to Gareth — *properly*. Did that mean they didn't belong to one another now? She'd always believed they did. The thought that she might be wrong now unnerved her.

Perhaps the desire for more was a simple matter of conditioning. She thought about her own parents' devotion to each other throughout their near forty-year marriage. *No one can ever completely let go of the way they were brought up*, she reasoned. And now that she was staring her late twenties in the face, she was longing for the same thing — the security that made her feel protected while she was growing up.

But surely it had to be possible to possess that security without marriage. Erin closed her eyes and searched her heart. *No.* The answer came back with a startling clarity. No, she didn't believe that anymore. Marriage vows weren't only a nice touch at a wedding ceremony. They changed people. Not their personalities, or even the way they behaved towards each other. But the change was still there, a transformation that wasn't so much material as much as it was....spiritual?

Good grief, what am I turning into? Erin gave spiritual things about as much thought as she did flying backwards to the moon. But there wasn't much hiding from the reality — she had seen it in Ryan and Bianca, and in John and Joanna. She needed, like them, to speak the words, and to hear them spoken back to her. She thought about her elder sister Katrina's wedding some years before. She remembered that Katrina and her husband Emilio had prepared thoroughly before their wedding, and years later they still seemed very happy together. Perhaps that was something the Catholic Church got right. Perhaps a church wedding wouldn't be such a bad idea.

Woah, wait up, girl. I'm getting ahead of myself. Gareth told me only hours ago that he's not ready for a change, at least not yet. Can't get married all by myself, now, can I? Another disconcerting thought rose up inside her. What if he was never ready? He asked her for more time, but what if no time was ever enough for him? He hadn't exactly been in a hurry to end their engagement so far.

Erin sighed. One thing was clear to her. Their current situation couldn't go on for much longer. Something had to change. She just needed to find a way to change it.

She stood some time longer by the window, staring out into the shadowy night until her eyes became heavy. Letting the curtains fall back, she took her wine glass half-finished back to the kitchen and headed back upstairs to hers and Gareth's bedroom. Entering the dark room, she took off her dressing gown and climbed back into bed, peering over at Gareth. The red glow of his clock radio provided too little light to see but as her eyes adjusted, she began to make him out in the dark. He was asleep, lying on his back with his arm up over his head on the pillow, his breathing deep and slow.

A pang gripped at her heart. All of a sudden, it felt as though they were intruding on each other. Invading each other's space in a way neither of them was entitled to. Such a strange feeling, after spending so much time living together in the same house, sleeping together in the same bed. She turned her back to him and moved right over to her own side of the bed, putting as much space as possible between them.

Yes, now was the time to act. She needed to convince him that this was the right way to move forward;

demonstrate to him how important this was to her. Practising Catholics weren't the only ones who could get married. She would think of some way to deal with this. With that resolve, she allowed herself to drift off to sleep.

*****

The following Monday morning, Erin was standing in front of the full-length mirror in her room, getting ready for the day ahead. It was early, and Gareth had left for work before her. Left before she had woken up, to be precise. She glanced down at the message on her phone that he sent her an hour earlier.

Sorry to dash so early, got some stuff in the office this morning that I need to work on before hours. Left some coffee in the pot for you. C u tonight.

Erin furrowed her eyebrows as she reached over to the bed for her handbag and slipped the phone inside. Turning back to the mirror, she reflected on the weekend. They'd barely seen each other on Sunday — Gareth had played tennis first thing in the morning while she'd slept in. They did have a little time together for a quick lunch, but then he'd left again to go to work. The hours he was keeping lately were crazy — worse than hers and she'd been working a lot too.

Or perhaps he's trying to avoid me because I'm making him feel uncomfortable. Well, he was doing a stellar job, if that were the case.

Erin brushed back her long, light brown hair and clipped it back at her neck. She sized up her outfit in the mirror. Grey pencil skirt and white, cap sleeve blouse. Yes, very corporate. If she wanted to take a step up at work, then it didn't hurt to look the part. The communications manager position had recently opened up, and she had applied. The job would mean more responsibility and less of the writing she enjoyed, but she thought she was ready for the challenge. Plus, if she got it, the job would give her a better salary. *And if my job is more lucrative, maybe that'll help Gareth feel more secure about our future.* She stepped into a pair of black high heel shoes, grabbed her bag and a black jacket and headed downstairs towards her car.

Fifteen minutes later she swung into the carpark of the neat, two-storey building where she worked. She jumped out of her Honda, beeped it locked with the remote and hurried towards the ground-floor office. Passing through the foyer, she pushed open the doors to the comfortable suite of offices to discover her close friend and colleague, Ingrid, standing behind the reception desk hanging up the phone. Ingrid was the agency's head graphic designer, a tall, attractive woman with short, dark hair and dark eyes, about five years older than Erin.

She glanced up and smiled as Erin walked in. "Morning, Erin. You're looking smart today," she said, tucking her bob behind her ear.

"Thanks, Ingrid," Erin said, warmed by the compliment. "You too — nice dress," admiring Ingrid's navy-blue shift dress, which showed off her elegant figure. Erin placed her bag up on the desk as Ingrid grabbed a pen and began scratching something on to a Post-It. "What are you doing out here? Did they demote you to reception?"

"Yep. Don't you think I'd look great on the front desk?" Ingrid said with a silly grin on her face. "Truly, though, I'm thinking answering phones might be preferable to the day's agenda. Phone conference with head office and then client meetings. And somehow they expect us to do some work in amongst all that." She handed Erin the Post-It. "Message for you, actually. Beth's not in yet." Beth was the agency's slightly vague, though well-intentioned receptionist.

"Well, Beth won't be in for a while yet — thanks," Erin said as she took the note from Ingrid. *Message for Erin, Please call Joanna Chapman.* Jo? She wondered what her pregnant friend who had been ill with extreme morning sickness could possibly be calling her about at 8.00 am. Perhaps she was ringing to arrange to catch up after the wedding. Still, it was awfully early.

There was no number with the message. Erin folded the note and slipped it in her diary, certain that she had Jo's number stored in her phone. She would have to look it up later. Ingrid was right. They had a heck of a day ahead.

"So, how was your friend's wedding on Saturday?" Ingrid asked as she began making her way to their cubicles at the back of the office.

Erin grabbed her bag and followed her. "Lovely; it was beautiful. They had a wonderful reception." Erin didn't offer any more information, the whole event being a sharp reminder of her own inadequacy. Reaching her cubicle she plopped down in her chair and leaned over to switch on her computer.

"Do you want to go out and grab a sandwich at lunch?" Ingrid asked, as she sat down at the neighbouring workstation.

"Yeah, okay. That is, if we have time to go to lunch today."

"Let's make sure of it," Ingrid said. "The weather's gorgeous. I'm not staying locked up in here on a day like this."

Erin murmured her agreement as she focused on her screen, opening up the text for a radio ad she'd been working on. As she reached over to grab the creative brief from her in tray, her eye fell on a photo of Gareth pinned to a corkboard on the wall of her cubicle. She'd taken it at a beach on the south coast last Christmas when they were on holiday together. He was smiling broadly in the photo, looking handsome with his sandy-coloured hair and blue eyes, dressed for summer in board shorts and a tee shirt.

He was certainly being infuriating, but studying a picture of him so happy, she didn't blame herself for falling for him all those years ago. Why was he so reluctant to commit himself to her? Turning back to her screen, she began working and tried to ignore the sense of unrest that was growing in her heart.

*****

The morning passed in a flurry of writing, meetings, two cups of coffee that went cold and countless interruptions. At 12.30 pm, Ingrid looked over at Erin and tapped her watch.

"Come on, Erin, let's go. I'm starving, and I'm going to go cross-eyed if I have to stare at this screen for one minute longer."

Erin laughed and grabbed her wallet from her bag. "Yes, let's escape before anyone notices!"

The two women wandered out of the office past Beth at reception. Beth, who was answering a phone call, smiled at them as they passed, and they stepped out of the building into the mellow autumn sunshine. A ten-minute walk brought them to a popular café that attracted most of its business from government and business staffers in the surrounding office buildings. With the lunch-time rush already underway, they waited a few minutes before buying sandwiches and drinks over the counter and then sat down together at one of the café's outdoor tables.

"So, tell me more about your friend's wedding," Ingrid said, taking a sip from her bottled water. "Did you take any photos?"

"Yes, I did," Erin replied, opening her orange juice. "I took some at the reception." She pulled out her phone and brought up the photos with a few taps, handing the phone to Ingrid and leaving her to scroll through them.

Ingrid spent a minute flicking through the photos, ooh-ing and ah-ing over Bianca's dress, the flowers and the bridesmaids.

Erin didn't respond.

"Is everything all right?" Ingrid asked, handing the phone back. "You're a bit quiet today."

Erin cringed as she realised how transparent she must be. Still, she and Ingrid had worked alongside each other and been friends for years. It wasn't surprising that she noticed something was up.

"Nothing," Erin said, shrugging. "I'm a little over the whole wedding thing, I suppose. I've been to so many in the last few months. Seems everyone's getting married except —" she paused, wishing she could keep her mouth shut.

"Except you?"

Ouch. It sounded so much worse when someone said it out loud. Frustrated, Erin let out a sigh and slumped back in her chair. She glanced down at her hand and touched her engagement ring with her right index finger.

"Yes! Except me. I don't know what I'm doing wrong. I even asked Gareth if we could think about setting a date, and he stonewalled me."

Ingrid rested back in her seat and regarded Erin for a second. "I've been wondering when this might start bothering you. Always the bridesmaid, never the bride and all that." She picked up her chicken salad wrap and peeled back the paper.

Erin wanted to point out that she hadn't been a bridesmaid at Bianca's wedding but decided to stay quiet.

"You know, I think there's a fairly simple solution to this," Ingrid said, then took a bite and began chewing slowly.

Erin jerked her head up. "Yeah? What sort of a solution?"

A group of young women wandered into the café's garden, sitting at a table close to theirs. She wondered how well the girls would be able to hear their conversation from where they were sitting. Erin leaned over the table, waiting patiently for Ingrid to swallow.

"Is there any chance you might tell me your suggestion sometime before the bell rings?"

"Sorry, I'm enjoying watching you squirm a little." Ingrid grinned and leaned in. "It's simple. Have you considered living apart until he decides to set a date?"

"What do you mean?"

"I mean, removing all the benefits until he decides to commit," Ingrid said.

It took a moment for Ingrid's meaning to dawn on Erin. "You mean no sex until we get married?"

"Woah, you're quick on the uptake," Ingrid said, her dark-brown eyes widening in mock awe. "That's right. Living apart, with no overnight visits, or separate rooms at the very least, until he bites the bullet. That should give him something to go on with." Ingrid took another bite of her sandwich.

Erin sat back and let the idea sink in. She thought back to Gareth's careless comment about her Catholic guilt in the car after the wedding, his desire for her the moment she got into bed and how used she'd felt afterwards. Why on earth would a guy like Gareth, or any other man like him for that matter, be motivated to get married when they thought they were basically married already?

She wondered now why she hadn't thought about this before. Perhaps in her resolve to shun the dictates of her upbringing she wasn't considering how it might be working against her.

A flutter of excitement began to rise up inside her. "Not a bad idea, Ingrid. How'd you come up with it? Is that how you got Jim to marry you?" Erin smiled as she peeled back the paper on her own sandwich.

Ingrid laughed. "No, but a friend of my sister's did the same thing with her husband years ago, and it worked a charm. I think they're still married." Her brow furrowed as though trying to recall.

Erin ignored the last part of what Ingrid said and went on. "Well, if it could galvanise him into action, it might well be worth it." There was little doubt it was quite drastic, but she needed something drastic to jolt him out of his coma. Surely, if she put this to Gareth, he would understand how important this was to her. Yes, it would show him how much she valued him and their relationship, that she would be willing to put herself through such an upheaval to cement their future. This was definitely the way forward.

Erin suddenly felt hungry and bit into her smoked salmon sandwich, enjoying the flavours, the feel of the warm sunshine on her hair and this new sense of freedom Ingrid's suggestion had given her.

"Do you think that would work?" Erin said, not needing an answer to the question and grabbed by an enthusiasm she hadn't felt in ages.

"Well, it'd certainly set the proverbial cat amongst the pigeons. Bit of a shake-up is just what the poor bloke needs." Ingrid sipped from her water. "What do you think you'll do about it?"

Erin thought for a moment. "I suppose I should be the one to put my money where my mouth is. And I don't think moving to the spare room would be the best solution. I guess I should move out for a little while."

"Maybe you could stay with your mum and dad for a while. Get married from the family home...how traditional!"

"Ha ha, you're so hilarious," Erin said. "It's easy for you to make fun, perfect husband, perfect marriage, perfect *everything.*"

Ingrid's face fell.

Erin bit her lip, wishing she could take back the last part of what she said. There was no doubt Ingrid had a wonderful marriage. Whenever Erin saw Ingrid and Jim together — like when he came to pick her up from work last Friday — it was clear that he still worshipped the ground she walked on, even after ten years of marriage.

But Erin knew things weren't perfect for them. They had

been trying for about six years to have a baby with no success, and Ingrid had tried everything from acupuncture to IVF. Over the last year or so, Ingrid seemed to have reached a quiet resignation towards her infertility, but Erin knew it was a deep wound that Ingrid had no choice but to carry round inside her.

"Sorry, that kind of slipped out. Not terribly subtle, am I?"

"No, but I wouldn't have you any other way," Ingrid said. "So, you think this is the right move for you and Gareth?"

"Yes, absolutely. I feel like we're in limbo. The time has come to commit for real or not at all."

"You're not worried he'll say no?"

Erin was momentarily jolted out of her comfort zone. Would he? Surely not. Not after all this time together. They were engaged to be married, not engaged to be....*engaged.* "No," she said after only a brief pause. "We've been together for so long. We belong together, and he knows that as well as I do."

"Well, then I guess your next step is to call your mum."

Erin winced. "Yeah, I guess it is," she said, wondering how her parents would react. Devout Catholics, neither of them had been thrilled when Erin had moved in with Gareth. Since then her relationship with them had been a little strained, at best. It wasn't her parents' fault, but Erin believed she had the right to live with whomever she chose, even if it was her boyfriend, and they didn't approve. She tried to think of somewhere else she might be able to stay, but there wasn't anyone else she would feel comfortable living with, even if it were only temporary. And it might help to repair what was damaged in her relationship with her mother and father.

Erin tried to quell a mild surge of anxiety and glanced down at her watch. "Maybe I'll even give Mum a call before we go back for the afternoon."

"My, you are keen. Looks like this is happening. In which

case I want gold edging on my wedding invitation."

Erin laughed. "Nah, it'll have to be silver, to match the white gold of my engagement ring," she said, holding her hand up and watching her diamond dance in flashes of light and colour as its facets caught the early afternoon sunlight.

The two women continued chatting as they finished their lunch and then made the short stroll back to their office. As they arrived at the entrance of the building, Erin stopped and pulled her mobile phone out of her handbag.

"I'll be in in a few minutes," she said to Ingrid, squinting down at her screen while she tried shading it with her hand.

"Yep. Good luck," Ingrid said as she pushed open the wide front doors and disappeared inside.

Erin wandered round to the side of the building where there was a small covered porch that was often used by the smokers in the building for their cigarette breaks. Finding it unoccupied, she pulled up her parents' landline number on her screen and pressed dial. After three rings, Judith Rafferty answered.

"Hello?" her mother's familiar and sweet-sounding voice came over the line. The anxiety that began creeping up on Erin earlier turned up a notch as she tried to formulate a way to explain things to her mother.

"Hi, Mum, it's me. How are you?"

"Erin! I'm fine thanks, darling. How are you?"

"I'm okay, thanks." Erin paused for a moment, wondering how to proceed. "How's Dad?"

"He's fine. He's out the back at the moment, nailing down some loose boards on the deck. Is everything okay? You don't usually call in the middle of the day like this. Are you all right?" Judith asked, with what Erin recognised as concern in her voice.

"Everything's fine. I'm about to go back to work after my lunch hour, but I wanted to talk to you about something."

"Yes, of course. What is it?"

"I was wondering," Erin sucked in a short breath. "How would you feel about me moving home for a little while?"

Judith paused for a brief moment before answering. "What's brought this on?" she asked. "Is everything going all right with Gareth?"

"Yes. Well, no. Not really, Mum, but not in the way you might think." *I'm not making any sense at all.* Erin's grip on the phone tightened. She'd been so adamant about doing things her own way when she moved in with Gareth. What was her mother going to think now?

She swallowed and went on. "Gareth and I want to set a date for our wedding. Well, *I* want to set a date. Gareth is being kind of resistant. I suppose he's comfortable with things the way they are. Anyway, I'm thinking that if he and I could agree on a date, then we could live separately before getting married so, you know...he doesn't end up backing out."

Listening to herself, Erin wondered how she could sound any more pathetic. What kind of desperado was she, blackmailing a man into marrying her? Was she doing that? Well, no, he was the one who had proposed. Five years ago. What if she'd insisted on getting married before moving in together back then? Like her mother had encouraged her?

If she'd ever paved the way for an epic "I told you so," then this was it. She closed her eyes and scrunched up her face in disbelief at herself, waiting for her mother to respond.

"I see. Have you spoken to Gareth about this yet?"

"No, not yet. I'm planning to soon, but I wanted to have a better idea of what to tell him. To have a plan in place." Erin's throat tightened and she tried to swallow a lump that was starting to form. "I'm tired of everything the way it is, Mum. Things aren't going anywhere." She suppressed a little sob as a sudden wave of sorrow washed through her and the realisation of how much time she had wasted began to dawn on her.

"There, there. Don't worry." Her mother's soothing tone sounded through the phone into her ear. "I'm happy that you don't want to live in a de facto relationship anymore. Of course, you can come home for a while. You can come home for as long as you like."

"Thank you, Mum, I appreciate it. So much." Erin exhaled in relief. She might have realised her mother wouldn't be judgmental or condescending.

"I'm wondering, though. Would you still like to come home if Gareth doesn't want to set a wedding date? If he decides he doesn't want to marry you now, what will you do?"

Hearing that question for the second time in an hour, Erin sensed the foundations of her well-constructed wall of defence beginning to shake.

"If I didn't think this...course of action was going to help move things along, I wouldn't be taking it."

"I know. But I can see how important this is to you. I don't want to see you compromise what you want, and I think you need to consider how to move forward if Gareth tells you he's not ready to get married soon."

Erin didn't think it was a good idea to mention that Gareth had *already* told her he wasn't ready to marry her anytime soon.

"Look, I'm not worried about that, really. I just think the time has come to move forward and that once I make it clear to him what I want, he won't have a problem."

Judith let out a concerned sigh. "Well, you're a grown woman, and I'm sure you can deal with this. Whatever happens, you know your father and I are here for you."

A sweet relief that her mother hadn't pushed her flooded through her heart. "Thank you again, Mum." She glanced at her watch. "I need to go back to work now. I'll be in touch again soon, okay?"

"All right. Take care. I love you."

"Love you too. Bye." Erin pressed the end call button and dropped her phone back in her bag. There. All she needed now was to talk to Gareth. *Which would be another thing entirely.*

Erin strode back towards the front of the building. All in a moment, she remembered Joanna. She stopped and fumbled around in her bag for her phone again. There wasn't time to call. A text would have to do. She found Jo's number in her phone and quickly typed.

Sorry I missed your call this morning, Jo, haven't had a chance to call back, things are crazy. Will try calling you tonight. Great to see you on the weekend. Take care. Erin.

Still wondering what Jo had called about, she hit send and began refocusing her mind on the work she'd left an hour ago. She would just have to find out from Jo later.

Chapter 3

Later that evening, Erin turned the key in the front door of her apartment. Darkness greeted her as the door swung open, telling her immediately that Gareth wasn't home yet. Relieved, she stepped inside and closed the door behind her, reaching to turn on the lamp in the entry so Gareth wouldn't arrive home in the dark.

She left her bag and keys on the small, glass-topped table in the entry and went straight to the kitchen carrying the bag of groceries she had picked up on her way home. If she got to work straight away, dinner would be ready when he arrived home.

Erin switched on the soft recessed lights over the kitchen bench and the lamps in the adjoining dining area. Placing her phone on the bench, she switched on their Bluetooth speaker, selected her favourite playlist and began unpacking her shopping bag.

The best way to try to revisit the subject of a wedding date with Gareth would be with a home-cooked meal, she had decided earlier that day. Like most Aussie blokes, Gareth loved his steak, and it was a good pick for a weekday dinner as it didn't require too much preparation.

After quickly making a coriander salsa and putting some mini corn cobs on to boil, she dropped a knob of butter into a hot frypan and waited for it to melt. When it was melted enough, she placed two beef eye fillets in, ground some pepper and Cajun spice over them and began thinking back over the afternoon.

Work had been crazy all day, but her boss had contacted her about the communications manager position and set a date for a formal interview for the following week. There was only one other person in the agency applying for the job, someone with far less experience. The likelihood of her getting the job was strong, and the thought of the higher pay along with more respect and responsibility excited her. She'd sent a quick text to Gareth straight away to let him know but received no response from him about the job. Just a short reply telling her he'd be home before 7.00 pm.

At that moment, her phone sounded the familiar text message noise, and she leaped over to grab it, wondering if Gareth was going to be late. Tapping the screen, she read the sender's name: Joanna. She smiled to herself as she opened the message.

Sorry, Jo is no longer on this number.

"Oh, for heaven's sake," Erin said aloud in exasperation. So Jo was on a different number now. That would explain why she had called Erin's office instead of her mobile; if Jo's phone had been lost or stolen, she might have lost all her contacts as well as her number.

At least the person who now owned Jo's old number sent a message to tell her so. *Thanks.* She tapped a quick reply and pressed send. Sighing, Erin put the phone down on the bench again. She picked up the tongs resting next to the hot plate and turned the fillets. Perhaps a call to one of their mutual friends later would help her reach Jo.

Fifteen minutes later, Erin turned down the heat on the steaks and sat down at the dining table, casting an eye over the hurriedly set table. Wine glasses next to her good plates and cutlery, tea lights flickering in frosted glass candle holders and a bottle of merlot in the centre. The ticking clock on the wall drowned out the soft ballad playing on low volume, and her eyes turned towards the time. 6.45 pm. How much later was he going to be?

Just as she began berating herself for cooking the meat too early, she heard the lock in the front door click and Gareth enter the apartment. Her heart gave such a colossal thump, she thought it might jump right out of her chest.

Get a grip, Erin. It's Gareth, not the Boston Strangler. She drew in a deep breath in an effort to calm herself down, but there was little doubt this evening together was going to mark a change in their relationship. *Am I ready for this? Do I know what I'm trying to do here? And what do I do if he insists he won't get married, like Ingrid and Mum warned me?*

Well, no time for worrying about all that now. She was going to do this. The front door clicked shut, and she heard Gareth place his keys on the entry table. She quickly ran her little finger over her lips to smooth out her lip gloss, then reached behind her neck and removed her barrette, taking a second to smooth down her long, thick hair.

"Erin, you home?" he said, appearing in the doorway from around the corner.

Erin attempted her most winning smile at him from across the dining table. "Hey, love, how are you?" she said, getting up and crossing the floor to greet him. "This is the first time we've seen each other all day. I missed you today."

As she closed the space between them, she was immediately struck by how tired he appeared to be. His eyes were drawn and slightly bloodshot as though he hadn't slept the night before.

"Are you okay? You seem exhausted. What sort of a day did you have?" She reached out and put her arms around him, hugging him gently and kissing his cheek as she did so. He responded by putting his hand on her shoulder and pulling away sooner than she wanted.

"Yeah, work was full on. Plus, I didn't sleep much last night."

"I thought so. I haven't seen you this tired in a long time." Erin gestured to his seat at the table. "Why don't you sit down and have a glass of wine and relax? Dinner's good as ready."

Gareth appeared agitated as he eyed the table setting.

"What's all this?" he said, rubbing his right arm as he moved away from her and perched on the edge of one of the chairs at the table. "You don't usually do this for dinner on a weekday."

Erin sized up her fiancé, wondering how she should proceed. Clearly, he was exhausted, but he appeared nervous, something she found strange.

"Well, actually there's something I want to talk to you about," she said, reaching for the bottle of wine on the table. "Thought this might be a good setting for it." She unscrewed the bottle top and filled his glass halfway, handing it to him with a smile.

Gareth returned the gesture with a weak smile and accepted the glass, holding it for only a second before placing it back on the table.

"So, tell me about your day," Erin said as she picked up the plates from the table and stepped over into the kitchen to serve dinner. "I didn't hear from you much. Things must have been crazy."

"Yeah, it was. Just the usual," he said as he began fingering the stem of his wine glass. He took a deep breath. "I got a call from John Chapman today."

"Did you? That's funny, because Joanna has been trying to reach me today as well. She called me at the office before I arrived this morning. I've been trying to reach her on her mobile, but she's not on that number anymore." Erin finished serving each plate and carried them over to the table. As she placed Gareth's plate in front of him, she noticed with alarm that his face had turned white and his fist was gripping his wine glass stem with such ferocity she wondered if he might break it.

"Are you all right, Gareth?" she said, leaning over and placing her hand on his forehead. "Your face has lost all its colour. Do you feel sick?"

Gareth took her hand from his forehead and stared at her.

As Erin peered back, she noticed there was an oddness in his gaze, as though he was far removed from her and the world they had built together. Little darts of worry began to pierce her heart as she struggled to understand what was wrong with him.

"Erin..."

At that moment her phone began to ring. "Oh, you've got to be kidding me!" she said, getting up and reaching for her phone on the edge of the bench. "Don't worry, I won't answer it. I don't recognise the caller, but it's probably Jo calling from her new number. I'll ring her back later," she said, hitting the decline button.

"Erin, I know what Jo is calling about," Gareth said, regarding her with a tortured expression, like someone about to deliver devastating news.

Fear entered Erin's heart. Later, when she thought back on that moment, she likened it to the feeling one might have on waking up, relieved, from a bad dream, only to realise the nightmare was, in fact, true and whatever horror haunted you in your sleep was still there, waiting when you opened your eyes. Confusion, coupled with a sense she was losing control of the evening, began to overwhelm her. Placing the phone down, she grabbed the end of the bench.

"Gareth, what are you talking about? What's wrong?" she said, searching his face for some explanation, some confirmation that everything was all right and that she had no reason to be anxious.

Gareth paused for what seemed like forever. Erin held on to the bench, trying to second-guess what he was about to say.

"I'm involved with someone else."

Time stood still, and Gareth's words didn't penetrate straight away. She stared at him for a moment, stunned, and clutched the bench tighter.

"What?" Her voice came out at the end of her breath and

sounded weak and foreign to her.

"I'm sorry. I owe you an explanation. Nothing is coming out the way it should, the way I'd planned it in my head." Gareth got up from the table and paced over to the window on the other side of the room before turning around and facing her again.

"John called me today. On the weekend at the wedding he overheard me — talking — with some of the other guys. I ignored a call from him last night, but he called me again today. He must have told Jo as well."

Erin's heart began pounding, and her chest began to tighten. Her breathing became shallow as she struggled to comprehend what she was hearing.

"You were talking behind my back? With our friends, at Bianca's wedding, about some other woman?"

"Erin," Gareth said again, his eyes imploring with her. "I hate to break it to you like this. I've been trying to figure out what to say. John told me that if I didn't tell you straight away, he and Jo were going to."

Erin's head started pounding in unison with her heart, and the room began to spin. She stumbled to the table and sat down on one of the chairs. She eyed Gareth's glass for only a second before picking it up and gulping half of it down.

"Who? How long?" she said, placing the glass down as a sob began to make its way up from deep in her gut.

Gareth cast his eyes downward. "Michelle. From my division. About two months ago."

Erin had met Michelle at Gareth's work Christmas party last year. An attractive, leggy, twenty-two-year-old blonde whom Erin dismissed at the time as nothing more than a bimbo with an accounting degree.

"And did you...have you...." she didn't allow herself to finish the sentence, trying to suppress a wave of nausea that began to rise up from inside her, like an oncoming tsunami after an earthquake. *Please, no....*

Gareth paused an agonising second before he answered. "Yes," he said, his face resolute.

Erin put her hand to her mouth and bolted to the kitchen sink, retching. The red wine she drank a moment earlier spilled out. She retched again, but her empty stomach produced nothing other than bile.

"Oh my God!" she cried, leaning over the sink.

Gareth rushed to the kitchen and grabbed a glass from the cabinet, pouring some water from the tap and handing it to her. She took the glass from him and swallowed the water down. Her stomach again began resisting any substance entering it and came close to rejecting the water. Refusing to give in to her own body assaulting her from inside, she supported herself by leaning on the edge of the sink, drew in several deep breaths and tried to clear her mind.

"Did you see her yesterday, when you went into work?" she cried, her voice coming in jagged rasps.

Gareth's eyes seemed to plead with her not to ask him. "Yes."

Erin stood straighter. "So on Saturday night when I asked you if you wanted to set a wedding date, and you had an opportunity to tell me you'd been cheating on me, you chose to tell me you'd discuss the wedding with me later?"

"No, I didn't mean to —"

"And then when we got home and you had *another* opportunity to tell me, to say nothing of the countless opportunities you've had in the last two months, you instead decided to have sex with me in an effort to...what, exactly? What kind of sick individual who's supposed to be in a stable relationship has sex with two different women in one weekend, Gareth?" The words spilled out in a big jumble, mixed in with sobs that racked her entire body. "Who, Gareth? Who?" she screamed, her own voice no longer recognisable to her.

"I know," Gareth said, stepping towards her as though

wanting to console her, but unwilling to touch her to do so. "It was a terrible thing to do to you. I guess it was the grog at the wedding and our history and...this thing with Michelle...isn't something I had a whole lot of control over. It just sort of *happened*."

Erin wiped at her mouth with the back of her hand. "Liar. These things don't just *happen*. You *let* it happen!"

"I thought it was something I could manage to tell you. I wanted to level with you, I really did. And it didn't go over the line until...recently. I know it was the wrong thing to do, to keep it from you and not tell you the truth sooner. It's been getting to me more and more. I could barely sleep last night."

Erin tried to straighten herself and faced him. "And so, what are you telling me now? Is all this something you regret and want to end, or do you want to...to...." Again, unable to complete her sentence she peered into Gareth's face, searching for some sort of answer.

"I want to be with Michelle. I'm so sorry."

Erin stared into Gareth's eyes, dismayed by the strong and quiet resolve she saw in them. In spite of the havoc the disbelief was wreaking on her senses, a startling clarity began to open up in her mind. This was it. The answer to her ultimatum, and she didn't even get a chance to tell him. In only a few moments, her life, the better part of her adulthood, all she loved and longed for, gone.

An invisible fist, cold and hard, uncurled its icy fingers and reached inside her chest wrapping itself around her heart. The hope for the future that filled her only moments ago evaporated, leaving a horrible, painful emptiness in its place. Tears filled her eyes and began to course down her face.

"What about our life together, Gareth? We've been together for so many years! We're engaged to be married! How could you have done this? I thought you loved me! I thought you loved *me*!" She slumped again on the edge of sink, this time seeing over the bench to their dining room, her intimate dinner going cold on the table.

"I'm so sorry to do this to you. But...I think this has been coming for a while now. We've been together so long we got into a rut. I think things got to a point where we didn't realise that we'd grown apart, that we're not suited to each other anymore. Can you honestly tell me you were happy with our relationship the way it was?"

Hearing him speak about their life together in the past tense tore at her heart. She turned her head to meet his gaze and stared at him through her tears. "Yes, Gareth. I'm happy with you. I've never looked at anyone else. Not since the first day I met you."

You stupid girl. Here he was telling her he didn't love her anymore. Putting off their marriage, using her, and all the while waiting for someone better to come along. How could she not have noticed? Why hadn't she seen this coming?

"Gareth, how could you? I feel like such an idiot!"

"Erin, please, let me—" Gareth said as he stepped towards her.

Not giving him the chance to finish his sentence, she pushed past him and raced up the stairs to their bedroom. Earlier in the day she began preparing herself to leave Gareth temporarily in an attempt to hang onto her future with him. Now, only one, solitary thought prevailed in her mind. *Get out. Get out of here as fast as you can.*

She pushed open the bedroom door, almost falling headfirst into the room as she did. She flung open the wardrobe, retrieved her overnight bag and began filling it, weeping as she randomly stuffed in clothing and toiletries. When she was done, she yanked the zipper closed and stumbled past her dresser, taking a fleeting glance at a framed photo sitting next to her cosmetics mirror. It was a selfie shot of the two of them she'd taken on the balcony in the apartment shortly after they got engaged. She stopped and picked up the frame, staring down at their joyful faces through her tears, Gareth's arm wrapped around her, holding her close. They'd been so happy that day.

In an instant, a vision of Gareth holding Michelle came crashing into her mind, and her voice broke with a fresh sob. She turned and hurled the photo across the room. It hit Gareth's bedside table, chipping the polished timber surface and cracking the glass in the frame before it landed with a thump on the floor by his side of the bed. She strode out of the room without looking back.

After storming down the stairs, she barrelled through the kitchen past Gareth, who was still standing there.

"Please, Erin, you don't have to leave," he said. "I'll....I'll go. You shouldn't have to leave. Please, I feel so terrible about doing this to you."

"Well, maybe you should have thought about that before you did it, Gareth," Erin said, snatching her phone from the bench. She strode into the entry, grabbed her bag and keys and reached for the front door.

Gareth followed her, grabbing her arm as he did.

"You never told me what you wanted to talk to me about."

Erin stopped and turned to face him, shaking her arm free of his grasp. *What?* Didn't he have the decency to let her go with dignity? What further humiliation could he possibly cause her? Hot fury fired up in her veins. Fury at him for making such a fool of her. Fury at herself for *allowing* him to fool her so.

Raising her hand, she let it fly and struck him hard in the face.

He stumbled backwards, shock evident on his face.

"I wanted to tell you that from now on, I'm *never* allowing you to take me for an idiot again. *Ever.*" With that she turned on her heel and walked out the door, slamming it shut behind her.

Chapter 4

Thunder rumbled ahead of Erin in the east as she sped down Wentworth Avenue, doing her level best to avoid breaking the speed limit. The sobbing that racked her body minutes earlier subsided, but her breath kept coming out in shaky gasps.

Droplets of water began appearing on the windscreen as she turned onto Canberra Avenue, a light sprinkling to start, then heavier, forcing her to turn on the windscreen wipers. Back and forth, back and forth the wipers swished, sweeping the rain away, keeping the road ahead visible, seeming to speak to her as they wiped the glass. Back, forth. *Gareth doesn't love you.* Back, forth. *Gareth doesn't love you.*

What happened just now? Erin's mind raced as the rain began hammering down on the car, trying to make sense of her exchange with Gareth moments ago. It *didn't* make sense. She and Gareth were happy together. They loved each other. Hadn't he told her he loved her? Told her so often, every day for years...well, no, maybe not lately. The two of them had been so busy lately; some days they barely spoke. When was the last time Gareth said he loved her?

The wiper action became mesmerising as she struggled to remember the last time they had spent time talking together, closely. How long ago did he say he'd been seeing that...that tramp? Two months? Was that how long it had been since they'd really talked to each other? No, it must be longer. How did this happen? Did that brat seduce him or was he so bored he was just waiting for an opportunity to get out? And why, oh why, did she not suspect anything?

A voice that Erin couldn't hear with her ears suddenly

cut into her thoughts. *Slow down, now*. Unaware her concentration had slipped, she refocused her gaze on the road, only to find herself approaching a red light at a horrifying speed. A bolt of sheer terror shot up her spine, paralysing a scream that tried to form in the back of her throat. Time stood still as she slammed on the brakes, the whizzing traffic coming closer and closer.

I'm not going to stop in time. The thought tore through her like a knife. *Oh, God, I'm not ready to die*. The car screeched to a halt only half a metre short of the intersection's pedestrian crossing.

Erin's heart hammered as she gasped aloud, overcome by how close she had come to ploughing into speeding traffic. Her hands began to shake, and she grasped the steering wheel tight in an effort to steady them. Fresh tears formed again in her eyes.

"Oh, Lord," she said, finding herself praying aloud. "Oh, Lord, help me. Help me, or I'm never going to get out of this car in one piece."

The interior voice she perceived earlier spoke again. *Be still, I am with you*.

Puzzled but not frightened, Erin placed her head back on the headrest, allowing herself to breathe in and out slowly. A warm calm settled over her shattered heart.

Be still, I am with you.

Erin closed her eyes for a moment and rested.

After what seemed hours later, a car horn sounded behind her. Glancing up, she noticed the traffic light had turned green while the driving rain had eased to a shower. She raised a hand in a polite wave and drove on, wondering how long the driver behind her had been waiting. Drawing in a deep breath, she relaxed into the sudden calm that had settled over her.

About fifteen minutes later, she pulled into the driveway of her childhood home in Queanbeyan, a town just outside of Canberra. She stared at the neat, cream-coloured brick house, made clearly visible in the early autumn evening by the light of the street lamp on the opposite side of the road. She turned off her lights and then the engine. The calm that had covered her at the intersection started to fade as interior pain began to grip her senses again, causing her head to pound. She peered through the car windscreen at the front window of her parents' home, the light from the living room lamp seeping out from behind the closed curtains.

Erin glanced sideways at the passenger seat, the overnight bag she'd hurriedly thrown together sitting there. *Oh, God, what are they going to think?* She hadn't given a thought to going anywhere else after walking out on Gareth. Erin didn't know two kinder people in the world than her mother and father. But aside from their disapproval about her living with a man outside of wedlock, they had never liked Gareth. And now, here she was, sitting in their driveway with her life in tatters. Just like they said might happen. A failure.

Tears welled up in Erin's eyes again. She sighed as she pulled the keys out of the ignition. *To hell with it.* Right now, her desire to throw herself into her mother's arms outweighed her fear of disapproval.

She snatched up her bag, jumped out of the car and slammed the door behind her. Barely stopping to lock the car, she fled to the front door and pressed the doorbell, counting the agonising seconds till someone opened. She heard the muffled sound of her mother's voice inside and footsteps approaching. The door swung open to reveal her father, Liam Rafferty. His face lit up.

"Erin!" he said, stepping back to make space to let her in. "I didn't know you were heading over. Lovely to see you. What brings you here at this hour?"

"Oh, Dad." Erin fell in through the doorway, throwing

her arms around her father. "He doesn't love me anymore!"

*****

"Thanks for looking out for me, Jo," Erin said tearfully into her phone later that evening from the sofa in her parents' living room. Jo had reached her on the phone after she arrived at her parents' house, and Erin had recounted the painful evening to her. Her mother sat beside her, gently patting her back, while her father sat in an armchair opposite.

"I can't believe he'd do this to you," Joanna's mournful tone came down the line. "If only I'd been able to reach you sooner. Maybe if I had, it would have been easier for you when you faced him."

"Don't you dare take any blame for this," Erin said, in an effort to comfort her pregnant friend. "Besides, nothing could have prepared me for that...that...expression on his face." She swallowed and struggled to keep her voice under control. "Anyway, you have enough on your plate right now."

"Erin —"

"Listen, don't worry about me now. Just take care of yourself and that baby of yours. I really should let you go now."

"I'll check in on you soon, sweetie. Night night."

"Night, Jo."

She ended the call and switched off the phone, dropping it on the coffee table. Wretched thing. It had been nothing but a herald of disaster all day.

She picked up the cup of tea her mother had made her earlier. It had gone cold, but thirst and a low blood sugar level compelled her to gulp down the tepid beverage. She placed the cup down and let out a long, shaky sigh, her face contorting in a fit of sobbing for the hundredth time that night. She lent her head on her mother's shoulder.

"My poor, darling girl," Judith said, placing her arm around Erin's shoulders. "I wish I knew what to say to ease this pain. We truly are sorry you're going through this."

"Thanks, Mum," Erin replied, grabbing a tissue from the box on the coffee table and wiping her eyes. "Funny thing that 'sorry' word. Everyone's said sorry to me this evening. You, Jo, even Gareth. He said it over and over before I left." She stopped and thought for a second. "Maybe he'll regret what he's done and change his mind. It wouldn't be the first time a man gives up his mistress and goes back to his wife, don't you think?"

Judith and Liam exchanged a glance that told Erin they thought otherwise.

"Except for one thing," Liam said gently, leaning forward in his chair. "You and Gareth aren't married, love."

Erin felt her insides bristling. "Please don't start, Dad. I know you never liked Gareth. I know you've never liked me living with him. But I've been with him for years. It felt like we were married, or at least like we should have been."

"It did to you," Judith said. "But clearly it didn't to Gareth."

"But, Mum, he's everything to me. I can't just let go of him. I can't. What am I supposed to do now?"

Judith sighed and placed her arm around Erin's shoulders.

"Nothing for the moment. Gareth may change his mind, or he may not. Either way you don't need to do anything." Judith stroked her hair. "You've had your heart broken, and you need to take time to recover from the shock of what's happened. It will take time to heal, but you will. It may not seem like that now, but I promise, you will."

"That all sounds so final, Mum. I can't face it. I can't." Erin began sobbing again. Rage churned in her gut as she remembered the look on Gareth's face when he told her about Michelle. "I can't bear the thought of him with that bitch!" she said through gritted teeth.

Her mother held her. "I know you don't want to hear this, but the Lord isn't done with you yet," Judith said. "You will survive this and go on to see a brighter day."

Erin remained crying in her mother's arms while her father got up and returned with another cup of tea.

"When was the last time you ate something?" he said as he placed the cup in front of her on the table.

"Lunchtime," Erin replied, sniffing. Lunchtime. It seemed like centuries ago.

"Would you like something to eat? Your mother cooked one of her legendary roasts tonight."

Erin attempted a smile. "Thanks, Dad, but I don't think I could keep anything down."

"At least try and eat some fruit. You look so pale." He went to the kitchen and returned with a banana, placing it in front of her.

Judith released her and stood up. "I'm going to go and check your old room, make sure there are enough blankets and the like."

"Thank you, Mum," Erin said, wiping her eyes again. "I know you weren't quite ready to have me back. I'm sorry to land in on you like this."

"It's fine. You'll just need to be quiet when you go to bed because Lily is sleeping in Katrina's old room." Six-year-old Lillian was her sister Katrina's eldest child. "She's having a sleepover with us for the school holidays."

"Okay." Erin wondered how on earth she would deal with her when Lily woke up in the morning. Lily was an enchanting child, but Erin didn't feel up to being bombarded with the questions and excited chatter that Lily would doubtless be brimming with after spending the night at Grandma's and Grandpa's house.

"Don't worry," Judith said, apparently reading Erin's thoughts before disappearing up the hallway. "Getting in touch with family might be exactly what you need right now."

Erin peeled the banana and sipped at the second cup of tea her father brought her and managed to get both down. He sat in his armchair and watched her as she ate and drank.

"Dad, why is this happening to me?" She swallowed the last of her tea and rested back on the sofa as she waited for him to reply.

"I wish I had the answer, my dear. I think you just need to wait for what comes next, like your mother said. I was very happy when she told me today you wanted to end your de facto relationship with Gareth and marry him."

De facto. Why did they insist on using that term? It sounded so cheap to Erin. She decided to let it slide and simply listen.

"It's difficult to see this in perspective right now, but it appears to me that you got at least the first part of what you'd wished for. You didn't want to go on living in limbo anymore. However painful the result is, you're no longer in that limbo."

"All due respect, Dad, I think I'd have preferred limbo to this," Erin snapped.

"Would you? Seems to me in order for you to call us and ask to come home for a while you were pretty keen to move things along," Liam said. "It hasn't worked out the way you'd hoped, but you were being true to yourself. What motivated your actions today is a good thing. Perhaps the fact that Gareth's infidelity was revealed to you today, the day you decided to change things, was all in God's plan for you."

As much as Erin loathed hearing her parents harp on about God's divine plan, she paused and considered. She remembered the voice that spoke to her in the car, warning her to stop before she drove headlong through a busy intersection. It was so strange. In recent years she'd almost stopped believing in God altogether, though she could never entirely let go of what belief remained in her.

Well, if God loved her, He had a funny way of showing it. Here she was, trying to get married to the love of her life and what did God allow to happen? Total humiliation and complete ruin. She rested back in the chair again and closed her eyes.

"I don't know, Dad. I can't think straight."

"Don't worry," Liam said, his voice reassuring her. "Everything will become clearer with time."

A profound fatigue settled over her, and she opened her eyes only when her mother came back into the room and spoke to her.

"Do you want to try and sleep now, honey?" she said. "Rest and we can tackle this again in the morning."

Defeated, Erin murmured agreement. She got up and kissed her father. "Good night, Dad," she said, trying not to cry again. "Thank you for listening to me all evening."

"Good night. I wish you were here under happier circumstances, but I'm still very glad you're with us. Don't you worry, now." Her father grinned up at her.

Don't worry? Worry was the least of her problems. Not dying from the inside out was a more immediate concern.

She turned and followed her mother down the hallway to her old room.

"I've put out an extra blanket at the end of the bed," Judith said. "The nights are getting cooler now. I'll put an electric blanket on tomorrow."

Erin peered around her old room. It had been some time since she'd checked in on it. Recent visits to her parents were usually brief and didn't involve leaving the main living areas. Gareth rarely came with her, knowing her family disapproved of him. She'd always believed her alliance should be with him even though it pained her that he barely gave them the time of day.

She wondered how long it had been since she'd even opened the door of her old room. A couple of years, at least. It looked much like it had the day she'd left home to move in with Gareth five years ago. Cozy and modestly furnished, her desk still in the corner where she'd completed all her high school and uni studies, with a single shelf hanging above it from the wall, still holding some of her old books. A pine dresser with the pine-framed mirror stood at the other end of the room. Her single bed in the middle, complete with the blue-and-white zigzag doona cover and pillowcase that had been on the bed the last time she'd slept in it. Her leadlight table lamp on the dresser cast a warm, soft glow of subtle greens, pinks and yellows. The room was almost completely unchanged.

Almost, but not quite. A few religious items had found their way back in: a statue of the Sacred Heart stood on the dresser close to the lamp, a gift given to her for her Confirmation. A framed picture of Our Lady of Guadalupe sat on the desk next to a family portrait and a crucifix hung above the doorway.

Erin reached down and picked up the overnight bag her father had placed there and dropped it on the bed.

"Thank you for looking after me," she said, reaching out to hug her mother. "Especially since I haven't been such a great daughter and...." the words trailed off. Judith put her arms around Erin and squeezed her. As Erin hugged her mother, her eyes fell on the family photo on her desk. She swallowed the lump rising in her throat and released her mother. "Mum?"

"Yes?"

"I wish David was here. I wish I could see him again, even for a minute."

Judith nodded. "Yes, me too. Every day." She reached up to a locket on a chain around her neck hanging alongside a crucifix and miraculous medal. She opened the locket and kissed it, Erin knowing whose picture was in it. Then Judith clasped the crucifix and kissed it too. "I know he's close to you now."

"Who, Jesus or David?" Erin asked, only half-joking.

"Both." Judith traced the Sign of the Cross on her daughter's forehead.

Erin closed her eyes and accepted her mother's blessing, for once not objecting to one of Judith's demonstrative displays of faith.

Judith stepped towards the door then turned to face Erin in the doorway. "Sleep, if you can. I'll be here if you need me."

"Night, Mum."

"Goodnight," Judith said, closing the door behind her all but an inch.

Erin flopped down on the edge of the bed, opened her bag and pulled out the pyjamas she'd packed. They weren't the ones she'd worn the night before. Those were still under her pillow back at home. Home. But home wasn't home anymore. Not now that her beloved had rejected her.

Alone in the quiet of her childhood bedroom, a newfound loneliness crept up and sliced through her. Her mind spun, disoriented by the day's events that had taken her from hope to bitter betrayal and rejection. Gareth, *her* Gareth, in the arms of another. All hope she had for a life with him; a wedding, a home and children, gone. In only one day her life rewound by five years. Only she wasn't twenty-one anymore. Her heart fired up with the burning resentment of one who has been robbed of something precious that can't be replaced.

Surely this couldn't be happening. Surely it wasn't permanent? Gareth could change his mind. It was possible, wasn't it?

What was he doing right now? He'd probably left their flat the minute she was gone to be with *her*. Or perhaps he'd stayed, and she was over there. In Erin's flat. Her home that she'd spent years living and loving in, furnishing and making it look just the way she wanted. Erin clenched her fists. The thought was almost too much to bear.

Spent of tears, she tried to relax, inhaling and exhaling slowly. Her head began pounding again, and she reached for her cosmetics bag to get some paracetamol. She punched out a couple of tablets and grabbed a bottle of water on the desk. Gulping them down, she placed the bottle on the desk, eyeing her family's photo once again.

It was an old photo, taken about fifteen years ago when she was only eleven. Erin remembered how she'd sat on the sofa between her mother and her older brother David. Katrina sat on David's other side while her father set up the camera timer, then sat on the sofa next to Katrina before the picture was taken. Everyone was sitting down together as David had been too sick to stand. He'd died only a month later, just after his eighteenth birthday.

Erin calmed a little as she stared at his image, with his beautiful smile and his face utterly devoid of bitterness or resentment. How strong he'd been in the weeks before his death. So reconciled to the hand he had been dealt. She remembered wondering how it would be possible to smile for the photo when she knew David wouldn't be with them much longer. But he had put his arm around her and held her through her sadness. What a wonderful brother he had been. Even through the busiest times in her life, there wasn't a day she didn't think of him. She reached over and picked up the photo frame.

"I really miss you, Dave," she whispered. "What am I going to do now?" She closed her eyes and waited for an answer.

Nothing.

"That's okay," she said after a moment, tracing over his image with her finger. "You can tell me what to do later." She placed the frame back on the desk next to the small drawing of a Willie Wagtail that David had sketched for her when he was a teenager. Erin had framed it after his death and kept it alongside the family portrait. A skilled illustrator, David had done a beautiful job of portraying the dark-feathered native bird, with its distinctive patches of white on its breast and over its eye. Willie Wagtails had been David's favourite bird species. Occasionally, when she saw one darting about in the gardens near her flat, or when she went out on a bush walk, she would think of her brother most especially. In those moments, it felt as though David was close by — just around the corner maybe, or waiting for her when she got home.

She picked up the drawing and kissed it, then she reached for her pyjamas and got ready for bed.

After switching off the lamp, she pulled back the doona and climbed into bed. The sheets and pillowcase smelled laundry fresh, as though washed only recently. She wondered why on earth her mother had kept her room as it was for so long, when they could have converted it into a reading or exercise room.

Her thoughts then turned to her little niece Lily, sleeping peacefully in the room next door, in Katrina's old bed. Beautiful child, innocent and carefree, oblivious to the pain that life would one day deal out to her, in some form or other.

And now here Erin was too, all tucked up in bed like her tiny niece, safe and sound in Grandma's and Grandpa's house. Only she wasn't a child like Lily.

She got up quietly and opened her door, stepping out into the dark hallway lit only by a night light in a power point in the wall. The door to Katrina's room was slightly ajar, and Erin pushed it open and peered in. She could make out Lily's form in her sister's old bed, breathing softly, her little arm draped over a large teddy bear. *Sleep peacefully, Lily-girl, for both of us.* Erin stared at her for a second longer before closing the door and returning to her own bed, wondering when she might have children of her own.

The icy fist that was wrapped around her heart squeezed a little harder as she pulled the covers up to her chin. She buried her face in her pillow and cried herself to sleep.

Chapter 5

Pale light spilled into the room around the edges of the Roman blinds. The sound of screeching cockatoos starting their early morning ritual of waking everyone who could hear them filled Erin's ears. *But there are no flocks of cockatoos near our flat,* Erin thought, and suddenly realised she wasn't at home. She opened her heavy eyes, struggling to remember where she was. Slowly the room came into focus, and the events of the day before came flooding back.

Erin closed her eyes again. *Oh Lord, what a night.* She had slept fitfully, with distorted dreams of Gareth plaguing her through the night. Exhaustion eventually took over, causing her to sleep deeply towards the early morning and left her feeling as though lead weights were strapped to her limbs and eyelids. She lay still for a moment and tried to ignore the thumping of her aching heart. Eventually, she reached for her wristwatch on the bedside table and struggled to read the time, but it was too dark with the blinds shut. Mustering all her strength, she got up and stumbled to the window. She pulled up the blinds a bit and peered bleary-eyed at the time. 6.40 am.

She threw the watch down on her bed and pulled the blinds up a bit more, staring out the window into her parents' back garden. A large claret ash tree met her gaze, the one that had stood in the yard for as long as Erin could remember. At this time of the year the leaves became such a sublime colour of red, it made her heart ache. Now her heart was aching relentlessly but not with the vivid autumn beauty. She leaned her head against the window and closed her tired eyes again. *What now?*

Sounds from the kitchen let Erin know that someone else

in the house was awake too. She reached into her overnight bag for her dressing gown, pulled it on and made her way to the kitchen, where she found her father preparing coffee and toast. He smiled as she entered the room.

"Good morning," he said, handing her a cup of white coffee. "Did you manage to sleep at all?"

"A bit," Erin said, accepting the coffee and sitting down at the table. She raised the cup to her lips and took a sip of the hot drink. "But I feel completely zonked out."

"I'm not surprised," he said, compassion filling his voice. "Do you think you should call in sick today? Give yourself a day or two to process everything?"

"I hate to admit it, but I think you're right," she said, the coffee settling like ash in her stomach. "There's this big promotion I'm trying to get; it's such a terrible time to be missing work." She slumped down in her seat as the tears started to form. "How on earth does a person go about breaking up with someone after this long together?"

Liam Rafferty placed down the coffee plunger and regarded her steadily. "We'll just take one thing at a time. Like your mother said last night, you've been through a terrible shock. We'll help you."

Erin's eyes darted up to her father. Though he was never one to speak a bad word about anyone, his familiar tone told her that he wasn't amused with the way his daughter had been treated and wouldn't be tolerating any nonsense.

"Here, try and eat some breakfast, Erin," he said, placing a plate with two slices of Vegemite toast in front of her.

"All right," Erin responded, listless, the smell of the warm toast making her stomach turn.

"Katrina will be in today to pick up Lily," Liam said, pouring another cup of coffee. "It might help for you to talk with her."

"Yeah, all right," she said again, watching her father as he prepared the second cup of coffee to her mother's liking. Clearly her parents were more than happy for her to be back under their roof and keen to integrate her back into the family she had chosen to isolate herself from in so many ways.

Perhaps they were right. Yesterday, everything had seemed within her control, or at least there was hope for what the future might hold. Today...well, today indeed. It was like mutiny on board the ship of her life. Yesterday she had been captain, exploring unchartered seas but still confident in her navigational skills. Then without warning, she had been thrown overboard while Gareth took hold of the ship's wheel and sailed off into the distance with....

Erin's train of thought was abruptly derailed by the sound of her niece approaching the kitchen. She burst into the room followed by Judith, the little girl dressed in her nightie and holding the teddy bear Erin had seen her sleeping with last night.

"Good morning, Grandpa," she said, dropping the teddy and leaping up into Liam's arms. "Is there any toast for me? And a cup of tea too? But I like lots of milk in mine, more than Grandma."

"Yes, Lily," Liam said, smiling. He glanced over at Erin and winked. "Did you see who's here?"

Lily glanced across the kitchen to the table, sleep still in her little eyes. Her face lit up, and she wriggled down out of Liam's arms.

"Aunty Erin!" she shouted and raced over towards Erin. She put her arms out and jumped up into her lap. "I haven't seen you for so long! What are you doing here?"

All Erin's apprehension at dealing with Lily's boundless energy evaporated as soon as the little girl threw her arms around her. Erin wrapped her arms around her in return and silently poured her grief into the child's embrace.

"Oh, I just thought I'd come and visit last night. Grandma said I could stay the night and see you in the morning," Erin replied into Lily's hair.

Lily released her arms from around Erin and peered into

her face. Erin regarded her pretty niece. In appearance, Lily was a mixture of both her parents. Katrina was fair-skinned with dark hair and blue eyes, features Katrina had inherited from Liam. Erin favoured Judith's looks: fair-skinned also, but with lighter hair and green eyes. Little Lily had Katrina's eyes and dark hair, but also her father Emilio's Hispanic skin tones. *Such a beauty. How many hearts are you going to break?*

Lily took Erin's face between her hands and kissed her on the nose.

"Poor Aunty Erin. You look like you've been swimming in a sea full of sad." She glanced down at Erin's plate. "Maybe that's why Uncle David came to visit me last night."

What?

Erin felt the earth shift beneath her feet and, for a moment, thought her heart might stop. Had she heard Lily right?

"Lily, what do you mean?" Erin asked, her throat going dry. In the corner of her eye she noticed her parents exchange a glance.

Lily stared at her for a moment, appearing bewildered. She pointed to a photo of David on the dining room buffet. "Uncle David. I see him when I dream sometimes. Although I never met him, you know, because he died before I was born." Lily talked in a matter of fact way as though this information were as ordinary as old running shoes.

Judith spoke up from where she stood rinsing a dish at the kitchen sink. "Did he say anything to you, Lily?"

"Not much. He just smiled at me and said, 'Tell Aunty Erin to stay put for now,' that's all." With that, all was well in Lily's world, and she slid off Erin's lap and sat in the chair next to her. "Can I have a bite of your toast?"

*****

Later that morning, Katrina arrived with her other children, four-year-old Bruno and the baby, three-month-old Marie. Judith and Liam took the older children outside to play in the cubby house Liam had built and left the two sisters together.

Erin sat at the kitchen table while Katrina sat opposite her, pushing her sleeping infant in a stroller with gentle back-and-forth movements. They had a view through the glass sliding door in the dining room that led to the Rafferty's back yard. Erin watched as Lily and Bruno played in and around the cubby house, throwing small chunks of bread on the grass to feed the magpies. With the children out of earshot, Erin allowed the tears to flow freely, pouring out her grief and anger in a big jumble of words and sobs while Katrina sat listening.

"I don't know how I could miss something like this," she said, wiping her eyes with a tissue. "I've been so busy, I didn't notice any of the signs."

Katrina nodded. "I was never that fond of Gareth, but I didn't think he would ever do something like this to you. I was pretty sure you two would marry eventually," she said, passing Erin another tissue from the nappy bag hanging around the stroller. "I know it's almost impossible to see this now, but it might be a good thing this happened. And perhaps you didn't notice the signs that something might be wrong because the whole situation was wrong to start with."

Here we go again. On another day, Erin might have tried to quell the indignation that rose up inside her. But fatigue and grief shredded any resolve that might otherwise have caused her to bite her lip.

"Honestly, Katrina, what is it with you and your bloody-minded Catholic morality?" she snapped. "When are you going to pull yourself into the twenty-first century? Yes, I wanted to seal my relationship with marriage, but what I had with Gareth was just as valid as your relationship with Emilio."

Katrina continued pushing the stroller back and forth. She fixed her gaze on Erin, her demeanour remaining calm with no sign of reacting to Erin's angry outburst. "What you had with Gareth was nothing like my marriage to Emilio. Emilio has never used my body for his own advantage. He pledged himself to me with vows before God and man that joined us in a holy covenant before he joined himself to me physically."

"Yeah, but...." Erin tried to cobble together a response.

"Yeah, but what? You told me a second ago that you wanted to get married because it didn't feel right anymore."

"I guess that's true. But I don't think we were using each other just because we lived together without being married."

Katrina stopped for a second and stared through Erin. "Truly? Are you telling me that you never felt used by Gareth, not even once?"

Erin thought back to the last time with Gareth, him turning his back on her and falling asleep the moment he was satisfied. She recalled the loneliness that welled up inside her while she struggled to convince herself she wasn't simply a thing that had served its purpose and was no longer needed.

"Maybe," Erin said. "But you can't tell me it was only because Gareth and I aren't married."

"Of course not," Katrina replied. "Married people still have to guard against using one another. But let me tell you a couple of things about that Catholic morality you're so dark on." Marie stirred in her sleep and raised her thumb to her mouth. Katrina got up and pushed the stroller into the living room, closing the door behind her. She sat down again at the table with Erin.

"You know that sex is powerful. It has the power to make or break *everything*. It joins two people and makes them one. Having sex outside of the marriage covenant simply serves to fragment people. The Church knows this; it's why sex is reserved for marriage. To safeguard the act and allow you to be completely free in your relationship with the one you love. Not to cramp your style."

Erin shook her head. "It's just so antiquated. No one saves sex for marriage anymore."

"That's true. And a huge number of marriages that start with cohabitation end in divorce too. You can't 'try before you buy' with a person, Erin. A human being isn't a commodity to be used, like a car or mobile phone or reusable food pouch. It doesn't work that way."

People as commodities? The thought made Erin stop and think. A "trial marriage" she'd always thought of it. It seemed a practical approach. Lots of people thought so too. "So what you're saying is my try-before-you-buy period has ended with me being returned to the manufacturer, and I've wasted the last five years of my life?" *Oh, God, please don't let that be true.*

Katrina reached out across the table and took Erin's hand. "No, of course I'm not. I'm trying to tell you that you're worth so much more than the way he's treated you — more than what you settled for. I would never have wished this on you, none of us would. But now it's happened, it could be time to rethink a few things."

Erin drew a deep breath and let out a shaky sigh. "Maybe. Up until yesterday I would never have considered a rethink of my life. A couple of strange things have happened to me in the last few hours." She recounted her experience at the traffic light the night before and Lily's dream about David.

Katrina nodded. "Yes, that's happened a few times now. We're getting used to it. A year ago she said to me, 'Uncle David says I need to be an extra good girl now because you have a baby in your tummy!' I was only about three days pregnant with Marie. Even the super-sensitive pregnancy test didn't show up positive until a week later."

Erin looked over at the photo of David on the buffet. "Do you really think David is watching out for us?"

Katrina peered into her face, her eyebrows furrowed. "Of course. Why wouldn't he?" she asked.

"I couldn't believe it when he died. I never understood how you and Mum and Dad went on believing in a kind, loving God. If God's so kind, why didn't He allow David to live?"

"It was hard for you when he died. You two were very close." At that moment, Marie let out a little cry. Katrina got up from the table and went into the living room, returning with her infant daughter. She sat down again, lifting her shirt up on one side and arranged Marie comfortably in her lap to feed her.

Marie latched onto her mother and put her little hand up to touch Katrina's face.

Katrina smiled down at her daughter, taking the tiny girl's hand in her fingers and went on.

"You were young when David died, but you weren't that young. Even Lily understands something about life and death. David dying young didn't mean he didn't live to the fullest the days God allotted him. We all went on because we believe we'll see him again one day. One more benefit of our bloody-minded Catholic morality," she said, winking at Erin.

Erin put her head down on the table and reached out for Katrina's hand again. "I wanted to stay with Gareth forever. Why did this happen to me?" she said, her voice cracking.

Katrina reached out and grabbed her hand again, her other arm holding Marie. "I don't know. But I suspect it's because God has something else in mind. I know it's hard, and it hurts. But not everything that hurts is bad. Many times it's through pain that we learn and grow the most."

Erin pondered this, and the storm raging inside her calmed somewhat. She looked up at her sister's tired face. "Thank you, Katrina. I know you have enough on your plate without dealing with me and my dramas."

Katrina released Erin's hand and lifted Marie up over her shoulder, patting her back. "No problem. We're family. I'm always here for you."

"Yes, you always have been. It's me that hasn't been there for you."

Katrina shrugged. "Plenty of time for that. Just focus on getting things right for yourself. The next phase of your life is going to be hard, Erin. There's no escaping that. But it won't be impossible. Whatever comes next, be brave. It'll be okay, I promise you."

*****

Erin stood in front of the bathroom mirror in her parents' home, applying the last of her makeup before work. She placed the lid back on her lipstick and dropped it in her makeup bag, glancing back into the mirror to look at the result. As she stared at her reflection, she began wondering why she bothered applying the stuff at all. No amount of lipstick and highlighter could disguise the effects of a major breakup.

Night after night of broken and restless sleep, round-the-clock tears and a constant effort to act like everything was normal had left her exhausted. Now it was really showing. The dark circles were telling but didn't say as much as the pain that was so deeply etched on her face, random strangers were making sympathetic comments to her. She almost didn't recognise herself anymore. How much more of this was she supposed to take?

Four weeks had passed since the night she walked out on Gareth. During that time she hadn't spoken to him at all. Gareth tried calling her a few days after she left, but she had ignored the call and asked her father to return it later.

She was unsure why she had done that. While part of her desperately hoped he had changed his mind, the renewed contact with her family awoke some strange form of self-preservation in her. It was like she didn't trust herself to resist him if he *did* want her back. What she couldn't figure out was why she would *want* to resist him. Didn't she love Gareth and want to be with him? Yes. Could she forgive him his tryst with this other woman? *Again, yes, in time,* she thought. But something else was at play in her heart, something that cautioned her against even speaking with him.

As it turned out, there was no fear of his wanting her back. The phone call was simply to tell her that he'd finalise everything with the lease, offer her access to the flat to retrieve her things and, of course, to say sorry once again. Liam had conveyed all this to her and said that he and Judith would retrieve her belongings from the apartment if she wanted them to, a gesture she accepted with gratitude. She knew she couldn't face going back to where it all fell apart.

Erin sighed. Shaking herself, she tried to focus on her reflection. *Yep, I really need the waterproof mascara today.* She reached into her makeup bag and began rummaging amongst the lipsticks and compacts. *Where is the stupid thing?* Just as she was about to upend the contents of the bag into the sink, her hand brushed something thin and plastic sitting right down the bottom. Not remembering what it was, she gripped it with two fingers and yanked it from the bag. Holding it up in front of her she saw straight away that it was her pill prescription, with three tablets left on the card.

Wow. She held the card in one hand and stared at it, shaking her head and feeling a bitter smile forming on her face. She hadn't taken the pill since the morning of the day she and Gareth had broken up. *And to think I'd been berating myself for not getting to the doctor earlier to get another prescription.*

Well, perhaps that was the one and only good thing that had resulted from this whole mess. It suddenly occurred to her now that she hadn't had a single headache in the four weeks since she'd been relieved of the pressure of taking it.

She turned the card over, gripped by a sudden resolve. *Well, I certainly don't need you anymore.* She pressed the final three pills into the sink, turned on the tap and washed them away. *Good riddance.*

At that moment, she heard her phone ring in her bedroom. Grabbing her contraceptive-pill-free makeup bag, she dashed out of the bathroom, down the hallway and into her room, picking up the phone from where it sat on the bedside table. A number that looked vaguely familiar appeared on the screen. She pressed call answer and put the phone to her ear.

"Hello, Erin speaking."

"Hi, Erin, this is Belinda calling on behalf of Doctor Hart," came a cheerful young woman's voice over the line. "Have I caught you at a bad moment?"

Erin's heart dropped down into her stomach. Debbie Hart was the doctor she had seen a week ago when Katrina and her mother had encouraged her to be tested for STDs. The thought horrified her at the time and caused her heart to break all over again remembering Gareth's infidelity, before it dawned on her that it was probably a sensible idea. Unable to face her usual doctor, she had taken her mother's recommendation to see Doctor Hart.

Doctor Hart had treated her kindly and with understanding, telling her she was doing the right thing getting things checked out and ordering some blood tests. When Erin had gone to the pathology lab opposite the medical centre and handed the humiliating request form to the nurse, she wished for the floor to open up and swallow her. The nurse had glanced quickly over the list of diseases to be checked for, looked back at Erin and smiled. They'd attended to her quickly, and since then, she had tried to put the whole experience out of her mind.

"Hello, are you there?" the receptionist on the phone asked.

"Yes, sorry, I'm here," Erin replied, attempting to sound calm and in control.

"I'm calling about some blood test results that Doctor Hart would like to see you about."

Erin felt herself come over faint and reached out for her bedpost, seating herself on the edge of the bed. She tried to speak but was unable to find her voice.

"Hello, are you there? Are you okay?" the young girl asked again, concern evident in her voice.

Erin tried to regain her composure. "I'm a bit concerned, that's all. Doctor Hart said that if the results were negative, I wouldn't hear anything. Did something come up that I should be worried about?" Her heart beat so violently she wondered if it would burst right out of her ribcage. *Please, no. Please don't let there be anything wrong with me.*

The receptionist paused as Erin heard her leafing through some pages. "No, no need to be concerned there, all the tests came up negative."

Erin released a breath she didn't realise she was holding. "Oh, thank God for that. You had me worried for a second. So why do I need to come in?"

"Something else came up in the test results that the doctor would like to discuss with you. There's an appointment this evening at 5.30 pm, would that work for you?"

"Um, yes, that would be fine, I suppose," Erin said, struggling to understand. "I'm afraid you've lost me though. If the results are negative, what is this about?"

"I'm sorry, I'm just following up on a request from Doctor Hart," she said. "I don't have any more information in front of me other than what I've told you."

With her sanity ready to topple over the edge, Erin doubted she could wait a whole day to find out what was going on. "Is it possible to see Doctor Hart earlier?" she asked.

"How much earlier? 12.00 pm?"

How about right now? "Look, I'm anxious to deal with this," Erin said. "I could come in before work, does she have anything early?"

The receptionist paused for a moment as Erin listened to her tap away at a keyboard. "Actually there's been a cancellation for this morning, 8.30 am. Can you be here by then?"

A quick glance at her watch revealed it was almost 8.15 am and the medical centre was only a ten-minute drive away. "Yes, I'll take that appointment, thank you."

"Of course. We'll see you here soon then, Erin. Bye."

Erin hung up without saying anything further, the indomitable cheer in the girl's voice grating on her raw nerves. Why was everyone being so bloody cheerful when her life was falling apart?

A short while later Erin sat in the waiting room. The medical centre was a place of practice for a number of doctors, evidenced by the half dozen or so doors along the length of one wall, each with the nameplate of a GP. The young receptionist who had called her earlier sat at the front desk close to the entrance, answering a steady number of calls, filling up the doctors' schedules for the day.

The sizeable waiting area was almost empty except for one other person, a young woman dressed in smart business attire like her, tapping away on her phone. Bitterness crept into Erin's heart as she wondered if that girl was here checking for possible damage to *her* body after her boyfriend had diced *her* over for another woman. Erin guessed not. She looked far too confident and well rested to be here for that.

The rumbling of Erin's empty stomach interrupted her pernicious line of thought, and she reached into her handbag for the protein bar she'd snatched from the kitchen cupboard that morning. Opening it, she ate a few mouthfuls, wishing there had been time to get a cup of coffee before flying out the door. Proper eating was another thing that she had let slip. Coffee, solely for the purpose of staying awake, and whatever small amount of food that kept her from fainting was all she was getting by on. She knew she'd lost some weight too, with her fitted work skirts feeling a little roomier around the middle in recent days.

Before she got a chance to resume fantasising about how much better off the other woman in the waiting room was, Doctor Hart appeared from behind one of the practitioners' doors.

"Erin Rafferty?" she said, smiling in Erin's direction as she held her office door open to let her inside.

Embarrassed, Erin stuffed the half-eaten sugar-fix back in her bag and hastened into the office.

"Sorry," Erin said after swallowing a mouthful of chocolate chips and oats. "I didn't get any breakfast this morning."

Doctor Hart closed the door to the small, narrow office behind Erin, stepped over to her desk and gestured for her to sit down on a seat positioned at the side of the desk.

"No problem at all," she said, sitting down in her swivel chair and turning to face Erin. "Now, tell me, how have you been?"

The genuine concern in Doctor Hart's voice and expression was unlike anything Erin had experienced with other doctors. The way she asked that simple question convinced Erin she was truly interested in the answer and would do what she could to help make things right. Erin swallowed a rising lump in her throat.

"I'm about as good as can be expected, I suppose," she said.

"Yes, you're going to need to give yourself some time. I know you have a lot of support, which is marvellous. You do need to be to taking care of yourself right now."

Unwilling to enter into further discussion about her private pain, she tried to move on. "Thanks, Doctor, but—"

"Please call me Debbie."

"Okay. I just wanted to say, I'm a little confused about why you wanted to see me about my results. The receptionist told me that the tests had come back negative."

Debbie turned her attention to her computer and began scrolling through something on her screen.

"That's right. No problems there. But something else did come up on your results that I needed to discuss with you."

Erin's heart gave a double beat and her mind started racing. "What? I don't have something bad, do I? Do I have cancer?" *Oh no.* Was that the reason she was losing weight? She knew firsthand how people got skinnier when they had cancer.

Before she had the chance to start hyperventilating, Debbie cut in. "No, no, nothing like that," she replied, reassuring her. "Actually, you're not sick at all."

"Then what do you need to see me for?"

Doctor Hart cleared her throat and leaned forward a little in her chair toward Erin. "Your test results showed you have a concentration in the hCG hormone."

"hCG?"

"Human chorionic gonadotropin."

Erin struggled to understand what she was hearing from the doctor. *Hang on. Why does that sound familiar? Isn't that the hormone that tells you whether....*

"It's the pregnancy hormone."

Erin froze for a second. "I'm pregnant?"

"Yes," the doctor said, nodding. "From the levels I'm seeing, you are about four weeks past conception."

Chapter 6

Pregnant?

Erin released an incredulous laugh and shook her head. "No, I couldn't possibly be pregnant. I was on the pill. I took it religiously. Every day at the same time."

Debbie let out an audible sigh and sat back a little in her seat. "If I had ten dollars for every time a newly pregnant woman spoke those words to me, I wouldn't need to win the lotto — I could provide the lotto office with the prize money."

No, this can't be right. I never missed one, despite the headaches. Not a single one.

As though reading her mind, Debbie continued. "The pill works in a few different ways to suppress ovulation. We know, however, it fails in this quite often and results in what's called a breakthrough ovulation. One of the reasons the pill is effective in preventing pregnancy is because even if an egg is fertilised, it depletes the endometrium to the point where the baby is unable to attach to the wall of the uterus, resulting in a chemical abortion."

"Chemical abortion?"

"Yes, no one speaks about this much. But technically, the combined oral contraceptive pill should be branded as a contraceptive/abortifacient, not simply a contraceptive."

What? Why hadn't she heard this before?

"The point is, despite its combined contraceptive and abortifacient capacities, the pill can still fail. And often does."

Erin stared at Debbie, still unable to accept what she was hearing. "Pregnant? I'm pregnant?"

"I realise this is difficult to take in," Debbie said. "But there isn't any doubt. You definitely are. I'm sorry this is happening to you at this time."

As she stared into Debbie's fixed expression, all hope that the result could be a mistake drained away. The sudden reality of the news struck her like a lightning bolt. A strangled yelp escaped from her throat. "Oh no!" she said and burst into a torrent of tears.

Debbie reached out for a box of tissues on her desk and offered them to her.

Erin grabbed a couple and sobbed while Debbie patted Erin's arm, waiting patiently for the tears to subside.

After a couple of minutes, Erin tried to regain her composure. "I can't believe this." She grabbed another tissue and wiped her face, staring at the doctor through her tears and willing her to make some kind of miraculous response that would somehow make everything all right.

Debbie smiled. "There, there now," she said. "This is a shock for you at a difficult time in your life. But it isn't the end of the world. A child is always a blessing."

Erin guffawed as she dabbed at her now-running makeup with the tissue. "Blessing? How can this possibly be a blessing? I'm at the lowest point I've ever been in my life. I'm not with the child's father. I lost my home. I'm staying with my parents. And now I'm supposed to be a parent myself? This could hardly be more disastrous."

"I understand. And I'll do all I can to support you as a doctor," Debbie said. She turned to her computer screen and began typing. A printer on the corner of the desk started whirring and after a second she grabbed a piece of paper from the tray. "I know you have support from your family, but these are the details for pregnancy support in the city, in case you'd like to speak to a professional counsellor." Then she took out a piece of paper from a notepad and began writing. "And here is the name of some pregnancy vitamins that you should start taking." She handed the page to Erin.

Erin stared at the doctor without taking the slip of

paper. "You're a doctor," she said. "How come you're not offering more...options?"

Debbie's face darkened a little. "I understand how overwhelming this is for you, believe me. I have been through this with patients many times before. And I can tell you from experience that destroying this life growing inside you is not going to give you any long-term answers. On the contrary, abortion is far more likely to give you long-term heartache. As a doctor, it's my job to care for human life at all its stages. For this reason I don't provide abortion referrals for any of my patients. There are plenty of doctors you can consult who will, but I'm not one of them."

Her tone was compassionate but resolute, and Erin could tell she meant what she said. Debbie paused to write more on another piece of paper. "I'd like to check you over now, okay?"

Erin nodded and cast her eyes down, wondering what her mother would say to her if she'd witnessed her conversation with the doctor. Or Katrina, or her father. Or Jo, or Ingrid...or David, if he were still alive. Almost everyone important to her who would have looked at her the same way Doctor Hart did when she implied she wanted a referral to an abortion clinic.

She closed her eyes as Debbie wrapped a blood pressure cuff around her arm. The icy fist that had taken up residence in her rib cage squeezed with a new ferocity. Relinquishing the last of her energy and dignity, she surrendered to the loneliness. Because the thing was, there really was no one else there. No one with her in this moment. Only herself and the doctor who would go on to tend other patients once Erin left her office and not have the burden of carrying her ex-fiancé's baby. Her parents had each other. Katrina had Emilio. Everyone in her life had someone. Now all she had was this helpless little life inside her that she didn't want.

How long had she tried to shake off the crazy Catholic guilt that she had carried inside all her life? Tried and failed. Despite herself, she knew she could never destroy a human life, no matter how soon after conception. Gareth had been right that night in the car after Bianca's wedding. She could never be totally rid of her faith. Her Catholicism was just going to continue haunting her, hammering her from all sides. And forcing her to have a child she couldn't imagine looking after.

*****

Erin sat in her car in the carpark at the medical centre, making no attempt to start the engine. She had left the appointment some minutes earlier with Doctor Hart encouraging her to make another appointment in a couple of weeks to discuss her plans for the pregnancy. Her bag sat on the passenger seat, along with the slip of paper containing the name of the vitamins and some stupid list of foods and drinks to avoid that made her wonder how she was going to nourish herself. Not that she was doing such a good job at that anyway.

"Pregnant. I'm pregnant," she said out loud to herself. The words sounded so strange and impossible. She didn't feel pregnant, but she didn't know how pregnancy felt anyway. She'd been feeling so terrible she'd hardly have noticed. Four weeks, the doctor said. It was probably too early for any noticeable signs.

When had it happened? Was it the night of Bianca's wedding? Yes, most probably.

A sadness too deep for tears welled up inside her. In a different context, this news could have been so very welcome. A little life was starting to grow and develop inside her. *I am going to be someone's mother. Someone's mum.*

If only things with Gareth had gone differently. If only she had been able to make him happy, and he'd remained faithful to her. Or if only she'd found some excuse to brush him off that night....

Stop. There was no point wishing things to be different. All the wishing in the world couldn't turn back the clock, couldn't change Gareth's mind, or his heart. Where was God in all this? If He was an all merciful, all loving God as He claimed, why was He allowing her to sink further and further into ruin?

Erin's phone beeped inside her bag, snapping her out of her thoughts. She pulled it out and found a message from Ingrid.

You coming in today?

Erin checked the time on her phone. Doctor Hart had given her a leave certificate, so she didn't have to go to work if she didn't want to. The thought of facing everyone in the office made her want to curl up in a ball and die, but what other choice did she have? It was a late start, but her work output had been terrible, and she needed to perform if she was going to hang on to her job.

It wasn't like anyone would be able to tell she was pregnant. She had missed her chance at her promotion so she wouldn't be climbing the ladder anytime soon. All she had in front of her this moment was to keep going.

Yep. Be there in 20 minutes.

*****

She slipped into the office past the reception desk, casting a perfunctory glance at Beth and mumbling some pleasantry in response to her cheerful greeting. She made her way as surreptitiously as possible to her desk and sat down. Three of the surrounding workstations were empty, Erin gratefully remembering that a couple of the graphic design staff were on holiday and another was in a meeting with clients. Trying to settle and make herself appear as though she'd been sitting there all morning, she switched on her computer and glanced down at the clean coffee cup sitting on her desk. *First things first if I'm gonna get through today.*

She picked up the cup and headed straight to the staff kitchen for the coffee pot. A couple of women from the HR department were leaving the kitchen as she entered, smiling and greeting her as they passed. Erin stood back for them, then stepped into the kitchen. Some wonderful soul had made a pot of coffee and left it about half full. She grabbed the flask from the hot plate, poured herself a cup, and added some milk and a bit of Stevia from a private stash that she kept at the back of the pantry in the corner. Lifting the cup to her lips, she heard a voice behind her. She swung around to discover Ingrid standing in the doorway.

"Hey, you," Ingrid said, relief evident in her voice as she approached Erin at the coffee pot. "I was beginning to wonder if you were going to get in okay." She made a sudden stop a couple of steps short of Erin and stared at her, an alarmed expression on her face.

"Yeah, I'm here. Only just, but I'm here," Erin replied, trying to quell a queasy sensation in her stomach. "What's wrong?"

Ingrid was still standing there, staring. "I hate to say it, Erin, but bloody hell. Did you get hit by a truck this morning? Need an aspirin?"

Erin rolled her eyes. "Thanks. What do you expect from me at the moment, Ingrid?"

Ingrid took a step closer and peered into Erin's face. "No, really, have you been getting enough sleep? If I didn't know better, I'd think you were...." Ingrid stopped short.

With that, Erin's secret was out. She'd barely spoken three words to Ingrid, but Ingrid knew. It was written all over her face.

"You're not, are you?"

Ingrid's face blurred in front of her as the tears started to form. She nodded and placed her cup down on the kitchen bench. "I was at the doctor this morning."

"Oh, Erin." Ingrid stepped forward and put her arms around her, enfolding her in a hug. She held her for a moment before pulling back, gazing at her sympathetically, a slight smile on her face. "You do realise you shouldn't be drinking this then, don't you?" she said, nodding her head in the direction of the coffee cup.

The intense pressure burst, and Erin laughed through her tears. "Yes, you're right, I shouldn't," she said and tipped the coffee down the kitchen sink. "Ingrid, I'm in such shock. I wasn't expecting this. I don't know what I'm going to do." She peered towards the door to make sure no one else was in earshot.

"What did the doctor say?"

"Not much, only that according to the blood test I'm about four weeks past conception, which makes me six weeks pregnant, apparently." Erin couldn't believe the sound of her own voice as she said it.

"Are you going to tell Gareth?"

Erin let out an irritated sigh. "I don't know, Ingrid," she replied. "I only found out an hour ago. And what good would telling him do? I mean, how great is this? Dumped, homeless and knocked-up in only four weeks. A real trifecta. I wonder if I've broken some sort of international loser's record?"

Ingrid smiled and reached out for Erin's empty cup. She rinsed it, then took a jar of green tea from the pantry.

"That's not totally fair. You're not homeless now, are you?" She filled a cordless electric kettle to halfway and set it to boil.

"No, I suppose not."

Ingrid placed a tea bag in Erin's cup. "That's right. You have a wonderful family taking care of you. And how could you be a loser when you have me for a friend?"

Erin smiled in spite of herself. A lull fell between them, and they stood alongside each other, listening to the sound of the kettle heating up the water.

"It's ironic, isn't it?" Erin said after a moment, staring down at the floor but not seeing it. "Here I am, pregnant at the worst possible time in my life. And here you are, desperate to have a baby but unable to. How did it turn out that way?"

"Who can tell?" Ingrid replied, turning to face her. "But I want you to promise me you won't do anything to end this child's life."

Erin jerked her head up to meet Ingrid's gaze, surprised not so much by her candour as her point of view. She'd always thought Ingrid was fine with abortion. The temptation to dismiss her cold and tell her to mind her own business rose up, but she checked herself. "No, I won't," she said after a moment's pause. "I can't say the thought didn't cross my mind for a second. But, no. I don't think I could ever do that."

An expression of relief passed over Ingrid's face. "Good. I never thought I'd say something like this, but since the time Jim and I tried IVF, I've thought about the number of embryos that got flushed away during the whole process. The ones that got frozen, the ones that got inserted, then died. I couldn't do another round after that. Our children. Little lives at their very beginning. Lives that we just disregarded." Ingrid sighed and toyed with the tag of the tea bag in Erin's cup. "I tried to tell myself they weren't people, that it was just organic matter that could one day become a child. But I was kidding myself. I should never have done it. I regret it. I regret it every day."

Erin stared at Ingrid but said nothing.

Ingrid released a sad little laugh. "Listen to me. I'm beginning to sound as Catholic as your mum and dad, aren't I?"

At a loss for words, Erin simply reached out and patted Ingrid's arm as they waited for the kettle to shut off.

Ingrid picked it up and poured the boiling liquid into the

cup, allowing it to brew for a few moments. After adding a dash of cold water from the tap, she handed it to Erin.

"Come on, now, drink this and chin up. If it doesn't kill you, it'll make you stronger."

Erin smelled the tea and wrinkled up her nose. "And if it doesn't make you stronger, it'll give you diarrhoea."

Ingrid laughed. "See? At least you can make a joke."

Erin grimaced. "Not sure how I managed that, under the circumstances. How could things get any worse, Ingrid?"

"Oh, things can always get worse, my dear. But they probably won't."

"Why not?"

"Because these things always come in threes, like you said. The next thing to happen to you is going to be wonderful. Just wait and then tell me if I'm wrong."

*****

Late in the evening, Erin sat up on her bed, clad in her flannelette PJs, leaning against the bedhead. The sharp chill of the autumn evening seeped into the room through the open window, something her mother had done earlier in the day to freshen up her room for her, no doubt. She knew she should get up to close it and pull the crocheted blanket that sat folded at the end of the bed over herself to warm up, but instead she remained still. The chill filling the room was nothing to the deep, biting cold penetrating her soul.

Unable to tell her parents her awful news as they sat down to eat earlier, she instead chose to sit with them as they knelt to pray the Rosary together after dinner, a nightly ritual that had been part of their family for as long as she could remember. It was the first time she had joined them for the Rosary since coming home. The first time she had joined in since she was a teenager, truth be told. She had stopped saying the Rosary altogether sometime after David's passing.

It suddenly seemed strange to her that her rejection of God had begun with his death. David had been so devoted to the Rosary, prayed it so often, or simply listened when he was too sick to make the responses. He had died, peaceful, lying in his room, with a rosary in his hand. *What would you think of me now, David? Your recalcitrant little sister? Look at how I've messed up my life.*

She closed her eyes and lay back on her pillow. *Oh, God, I'm so tired.* An ache began to rise in her throat, and she yielded once more to the tears.

Jeremiah.

Erin opened her eyes with a start. *Oh, no, not again.* More voices. No, wait. Not *more.* The *same* voice. The one she heard in the car the night she left Gareth.

Jeremiah? As in the Old Testament?

Jeremiah.

A pocket edition of the Jerusalem Bible sat on the shelf over Erin's desk, a Christmas present from her parents when she was a child. Getting up, she crossed to the desk to pull it off the shelf and perched herself on the edge of her bed. She held it in one hand for a moment and ran her fingers over the worn, blue cover, remembering how grown up she had felt when they gave it to her. Opening the front cover, a small piece of paper slipped out on to her lap. She picked it up and read it. It was a verse from scripture in David's handwriting, which he had given her some months before he died.

Erin, do not be afraid, Erin, do not be alarmed
For look, I shall rescue you from afar
and your descendants from the country where they are captive.
You will return and be at peace,
secure, and none shall make you afraid.
Jeremiah 46: 27

Erin smiled, and her eyes clouded over. The scripture

verse was addressed to Jacob, she remembered that, but David had put her name in place of Jacob's. It had been so many years since she'd opened her Bible and seen this scripture verse that her brother had penned to console her while he was dying. She lifted the paper to her lips and kissed it. The sadness had been so overwhelming when he died that it had been easier to turn her back on everything, including this beautiful gesture of consolation. How could she have forgotten about this?

Still, forgotten she had. She reread the verse. Despite her long-held rejection of her faith, the words reached into her heart, warmed the chill and consoled her in her loneliness. Was it possible that God was trying to find His way back into her life? How else could she explain the prompting to slow her car that night? To reach now, this night, for her Bible?

Erin's thoughts were interrupted by a knock at her bedroom door. "Can I come in?" Her mother's voice came from the other side of the door.

She placed the Bible at the end of the bed next to the bedpost and wiped her eyes. "Yes," she said, straightening herself.

Judith opened the door. "Is everything all right with you?" she said, the worry in her voice mirroring the concern on her face. "Erin, it's freezing in here." Judith went over to the window and reached behind the blinds, sliding the window shut. "You left in such a hurry this morning and you've hardly spoken a word since you came home," she said, reaching out to turn on an oil-filled heater that sat in the corner.

Erin watched as her mother took a seat next to her on the bed.

Judith's eyes fell on the Bible, and she looked at Erin with a smile. "Goodness, first you sit with us for the Rosary and now I find you with the Bible. What's going on with you, then?"

Judith's gentle attempt at humour broke through the last

of Erin's resistance. She leaned her head on her mother's shoulder and Judith put her arm around Erin's shoulders.

"I'm pregnant with Gareth's child," she whispered, burying her face into Judith's shoulder, unable to bear seeing her reaction.

Judith froze for a second, her grasp on Erin's shoulders tightening a touch. After a pause that lasted an eternity to Erin, Judith finally spoke. "Are you sure?"

"Yes. I went to see Doctor Hart this morning. She said my blood tests all came up negative for any diseases. But I'm pregnant, Mother. Undeniably, one hundred per cent pregnant." Erin lifted her head up to face Judith and met her gaze. "What do you think of that?"

Judith stared back at Erin, her face betraying none of the shock Erin expected to see there, only apprehension. "What are you going to do?" she said, a near tangible fear in her voice.

"You don't need to worry; I'm not going to...get rid of it," Erin replied. "But I did consider it for a second. Doctor Hart said she wouldn't refer me and that I'd have to find another doctor. But I knew, then, that I couldn't do it anyway."

Relief seemed to wash over Judith as her hold on Erin's shoulders relaxed a little. "And now you've been reading the Bible looking for answers?"

"I found a scripture verse that David wrote down for me once, something from Jeremiah." She opened the book cover, took out the quote and handed it to Judith, waiting while she read it. "I had this...idea that I should open my Bible."

Judith read the quote and gave it back to Erin. "That's beautiful," she said, her eyes tearing over. "I never knew David wrote this for you. How do you feel after reading it?"

Erin sighed deeply and leaned her head again on her mother's shoulder. "I don't know. I'm so lost, so...utterly bereft. I was before I discovered this pregnancy. Now, I'm completely overwhelmed. I mean, I'm going to be a mother! But I can't be, Mum. I'm done. I've got nothing left."

"Sounds like an excellent place to start putting things back together," Judith said, giving her a squeeze.

"I don't get it. I've just told you I'm pregnant. I'm unmarried. Why aren't you going off the deep end at me?"

Judith released Erin and stood, facing her as she sat on the bed. "Because you're not a child anymore. You're a grown woman, and you're able to face the consequences of your actions and decisions. Perhaps this baby isn't going to be born into perfect circumstances, but a child is always a blessing."

Erin thought back to that morning, when Doctor Hart had spoken similar words. "But having a baby on my own destroys my whole life," Erin said, her heart sinking like lead. "Gareth doesn't want me. No one's ever going to want me with another man's child."

"That's nonsense. Besides, for now, your father and I want you, and we'll help you every step of the way."

Erin lay herself down on the bed, the last of her energy for her life draining away through a gaping hole in the bottom of her existence. "No, Mum. I'm done. I'm as low as I can go. I can't go on anymore. I can't."

"That's why you need the Lord." Judith pointed up to the crucifix above the doorway. "See Him hanging there? He dragged that cross all the way to Calvary, after a night of beatings, after a flogging that would have killed an ordinary person, after receiving a crown of thorns that dug holes deep in His skin and through His skull, blinding Him with His own blood. He understands what it is to keep going when it seems impossible." Judith turned to face Erin and sat down on the edge of the bed again. "You won't be able to do this without Him. He's calling you. You need to return to your faith."

Erin turned over on her side, staring up at her mother. "And how do I go about doing that?" she said.

"Start by going to Mass. Go tomorrow."
"I don't know, Mum. It's been so long."
"Go, Erin. Listen. See what He has to say to you."

Chapter 7

Mark Ashcroft turned off his computer and pushed himself away from his desk. At 5.15 pm the small architectural firm where he worked had all but emptied. The meeting he'd been in during the afternoon had gone on longer than anticipated, and he didn't plan on sticking around any longer either.

He grabbed his keys from a drawer in a console under his desk, stood and lifted the jacket off the back of his chair, quickly putting it on. He switched off the lamp on his desk and turned towards his boss's glass-panelled office in the back corner.

Rob, the managing director of the firm, was still at his desk. Mark approached the office and tapped a knuckle on the door, which had been left open. "Heading off now, Rob," he said, lifting his hand in a wave.

"Night, Mark. And good input at the last meeting," Rob said as he lifted his phone receiver to his ear to make a call.

"Thanks. See you tomorrow," Mark responded with a smile and began heading out of the building, sending up a prayer of thanks for his job and the easy relationship he had with his employer.

Once out of the office suite, he bypassed the lift and took the two flights of stairs down to the ground floor to exit the building, then started jogging through the crisp evening air towards his car in a neighbouring carpark. While he was grateful for the chance to have impressed the boss in the last meeting, the delay was going to make him late for 5.30 pm Mass, and he didn't want to be any later.

Please, Lord, he prayed. *Let the traffic be clear between here and the cathedral so I'm not too late.*

Mark reached his blue Subaru, unlocked it and climbed in. He prayed a Hail Mary as was his custom before getting behind the wheel, and started the engine, driving cautiously out of the carpark. The sun had all but set and visibility was low.

Driving down Cooyong Street towards Parkes Way, he again felt grateful that his office was on the outer part of the city area, making it quicker to exit on to the main drag. Not that Canberra City was that big or difficult to drive through. You could walk the entire length of the business district in about fifteen minutes.

He chuckled to himself as he drove, wondering what people in Sydney or Melbourne would think of him, complaining about Canberra traffic. He'd barely been able to believe how beautiful Canberra was when he'd arrived two years earlier. Now he was getting used to it, becoming spoiled. It was easy to become used to living in a town that had all the benefits of the city but with no pollution, easy driving and no more than twenty-five minutes' drive from the countryside in any direction.

He began praying again as he picked up speed on Parkes Way and headed towards Kings Avenue Bridge which would take him towards the cathedral. *Thank you, Lord, for the blessings you have showered on me since coming here. Please prepare my heart to receive you, Body, Blood, Soul and Divinity in Holy Communion. And please hear and answer my prayer for a Catholic spouse, that I may give You glory by laying down my life for my wife and family the way You lay down Your life for the Church.*

Mark glanced again at the time lit up on his dashboard. Yes, he would be a few minutes late, but not too much. He could enter quietly and sit down the back so as not to disrupt the Mass.

*****

Erin stepped into a small foyer at the side of the cathedral. She skirted her hand across the holy water font and pushed open a creaky, wooden door that led into the side chapel. A pew towards the back of the chapel was empty, so she slid in along the seat and huddled in the corner, close to the wall, trying to make herself invisible.

From the safety of her corner, she observed the rest of the small congregation in the pews ahead, all waiting, like her, for the 5.30 pm Mass to start. A few young single people arrived from work and some older folk. A young couple sat side by side in a pew close to her on the other side of the aisle. A woman a few rows ahead, in her forties maybe, sat with two teenage girls still wearing their school uniforms. An eclectic group of people with little in common, it appeared, except for their shared faith.

Erin gazed past them towards the sanctuary. The altar was prepared for Mass and a key sat in the lock of the tabernacle door, ready for the priest to open to retrieve hosts for Holy Communion. A crucifix on a stand was placed to the right of the altar facing the people, while a smaller one had been placed on the altar for the priest. The other congregants were kneeling or sitting, their heads bowed in prayer or reading from the missals that were left in the pews.

She glanced back towards the crucifix and in her mind's eye, threw herself at God's feet. *All right, I'm here.* What was it God wanted to say to her? What could He possibly say to fix this horrible mess she found herself in?

What are you doing here? A suggestion, not of her own thoughts, entered her head. *Get out of here now, as quick as you can. You're right at the back — slip out and no one will notice. No one bothers with this rubbish anymore.*

At that moment, someone in a pew further ahead rang a bell and everyone stood, opening missals and reciting the entrance antiphon for the day.

Erin shrugged off the thought, picked up a missal resting on the seat next to her, and turned the pages to find the right place.

A young priest dressed in white vestments entered the

chapel from a side entrance and processed up the aisle. He genuflected, ascended the three steps up into the sanctuary to the altar and bent down to kiss it. When he stood up and faced the congregation, Erin recognised him immediately. It was Father Nick Bentley, the priest who had married Bianca and Ryan.

Father Nick raised his hand to his forehead to make the Sign of the Cross. "In the name of the Father, and of the Son, and of the Holy Spirit," he said.

"Amen," Erin said, joining in with the rest of the congregation.

"The grace of our Lord Jesus Christ, and the love of God, and the communion of the Holy Spirit be with you all."

"And with your spirit."

"Brothers and sisters, let us acknowledge our sins and so prepare ourselves to celebrate the sacred mysteries."

The chill in her soul warmed somewhat, the same way it had when she read the verse from Jeremiah the night before. She paid attention to Father Nick as he continued with the Mass, marvelling at his fervour and devotion.

How strange it seemed to her, seeing such piety in a man so young. They were the same generation; he couldn't be more than a couple of years older than her. What was it that he experienced in his youth that had compelled him to become a priest? What did he see that she missed?

Father prayed with the congregation through the penitential act and opening prayer and then everyone sat down. A young woman sitting at the front stepped up to the ambo to read the daily readings, and Erin continued to fumble through the missal. Just when she found the right spot, her attention was diverted by the creak of the chapel door behind her. A young, dark-haired man carrying a daily missal walked past and slipped into a pew a few rows ahead of her. He knelt for a few moments before sitting down and opening up his book. Erin turned her attention back to the missal while the reader continued.

When the young woman finished the readings, Father stepped over to the ambo and everyone stood while he read from Saint John's Gospel. Then he kissed the Lectionary and motioned for everyone to sit while he stayed standing.

"Now, I don't want to keep you long, I know it's been a long day, and you're all looking forward to getting home." He paused and smiled while a couple of people in the congregation chuckled appreciatively. "But I wanted to focus on a particular verse from today's Gospel reading.

"'Peace I leave with you; my peace I give to you. Not as the world gives do I give it to you. Do not let your hearts be troubled or afraid.' I'd like to share a few thoughts with you that come to mind when I read it. In my dealings with so many of you, and also in my own life, I know how difficult it can be to follow the Lord in this crazy world. But when we read this verse it calls so clearly to mind the love of Jesus."

Erin saw several people nodding.

"It is quite something to become a saint and let the Lord work on us and through us. I'm sure you're all familiar with the prayer of St. Francis, "Make Me a Channel of Your Peace." Like this verse from Saint John, this prayer truly calls to mind all Jesus has done for us, all He has given of Himself for us and all He calls us to. At its essence, it is a prayer that reflects how we are nothing without Him; that it is He who gives us our identity and imbues our lives with meaning. It tells us that if we are to experience a profound and lasting peace and to bring peace into the lives of others, we need to pursue Jesus and His will. We need to make ourselves available to Him to use us when and how He wants. He is always looking for generous, selfless hearts in which to work His marvels. And if we allow Him in, asking Him to make our heart like His, He will.

"I know at times even the most faithful of us can feel let down or a little lost. Life is hard. It's full of uncertainty.

But during those times when we feel doubtful or afraid or lost, there's one thing we can always be certain of. Allow Him in, and He will work His marvels in our hearts, marvels in our own lives and in the lives of others. He will. If nothing else is certain, Jesus is. He will never change, and He will never leave us. Of course, the Blessed Mother of God is our prime example of perfect faith and trust in her Son's will. Mary always has our best interests in her heart and will never fail to lead us to her Son. In the words of Saint Josemaria Escriva, 'without Him, we can do nothing, whereas with Him we can do all things.' Words to live by."

Father Nick stepped back and moved towards the altar for the next part of the Mass.

Erin continued to watch him closely. When it came time for Holy Communion, Erin stayed seated, keeping her head bowed down and pondering the young priest's homily.

Seek Jesus' will? Work marvels in the lives of others? Her mother had encouraged her to come to Mass and listen, hear what God had to say. And this was it? An old anger she didn't realise she harboured began to rise up inside her.

You want me to do Your will? Hasn't Your will had enough of a say in my life? Why did my brother have to die so young? Why did Gareth leave me? Why did You allow me to fall pregnant? Is this all You have planned for me? Sorrow and disappointment? Sorry, Lord, but I just don't understand it. Why have You brought me here? Are You truly here with me like Father Nick says? If so, why do I feel so alone?

Erin sat through the remainder of the Mass without participating. At the final blessing, she kept her head down and her eyes shut.

"May almighty God bless you, the Father, and the Son and the Holy Spirit."

"Amen."

"Go forth, the Mass is ended."

"Thanks be to God."

Erin opened her eyes and looked on as Father Nick kissed the altar again, genuflected and processed back to the sacristy. She bent her head again and remained in her pew for a few minutes, struggling with the conflicting feelings that bombarded her. She contemplated the consolation she felt on reading from the scriptures the night before, and now, hearing Father Nick pray and teach, but was simultaneously confronted with an overwhelming sense of betrayal. Surely a loving God wouldn't have allowed all this mess to happen to her.

No, I won't be drawn into this with You. You can't do this to me.

Then a thought occurred to her. Did God do this to her, or did she do it to herself? Through her own action and inaction? In the clear light of day, she knew she couldn't blame God for what happened with Gareth and with this pregnancy. She had used her own free will to make choices, and these were the results that flowed from them. She knew God did not condone the way she behaved. Perhaps if she had listened years ago, she would be in a very different place right now.

But David's death? Why did God allow it? He was her parents' only son; her and Katrina's only brother. The light of their family in so many ways. Why had God seen fit to take him away?

I just can't get past it, Lord. I'm still so furious with You for allowing him to die. Where were You on the day I stood next to David's lifeless body? If You want me back, if You're truly there, You're going to have to help me. Please, help me.

Erin opened her eyes and peered up. Most of the congregation had left, and there were now only a few people remaining, an older couple and the young man who had come in late. She got up and stepped out of the pew, genuflecting towards the tabernacle before she left the church, an act she did without thinking. It surprised her how quickly the old rituals came back to her.

Hurrying outside, she headed towards her car in an undercover carpark that was right outside the small Manuka shopping area close to the cathedral. She unlocked the car and climbed in, yawning. The evenings were becoming noticeably cooler with each passing day and the cold made her feel horribly tired. She put the key in the ignition and turned. The car sputtered but didn't start.

"No! You've got to be kidding me," she said aloud. She turned the ignition again. Nothing. Glancing down at the dashboard, she realised she'd left the headlights switched on. "All right, Lord," she said, groaning, and slumped back in the car seat. "You've got me. What are you trying to tell me?"

*****

Mark finished his prayers after Communion, made the Sign of the Cross and got up from the kneeler in his pew. He moved to the end of the pew and genuflected to the tabernacle, taking a moment with this final act of worship at the end of Mass. *I'm leaving now, My Lord, but not without You. Please stay with me always.*

He stood and left the now-empty chapel. Stepping out into the fresh evening, he breathed in, relishing the feel of the crisp air in his lungs. With daylight saving now ended, the sun had completely set after evening Mass, and Mark began thinking of the winter ahead. The Canberra winters had perhaps been the hardest thing for him to adjust to, with the temperatures dropping much lower than in his home town of Newcastle. While it didn't snow in Canberra during winter, you could often see snow to the west on the Brindabella mountain ranges.

Mark strode across the road to the carpark and towards

his car. He beeped it unlocked and opened the driver's side door. He was about to climb in when he heard the sound of an engine stalling. Turning around he saw a young woman in a car about five or six spaces down from him get out of her car and raise her mobile phone up towards the ceiling.

Oh no, she looks a little stuck.

"You right there?" he called out to her.

Her head turned in his direction, and she lowered her phone.

"Yeah, thanks. There's just not much phone reception in here," she responded.

"Do you need a hand with anything?" he said.

She paused and stared across at him. Mark could sense her hesitation, and his heart went out to her. He knew it couldn't be easy for a woman to discern whether to engage in conversation with a strange man in an almost-deserted carpark. Not wanting to alarm her, he refrained from approaching.

"Um, I left my lights on, and the battery died," she said. "I'm trying to call roadside assistance to get them to come out and jump start me, or possibly replace the battery. I don't know." She raised her phone to the ceiling again.

"I have some jumper leads in the car," Mark said. "I could help get you started. That would save you waiting for them to arrive."

"Oh, that'd be terrific. Do you mind?"

"Not at all, just a tick."

Mark jumped in his car and drove it over to hers, parking it so the bonnets of both cars were close enough for the leads to reach. He got out and retrieved the leads from the boot and brought them to the front of the car.

She opened and lifted the bonnet of her small Honda. "Thanks for this, I really appreciate it," she said, turning to face him.

"No problem. Glad to help. I'm Mark, by the way."

"I'm Erin," she replied.

Mark smiled at her, momentarily taking in the young woman before him. Though it was nighttime, the carpark was well lit enough for him to see that she was extremely pretty. She had long, light brown hair pulled back in a ponytail that fell over one shoulder. Her complexion was fair with just a dusting of freckles over her nose, and she had intelligent, green eyes that immediately brought warmth to his cheeks. He quickly turned his attention to his own car.

Lifting the bonnet of his car, he connected the leads to both cars. "Hop in now, and start her up," he said.

Erin climbed in her car and started it, this time the engine responding. She got out again.

"Thanks, this is great. You've saved me at least an hour of waiting in the cold."

"We should leave this running for a few minutes, just to make sure it doesn't conk out again on your way home."

"Okay. I can't believe I managed to kill the battery. I only had the lights on for half an hour."

"Sounds like the battery might have been on its way out anyway. You should get it replaced soon."

"Yeah, I guess I should. I don't normally take care of the cars." Erin cast her eyes down suddenly, giving Mark the impression that she wished she hadn't spoken. He stared at her hands, which were folded in front of her. They were ringless. Perhaps she had a boyfriend? How could she not? *Tread carefully now. Don't freak her out.*

"I'm just glad you were okay accepting my help. I wouldn't blame you for feeling uncomfortable talking to a stranger at night."

"I saw you in Mass earlier, so I figured it would be all right," Erin said, lifting her eyes to meet his.

"You were at Mass?" he responded, wondering how on earth he could have missed her. "I didn't see you."

"I was sitting down the back. You walked past me when you came in."

Mark's heart started beating a little faster. This beautiful girl was at Mass this evening?

"I come here after work whenever I can make it," Mark said. "Father Nick became assistant priest recently. I know him pretty well, actually. He's a good pastor and teacher."

"Mmm. It seems like he really believes in what he's saying," she said, pushing her long ponytail back over her shoulder.

"I haven't seen you here before. Do you normally go to another parish?"

Erin hesitated a little before speaking, shadows passing over her eyes. "Yeah, I'm from another parish. But I don't usually go to weekday Mass."

That seemed strange to Mark. He knew from experience that only people who really loved their faith made the effort to come to Mass during the week. Especially on a dark and cool evening. *If she doesn't usually come during the week, I wonder what made her come today?*

"Well, it's good you were here today. Hopefully we'll see you back again." Mark hoped he came across in a friendly, Christian manner that didn't sound as though he was being pushy, or worse, a bit creepy.

"Maybe," she said, avoiding eye contact. "I'll have to see."

Mark regarded her closely for a second, wondering how to proceed with the conversation. Remembering that to her he was just a stranger in a carpark, he refrained from enquiring any further. He allowed the engine to idle a few more moments, then spoke again.

"I think you might be all right now. You should keep it running for a few minutes once you get home." Mark detached the leads and lowered the bonnets on both their cars.

Erin stepped over to the driver's side of her car and opened the door. "Thanks again for your help. Hope I didn't hold you up too much," she said with a smile.

"It's fine. Like I said, no problem at all."

"Take care."

"You too."

Mark watched as she climbed into her car, backed out and drove out of the carpark exit, disappearing into the chilly evening.

Mark rolled up the leads and placed them back in the boot of his car, slamming it shut. He climbed back in behind the driver's seat but didn't move. He knew the next logical step for him was to simply drive home as he had planned. But instead, he re-parked the car, got out and headed back towards the cathedral.

Approaching the side door to the chapel, he found it was still open. Stepping inside, he saw the church was still lit and heard movement in the sacristy. He knew his priest friend would want to lock up soon, so he went quickly to the front pew.

He knelt at the end of the pew closest to the aisle, as close to the tabernacle as he could get. He gazed up at it, calmed by the red flickering of the tabernacle lamp alongside, indicating that the Real Presence of the Lord of heaven and earth was inside. *How extraordinary.* The creator of the whole universe contained in a small metal box in all the Catholic churches in the world, waiting patiently for people to come and love Him.

He thought back to his encounter with the young woman in the carpark. *Erin.*

So brief, so few words exchanged, yet he was sure he would have trouble sleeping that night because of it. He couldn't quite place what it was about her that made such an impression on him.

She was beautiful, to be sure, and it was clear that she was well educated from the way she dressed and spoke. And she was a Mass attendee, something that came down in her favour with him. But there was something else about her that haunted him.

He closed his eyes and prayed silently for a moment. He

opened his eyes and turned his gaze towards the tabernacle. All in a moment, it became clear to him.

She was sad.

Mark lowered his head. *Lord, please shower Erin with Your blessings. Be with her through whatever trial she's going through. Grant her peace, serenity and happiness and hold her safe in Your heart. And, if it's okay with You, Lord, please let me see her again.*

Chapter 8

The next evening, Mark once again arrived at the cathedral for evening Mass, this time a few minutes early. Crossing the street towards the chapel entrance, he admitted to himself that while he hated being late for Mass, the possibility that Erin might turn up fired him with a little extra motivation to arrive on time. He endeavoured to measure out his paces as he approached the church, resisting the temptation to bolt through the chapel door to see if she was there.

He stepped into the chapel foyer, blessed himself from the holy water font and pushed through the creaky door into the chapel. Casting his eyes quickly across the pews, his heart almost stopped when he saw Erin seated a few rows from the back.

She came back.

The elation he experienced on discovering her there surprised and alarmed him. Reminding himself that he knew practically nothing about her, he made his way to one of the centre pews where he usually sat. He glanced sideways at her as he walked past, but she didn't look up.

Mark knelt down and tried his best to recollect his thoughts, prepare himself for Holy Communion and give thanks for his many blessings. He also decided to offer prayers at Communion for Erin's intentions, and for relief from whatever heartache he was sure she was going through.

Father Nick was scheduled to pray Mass again that day. The young priest processed into the chapel and ascended the sanctuary steps. As he made the Sign of the Cross, Mark immersed himself in the Mass, praying that he could conform himself as perfectly as possible to God's will and to be an instrument through which God would work His marvels.

After receiving Holy Communion, Mark prayed for Erin. He also prayed for wisdom to discern the feelings he was having around her, feelings he realised were disproportionate with the two fleeting times he'd seen her in the last twenty-four hours. *If this is out of place, please show me.* Peace settled over him and by the time Mass ended, all traces of anxiety were gone.

His prayers after Communion went for so long that by the time he opened his eyes, the chapel was almost empty. He turned around to see if Erin was still in her pew, but the pew was empty. He got up out of his seat, genuflected and made his way out of the chapel, disappointed that he had missed an opportunity to talk to her again. Berating himself for his disappointment, he pushed through the chapel door into the small side foyer and almost bowled straight into a young woman stopped by the brochure stand, poring over a couple of pamphlets. She glanced up when he came through the door, and he stopped short. It was Erin.

"Oh, hi!" he said, backing up a little. The disappointment that had settled on him only a second earlier evaporated entirely, replaced by sheer joy. *For Pete's sake, don't let it show.* "I'm so sorry. I almost knocked you over there."

"Oh, hello. Don't worry, you didn't bump into me." She smiled up at him, causing his heart to flip-flop.

"Mark? Right?" she said, regarding him briefly before peering down again at the pamphlets in her hand and placing them in her handbag.

"Yep."

Erin stepped towards the door that led to the street. Mark pulled it open and stood back, allowing her to pass. She smiled politely at him, seeming to wait for him to follow her, something he was only too happy to do.

"So, did you get that car battery fixed?" Mark asked,

falling into step beside her as she headed for the carpark.

"Yeah, I did, thanks. I borrowed my dad's car today; he's taking care of the battery for me," she said, thrusting her hands in the pockets of her coat as she checked the road for traffic.

Dad? So, maybe no boyfriend?

"Thanks again for your help yesterday."

"No problem, glad to help." They crossed the road together and wandered towards the carpark. Mark glanced at her from the corner of his eye as they walked, her head bent slightly and hands in her coat pockets. He wondered what she was thinking. She clearly maintained her polite exterior, but he sensed in her the sadness he had picked up on yesterday. She appeared distracted, perhaps by what she was reading in the foyer earlier, but didn't appear to mind his presence. He racked his mind for ways to continue the conversation.

"So, do you work around here, Erin?"

"Yes, quite close by, in Kingston. You?"

"Over the bridge, in Braddon," Mark replied, at a loss for something else to say. He dearly wanted to stay in her company but was unsure of the best way to keep the conversation going, or how to secure a chance to see her again once they reached their respective vehicles. Perhaps he would have to be content with glimpsing her occasionally at daily Mass, if and when she decided to attend.

They reached the carpark, and Erin began heading towards a white Camry when, all of a sudden, she stopped short and turned to face Mark, her forehead creased in a frown.

"I hope this doesn't seem too forward, but I was wondering if I could ask you something," she said. "You said you come to Mass often. That must mean you really believe in the Catholic faith, right?"

Where is this going?

"Yes, I do," he replied, wondering what she would say next.

"Can I ask you, what's your take on—" she rummaged around in her bag and pulled out the two pamphlets she put in there a minute before and held them out to him "— these?"

Mark stepped towards her and took the pamphlets. He immediately recognised them as publications from a Catholic pro-life organisation in Sydney, a series that Father Nick had started making available in the cathedral. One was about the pill, which explained how its use is contrary to human dignity and the significant health risks associated with taking it. The other about a form of Natural Family Planning called the Sympto-Thermal Method.

"These are excellent," he said. "They're all in line with what the Church teaches. I particularly like the one about Natural Family Planning." Mark handed the pamphlets back to her. "This method is easy to use and works well, not only in family planning but also helps in keeping relationships together. That's what's great about a series of brochures like these. They don't simply point out what's wrong with contraception and leave you floundering. They offer an alternative that isn't damaging to our relationship with God or our bodies."

"Right," she said, taking them back and sliding them back in her bag. "So the Church does still teach against contraception?"

"Yes. The Church hasn't wavered on this teaching ever, though there has been a lot of confusion over the years."

Erin nodded and glanced down for a few seconds, placing her hands back in her pockets. "Sorry, I realise this might strike you as a little odd, a near stranger grilling you on Church teaching."

"It's fine. In fact, you'll find it helpful to talk through the questions you have, rather than nut things out alone. I know I did, a lot, when I started practising again."

Erin's head darted up, and her eyes widened a little. "You mean, you haven't always practised?"

Mark nodded, staring back at her, basking in the thoughtful expression on her face as she processed this information. *Do it. Ask her out. Now.*

He took a deep breath. "Listen, is there anywhere you need to be right now? Cause if not, maybe we could...go get a coffee or something and you could talk through anything bothering you?"

Erin immediately appeared taken aback, as if his question were the absolute last thing she expected to hear. *Oh no.*

"Oh gosh, um...." she raised her hand to her shoulder and pushed her hair back over it, as she had done the night before. "Um..."

Oh no, mate. Now you've blown it.

Mark was on the verge of dashing towards the nearest wheelie bin to throw himself in when, all in a second, her demeanour changed.

"Yeah, okay," she said, smiling up at him. "I don't have anywhere I need to be."

Mark smiled back. *Touchdown!*

*****

Ten minutes later, Mark and Erin sat at a table by the window in a popular bistro in the Manuka district. Happy hour was already well underway, but thankfully most of the patrons kept to the bar at the other side of the restaurant. The dinner rush hadn't yet started, leaving them both in relative peace. Mark contemplated Erin as she sat staring out the window, a wistful expression on her face. *What is she thinking? Is she regretting coming out with me?*

A tall, slim waitress in fitted black jeans and black top approached their table. "Here for a drink or for dinner?"

she asked, grasping an electronic ordering pad and stylus.

"Just a drink," Mark said. "I'll have a Corona, thanks."

"A mineral water for me, thanks," Erin said, glancing up at her and seeming a little uncomfortable.

The waitress tapped on her device. "Be right with you," she said smiling and strutted off towards the bar.

Mark leaned forward in his seat a little, keen to set Erin at ease.

"So, you said you work close by. What do you do?"

"I'm a copywriter. I work for an advertising agency," she replied. "What about you?"

"I'm an architect."

"Cool. That sounds like fun."

"Yeah, it can be. I have to say your job sounds pretty cool too."

"Sometimes it is. Mostly I sell stuff. Appealing to the needs of the consumer. I'm not so great at writing catchy slogans. I'm better at writing about the product the client is trying to sell, for brochures, websites, radio ads, stuff like that. I've always loved writing. I never wanted to do anything else."

Mark nodded. "It was the same for me, but with drawing. I've always loved it. My interest in architecture sort of grew out of that. "

"It's supposed to be a good thing to work doing something you love," Erin said, without conviction. She paused and gazed out the window. "I applied for a promotion recently, something with a bit less writing but more responsibility. It made sense. Climb the ladder. I found out today I didn't get it, though." She sighed and glanced down at her hands.

"I'm sure you were an excellent candidate. I think your supervisors must have made a mistake."

"No, I don't think they did."

The waitress returned with a Corona and a Pellegrino, placing them on the table before flouncing off to serve another customer.

Mark regarded Erin as she opened her bottle and poured it into a glass. She took a small sip then placed it down. Then she lowered her head and lifted her hands to her face.

"Oh, my God, what am I doing?" she whispered to herself. Horror filled him as her shoulders began shaking with silent sobs.

"Are you all right?" he said, his heart instantly morphing from a functioning organ to a puddle of sludge in his ribcage. "Is something wrong?"

"Yes, something's wrong," she said, her voice breaking. She reached down to the floor for her bag and placed it on the table in front of her. "There are so, *so* many reasons why I shouldn't be here."

Oh no, she wants to leave. Did he do the wrong thing asking her out? He knew there was something upsetting her. He should have been more sensitive, left her alone. But he had no idea she was going to break down like this.

"Hey, don't worry, it'll be okay," he said, struggling to find the words that would ease her distress. "You don't have to stay. Give yourself a minute, and I'll walk with you to your car."

Erin nodded, and the tears started to flow. She reached into her bag for a couple of tissues and dabbed at her eyes. Placing her face in her hands again, she began crying in earnest.

Mark watched her while she sobbed, praying the right words would come to him when she calmed down. Her sorrow was palpable. With each sob, it was as though an invisible knife was paring slices off her soul. And with each sob, he found himself suffering a little with her. What was it? The death of someone close to her? A broken relationship? Finally the torrent subsided, and she managed to speak.

"I'm so sorry. I'm not normally this loopy," she said

sniffing and stuffing a soggy tissue in her bag. "Bursting into tears in front of someone I only just met."

"Please don't apologise. I'm more sorry about the distress you're going through."

"No, no, I...." Erin took a deep breath and put her hands on the table in front of her. "My engagement ended about four weeks ago. My fiancé, Gareth, who I'd been living with for five years, just up and found someone else. I didn't notice any of the signs. I wasn't prepared for it."

Woah. A fiancé? *Five* years? Mark hadn't anticipated something like this. What a doozy. Only four weeks ago? A serious case of someone on the rebound if ever there was one.

"Erin, how awful. I'm so sorry."

"It's okay; it's not your fault. But the whole thing has wrecked me. And to top it all off, I...." she stopped abruptly, as though she caught herself about to say something she didn't plan to. She swallowed and collected herself before continuing. "Anyway, I've been staying with my parents since Gareth and I split. I can't find my bearings. I'm just so lost."

"Understandably."

"My family is pretty Catholic. I haven't been to Mass, or Confession, for a while. Years and years, actually. My mum encouraged me to go to Mass. She said I need my faith to help me."

"Sounds like your mother is a wise woman."

Erin peered at him, her lovely eyes red from crying. "Yes, I can tell you feel the same way she does. And my dad and my sister and her husband. I've always thought that Catholicism — I don't know — went out of fashion ages ago. I didn't think anyone practised much anymore. I thought my family was a bit...."

"Strange?"

She smiled a little. "I guess so."

"Look, you're not wrong in that a lot of Catholics, in this

country at least, don't practise their faith. But that doesn't make our faith less true. It doesn't make it less relevant in our lives, or less vital to our living out our humanity to the fullness that God intended."

Erin stared back at him, her expression telling him she was trying to take in what he said, but remaining confused and unconvinced. It was obvious the last thing she needed at this moment was a lecture. Mark decided to change the subject.

"This thing with your ex-fiancé, it'll get easier with time."

She shook her head slowly, appearing mournful and tired. "So they say. But it sounds like an empty platitude to me."

"No, it really does. Then, one day, it won't hurt you much anymore."

"How do you know?"

Mark drew in a breath and paused for a moment. "Because I had a girlfriend once who did the same thing to me."

Erin's eyes widened and again he could see surprise at this revelation. "We weren't engaged, and we hadn't lived together for as long as you and your fiancé, but it was one of the worst things that happened to me."

"You lived with someone? For how long?"

"Two years."

"Wow." Erin sat back and seemed to contemplate him for a second, distracted momentarily by this information. "Looks like I summed you up all wrong."

He smiled. "Never judge a book by its cover."

"So what made you become...." Erin paused, seeming to fumble for the right word.

"Become what?"

"Well, become all holy?"

Mark laughed aloud, amused by her assessment of him. "I'm not that holy, Erin."

"Sorry, but you know what I mean. I've seen you the last

couple of days, how...how prayerful you are. How did that happen in someone who didn't have any time for his faith before?"

"Well, I'd love to tell you that story some day. But I suppose, in the end, I couldn't resist."

"Resist what?"

"Resist my God, calling me to Himself."

Erin didn't respond. She reached for her glass but didn't drink anymore.

Mark studied her face, clouded by sadness, doubt and fatigue. A woman at crossroads. Vulnerable. A sudden and overwhelming desire to enfold her, to shield and protect her from the storm that raged around her, pierced through him.

This is crazy. He'd only met her yesterday. Spoken with her twice. What was the matter with him? There were only a couple of people from Canberra he'd told about his conversion and his past relationship. Now here he was, telling someone he'd only just met.

Yet, he realised it probably helped her. *For what reason have You allowed Erin into my life, Lord? Brought me into hers? Is it to help her find some direction? Or something more? Please shine Your light on this situation. Don't allow my feelings to get in the way, if it isn't Your will.*

Erin's eyes closed for a moment. She drew in a deep breath and yawned a little, quickly covering her mouth with her hand.

"I'm so sorry," she said, once she finished yawning. "But I think I should probably get going. I might fall asleep at the wheel if I don't head home."

"Excellent idea. You could do with a good sleep, I think. I'll walk with you."

Mark went to the register and paid for their drinks, then rejoined Erin at the table. They walked the short distance back to the carpark, exchanging only a few words. He walked with her right up to her car and waited while she got it started. She rolled down the window and turned towards him.

Mark stepped back from the car a little. "Make sure you stay awake now. Turn on the radio or something."

"Don't worry, I will," she replied. "Thanks for this evening. It was good of you to listen."

"All good. You take care now."

"You too. Maybe I'll see you at Mass again?"

Mark's heart surged within him, warming him in spite of the evening chill. "Of course. I'm glad you want to come back."

"I'm not sure where else to go right now."

"There's nowhere better."

Erin smiled. "See ya," she said, rolling up the window.

"Bye," Mark said, and watched her drive off into the night again, trying to ignore the feeling that she was driving away with his heart.

Mark wandered over to his car and got in, grasping the steering wheel tight in his hands. He thought back over the last half hour. It was like he'd lived a lifetime in those few minutes. How could everything change so much in such a short time?

"Get a grip," he said out loud to himself. "This was nothing. Just some girl I had a fifth of a drink with who's been through a breakup. She's not even a practising Catholic. Forget about it."

He closed his eyes and instantly beheld her in his mind's eye, seated across from him at the restaurant only minutes earlier. Downcast, lonely. And absolutely exquisite.

"Oh, heck, who am I kidding?" he said out loud to no one. He knew full well there was no way he would be forgetting about Erin. How did this happen? It had been so long since a girl had captured his attention like this. There had been no one, not since....

No. He'd already brought up one painful memory about

her this evening. There had been so many awful times, so many bad memories to choose from. He knew from experience that dwelling on them achieved little.

Especially *that* memory. The day that she—

Mark's throat constricted, and his eyes started stinging with tears. He let them fall for a moment then brushed them away, refusing to indulge them. He had grown used to this pattern. Some wounds were too deep to heal completely.

He sat up straight and started the engine. Erin had baggage, but she wasn't the only one. If there was any way he could use what he'd suffered to help ease her burden, nothing was going to stop him.

*****

Erin opened the front door of her parents' home and stepped inside, the warm air in the heated house wrapping around her like a blanket. She yawned and closed the door behind her. No sooner had it clicked shut than she heard her mother's voice calling from the kitchen.

"Erin, is that you?

"Yes, I'm home," Erin replied, taking off her coat and heading into the kitchen. She found Judith sealing the lid on some leftovers and placing them in the fridge.

"Hello," she said, closing the fridge door. "I've saved some dinner for you. Are you hungry?"

"More empty than hungry," Erin said, taking a seat at the kitchen table and dropping her bag and coat on the seat next to her. "I suppose I should eat something."

"You suppose correctly," Judith said, reaching for a plate on the kitchen bench and placing it in the microwave. "You've lost enough weight already. You don't want to lose any more if you can avoid it. Though you might have trouble keeping things down in the first trimester."

"Please, don't remind me, Mum," Erin said, groaning. "The fact that I'm pregnant will become obvious soon enough when my stomach begins expanding to occupy all available space."

Judith chuckled but didn't respond. Erin marvelled at how well her parents had taken this unexpected development in their lives. If only she were taking it as well as they seemed to be.

"Where's Dad?"

"You missed him by a few minutes. He's gone to help the Missionaries of Charity sisters with the soup kitchen at Ainslie Village."

"Oh, of course. I forgot."

The soup kitchen was something Liam Rafferty had been helping with for many years, along with a number of other efforts both he and Judith participated in. The MC sisters, or Mother Teresa sisters as some thought of them, had a small convent and women's refuge in Queanbeyan, a few streets from where her parents lived. Erin had always liked them as a youngster, dressed in their distinctive white and blue sari, the same as their foundress. Always smiles and cheer, kindness and love. Erin tried to remember the last time she had spoken with any of the sisters.

"How was your day today? Did you go to Mass at the cathedral again?" Judith asked, disrupting her thoughts. She got some cutlery out of the kitchen drawer for Erin then proceeded to wipe down the sink.

"Work was fine. I'm keeping on top of things. And yes, I did go to Mass again."

"Good," Judith said but didn't press any further.

Erin knew her mother well enough to know she had no intention of intruding into what Judith considered an immensely private experience, which was fine with Erin. She wasn't ready to discuss religion with her mother just yet anyway. Her thoughts wandered instead to her encounter with Mark.

"Something kind of...unexpected happened after Mass today."

"Really? What?" Judith stopped her activity in the kitchen and turned to face Erin.

"You remember I told you yesterday someone at Mass helped me start my car after the battery died?"

"Yes," her mother replied, sounding intrigued.

"Well, I saw him again today. We walked to the carpark together from the church, and I was about to go home when...when he asked me for a coffee."

"And?"

"And I went. I wasn't going to. But then I changed my mind. I'm not sure why."

Judith bore a quizzical look into her, which Erin met full on. "Well, I'm not surprised you're being noticed," she said. "It happened all the time when you were with Gareth, but you never cared about anyone else while he was around. But do you think you should be accepting coffee invitations from men at this particular time? You're very...."

"Very what, Mum?"

Judith sighed and put the dishcloth on the edge of the sink. "Very vulnerable. What do you know about this man?"

"Not much. But you don't have to worry. After the meltdown I had in the restaurant, I doubt he'll be asking me out again."

"You had a meltdown?" Judith said, raising her eyebrows.

"Yeah. About two minutes after we arrived, I burst into tears. Being out with someone other than Gareth after having been with him for so long, it was too much, too soon."

"What did he say when that happened?"

"He was kind. He seemed to understand. I told him about Gareth, and he told me he used to live with a girl who ended up leaving him too. Now he's practising his faith again. I found that interesting."

Judith nodded but said nothing.

Erin stared at her mother. "What? Just tell me."

"This man asked you out."

"Yes. So?"

"Well, clearly he's interested in you. Did you make plans to meet up again?"

"No. Look, I told you not to worry. Like I said, my life is far too...unhinged for anyone to take me seriously at the moment. I'll be fine. I just...."

"What?"

Erin paused, trying to make sense of the evening, to form a clear sentence to articulate her thoughts. She knew she was too much of a mess for someone like Mark, and he would certainly realise that. But that didn't worry her, and it wasn't uppermost in her mind after talking with him. Something was different. She felt lighter, less burdened. Like sharing some of the mess with Mark had diminished the load.

"It was like an answer to prayer."

"An answer to prayer?"

Erin saw she had grabbed her mother's interest. "Yes. I realise that sounds weird coming from me. I can hardly believe I'm saying it. I was praying in Mass last night for help. Help with everything, everything I've been angry with God for. Then, my car didn't start, and he was there. I didn't think much of it. But then today I saw him again and told him about Gareth, even though I didn't plan to. And again, it helped. *He* helped. In spite of everything, I feel a little bit better."

Her mother stared back, seeming to process this information.

A surge of weariness enveloped Erin, and she yawned again. "Oh, listen to me," she said. "I've done nothing but yawn all evening."

"Good. It shows you're relaxing. You're exhausted. You haven't slept well for weeks." Judith picked up the cutlery and brought it over to Erin, placing it down in front of her.

"You're right. I haven't felt this relaxed since before that night with Gareth," she said, arranging the knife and fork in front of her. "Longer. Much longer. I think I could sleep and sleep."

"Then you should. Have something to eat and go to bed. You need to rest."

Erin smiled. "Mark said the same thing."

"His name's Mark?"

Erin nodded. "Yep. He seems like a nice guy."

"Yes, you said that. What does he look like?"

She thought for a second. "Dark hair, a bit wavy. Brown eyes, I think."

"Tall?"

"Yes. Well, a fair bit taller than me, I suppose."

"Good-looking, then?"

"Mum, I can see where you're going with this. Don't bother."

Judith chuckled again. "Well, you're the one who got rescued by a tall, dark, handsome stranger. I'm just trying to put the pieces together with the sparse information you're giving me." She retrieved the plate with lasagne and steamed vegetables from the microwave and placed it down in front of Erin. "I must say, it's lovely to see a smile on your face." She took a seat next to her at the table.

Erin picked up her fork and tasted her mother's cooking. "This is delicious," she said. "I haven't eaten your lasagne in so long."

"I made lasagne a couple of weeks ago," Judith said, smiling and rubbing Erin's arm. "You tried some but didn't finish it."

"I didn't? I don't remember." Erin ate another mouthful, relishing the familiar flavour of her mother's cooking. She paused and thought for a second. "Perhaps I could help out with the cooking a couple of nights a week for you and

Dad, or on weekends, seeing I'm living here at the moment."

"That's thoughtful, sweetheart. Thank you."

Erin placed down her fork for a moment and reached for her mother's hand. "No, thank *you* for taking care of me. A few weeks ago, I never would have believed I'd need this kind of care. But now, I shudder to think what I would have done without you and Dad. Especially with this...new development." She reached down with her other hand and placed it on her stomach.

"Ah, Erin. 'We know that in everything God works for good with those who love him, who are called according to His purpose.' Romans 8:28."

Erin lowered her head. "But I haven't loved God. I don't think that verse applies to me."

Judith leaned forward and smiled. "Yes, it does, my dear," she said. "You cried to the Lord for help, and He helped you. Remember, just because you forgot about Him for a while doesn't mean He's forgotten about you."

Chapter 9

"Blood pressure 110/70," Doctor Hart said, removing a cuff from around Erin's upper arm. "Good."

Erin sat in Debbie Hart's office for her first visit since discovering her pregnancy. She exhaled and pulled down her sleeve over her bare arm.

Debbie entered some details into her computer. "Are you planning on being a private or public patient?"

Erin gulped. She couldn't imagine herself paying the excess on a birth in the private system, especially if she needed a caesarean. "Public, I think."

"Fine. The public system is excellent. You'll meet regularly with a midwife and once or twice with an obstetrician over the course of the pregnancy at whatever hospital you choose. Make sure you register soon. Your first appointment with them should be at around sixteen weeks."

"Okay," Erin replied. *Sixteen weeks*? She placed a hand on her still-flat stomach. How big would she be so far in? She was able to hide her pregnancy easily at this point. What would people say when they found out?

With the medical part of her examination finished, Doctor Hart turned towards Erin. "Do you have any questions?"

"I do, actually," Erin said, thinking of the pamphlet on the pill from the cathedral foyer. "Not about the pregnancy though, just something I read recently in a leaflet — about the pill. It said the pill is a human carcinogen. Is this true?"

"Yes," Debbie replied. "The combined oestrogen and progestin pill is a Group One human carcinogen. The World Health Organization declared this in 2005."

"Yeah, so I read." *Unbelievable.* Erin had been pondering

this information since the night she read it, dubious at first about its accuracy. She had been certain Debbie, a medical professional, would reassure her this was an exaggeration at the least. She thought back over the hundreds of times she placed the artificial hormones in her mouth and swallowed without a second thought for the havoc it might be wreaking on her body. Why had she not checked this out more thoroughly a long time ago? A hot ball of anger began forming in her gut, and her body tensed up a little.

"Why didn't anyone mention this to me before? My GP wrote me scripts for the pill again and again and never mentioned this. Nearly all my friends are on the pill. If it's so dangerous, why does the medical community hand it out like lollies at a kid's birthday party?"

"Honestly, I'm not sure many of them are aware of the risks," Debbie replied. "Pill usage is so engrained in our society as a way to prevent pregnancy, many of them might ignore the risks even if they did know. I refuse to prescribe any brand of OCP, not even to treat complaints like painful or heavy periods, as the pill only masks the complaint without providing any treatment. There isn't anything the pill is prescribed for that can't be solved or treated another way."

"But this is outrageous. I would never have taken the pill if I'd been aware of all this." She remembered washing the last of the useless pills down the sink, weeks before. *Better late than never, I suppose.*

"You're right. Most women say that when they discover the truth."

"What are the alternatives?" Erin asked.

Debbie leaned back in her chair. "All hormonal contraceptives carry a degree of risk. Other types are messy or unreliable or both. And no form of artificial contraception, no matter how reliable, is completely failsafe. Besides which, and very importantly, the menstrual cycle is a completely normal part of a woman's physical make up. I take exception to using artificial hormones or barriers to obliterate a perfectly healthy process."

"So what do you tell your patients who want to put space between their children?" Erin waited, though she sensed the answer Debbie would give her.

"There are some extremely reliable natural ways to manage fertility. Natural Family Planning is largely dismissed as unreliable, but nothing could be further from the truth. I always point patients in this direction." Debbie paused. "If you need any advice on this in the future, let me know."

"Thanks," Erin replied, wondering if she would ever need advice on family planning again.

"And how are things otherwise?"

"All right, thank you. My family is supporting me. I guess I'm still adjusting, but I'm getting by from day to day."

Erin didn't need to lie. More than two months had passed since breaking up with Gareth. She knew she should still be feeling as though a train had run her over. The sadness Gareth's rejection had left in her heart remained, but it didn't overwhelm her. The compulsion to cry at the slightest thought of Gareth, or of being a single mother, had passed. Perhaps her instinct to survive for the sake of her child was predominating, or perhaps it was because her family cared for her so well.

Or maybe, she had to admit, it was because she had been going to Mass so frequently. Her reluctance to attend in the beginning had been outweighed by her desperation to find answers. The answers she was seeking were still hidden from her, but despite her doubt, she daily found herself craving the peace she experienced while sitting at Mass, surrounded by the prayers of the other parishioners, quietly forming her own, hoping beyond hope that they might be heard. On the one hand, a part of her reasoned that she was being ridiculous, but no amount of reasoning could talk her out of the consolation she found from daring to believe her problems were not being carried by herself alone.

"Glad to hear," Debbie said. "You're healthy and everything is progressing well. Whatever you're doing, keep it up."

*****

Erin stepped out of the medical centre into the beautiful late May morning. An extended autumn had resulted in warm daytime temperatures lasting longer than many Canberrans had expected and Erin was grateful. A soft, mild breeze blew gently, and the sun shone down on her, warming her face and hair and soothing her soul. She breathed deeply and closed her eyes, tilting her head towards the sunlight. She couldn't remember in recent months a more impeccable day.

Lucky I'm not going in to work today. Erin had several leave days owing and had applied for one to take care of this most recent doctor's appointment. So far, only her family and Ingrid were aware of her pregnancy, and she wanted to keep it that way, for now at least. She took in another deep breath and soaked in the sunlight for a second longer before walking towards her car. The morning was getting on, and she planned to go to the cathedral for lunchtime Mass and enjoy a peaceful afternoon.

Erin got into her car and drove towards the cathedral. She hadn't yet attended a midday Mass and wondered if Father Nick would be officiating. Though tempted to talk to him on several occasions, she had still to work up the courage. There were many questions she wanted to ask, not the least of which concerned her recent discovery about the pill and how this fitted in with Church teaching. She thought perhaps Father Nick could provide some answers. Perhaps one day she should approach him and ask if he had a moment to talk.

As she got closer to the cathedral, her thoughts turned to Mark. Erin had been hoping to see him again at each Mass she'd attended recently, but he hadn't been there since the night they'd gone for a drink. *I'm so crazy; I probably frightened him away from his own church.* Yeah, it would be just like her to do that.

No, surely that couldn't be it. Maybe he was just busy at work and couldn't make evening Mass. Chances were they'd bump into each other again soon. She hoped so. She wanted to apologise to him for her behaviour, reassure him she didn't normally act like that. Bursting into tears and then almost falling asleep in her mineral water. How embarrassing.

Minutes later, Erin arrived at the cathedral chapel and sat in the pew a few rows from the back, a spot she'd come to think of as her own. She knelt and closed her eyes, trying to form a prayer to the God she had come to be certain was, in fact, there.

Lord, I'm no longer tempted to believe You are simply a myth I rejected in my youth. So, what should I do now? I'm still so confused. So much has changed for me. Many things I believed to be firmly set have come crumbling down around me, and I can't find my way forward. And now there's a life growing inside me. A little person who needs me to be strong. Please, show me the way.

She sat up and began leafing through the daily missal her father had lent her, which was more comprehensive than the ones available in the chapel. Someone from the congregation rang the bell for the start of Mass and an older priest, one Erin didn't know, processed down the aisle and began ascending the steps to the sanctuary. She stood with the rest of the congregation to recite the entrance antiphon and watched while Father bent down to kiss the altar. As her eyes momentarily glanced across the pews ahead of her, she noticed a tall, familiar figure standing in a pew close to the front on the other side of the chapel. *Mark.*

An unexpected rush of joy rose up inside her, and a smile instantly formed on her face. Surprised at herself, she lowered her head, wondering if her reaction was visible to anyone standing nearby. *Thank goodness I'm sitting at the back.*

During Mass, Erin did her best to focus but found herself distracted occasionally by Mark's presence. At Communion time, she stayed in her pew as she always did and watched Mark as he got into the line with the rest of the congregation. She hoped he might glance over and see her as he walked back, but after receiving the Host he seemed transfixed, kneeling down as soon as he returned to his pew, head bent, and hands joined in prayer.

When Mass ended, Erin decided to stay and wait for Mark to leave so she could try and talk with him. He stayed kneeling while the chapel quietly emptied around them.

Finally he got up, stepped out of his pew and genuflected towards the tabernacle before turning and heading down the aisle to the back of the chapel. Erin stood and stepped into the aisle, waiting for Mark to glance in her direction. She smiled as he paced towards her, his eyes finally meeting hers. He stopped short and his face lit up.

"Erin!" he said, grinning. "How are you?" He peered down at her with sparkling brown eyes, giving Erin the instant impression that he was truly interested in her answer, not simply muttering some pleasantry.

It was the first time Erin had seen Mark in the daytime, and she found herself a little overwhelmed. She remembered her mother asking her if Mark was attractive. Seeing him today, dressed casually in a dark grey button-down shirt, black jacket and jeans, she realised now that describing him as simply good-looking would be rather an understatement.

"I'm okay, thanks. How are you?"

"Pretty well," he said, and gestured with his hand for her to walk ahead of him. "After you."

Erin smiled again and walked ahead of Mark out of the chapel and onto Franklin Street into the lunchtime bustle. Traffic was building up along the small Franklin and Furneaux Street intersection, and the shopping and restaurant district across from the cathedral was buzzing with activity. Everywhere around them, people were out strolling, enjoying the unusually temperate day.

"How's this weather?" Mark said, removing his jacket. "Who would believe we could get a daytime temperature like this so far into May?"

"Oh, I know," Erin replied. "They're predicting twenty-two degrees today. It might be the last of the fine weather though, so enjoy it while it lasts."

"I reckon." Mark didn't make any attempt to walk towards his car or the shops across the road which Erin took as a sign he wanted to stay and talk for a moment. She tried to clear her thoughts and come up with something sensible to say.

"So nice to bump into you again, after all these weeks," Erin said, hoping he might explain his absence.

"Thanks. A big project at work has prevented me from making evening Masses for a while. Lots of late nights. But I've been praying for you."

"You have?" So he *had* been working late. And he'd been praying for her. The warm rush she felt earlier returned, causing her to smile again, and she glanced down for a moment, hoping that her face didn't show what was in her heart. "Thank you; how thoughtful."

Then the memory of their last encounter came crashing back into her consciousness, and she started to fidget, nervously rearranging her bag strap over her shoulder.

"I'm glad you're here today. I just wanted to apologise to

you for the other night. I was a total mess, and you were so great about it."

Mark shook his head. "It was fine. You're going through a tough time. I understand. If I was any help to you, then I'm glad I was there."

Erin nodded, relieved that she had dealt with that issue. Mark didn't seem to be in a hurry to leave, and she wondered if he needed to return to work.

"Well, I don't want to keep you. Are you working today? You don't appear to be dressed for the office."

Mark chuckled. "No, actually I have a day off to make up for all the overtime."

"You get flex-time at your work? Lucky you."

"What about you? You headed back to the office?"

Erin was dressed differently from the way she would for work in a tunic top, jeans and ankle boots, but she didn't expect a guy to notice details like that. Though she was dressed casually, she'd decided that morning to put some extra effort into her appearance, something she'd been tempted to dispense with. Now, talking with Mark, she was deeply thankful she'd made the extra effort. "No, I'm off work today too."

"Do you have any plans for lunch?"

Erin's heart beat irregularly for a second. "No, I'm free this afternoon."

"I was going to get a sandwich in Manuka and eat down by the lake to make the most of the weather. Would you like to come with me?"

Oh, Lord, he's asking me out again. She could hardly believe he was still interested in talking to her after her witless performance the last time she met him.

Was this such a good idea? Her mother's words of caution came to mind. Judith was right, she was vulnerable at the moment. And felt it. Not in a place to start new relationships.

But there was something about Mark she found disarming. He seemed so utterly without guile, like she was completely safe with him. No pressure on her in any way at all. And he was only suggesting they eat a sandwich down by the lake, something she would do with Ingrid or any of her friends.

She hesitated for only a second before answering. "Okay. That'd be nice."

*****

After buying sandwiches and drinks in Manuka, they walked back to Mark's car, making small talk as they went. Mark took them the short drive to Bowen Park down by Lake Burley Griffin where they found a park bench overlooking the water. Mark sat down, and Erin took a seat next to him.

"So, Erin, are you from Canberra?" Mark asked, peeling back the paper from around his sandwich. "Most people I meet here are from somewhere else originally."

"Yes, I'm from here," Erin replied, twisting the lid off her orange juice. "My dad's family have been in this district for a long time, since the 1840s. But I'm not strictly from Canberra. I grew up over the border in Queanbeyan."

Mark arched his eyebrows, appearing impressed. "A real local. I don't spend much time in Queanbeyan."

"It suffers a bit of knocking by Canberrans, but Queanbeyan is a lovely town. What about you? Are you from here?"

Mark shook his head. "No, I'm from Newcastle. I moved here about two years ago."

"So what brought you to Canberra? I would have thought a move to Sydney would make more sense for someone from Newcastle."

"Actually, I did move to Sydney first. I spent a year at Good Shepherd Seminary at Homebush before coming here."

Erin almost choked on her drink. She placed it down on

the bench next to her and turned to face him.

"Are you serious? You studied for the priesthood?"

Mark laughed, clearly amused by her reaction. "Yes, but it wasn't for me. I discovered while I was there that God definitely wasn't calling me to be a priest. It was a terrific experience, though. I made a few lifetime friendships while I was there. It was a healing time for me, in many ways."

"Healing? You mean after your split from your girlfriend?" Erin bit her lip, wondering if it was wise to mention the ex-girlfriend again so early in their conversation.

Mark merely nodded. "Yes, partly that, though our breakup was a couple of years before entering the seminary. After I left, I didn't want to go back to Newcastle. I mean, I still love it, and my mum and sister are still there. But I wanted a fresh start. I found a job ad for a position at an architectural firm here and I got it."

"Wow. What a ride."

"You could say that, but everything's worked for good," Mark said as he smiled at her.

Worked for good. There was that verse again, the one her mother had quoted from Romans. *With those who love Him, who are called according to His purpose.*

"And how've you been since everything happened?" Mark asked, a note of empathy in his voice.

Erin thought a second before answering. "Not too bad. I mean, I'm still sad. I miss the familiarity of my life with him. But I'm not as raw as I was at first. When we first broke up, I wondered how I was going to go on living without him. I cried at the very thought of it. But that seems to be over now. Perhaps I'm all cried out."

"Could be," Mark replied. "Or possibly, deep down, you know you're better off and finally have a chance to come into your own."

Better off? The thought hadn't occurred to her. After Gareth's rejection, she had simply thought of herself as not good enough. For Gareth or anyone else. Was Mark implying that it was Gareth who wasn't good enough for her?

Taken aback by this revelation, she wondered if Mark had come to the same conclusion after his girlfriend left him. "Are you speaking from experience again?"

"Yeah, I am. I'm not saying this is the case for every relationship. But a relationship where one partner is lying can't help but harm you. Especially a relationship which is out of God's order. Sometimes the relationship is worth saving and sometimes it isn't. In my case, once that relationship ended, the injury caused by the lies started to heal."

Erin pondered this. "And by 'out of order,' you mean a relationship with sex outside of marriage?"

"Absolutely," Mark said, sounding as though this were the most obvious and logical conclusion in the world.

Erin nodded. "Up until recently, I would have laughed at anyone who said that to me. But I guess I was coming to that point without realising it. The night we split I was going to try and force him into setting a wedding date. I wanted us to live apart until after the wedding to try and stop him from backing out. I felt so stupid afterwards. Like I was giving him a motivation to hurry up. A motivation! And all the while, he was off getting it somewhere else. I dunno, having to resort to that after so many years...maybe a part of me already knew it was over."

"You deserved better, and you knew it. You're worth so much more than the way he was treating you. You did the right thing, expecting him to step up, regardless of how it turned out. Never doubt that, not for a minute."

Erin eyed Mark and puzzled over him. His resolve to live this particular way, his total conviction that this way was the only way to proceed with his life. Here was a man who had probably experienced much of what could be experienced in life and this was where he had ended up: a devout, daily-Mass-going Catholic, sitting on a park bench with her. The curiosity he had spiked in her that night weeks earlier resurfaced, and she found herself wanting to learn more about him.

"So, you mentioned that you have a mum and a sister in Newcastle. What about your dad?"

"My dad died when I was thirteen. He was hit by a car walking home from work one afternoon."

Erin gasped. "Oh, Mark. I'm so sorry." *Brilliant, Erin. Stuck your foot in it again.* "That must have been terrible for you and your family, losing him so suddenly."

Mark nodded and glanced down at the footpath. "Thanks. He didn't die straight away. We thought he might recover, but he died a few days after the accident from complications. But at least we got a chance to tell him we loved him before he died. He could have died instantly. Plenty of people do when they're hit by a vehicle. I didn't think of that as a blessing when it happened, but over time I developed a deep sense of gratitude for those days we had with him. The driver wasn't drunk or using drugs, he just lost concentration for a moment. I was so angry at him, but before Dad died, he encouraged me to forgive the guy who hit him. He said it was an accident."

Tears formed in Erin's eyes. "I'm so sorry," she said again. "It must have been so hard for you, a young boy growing up without his father."

"It was. I was devastated. I didn't cope well with his death. My parents had a mixed marriage, Dad was Catholic, but Mum isn't. Dad was the one who took my sister and me to Mass and instructed us in our faith. Mum is Anglican, but she's never practised much. After Dad died, Mum didn't bother much with our religious instruction. I started going off the rails eventually and got into a fair bit of trouble."

"Really? What sort of trouble?"

"Some juvenile crime. Nothing too sinister to start with,

a bit of shoplifting, graffiti. But then I got in with a bad crowd, and there was some other stuff, stealing cars, some break and enter."

"Wow," Erin said, trying to picture the good-looking, clean-cut man beside her as a young criminal. "So, how did you get yourself sorted out?"

"One day I ended up in children's court, and the judge I appeared before really knew how to deal with troubled kids. Thankfully, she didn't put me in detention. There was community service, though, and she referred me for mandatory counselling with a guy who helped me get some direction. He was a man about my father's age who'd seen it all; there was nothing I could pull over him. I found out years after my counselling ended that he was a practising Catholic, like Dad."

"Then what?"

"Well, I didn't come back to the faith at that time, but on reflection I can see that his presence in my life sowed the seeds for my return to the Church. At that time, the best I could manage was to end my burgeoning career as a criminal and finish my education. I did well at school and enrolled in architecture at the University of Newcastle. But during my late high school and uni years, I traded one set of troubles for another when I turned my attention towards women."

"Oh."

Mark took a deep breath and let it out slowly. "I have a horrible time admitting it now, but I was fairly promiscuous for a few years. Somehow it didn't interfere with my studies, and miraculously, I never contracted any diseases. But I still shudder when I remember how many times I used women for my own enjoyment, then cast them aside. Someone's daughter, future wife, future mother."

"Well, I'm sure it wasn't all your fault, Mark. Obviously, they were consenting."

"It doesn't matter. It just made both parties guilty of the

same crime. Using another person as a means to an end."

Erin said nothing, remembering Katrina's similar advice to her on that first day after she left Gareth.

"Women and men experience sex differently anyway," Mark went on. "When a woman pursues a man or accepts his advances, it isn't always because she's after sex from him. She's seeking someone to love her, to assure her she is cherished and valued. I realised that at the time, but I didn't care."

Erin peered sideways at Mark's face, his brow knitted, momentarily lost in thought, as though recalling times from his past he would happily take back.

Was this guy for real? She had never heard a man their age speak like this before. Even the married men in her circle of friends had had their fun before settling down. She couldn't recall any of them ever expressing regret about it. Mark obviously had a tremendous respect for women, and not only women collectively, but each woman as an individual. She hadn't encountered an attitude like this in any men outside those in her own family.

Now it made sense to her why she felt so safe with him. Was this what the Catholic faith did for people? Turn a serial womaniser into someone who reverenced women and somehow understood them? The revelation unnerved her slightly, but in spite of herself, it awed and uplifted her also.

"Amazing," she said. "You don't often hear someone from our generation talk like that."

Mark turned to face her. "It's all true, though. I came to realise that in time. I think sometimes how I'd feel if someone treated my sister or my mother like that, how furious I'd be with whatever guy used them that way. All men should have an attitude like this towards women."

Erin was eager for him to continue but worried she might be intruding by asking him to go on.

"I hope I haven't offended you in any way with this

rundown of my past," Mark said, appearing a little reticent, as though regretting going into such personal details with her.

"On the contrary, please continue," Erin said, hoping she didn't appear too anxious to hear more. "I wouldn't mind hearing how you got by after things...went sour with your ex-girlfriend. Only if you don't mind talking about it, that is."

"No, of course not," he said, smiling at her once again, making her feel as though nothing she asked him would be too much trouble.

"I'd been working as an architect about six months when I met Natalie through a work colleague. She was different. Not like any other woman I'd met before. Things started off great; we went out for about a year before we moved in together. After that, it got harder. Our relationship became turbulent, emotionally speaking. There were some difficult times, a lot of arguments." Mark paused for a moment then cleared his throat before going on. "Then one day, I came home, and she told me she was leaving me for another guy. Like you, I was completely shocked; I didn't see it coming."

Erin shuddered inwardly, remembering the evening weeks earlier with Gareth. "I know how that feels," she said.

"After it ended, I was very low. Depressed, actually. I didn't know what to do with myself. I was tempted to return to the life I'd had before I'd been with Natalie, but for some reason, I didn't."

"You must have really loved her."

"I did, but I didn't show her. And it wasn't just that. There were...things that happened in the relationship, things we said — did — that couldn't be taken back. I drove her to leave in a way. She wanted to get married, and I kept refusing, putting her off. I didn't see what I was doing to her when I did that."

Mark paused, but Erin kept silent, waiting for him to continue.

"Anyway, I was out one Friday evening and I passed this guy preaching on a street corner. I'd seen him there a lot, everyone had. He would stand there week after week, talking about Jesus and quoting Scripture. Handing out prayer cards with the Divine Mercy image to anyone who would accept one."

The Divine Mercy. Erin knew the image, which had been on the wall in her parents' home for as long as she could remember. It was a vision of Jesus seen by a Polish nun named Faustina Kowalska, now a saint, during the 1930s. In it, Jesus appeared with white and red rays streaming from His heart, representing the blood and water that flowed from His side at His crucifixion, pouring out His mercy on the world.

"I know it. *Jesus, I trust in you,*" Erin said, quoting the line that was written underneath the image. She remembered the story of Jesus asking Saint Faustina to have the vision of him painted and spread around the world with those words displayed underneath the image.

Mark smiled at her, his eyes lighting up. "Yes. I'd never seen it before. I didn't have any intention of looking at it that night either. I decided to try and dodge him by crossing to the other side of the street when I spotted a group of men approach him, three of them. Before I knew what was happening, they were attacking him. They threw him to the ground then started hitting and kicking him over and over."

"Oh, no, how awful!"

Mark nodded. "It was horrible. For a split second I just froze. Then without thinking I just raced in and tried to pull them off him."

"Did you get hurt?"

"Yes, but only a bit, amazingly enough. I got a black eye and some other bruises, but otherwise, I was fine. Luckily for me, a couple of other guys who saw what was happening came to help, and together we managed to distract them. The police turned up quickly, but the poor guy they attacked was badly beaten up. He was taken straight to hospital."

"Was he okay?"

"He was, after some time."

"That was brave of you. You must have been so shaken up afterwards."

"Well, that's the strange part. I came close to being beaten senseless. The police questioned me as a witness, and the paramedics checked me over. But all I could think about was the guy these thugs were hitting. See, the whole time they were laying into him, he kept repeating one thing. 'I forgive you.' He said that phrase over and over as they were punching and kicking him."

Erin blinked back tears for the second time. She swallowed but was unable to find any words.

Mark went on. "I couldn't understand how anyone could say that while they were being so savagely attacked. I mean, they wanted to kill him. But he just loved them." Mark paused and stared out over the water. "Witnessing that — well, I sat there in the gutter afterwards, crying like a fool. It brought me, in my heart, straight to the door of my faith again. I understood that I could walk through and choose life, or stay on the outside, and go on wandering aimlessly through my barren existence, devoid of the light of Christ."

"And you started believing again, just like that?"

"I don't think I ever stopped believing. I just rejected Him. I stopped hearing His voice because I chose myself and my own desires over Him. But He had mercy on me and called me back. He calls us all to Him, but sometimes He allows certain things to happen to us to get our attention. At least, it was like that for me."

Erin nodded and followed his gaze out over the water.

They sat together for a few minutes in silence and finished eating. Erin folded up her sandwich wrapper slowly and thought for a moment about Mark's story. He fell away from Catholicism at a young age after a death in his family. But somehow, he'd found a way to let go of his bitterness and embrace the faith of his youth once more, despite having wandered away for so many years. Was it possible she could do the same? She thought again about how hard it must have been for him to grow up without his father.

"I'm sorry you lost your dad," she said.

Mark turned towards her again. "Thanks."

"I know it isn't the same, but I do understand what a death in the family is like. My elder brother David died of cancer when he was eighteen. I was young, only a primary school kid at the time."

"I'm so sorry. That must have crushed you."

"It did crush me. He was such a wonderful person. I can only imagine my parents' grief. They still deal with it, every day. But they were always so peaceful about it, despite their sadness. I think that's where I started to go wrong. I didn't allow God to console me. I was angry at Him for not saving David."

Mark grinned at her. "You and I have similar pasts."

"Yes, we do," Erin replied. "And I appreciate you sharing some of yours with me. Thank you."

"My pleasure, truly." Mark scrunched up his sandwich wrapping and stood up. "Come on. Enough deep and meaningful talk for one day. Let's walk for a bit and soak up this golden afternoon."

*****

"What's up with you, then?" Ingrid's voice came over the top of Erin's partition at the office later that evening, followed quickly by Ingrid herself. She leaned her elbows on the partition and rested her chin in her hands. "I thought you were having a day off. What are you doing here at this hour? Nearly everyone's left for the day."

Erin turned her computer off and looked up at Ingrid. "Yes, I know. But I saw an email from a client and needed to check on some work before tomorrow morning." She grabbed her coat and bag from where they were resting on the desk. "How were things here today? Did you miss me?"

Ingrid didn't answer, squinting her eyes and peering at Erin with mock suspicion. "Who are you, and what have you done with Erin?"

"What on earth are you talking about?"

"Nothing much. I'm only wondering what happened to my rejected, lonely, not to mention homeless, friend. You're far too cheerful to be her." Ingrid lowered herself so that only her eyes appeared above the partition. "I don't trust you."

Erin giggled. "You're such a goose, Ingrid."

"Yes, I am," Ingrid said, straightening up. "Seriously though, you look as though you had a wonderful day. You're glowing."

"Really?" Erin said, perturbed once again by Ingrid's uncanny ability to see straight through her. "I suppose I did have a good day." She felt a smile creep over her face as she thought back to her afternoon with Mark.

"Okay, that's it," Ingrid said, stepping around into Erin's cubicle. She grabbed a chair from a neighbouring workstation and sat down. "Stay put. You're not leaving until you give me an explanation for that silly grin."

Erin swivelled her chair around to face Ingrid. "There's nothing much to tell. I met this guy in Manuka one night several weeks ago, he helped me get my car started after the battery died. We've met a couple of times since then, including today. We had lunch together down by the lake. I don't know; it was pleasant. No stress or pressure. We talked a lot. He's had similar experiences to me. I suppose I feel better when I'm around him."

Ingrid grinned from ear to ear. "Didn't I tell you? I said the next thing that happens to you is going to be wonderful. Man, I love it when I'm right. What's his name?"

"Mark. But it's not like that," Erin hurried to correct her. "It's just friendly. I'm going back to Mass regularly again, and he goes too. And like I said, our life experience is similar — we've just been talking about it."

Ingrid paused and stared at Erin. "You know, for a woman who lived in sin for five years, your innocence is truly breathtaking."

"What do you mean?"

"This guy! Of course it's like *that*. What are you, six years old? A man isn't going to ask you out twice unless he likes you in a *more* than friendly manner, Erin."

Erin stopped short, the smile slowly slipping from her face. She thought back to exchanging phone numbers with Mark only a couple of hours ago, recalling his promise to check in on her again soon. "Really? Do you think I'm stringing him along if I see him again?"

Ingrid peered at her thoughtfully. "I think you're asking the wrong question. You need to ask yourself if you're interested in him too."

Erin scoffed and waved her hand at Ingrid dismissively. "Ingrid, how could I be interested in someone so soon after my engagement to the only man who's ever been in my life has ended? Too soon."

"Is it? There aren't any rules about moving on, Erin. Don't rule this guy out because of some self-imposed idea of how long you need to wait before getting over that bottom-dweller. If you meet someone, you meet someone."

Erin thought back to Mark sitting alongside her at Bowen Park earlier that day. His candour and honesty, his willingness to share so many personal details about himself with her. She remembered him smiling at her, making her feel like she was the only thing in the world that mattered in that moment. Funny how she had never noticed how fascinating dark hair and dark eyes were before Mark came along.

"He *is* lovely," Erin admitted. "I don't think I've ever met a guy so thoughtful and gentlemanly."

"See. Told you. You like him."

"I hadn't thought about it. Only that I'm just...happy when he's around. I didn't see him for over a month, and I thought about him quite a lot then too. I wonder why I didn't catch myself doing that?"

"You've had rather a lot to think about. Not the least of which is your little baby."

Ingrid's reminder of her pregnancy came falling down on her like a brick wall. "Oh, no, you're right," she said, her heart sinking inside her like a lead weight. "I didn't think about the baby all afternoon. How could I forget?"

Ingrid's teasing expression softened, and she reached out and patted Erin on the knee. "Hey, don't worry. You just forgot your troubles for a while. Getting pregnant wasn't exactly on your to-do list. It doesn't mean you won't be a good mother."

Erin considered for a moment the idea of her new friendship with Mark becoming something more. Did she want that? Examining the situation honestly, she had to admit she might. Ingrid's blunt assessment was right on target, as usual. She was increasingly drawn to Mark. But her pregnancy — how would he react to that? She couldn't hide it indefinitely. And how did Gareth fit into all this? She hadn't tried to tell him yet and wasn't sure she could.

"What am I getting myself into?" Erin muttered, half to Ingrid, half to herself.

"It's okay. If things go further, just be honest with him," Ingrid said, reassuring her. "Any guy would be lucky to have you, Erin, no matter the circumstances. If he doesn't see that, then he doesn't deserve you. It'll be fine."

"I hope you're right."

"Of course I am," Ingrid said, standing up. "Come on, time to pack up and go. We'll talk more tomorrow."

Erin stood and reached over for her bag and coat, thinking suddenly of the image of Jesus' Divine Mercy, the turning point for Mark in his journey back to the Church.

"Jesus, I trust in You." You asked us to trust in You. Well, Lord, I don't know what I'm doing, but I think I might try leaving it in Your hands for once. Mark trusts You. He trusts You so much.

And if Mark trusted then maybe it wouldn't hurt for her to do the same.

Chapter 10

Mark wheeled his bike through the side gate of his townhouse the following Saturday afternoon and locked the gate behind him. He unclipped the strap of his helmet, took it off and hung it around the handlebars of his bike. He took the bike around to the courtyard at the back of the house and let himself inside through the back sliding door. Closing it behind him, he headed straight to the kitchen, grabbed a glass and filled it with water from the kitchen tap, downing it in a few seconds.

A good ninety-minute ride had been just what he needed. The exercise had left him feeling invigorated and provided a much-needed distraction from all that had been going on in his mind and heart. He filled the glass with water again and stared out his kitchen window, which afforded him a view to the Tidbinbilla mountain range. Resting his gaze, he took in a deep breath and let it out slowly.

For the millionth time since he met her, Mark's thoughts turned to Erin. Since seeing her earlier in the week, he had found himself in a mixed state of delight and torment, the kind of emotional state that made it difficult to function normally. Spending the afternoon with her, talking to her, getting to know her and simply *being* with her had proven to be one of the most wonderful times he could remember having. He had waited a long time to meet someone who brought him so much joy and whom he wished, in turn, to make equally happy. The fact that she seemed to enjoy his company too only made the thrill more pronounced.

But the fact that she was so soon out of an engagement gave him pause about leaping forward with too much enthusiasm. It was likely she was too vulnerable to begin a new relationship any time soon. In addition, she seemed to be struggling with aspects of their shared Catholic faith, and this troubled him a great deal. He had been taking the matter to the Lord in prayer daily, almost hourly, but had yet to sense how he should proceed. *If in doubt, don't,* as his mother had always said.

He placed his glass down on the sink without drinking from it and tried to form another prayer. *Lord, if ever there was a situation I don't want to stuff up, this is the one. Please, make your will known to me. Help me to proceed along the path you have laid out for me, no matter where that should take me. Give me some direction.*

At that moment his phone beeped behind him, alerting him to a text message. He turned and grabbed it from the kitchen bench. It was from Father Nick Bentley, his friend from his seminary days.

Hi. Had a heck of a week. Pizza at your place after I've said 6 pm Mass?

Mark smiled. Though Nick was a few years younger than him, he'd been several years ahead of Mark in the seminary, having entered quite young. He'd been only a couple of years from ordination when Mark first entered. Mark had always respected the young man's deep spirituality, but he noticed a further change in Nick after his ordination: a deepening in his understanding of people, the humble authority he exuded when he read the Gospel and preached from the pulpit. Grace of state, Mark supposed. The transformation that took place in Nick's soul once he'd received the Sacrament of Holy Orders and became a minister of Christ, capable of absolving sins in the confessional, of changing the bread and wine at Mass into the Body and Blood of Christ.

Mark picked up his phone and started typing. *Sounds good.* He pressed send then waited a moment.

See you at 7.30.

Mark put the phone down and headed towards the shower. *Thank you, Lord.* Perhaps this was an answer to prayer. He knew he was going to burst if he didn't talk to someone about Erin soon.

*****

"You got any Diet Coke in here, Mark?" Nick called out from the kitchen that evening while Mark sat on the sofa in his living room.

"They'll bring some with the pizza. Do you want a beer instead?"

Mark heard the fridge door close as Nick made his way back into the living room.

"Yeah, why not? I'm finally off duty for the day." He slumped down on a single seater with a beer he'd retrieved from the fridge, handing another one to Mark.

"So how are you?" Mark asked. "You under a lot of pressure?"

"No, no pressure, just the usual. I mean, I love it. I love my ministry. I didn't realise I could be so happy. I've just had an incredibly busy week." He took the lid off his beer and took a sip. "What about you, how've you been?"

Mark drew in a breath, trying to formulate an answer when Nick's phone beeped from his jacket pocket.

Nick groaned and retrieved the phone. "I'm not on call for the hospital tonight. I hope nothing's wrong." He opened a message on his phone and cast his eye over it.

Mark observed Nick as a smile spread over his face. He quickly began typing on his phone then put it back in his pocket.

"My cousin, Ryan," Nick said. "I officiated at his wedding a while back. He's just told me his wife's pregnant."

"That's great," Mark replied. "To be expecting a baby so soon after their wedding."

"It is. I hope they ask me to do the baptism."

"I'm sure they'll ask you," Mark said, laughing. He

thought for a moment how childlike Nick was sometimes, almost like a little brother in some ways.

"Anyway, sorry about that. I was asking you how you were getting on. We haven't had much time to catch up lately."

"No, we've both been busy."

"So what's been happening with you? Everything okay?"

Mark put his beer on the coffee table in front of him. "A bit yes, and a bit no."

Nick frowned a little. "Sounds cryptic. Would you mind explaining that ambiguous comment?"

Mark drew in a breath. "I met someone."

Nick's frown disappeared, and his face lit up. "Mate, that's fantastic! Where did you meet her?"

"After weekday Mass, a few weeks back. Your Mass, actually. She couldn't get her car started, and I helped her."

"Daily Mass-goer, sounds good. What's she like?"

"Oh, wow. Where do I start?" Mark sighed and leaned back in his chair. "Her name's Erin, and she's absolutely beautiful. I could barely believe what I was seeing when I first met her. I don't think I've ever seen a prettier girl in my life. And she's wonderful to be around. We've only met up a couple of times but being with her lights me up inside. I feel like I could take on the world for her and have everything wrapped up by lunchtime."

Nick smiled and relaxed in his armchair. "Well, this sounds more than a bit okay. It sounds like a lot okay. Clearly you like her a lot."

"I do. So much I'm having trouble thinking straight. But there are a few things that I'm concerned about."

"What are they?"

"She was engaged, and it broke off recently. Her fiancé was cheating on her, and she didn't suspect anything. She's heartbroken. Aside from that, she's not a practising Catholic, not really. She's a cradle Catholic, but she hasn't practised for years and told me she's come back recently at her mother's insistence, to try and make sense of what's happening in her life. She has a few...issues with some key Catholic doctrine."

Nick nodded. "And I suppose that doctrine would be the Church's teaching on marriage and contraception?"

"Yeah. How did you guess?"

Nick swallowed another mouthful of beer then placed the bottle down on the coffee table in front of him. "Contraception and reserving sex for marriage are the two teachings people take issue with. Sex is always at the root of people's problems with the Church. You don't often find someone staying away from the sacraments for years because they object to the Nicene Creed or the outcomes of the Council of Trent."

Mark laughed. "No, can't say I've come across that either."

Nick shook his head and appeared sad. "Contraception and pre-marital sex are two of the hardest things to explain to young couples who've never been presented with the richness of the Catholic teaching on sexuality. The world has been gifted in the last thirty years or so with the teachings of Saint John Paul II, but no one seems to take notice of it. It makes me sad that they've never even heard of Theology of the Body."

Mark nodded. "Well, you've hit the nail on the head. It's that whole area she's struggling with. She appears to be reconsidering her rejection of the faith, and I've offered the best I can by way of explanations. Plus she has a family that are all deeply Catholic, from what I can figure." He drew in a deep breath and let out a sigh, relieved to finally share his struggle with someone. "I suppose I'm finding it troubling being so attracted to someone who I'm not aligned with in matters of faith. What do you think I should do?"

"You know better than anyone that people change. It

appears she's open to change, otherwise she wouldn't be anywhere near a church, let alone coming to Mass."

"But how should I proceed? I haven't told her straight out that I'm interested. I don't want to push her if she's not ready, but I don't want to lose my chance with her, if there is one."

"Let her reaction guide you. You can let on that you're interested without applying any pressure to start something she's not ready for. She's already been out with you a couple of times. You're off to a pretty good start."

Mark sat up a little straighter, Nick's words suddenly shining rays of light through the fog in his mind. "I suppose it is a good start."

"It is. You'll know how to proceed. You're a gentleman." Nick said. "But I'm wondering one thing."

"What?"

"Is her breakup with her fiancé the only reason she's coming back to Mass? Did she mention anything else?"

Mark frowned and shook his head. "Not really. Her brother died when she was young. She said she took that quite hard. But she didn't say there was anything else. Why do you ask?"

Nick shrugged. "In my experience, it's often something truly momentous that draws someone back to their faith when they weren't seeking it out. Earth-shattering events. Life and death."

"Oh," Mark said, his heart dropping in his chest again. That made sense, though. It had been the exact same way with him. But he hadn't considered the possibility there was more going on in Erin's life than he was aware of. Of course there could be. She would hardly have told him everything there was to know about herself. She'd only just met him.

"Don't worry. Maybe it is her engagement breaking up and unresolved grief about her brother. Those are both devastating. I'll keep this intention especially in my prayers. In fact, I'm going to offer Mass for you this week. But whether it's with Erin or someone else, I know things are going to work out for you, one way or the other. You're going to make a terrific husband and father one day. Soon."

Mark glanced across the coffee table at Nick and sensed a peace and confidence settle over him, like a soothing balm over a wound. He had prayed for some direction and the Lord was speaking through his friend. *Proceed, carefully.*

Nick went on. "Life is hard. You've had your fair share of trials, heaven knows. The Lord always asks much of those who are faithful to him. But your life is an extraordinary witness, Mark. Don't doubt that. I hope this is the one that works out for you, and you find the joy you're seeking."

Touched, Mark swallowed. "Thanks, Nick. I appreciate it."

Nick reached for his beer again. "Just keep praying for me."

"You bet."

At that moment, the doorbell rang. Mark stood and reached into his back pocket for his wallet.

"Oh, brilliant, I'm starving," Nick said. He reached into his pocket and pulled out twenty dollars. "Here you go, I'm pitching in."

"No, you're not," Mark replied, overwhelmed with gratitude that Nick was free to catch up. "My shout."

*****

The following Sunday morning Erin was in her parents' kitchen, preparing coffee for her sister, who had called in after Mass with her family. The children were playing outside with Judith, Liam and Emilio while Katrina had gone to retrieve some toys from the car. Marie was lying in a baby bouncer on the floor in the corner of the room. Erin was pushing down the plunger on the coffee pot when

Bruno dashed inside through the sliding door, hotly pursued by Lily.

"Bruno, come back here you...invertebrate!" Lily screeched, chasing her little brother around the kitchen table.

"Woah, Lily!" Erin said, reaching out to pick Bruno up as he raced into the kitchen to escape his sister. "That's a very big word. Why did you call Bruno an invertebrate?"

Lily stopped in front of Erin and glared at Bruno, her hands on her hips. "Because he has no backbone!"

Erin did her best to suppress a smile. "And why do you think Bruno has no backbone?"

"Because he stole my sunglasses!" she wailed. "And he won't give them back!"

Erin gently turned Bruno's face toward her. "Did you take Lily's glasses, Bruno?"

A cheeky grin spread across the child's face, and he nodded. "But only because Mr Fossil Head needs them!"

"Mr Fossil Head? Who on earth is Mr Fossil Head?"

Katrina appeared in the doorway carrying a Lamaze toy and a resin model of a human skull. "This is Mr Fossil Head," she said, sounding exasperated.

Bruno wriggled down and bounced over to his mother, quickly grabbing the skull from her hands and placing it on the kitchen table. He whipped the purloined glasses out of his little jeans pocket and put them on the skull.

"See? Doesn't he look funny?" he said with a mischievous giggle, picking up Mr Fossil Head and showing him to his mother, Erin and Lily.

Erin stared for a moment at the cheeky grin on Bruno's face and his model skull wearing Lily's star-shaped, pink glitter sunglasses and burst out laughing.

Lily stood scowling, feet rooted to the floor, not seeming to know what to do.

Bruno held the skull out to her. "Funny joke, Lily?"

Lily's frown slowly disappeared, and she started to

giggle. "Yeah, he looks a bit silly." She grabbed the skull from Bruno and bounced towards the back door. "Come on, let's show Daddy and Grandma and Grandpa!" The laughing children disappeared back into the garden as quickly as they had arrived, leaving Erin and Katrina in the kitchen.

"Oh, Katrina," Erin said, wiping her eyes. "Those two are hilarious. Where did Lily learn a word like invertebrate? And why does Bruno have a model of a skull for a toy?"

Katrina shook her head, letting out a sigh. "I have three children aged six and under, and I'm still sane. Relatively. Don't judge."

"At least the baby appears normal. So far."

Laughing, Katrina took the soft toy over to Marie and hung it from the arch over the baby bouncer. Marie smiled when she saw it and reached out her tiny hand to try and touch it. Katrina stroked her head.

"Give her time. I'm sure the other two will corrupt her soon enough."

"They're certainly good value. I haven't found anything that amusing in a while." Erin poured some coffee for Katrina. The aroma of the coffee wafted up towards her nostrils, turning her instantly nauseous. "Here you go," she said, stepping into the adjoining dining room and holding the cup out to Katrina. She scrunched up her nose and turned her face away from the smell.

Katrina stood and accepted the cup. "Ta," she said and took a sip. "You sick?"

"Yes, for a few weeks now. I'm not too bad. Apart from that and the tiredness, I wouldn't know I was...." her voice trailed off, leaving the sentence unfinished.

"Pregnant. It's okay. You can say it," Katrina said, taking a seat at the table. "Eat something. It'll calm the queasiness. Weird, but it works." Katrina glanced over to the kitchen bench to some chocolate chip muffins Judith had made for the children. "Ooh, have one of those muffins. They're always yummy!"

Erin peered over at the muffins, then shook her head, her stomach turning over once more. "Nah, they make me want to gag too."

"I wish they made me want to gag. I'm so hungry feeding Marie. I just can't lose these last few kilos."

Erin sat down next to her sister and observed her. She certainly was carrying a little extra weight these days, but with her dazzling blue eyes and dark hair, she still appeared as beautiful as always.

"You look lovely. Don't worry about it."

Katrina scoffed. "You're very kind, but I know what I see in the mirror. On scale of Audrey Hepburn to Old Mother Hubbard, where exactly do you think I measure up?"

Erin laughed again. "No wonder your kids are all crazy! You have no resemblance to Old Mother Hubbard, whatever she was like."

"Well, I would, if I wasn't sticking to a low sugar diet. So boring. Who wants a handful of almonds and a glass of water for morning tea, I ask you? I want a cappuccino and a chocolate frog. A big one."

Erin rolled her eyes. "You and your chocolate frogs," she said, remembering Katrina's penchant for the treats when they were younger.

Katrina sipped her coffee again, and Erin continued to observe her sister, relishing, no doubt, one of those rare moments in which there was nothing pressing for her to do. Erin found herself regarding her sister with a newfound admiration. Katrina had given so selflessly all through her marriage, both to Emilio and to their children. Erin had, on occasion, belittled Katrina's decision to stay home with her children instead of continuing with her career as a solicitor, at least in a part-time capacity. She'd had an amazing job with the Attorney General's department, and Erin knew she could go back any time she wanted. Whenever Erin had questioned her about it in the past, Katrina simply said that if it was necessary for her to work she would, but was grateful that Emilio was able to support them all so she could be with the children.

In the last few days Erin had been pondering how life would be as a single, working mother. She knew that she would have to return to work once her child was born and wouldn't have the option of staying home with the baby for any length of time. Her pregnancy was still in its early stage, and physically she was barely aware of the child inside her, aside from the first-trimester pregnancy symptoms that were taking hold. Nonetheless, a motherly bond with her baby was forming in her heart, and she had begun contemplating the practicalities of handling the task ahead of her.

"Earth to Erin," Katrina said, snapping her fingers. "You're a million miles away. What are you thinking about?"

Erin sighed. "Nothing. Just pondering it all. Seeing you, such a devoted mother. You're an example for me. I wonder how I'll go being a mum on my own."

Katrina gazed at Erin sympathetically. "You won't be alone. We'll all be here for you."

"Yeah, I know. I'm just trying to prepare myself."

"Have you talked to Gareth yet?"

Erin shook her head. "No, I can't. I can't face him with news like this after what he pulled. Not yet."

Katrina nodded. "How have you been since the breakup? You don't appear to be devastated anymore."

"Surprisingly, no. Not anymore. Missing him was sort of like missing something that wasn't there. I guess it hadn't been there for a long time. I'm going okay."

Katrina sat back a little and sized Erin up. "I must say, I'm impressed with how well you seem to be coping. You seem very...calm. Peaceful."

"Well, it might shock you to hear this, but I've been praying. Every day, almost. I've been going to Mass."

Katrina's eyes lit up, and her face broadened into a huge smile. "I'm so happy. I've been praying for this. So have Emilio and the children."

"Well, it's all still a little fuzzy to me, so don't get too excited just yet. But I must say, trying to communicate with God has made me more peaceful. I sometimes wonder why I'm not more stressed out."

"My peace I leave you, a peace the world cannot give, this is my gift to you," Katrina said, without commenting further.

"Yes, something like that," Erin said, recalling the verse from the Gospel of John that Father Nick had read the first day she'd gone back to Mass. The day she met Mark.

Her heart gave a little flutter at the thought of him, as it did almost every time she remembered him. It had been a few days since their conversation by the lake, and he hadn't been in touch again, though she felt sure he was still thinking of her and praying for her. She once again found herself trying to reconcile, in her mind, her continuing pregnancy and her growing affection and admiration for Mark. Perhaps it was best that he hadn't contacted her yet.

Another wave of nausea gripped her, and she put her hand to her mouth, waiting a moment while it passed.

"Oh, Erin," Katrina said. "You should try eating something."

"Okay, I will." She got up and stepped into the kitchen, looking again at the muffins on the bench. "How many calories in one of those, do you think?"

"Too many, if you need to ask!"

Erin peered down at her stomach. "How long will it be before I start to show?"

Marie began to fret in her bouncer, and Katrina reached down to pick her up. "Hmm, not sure. Everyone's different. It's your first pregnancy, so maybe not for a little while yet. I didn't start to show till after four months with Lily."

"Katrina, do you think there might ever be a guy who

would want me? As a single mother?"

"What sort of a question is that?" she said, pacing and patting Marie gently on the back. "Of course there will be! I'm already petitioning Our Lady for you. I'm halfway through a novena to Our Lady of Hope for that exact intention."

"You are? Thank you. How kind."

"What, is it working already?"

Erin drew in a breath. "Do you remember you once told me that it's a terrible thing to already be married when you meet the right one?"

Katrina nodded. "Yeah, I do."

"I think I understand that now. It would have been the wrong thing for me to marry Gareth."

Katrina's face suddenly lit up. "Meaning what? You've met someone else? Already?" She sat back down with Marie over her shoulder. "This visit keeps getting better. Details. I want details."

"I have met someone. It's still very new, but I'd love to talk to you about it, actually."

"Good-o. Start talking. And grab us both one of those muffins, will you?" Katrina replied. "I can't have them sitting there in front of me without eating one for a minute longer."

At that moment Lily and Bruno burst into the kitchen once again in such a state of fevered excitement it made Erin jump. Emilio followed them inside, closing the sliding door behind him.

"Mummy, Mummy!" The two breathless children bounced over to Katrina.

"Goodness, children, you're strung out to concert pitch," Katrina said, glancing up at her husband. "What have you been doing with them out there, Emilio?"

"Daddy said he can take us to Pine Island, Mummy!" Lily said, jumping up and down on the spot.

"Can we go now?" Bruno asked, pulling on Katrina's arm.

"Can we go right now? Please, Mum, it's such a nice day!"

Katrina peered over at Emilio with a look on her face that suggested his idea was less than inspired.

Emilio shrugged. "Well, it *is* a beautiful day, *mi amor*," he said, sounding both apologetic and eager at the same time.

Erin's heart went out to Katrina. "How about I come too? I can help Emilio with the kids while you sit with Marie."

"Oh, yes, Aunty Erin can come too!" Bruno yelled and started running around Erin in circles. "But you have to play with *only* me, okay?"

"Aunty Erin won't want to play *your* games, Bruno," Lily said, her arms folded and her chin in the air, a note of childish superiority in her voice. "She only wants to play with *girls*. Girls are more grown up."

"Hey, hey, I'll play with *both* of you," Erin said firmly, glaring from one child to the other.

Katrina chuckled. "I think someone's going to sleep well tonight," she said, shaking her head.

"I'd say so!" Erin said. "I doubt they'll last till bedtime."

Katrina shot her a wry expression. "I wasn't talking about them!"

*****

A short while later, Erin joined her sister's family at the Pine Island Reserve — a group of black cypress pines growing along the Murrumbidgee River. Complete with playground and picnic facilities, it was a popular spot with families. As a child, Erin had spent many a summer afternoon digging in the sand at the little inland beach and swimming in the safer parts of the river with David and Katrina. It surprised her how contented she felt now, pushing Bruno on the swing in the playground, spending some time at the beautiful location with the next generation in her family.

She was about to give Bruno another big push when he wriggled down off the swing and ran over to his father, who was standing by the slide waiting for Lily to come down. "Daddy, can we walk down by the river now?" Bruno said. "I've had enough of the playground."

"Yeah, let's go to the water," said Lily as she jumped off the end of the slide. She ran towards Bruno. "Maybe we'll see a platypus!"

"I'm not sure you'll see a platypus, Lily," Katrina said from her seat on the park bench where she sat holding Marie. "They're very shy."

"But there *are* platypuses in the Murrumbidgee River, Mum," said Lily emphatically. "We *might* see one."

Emilio glanced at Katrina.

"Just make sure they don't get wet!" she said.

"Would you like me to stay with Marie while you go down with everyone?" said Erin, knowing Katrina could never jump from rock to rock along a riverbank with a baby.

"No, it's okay. She's just drifted off to sleep," Katrina said, placing Marie gently in her stroller. "I'll stay with her in case she wakes up again and wants a feed. She's a little unpredictable at the moment. You go down with Emilio and the kids."

"Okay. Come along, Aunty Erin!" Emilio said, then turned towards Katrina. "We won't be long, *amor*."

"Take your time. I might actually read for a bit!" Katrina said eagerly, pulling her tablet out of her handbag.

Erin walked with Emilio and the children the couple of hundred metres down to an accessible part of the river. There was a chill in the early winter air, but with no wind and the near midday sun shining down on them, it was a most pleasant day to be enjoying the outdoors.

Erin sat down on a large, flat rock right by the water and stared out over the river. The sun glittered and shimmered off the Murrumbidgee, its waters splashing and rushing loudly over some protruding rocks and flowing rapidly downstream.

"Watch this, *niños,*" Emilio said, picking up a small pebble. He threw it expertly across the river, and it skipped five or six times before disappearing into the water.

The children gasped in delight. "Let me try!" Bruno said, picking up a rock in his little hands and throwing it in. It landed in the water a few centimetres from where he stood with a plunk. Lily laughed out loud while Bruno slapped his hand to his forehead and shook his head. "Oh, dear, silly me!" he said, his eyes crinkling, a funny grin on his face and a tone of self-mockery in his voice.

Erin smiled, marvelling out at how Bruno's resilient personality and carefree attitude shone through him, despite his tender age.

"How about we give Aunty Erin a try?" Emilio said, throwing her a pebble.

She caught it and stood up on her rock, tossing the pebble across the water, watching it skip three or four times.

"How do you *do* that?" Lily said, with equal measures of awe and frustration in her voice.

"It's just practice, Lily," Erin said, sitting back down. "Keep trying, you'll get it."

"Aunty Erin's not telling the truth. We're actually using our magical Daddy and Aunty powers, kids," Emilio said, mysteriously.

Lily rolled her eyes. "No, you're not. We need to get higher." She turned and pointed to a grassy spot a few metres further along the embankment. "Can we stand there and try some more?"

Emilio helped his children to the spot and gave them some more stones and pebbles to play with, then rejoined Erin back at the rocks. He threw another pebble across the water.

"So, how are you? You know, how are you feeling?" he said tentatively to Erin.

"I'm all right. Thanks. A little tired, a little nauseous, as I was telling Katrina earlier. But I'm okay." She picked up some pine needles and began twirling them in her fingers and turned to face her brother-in-law. "Did you always want children, Emilio?"

Emilio raised his eyebrows as if surprised by the sudden turn in conversation. "Yes, I did. But I didn't realise how much till I met Katrina."

"Right. So guys *do* want kids, then?"

"Yes, of course they do."

Erin nodded, thoughtful, but said nothing.

"*La oscuridad no es enemiga de la luz,* Erin."

"What?"

"Darkness isn't the enemy of the light. Only the lack of it. Shine the light and darkness scatters."

Erin shook her head. Emilio had a position as a lecturer in philosophy at the Australian National University. With a pang, she suddenly regretted never taking philosophy. "That's very Latino and poetic of you. I have no idea what you mean, but thanks anyway!"

"I mean, you've only had one experience. Not a very good one. He's not the one you should be measuring things by. Gareth isn't the only guy out there."

"You're right. I seem to be getting that message a lot lately."

Erin gazed out over the scenery and listened over the sound of the water for any birdsong she recognised. She heard the familiar trill of a superb fairy wren and noticed one darting about in some shrubbery quite close to her, the bright blue plumage on its head and face clearly visible against the greenery. A noisy friarbird sounded somewhere out of sight, which Erin recognised from its unique call — the "four o'clock" bird, her father had always called it, owing to its call sounding as if that phrase were sprinkled throughout its song. Erin sighed contentedly and allowed her beautiful surroundings to soak into her being. *In spite of everything, the world is still a beautiful place.*

The children called out for Emilio, and Erin watched as he helped them both down from the embankment. A vision of Mark doing the same thing suddenly entered her head, and she immediately felt herself blushing, though she was unable to tell whether it was from joy or embarrassment. She'd only just met him and already she was picturing him as a father to her child. Honestly. Thank goodness no one could read her mind.

In that moment, the air was filled with the sound of a kookaburra laughing. It was close, no more than thirty metres away, Erin guessed.

"Listen, Dad, can you hear?" Bruno said excitedly.

"Yes, I can hear!" Emilio said, placing a hand behind his ear in an exaggerated gesture, as though trying to listen more closely. "I think I know what it is too! It's, it's...yes, it is! It's a Mexican woodnymph!"

The children collapsed in fits of giggles. "No, Daddy! Silly, it's a kookaburra!"

"Oh yes, of course!" Emilio said, slapping his hand to his forehead. "It's a kookaburra! How could I confuse that with the Mexican woodnymph?"

Erin watched her niece and nephew with their father, chuckling to herself. *Yes, that's certainly where Bruno gets his humour from.*

"How about we go back up to Mum and Marie, then get some pizza and bring it back here for us all to eat?"

The suggestion was met with jumps and cheers of delight from the children, and they began making their way back towards the playground.

Once there, Lily sidled up to Erin. "Aunty Erin, I need to go to the loo, but I don't want to go into the toilets on my own. Will you take me?"

"Of course, Lily-girl. Come on." Erin took Lily's hand and began heading towards the toilet block.

"Don't go get pizza without me, Daddy. I'll be right back!" Lily called out to Emilio, pointing to the toilets.

"Okay, *hijita!* We'll wait!"

Right then, Bruno yelled out and pointed. "Hey! Everybody! Look at that!"

The family all turned to stare in the direction Bruno was pointing, only to see a common wombat emerge from behind the toilet block and start running across the picnic ground.

"Oh my goodness, *niños!*" Emilio said. "You hardly ever see those creatures! It's one of those, those, what do you call them? That's right! It's a nine-banded armadillo!"

The children laughed again and raced, in vain, to catch up with the wombat, its short legs carrying its large, barrel-shape body with surprising speed across the grounds and away from the children. "No, Daddy, it's a wombat! It's so cute and furry!" they called out to Emilio as they ran. "You're so silly, Daddy!"

The wombat reached the other side of the picnic ground and disappeared into a burrow in an embankment, but not before turning around for a moment to peer at the small children it had outrun.

Erin grinned from ear to ear and turned to see Katrina's reaction. Her sister was laughing as her children raced back towards her.

"Did you see, Mum? Did you see the wombat?"

"Yes, kids, I saw it. How about that?" Katrina glanced in Erin's direction and winked at her.

Erin winked back, feeling a sudden wave of gratitude for family and warm sunshine and peaceful flowing rivers and, yes, even her own life. It certainly wasn't ideal, but there was no doubt it could be an awful lot worse.

*****

Later that afternoon, Erin was in her room adding an elastic extender Katrina had given her to the button of her favourite jeans. A thickening middle had filled in for the weight she had lost weeks earlier, and her skinny jeans, while not impossible to do up, were certainly gripping her waist a little more snugly these days. Though her pregnancy would not be obvious for a while yet, she still found it perturbing how her body was changing, and how fatigued she had become.

With the extender in place, she breathed in deeply and then exhaled, allowing her stomach to relax, instantly relieved by the comfort afforded by the added stretch. She pulled on a relaxed-fitting light green jumper and sized herself up in the full-length mirror on the wall next to her door. *Yep, passable.* Better sleep and a more peaceful disposition reflected in her appearance, and she enjoyed looking more like she did before her life had gone pear-shaped. She placed her hand over her tummy and caressed it, staring at her reflection and marvelling at the reality that it was no longer just herself in the mirror.

Hello, baby. What are you doing in there? Erin smiled. She knew from what she had read that her child, while still small, was already jumping around inside her womb though it would still be some weeks before she would be aware of the baby's movement.

She checked the time on her watch. 4.00 pm. Still early. In the evening, she would be heading over to Jo's place for a girls' catch up with both Jo and Bianca. Her childhood friends had both rallied around her since her breakup with Gareth and had been calling and messaging her frequently. She had been touched by their concern and was eagerly anticipating seeing them both, despite the fact that she hadn't yet told them about her pregnancy. She thought maybe it was best to keep it to herself for the moment, especially seeing Jo was so advanced in what had been a difficult pregnancy of her own.

She grabbed a pair of gold ballet flats from the built-in wardrobe and placed them on the floor near her dresser. Flopping down on the edge of the bed she let out an enormous yawn. She lay herself down, arranged her pillow comfortably beneath her head and turned towards her window.

A flock of eastern rosellas, about twenty or so, had appeared in the now-bare claret ash tree that stood in the garden. "Rainbow birds," Bruno had called them earlier that day. With their bright red, yellow, green and blue plumage and patches of white on their little faces, it was easy to understand why her small nephew would choose that name. Parrot species were abundant in this region of New South Wales, but the eastern rosellas had always been Erin's favourites.

She watched them alight on the ground one by one to forage for seeds, her mind turning to the brief conversation she'd had with Katrina about Mark earlier. While Emilio was getting lunch for them all with the children, Katrina had shared her advice with Erin, advice that had more or less mirrored Ingrid's — honesty with Mark if things should develop further.

Somehow the idea of telling him about the baby didn't put her off in one way — he had a way of disarming her to the point where she thought she could tell him anything. But the uncertainty of his reaction when she told him, bringing with it the distinct possibility that it would halt any chance of a relationship, made her think twice. She once again wondered whether she was ready to be thinking of starting a relationship with someone new. Could she risk another rejection? She'd had enough of that to last her a lifetime.

Overwhelming fatigue welled up from inside her. She closed her eyes, and within seconds, the world faded out of existence.

Some indiscernible time later she was woken by the ring of her mobile phone. She opened her heavy eyes and turned over, reaching for the phone on her bedside table. *Stupid thing. Why didn't I remember to put it on silent before I lay down?* Focusing on the screen she saw

Bianca's name and quickly swiped it to answer.

"Hi Bianca," she said, making an effort not to sound like she had just woken from a deep sleep. "What's happening? Everything still okay for tonight?"

"Hi, Erin," Bianca said, stress evident in her voice. "No, it isn't actually."

The worry in Bianca's voice gripped Erin, and she propped herself up on her elbow. "Why, what's wrong?"

"It's Jo. She went into premature labour this morning, and John took her to hospital."

"Oh no. She's only seven months along! Is she okay?"

"She had to have an emergency c-section as the baby wasn't doing well. She's fine now, but the baby is in the neonatal unit. They had a boy; they're calling him Jacob. He's having difficulty breathing, and he needs around-the-clock care."

"Oh, no," Erin said again, her heart sinking. "Is he going to be all right?"

"The doctor said there's no reason to think he won't be fine after a while. But it's such a shock. Jo was going fine last night. Then today she's in hospital with a premmie baby."

"You sound like you're in shock too."

"I am a bit," Bianca said. "I'm still here at the hospital. I was wondering if you wanted to come over here too. Jo is up to having visitors, and she'd like to see you. Sorry it's not what we had planned for the evening."

Wide awake now, Erin sat up on the bed. "Of course I'll come. I'm on my way now," she said, reaching for her shoes and slipping them on. "I'll see you in a little while."

"Great. She's at Calvary Hospital. See you soon."

*****

Erin climbed the steps to the second floor of the maternity wing at Calvary Hospital carrying a small box of flowers and a blue teddy bear with "It's a Boy!"

embroidered on its chest that she'd bought at the hospital gift shop. She approached a desk where one of the midwives on duty was filling out some paperwork and got directions to Jo's room. After following a long corridor, she found the room where Jo was staying. The door was half-open, so she made a tentative knock to announce her arrival and entered the room. Jo was sitting up in a large hospital bed, her mother Anne, in a chair on one side and Bianca on the other side.

"Hello, is there a new mummy in here?" she said quietly, smiling in Jo's direction.

"Erin!" Jo said, then promptly burst into tears.

Erin approached the bed, leaving the gifts at the end of it and reached over to embrace the distressed new mother.

"If you didn't want to catch up this evening, there are other ways you could have gotten out of it besides going into labour," Erin joked.

Jo laughed through her tears and hugged Erin. "This is the last thing I would have imagined doing today," she said, her voice shaking, then letting out a sigh loaded with such emotion that Erin wanted to cry with her.

"Here, Erin, you take my spot," said Anne, standing and offering her chair to Erin. "I might go to the kitchen and grab a cuppa, let you young ones catch up."

"Thanks, Anne."

"See if you girls can distract her a bit. She's a bit emotional right now," Anne said, reaching out to pat Erin's shoulder.

"We'll do our best," Erin replied, winking at Jo.

Anne turned to Jo. "I'll be down the corridor, all right?"

"Yep," Jo whispered as her mother left the room.

Erin sat down next to the bed, where Anne had been. "How's the baby?" Erin asked, placing her bag down on the floor next to the hospital chair. "Is John with him now?"

"Yes, he's up at neonatal now. He needs help breathing, and he's a little jaundiced. They'll be taking me up again soon, but I wanted one of us to be with him all the time, at least at first."

Bianca smiled. "Welcome to parenthood," she said. "Your life for the next twenty-five years or so!"

Jo's lip trembled, and she started to cry again. "I just can't help thinking there was something I did that made him come early."

Bianca reached out and took Jo's hand. "No, don't. You've had a hard pregnancy as it is. You did everything you could to get him this far. Babies come early sometimes. We can just thank God that he's getting good care, and he's going to be all right."

Erin peered over at Bianca, wondering about her reference to God, something she'd never heard her say before. She wondered if it was Father Nick's influence, now that she was married to his cousin. He certainly seemed to have a remarkable effect on people, herself included.

"I just want to be up there with him now."

"You will be in a few minutes," Erin said. "Work on getting yourself better so you can take care of him. Here," she reached out for the teddy at the end of the bed and handed it to her. "Put this in his cot when he's a bit bigger."

"Thank you; it's lovely," she said, accepting the bear and stroking it. "I'm so happy you came. How are you getting on?"

"I'm all right. Don't worry about me; I'm going fine," she said, reaching for the flowers she'd brought and placing them on Jo's bedside table. "How are *you*? You must be feeling like you've been hit by a tidal wave after what you've been through today."

"I dunno," Jo said, rubbing her eyes. "The whole day has been a bit of a blur. The contractions came on so violently and before I knew it, he was in distress, and they had to get me to surgery." Her lip began to quiver again. "I only got to hold him for a few seconds before they took him away.

They had to sew me up and get me to recovery. I still don't have any sensation in my legs."

"Do you have a photo?" Erin asked.

Jo reached over to her bedside table and grabbed a mobile phone. "Yep, John took some on his phone and left it with me until I can get back with him and Jacob."

She handed the phone to Erin. Erin took it and looked down at the hurriedly-taken snap of the tiny, red child, surrounded by white latex-gloved hands, moments after being pulled from Jo's womb.

"Oh, he's beautiful, Jo," she said, handing back the phone. "You've done so well."

"Yes, you have," Bianca joined in. "You'll be with him soon. They'll want to get you two together as soon as possible. John will be down with the orderly in a few minutes."

"I know," Jo said, taking the phone from Erin and staring down at the photo. "It's the most incredible thing. I spent the whole pregnancy wondering how I'd feel when I first saw Jake. I mean, I always loved him, from the moment I knew I was pregnant, of course. But nothing prepared me for what it was like when I first saw him. It's like nothing I could ever have imagined."

"Yep, all the new mums say that," Bianca said, a hint of longing in her voice. "You're so lucky to finally be experiencing it for yourself."

Jo nodded and gazed at the photo on the phone. She placed it back on the side table. "Come on, you two, you're supposed to be distracting me till they take me to the baby."

"Well, this is supposed to be our girls' catch-up night," Erin said. "What about you, Bianca? How's married life treating you?"

"Fine," Bianca said, holding her hand up to her mouth and closing her eyes. She waited a second then lowered her hand again. "Ryan's good. Everything's great."

Erin bit her lip, trying not to smile, immediately recognising the signs Ingrid must have seen when she guessed Erin's secret. "How far along are you, Bianca?"

Bianca looked at Erin as though she'd been hit.

"Sorry, but it's a little obvious. You're positively green."

"I'm sorry, Erin, I didn't want to tell you yet. Not after all you've been through. I thought it was a bit selfish."

Erin shook her head. "Don't be silly. Congratulations! It's wonderful news. When are you due?"

"Early January," Bianca replied. "Summer baby."

January. Same as me.

"She certainly didn't muck around," Jo added. "She's only been married five minutes."

"Yeah, I think I got pregnant on my wedding night," Bianca said.

It struck Erin that earlier that day all three of them had been pregnant. "Funny that," she said, and laughed, half to herself. "I think I got pregnant on your wedding night too."

Bianca and Jo stopped short and their jaws dropped open in unison. "What?" Bianca said, tilting her head and staring at Erin.

Erin nodded, then lowered her head. "I know. It's terrible timing, but it's true. I discovered it after Gareth and I broke up. I didn't mean to tell you both now. It just kind of slipped out. I haven't told many people yet."

"You haven't told Gareth?" Jo asked.

"No, not yet," Erin replied. "Please, *please* don't tell him."

"No, of course not. We won't even mention it to Ryan or John yet. Right, Jo?" Bianca turned to Jo.

"You're pregnant?" Jo said, seeming to forget herself for a moment.

Erin nodded.

Jo's face lit up. "That means we're all going to be mums together! Don't you think that's amazing?"

Erin smiled. "Yeah, I suppose we will be, in a few months' time."

"Erin! You should have told us sooner," Bianca said. "We could have done more for you."

"Thanks, girls. I appreciate it. But I didn't want to say anything. I didn't want you to feel awkward around me. You're both newly, happily married, and I'm, well, I'm..." her voice trailed off, leaving the sentence unfinished.

"You're an outstanding mother, is what you are," Jo said.

Erin laughed Jo off with a wave of her hand. "I'm not a mother yet, Jo. But thanks."

"Of course you're a mother," Bianca said, a shocked look on her face. "You *know* you are. Once you're pregnant, where on earth do you draw the line between motherhood and not? And Jo's right. You're an amazing mum for taking this on all alone. Jo and I have the fathers of our children with us. I can't imagine what you must have been through."

"Thanks," Erin replied, her eyes filling with tears. "I'm glad I let that news slip out now."

The women talked together for a few minutes longer until John arrived with one of the orderlies to take Jo up to the neonatal ward. Erin and Bianca made their way downstairs to the main foyer area where Ryan was waiting for Bianca.

"We'll walk you to your car, Erin," Bianca said. "It's getting dark out there now."

The three of them walked to Erin's Honda. Ryan hung back as Bianca spoke to Erin. "Mum's the word, now," she whispered to Erin, reaching out to hug her. "Call me if you need anything. I'll be there right away."

"Thank you," Erin said. "And congratulations again. I'll see you soon." Standing at her car door, she watched Bianca link hands with Ryan and walk towards their own car.

*****

Forty-five minutes later, Erin opened the door of her bedroom and kicked her shoes off. "What a day," she said aloud, dropping her bag on the floor next to her bed and rubbing her face with the palms of her hands. The exhaustion that had overwhelmed her earlier that day began creeping up on her again and she flopped down on the edge of the bed.

She reached down into her bag for her phone and pulled up the photo of Jacob that Jo had sent her. She stared down at the image of her friend's new child. Precious little thing. So tiny and defenceless. So utterly reliant on those around him. Her thoughts then turned once again to her own baby, and she smiled. A sudden sense of joy like that of a gleeful child on Christmas morning rose up in her.

Joy? She smiled again. Yes, pure, unadulterated joy. Despite her weariness, the sensation flowed up from inside her like a cup overflowing, warming and soothing her, healing her a little from the pain of recent months. For the first time since learning of her pregnancy, she wondered about the baby's sex. A little girl, maybe? Closing her eyes, she placed one hand on her tummy, and pictured herself holding her new child. *I'll do everything I can to bring you safely to that day, little angel.*

A sudden buzz of her phone pulled her out of her peaceful reflection. The photo of baby Jacob disappeared, replaced by an incoming call. Mark's name appeared on the screen.

Mark! A small gasp escaped her, and she tapped at the screen. Her joy stepped up a notch, and her stomach knotted up slightly as she anticipated hearing the sound of his voice.

"Hello?"

"Erin? Hi, it's Mark. How are you?"

Erin released a breath and grinned from ear to ear. "I'm pretty good, actually. How are you?"

"I'm okay too, thanks. Is this a good time to call you?"

"Yes, of course. I just got home. I had to make an unexpected visit to Calvary Hospital this afternoon."

"What?" Mark's voice rose a notch. "Is everything all right?"

"Yes, it is, or at least, it should be," Erin explained briefly about Jo's premature birth. "I didn't get to see the baby, but she showed me a photo. He's so tiny."

"I'll keep your friend and her baby in my prayers. Should I let you go? You must be pretty wrung out."

"No, no, it's quite all right. It's so good to hear from you," she replied, knowing she'd be happy to sit on the phone all night if it meant continuing to hear Mark's voice. "To what do I owe the honour of this call?" There was a pause in the conversation, and Erin waited to hear what Mark would say.

"Honour? That's nice, Erin. Thank you," he said, sounding bashful. "Um..." he paused again. "I wanted to say hi. I've been thinking about you, praying for you."

"Thank you for your prayers, I really think they've made a difference."

"I'm so glad you're feeling stronger."

A lull fell in the conversation, and Erin wondered about the real reason Mark had called, hoping he wanted to see her again soon. Resisting the temptation to ramble, she waited.

Finally he spoke. "I was wondering, what are you doing tomorrow?" The next day was the Queen's Birthday holiday, the last public holiday before the Labour Day holiday in October. In truth, Erin had been planning to sleep a large part of the day, but she pushed that thought aside.

"I haven't organised anything."

Erin heard Mark draw in a breath. "Well, I was going to take a drive down the coast, and I wondered if you might like to come with me."

"The coast?" Erin laughed. "You do realise it's going to be

fourteen degrees tomorrow, don't you?"

"In Canberra yes, but it's going to be twenty and sunny at Bateman's Bay."

"No kidding. I didn't realise."

"Looks like I might need to educate you about the delights of the south coast."

Erin scoffed. "Yeah, right! I'm from Canberra — I can out-south coast you any day!"

Mark chuckled, the sound of his laughter lifting Erin's spirit. "So, you up for it?"

This time she didn't hesitate. "Yep. I'd love to."

Chapter 11

The stretch of road on the Clyde Mountain is a necessary obstacle between Canberra and Bateman's Bay, a journey that Erin had always dreaded making, thanks to her experience as a passenger with Gareth at the wheel. His handling of the winding turns descending the mountain road down to sea level had often come close to relieving her of her most recent meal. But now, sitting cozy in the passenger seat in Mark's car, she found the drive down the mountain road pleasant in spite of her pregnancy nausea.

"How are you going there? Some of these turns are a bit hairy," Mark said as he negotiated his way carefully around a steeply descending hairpin bend.

"Fine, thank you." Erin gazed out the front window at the wide expanse of native Australian flora spread out in front of them to the horizon. "Your driving is far less nauseating than my ex-boyfriend's."

Mark chuckled but didn't comment. Erin peeked sideways at him for the hundredth time since he picked her up a little over an hour ago, taking in his handsome profile as he confidently navigated the difficult stretch of road.

That morning Erin had introduced Mark to her parents and was struck straight away by how taken they seemed to be with him. Charming and polite, he had immediately won them over in a way she had never seen Gareth do. Years ago she had given up on the idea of having her parents approve of her choice of boyfriends and was surprised to find that their approval still mattered to her. The astonishing direction her life was taking seemed so surreal. Never would she have believed she was capable of such a change of heart.

"I was thinking we could drive past Bateman's Bay down to Broulee Beach," Mark said, interrupting her thoughts. "It's only another twenty minutes past the Bay, and it's such a beautiful beach to walk along."

"Sounds lovely. I love Broulee Beach. It's been years since I last saw it."

"Well, today's the day you go back."

"When was the last time you went?"

"Back in early March, when the weather was still hot. I love it. I try and get down as often as I can."

"Do you go alone, usually?"

"Sometimes I go alone; other times I go with Father Nick."

Father Nick. Erin had still not worked up the nerve to go and speak with him, despite her growing desire to seek his counsel. "How long have you known Father Nick? You seem quite friendly with him."

"Yes, he was in his final years at the seminary the year I joined. We're good friends."

Erin stared at the rosary beads dangling from Mark's rear-view mirror. "What's it like being friends with a priest?"

Mark laughed. "Just like being friends with anyone else. Priests are people too."

Erin suddenly felt a little silly. "Yeah, I guess you're right. I've never thought about it like that before. He's certainly the youngest priest I've ever come across."

"He's twenty-eight. I guess that is fairly young." Mark paused. "Can I ask, why did you want to know if I go to the coast alone or not?" he said, a hint of a smile in his voice.

Erin turned to look at him. "I suppose I'm curious as to how many other girls have sat here in your passenger seat."

Mark shrugged. "I've never been any good at being coy, Erin. You're the only one since I've moved to Canberra. The only one in quite some years, truth be told."

Erin's cheeks warmed. "You're a puzzle, Mark. There must be dozens of girls who would love to spend time with you. It's hard to imagine that I'm the first one in years. Though I must say — I'm very flattered that I am."

Mark turned briefly and smiled at her. "I'm happy to hear you say that."

*****

Another hour of driving and easy conversation later, they pulled up along the road running parallel to Broulee Beach. Mark got out and stepped over to Erin's side of the car, opening the door for her, a gesture that surprised and pleased her. When was the last time Gareth had stood back and opened any sort of door for her, car or otherwise?

"Thank you." Erin grinned up at him as she climbed out. "I didn't know this kind of chivalry still existed. What on earth have I been missing?"

Mark grinned. "Yes, we Knights in Shining Subarus are in pretty short supply these days," he said, making her laugh. He closed the car door behind her. "Shall we?"

They made their way down a narrow, sandy track next to where they parked that cut through low-lying scrub that led down to the beach. The weather was pleasant, as predicted, and the sun shone down on them from a cloudless sky. *A perfect day.*

Erin breathed in deeply as she made her way towards the beach with Mark close behind her, the salty breeze filling her lungs. The roar of the South Pacific Ocean breaking on the beach just a few metres ahead of them made Erin want to run so as not to waste a second in catching sight of those beautiful waves, in kicking off her shoes and feeling the sand between her toes. Her sudden eagerness caught her off guard. The last time she felt this excited about seeing the ocean, she had been a little girl.

She managed to restrain herself for the last few steps till they reached the end of the track and stepped out onto the beach. Erin stopped and stared out ahead and around her.

The sun sparkled blindingly off the ocean, and the beach stretched out for a couple of kilometres all the way down to Broulee Island at its southern end. There were a number of people walking up and down the beach, making the most of the weather and the public holiday. Even a few surfers were enjoying the waves, braving the now fairly cool water temperatures.

Mark came up and stood beside her. "Beautiful day," he said, staring out over the ocean.

"It certainly is," Erin replied, reaching down to remove her sand shoes.

"Isn't it a little cool for bare feet?"

"No way! How can you feel the sand under your feet properly with your runners on? Come on, you too. Don't be a wimp." She dropped her shoes down by the opening to the track that led back to the car.

Mark laughed. "Okay." He took off his runners and socks and threw them down next to Erin's.

"Come on; I'm up for a nice long walk," Erin said as she started off in a well-paced stroll down the beach.

Mark immediately followed, and they fell into step together. "Yeah, me too."

Erin slid her feet a little as she walked, delighting in the cool, powder-soft sand. "It's so lovely down here. I can't remember the last time I felt so enthusiastic about getting outside. This was such a great idea."

"I'm glad you're having a good day."

"I am. Thank you."

They walked together side by side, the conversation continuing to flow easily between them as they strolled all the way to the end of the beach, then turned to walk back again. About halfway up the beach, they stopped and sat down together on the sand to take in the crashing surf.

Erin couldn't believe how quickly the time was passing with Mark. Hours were passing her by like minutes, but the time with him revealed so much more to her about what he was like. His mild manner, his kindness and humility that shone through while they discussed topics in which he was far more knowledgeable than her, and yes, even his deep devotion to his faith were winning her over more and more. Now, sitting side by side, shoulders close but not quite touching, she thought again how lucky she was to be the one who was with him, instead of some other girl.

I wonder where this is going for him? Obviously, he wanted to be there with her. But as kind and gentlemanly as he had been, he hadn't yet given her any clear indication that he wanted anything more from her than a simple friendship. Still, this was only their third meeting. Or date? No, they were hardly dating. Or were they? Mark would be aware she was feeling vulnerable. Perhaps he was just waiting for some kind of confirmation from her?

Lost in thought, she stared out over the surf and glimpsed four or five dorsal fins riding the waves only a few metres from shore. She gasped.

"Did you see that?" she said, pointing. "Dolphins!"

"Hey, you're right!"

"I've never seen dolphins in the surf before. They swim so fast, don't they?"

The fins emerged again briefly on another wave a little further up the beach, then disappeared again. Erin laughed, unable to stop herself, the laughter bubbling up out of her.

How long since sheer joy for the beauty of the world around her had burst out of her like that? She didn't know and didn't care to remember. Perhaps this was the first time in her life. *Oh Lord, I'm so tired of analysing everything.* It seemed far more sensible to stop placing her newfound joy under a microscope and simply start enjoying it.

"Wow," Mark said.

Erin turned to look at him and found him staring at her.

"Wow, what?"

"I can't believe how different you are from the first time I met you. You're like another person. You seem so..."

"Happy?"

"Yeah, you do."

"I think that's because I am."

"What's changed?"

Erin paused and thought before answering. "I suppose part of it is realising that being with Gareth was bad for me. I wasn't aware of it while we were living together. And I would never have left him, not ever. I never thought I'd say this, but I think him leaving me was a blessing in disguise. I don't feel rejected anymore. I feel free."

"A good reason to be happy. And what's the other part?"

Ooh, watch now. Choose your words carefully. "I'm grateful for all the other blessings unfolding in my life. Exploring my faith again for the first time in years. Friendships. More contact with my family. And —"

"And what?"

"And you."

"Me?"

Erin turned to look Mark full in his face. "Yes. Meeting you has — has had a — a profound effect on me. Your — friendship is making a real difference to me." She glanced down, embarrassed, and began tracing with her fingers in the sand. "I'm starting to believe in God again because of you. I didn't see it straight away, but my life started turning around from that first time I met you."

There was a pause in the conversation, and Erin kept her head down, a sensation of warmth rushing to her face. *What's the matter with me? Why can't I just keep it together when I'm around him?*

"My life turned around when I met you too."

Erin's heart quickened a little. "But your life is all figured out already. What possible difference could I make to you?" She dared then, to glance up, and found the answer.

It wasn't necessary for him to speak. It was in his expression, undeniable. The look on his face told her more about what was in his heart than anything he could have said in words. She peered into the dark eyes that were staring into hers with such tenderness. A man in love was a difficult thing to mistake. He loved her! There was absolutely no doubt in her mind.

Joy gripped her anew, her heart so overflowing with the sensation that she thought it might burst. She smiled up at him, wondering if her eyes were as betraying as his. She held his gaze for a moment, waiting to see if he might kiss her.

Instead, he turned slightly towards her, reached out and took her hand in his. "I can't begin to tell you the difference you're making in my life. You have such a beautiful heart. I'm so inspired by your courage." Erin sat there almost breathless. This was the first time he'd touched her, and she felt completely overcome by the innocence and total *reverence* with which he did so. The experience was unlike anything else she could remember. She silently thanked God she was already sitting down, otherwise she knew her knees would never have held her up.

Mark went on. "You've been through so much. You're still suffering. But I want you to know, I'm here. Whenever ...*if* ever you're ready to...to take things further. I'll be waiting for you."

Erin drew in a breath. *Oh, God, am I ready?* No, nowhere near ready. Not because she didn't want to be with him. That would never be true. The advice Ingrid and Katrina had given her began throbbing in her ears. *Be honest if things develop further.* No doubt this was "further." That point had been reached about thirty seconds earlier. Could she tell him? Now?

There could be no competition. She knew in her heart

that her child came first. Their bond was growing daily, mother and baby, and Erin was profoundly aware that she was the only one in the world her baby could rely on. Her desire to fulfil her child's needs ran deep and strong in her, and there was nothing she could allow to get in the way of that. What Bianca said was right. Once a woman was pregnant, there was no line of demarcation between being a mother and not. Before she could be Mark's girlfriend or anything more, she was now — first and foremost — her child's mother.

But the fear of Mark rejecting her now stared her in the face. Would he reject her? Maybe not, but possibly. The thought was just too awful to bear.

She turned towards Mark, doing her best to steady her beating heart. "You're right. I am still suffering. Things are ...complicated for me, still. You deserve someone who isn't so...so all over the place."

"Erin," Mark said, keeping his strong but gentle hold on her hand. "I'm all over the place too. Everyone is. And I *don't* have it all figured out. If I did, I wouldn't need my God so much. And that suits me just fine. Being broken is part of our human condition. Life *is* complicated, I understand. I don't want you to do anything before you're ready."

Could he be any more amazing? Erin did her best to calm herself, staring into his handsome face, becoming every moment more lovely to her.

"Thank you. Maybe if we just...I don't know, take things slowly?"

What? Define slowly, Erin. What are you asking him? Any slower and you'd be going backwards, girl.

But Mark didn't hesitate. "Of course. I meant what I said. I'm here for you, whenever you're ready."

"Thank you."

They sat together in silence, their hands joined. After a moment Mark spoke again. "I just have one thing to ask you."

Erin sucked in a small breath. "What?"

He leaned in towards her. "Are you hungry?"

Erin burst out laughing at his unexpected question, grateful for his diffusing the intensity of the moment. "Yes, actually, I am."

"Good, me too. Feel like fish and chips?"

"Yep." They both stood up, Mark helping her to her feet.

As they continued their walk back up the beach, Erin thought about the tiny life she carried inside her and how close she had come to telling Mark. Guilt that she'd failed to do so crept up on her, spoiling, in some part, the joy of the day. Didn't he deserve to know? Yes, and she knew she must tell him soon. She would.

Thank you, Lord. Thank you for Mark, for sending him to me. Help me to level with him, give me the courage to do it soon. Please don't let me lose him. Please.

When they got back to Mark's car, Erin noticed again the rosary beads hanging from the rear-view mirror. She reached up and touched them and shifted herself around to face Mark in the driver's seat.

"Mark, do you think we could pray the Rosary together on the way back home later?"

Surprise, then delight, lit up his face. "Of course!"

"You might need to help me. I'll be a little bit rusty remembering the right mysteries."

But from the way Mark looked at her, she guessed he wouldn't mind helping her with that. At all.

*****

"So after that you didn't tell him?" Ingrid's voice floated over the top of the change room curtain at the back of a women's clothing boutique in Kingston during their lunch hour later that week.

Erin sat outside the change room on a comfy sofa, the type they put in dress shops full of garments with price tags meant specifically for shoppers who were not faint of heart.

"No, I didn't. I came awfully close to telling him, but I just couldn't do it." Erin propped her elbows on her knees and placed her head in her hands. "Ingrid, it was such a beautiful day with the beach and the ocean and, and *Mark*. He's so incredible. I just didn't have the courage. What could I have said? 'Thank you for asking me out on this gorgeous date with you. I'm so enjoying this chance to get to know you better. By the way, remember that idiot who dumped me a few months back? Did I mention I'm pregnant with his baby?'"

"Yes, I agree that would have killed the moment," Ingrid said, pushing the curtain aside to show Erin the rose-coloured, cap sleeve dress she'd tried on.

Erin glanced up. "Ingrid, you look amazing in that," she said with a tinge of envy. "You're one of the few women I know who can get away with wearing a dress like that so elegantly. You should definitely get it."

"Thanks. I do like it. And Jim did want me to get something nice for our tenth anniversary." She stepped over to a rack close to the change room and pulled off an emerald green A-line dress in Erin's size and handed it to her.

"Why don't you try on something? You need a distraction. This one's gorgeous and it matches your eyes."

Erin laughed and waved Ingrid away with her hand. "And wear it where? My twenty-week ultrasound?"

"There is life after pregnancy, Erin. You won't be pregnant forever, believe it or not." Ingrid placed the dress down on the lounge next to Erin and stepped back into the change room, pulling the curtain closed. "How far along are you now?"

"About twelve weeks, give or take."

"If you don't tell Mark soon, he's going to find out

anyway. You're going to pop in the next few weeks. You don't want him finding out like that. It'll be hard to tell him initially, but you'll be able to get on with things once you do. Why are you so scared to tell him?"

"Apart from the fear of him running for his life and never looking back? Gee, I don't know."

"The man is obviously completely gone on you. Have some faith in him. I think you might be pleasantly surprised."

"Possibly." Erin waited while Ingrid changed and went to the front of the shop to buy her dress. Erin put the green dress back on the rack and joined Ingrid out the front of the shop.

"Oh, this will interest you," Ingrid said as they sat down at a café opposite the dress shop. "Did I tell you that my sister stopped taking the pill? I told her what you said about it being carcinogenic and abortifacient, and she saw that as the final straw. She said it was making her feel like crap and blasting her libido to oblivion as well. She's not sure what to replace it with though. I didn't know what to tell her, apart from the usual."

"She shouldn't use anything artificial," Erin said, thinking about a recent conversation with Mark on that very topic.

"Why not? I mean, as long as it's not polluting her body, it'd be okay, wouldn't it?"

"Not really. Barriers and chemicals don't belong in a relationship like that. I mean, think about a much lesser relationship like what we have as advertisers, with our clients. Imagine if we'd met with one of our customers — say, Brendan, from yesterday. And just as he was leaving and we went to shake hands with him, he put his hand in his pocket and put on a latex glove?"

Ingrid frowned, then gave an awkward laugh. "That'd be kind of weird, I suppose. Insulting."

"It would, wouldn't it? How much less appropriate is it,

then, in a committed relationship like a marriage? Where you're supposed to love each other more than anyone else does?"

"Okay, fair enough. But natural methods don't actually work, do they?"

"Yes, they do, as far as I'm aware. My doctor is a big fan of them. She told me modern forms of fertility awareness are over ninety-nine per cent effective. I know my sister uses a natural method using basic observations and temperature taking and all her pregnancies were planned."

"You're joking."

Erin shook her head. "No, and believe me, I've been checking it out. Did you also know that there's been research done on the divorce rate of couples who use natural methods of family planning, and it's very low? They reckon as small as five per cent. What's the average divorce rate in countries like Australia or Canada or the USA?"

"Probably at least one in three. Maybe half. It'd be high."

"There you go." Erin sighed. "You know, I always thought the Catholic Church was totally backward for teaching against contraceptive practices. But lately I've been seeing that the Church's way of doing things is far more considerate and caring of people. They're far more interested in giving women freedom to manage their fertility and their bodies than the pharmaceutical companies. I always thought the Church needed to keep up with the times. Now I wonder if maybe the times haven't caught up with the Church."

Ingrid observed Erin with a bemused smile. "Been discussing these things with Mark?" she said, her tone sounding as though she already knew the answer.

"Yes, I suppose I have."

"This man is really changing you. And it's not a bad change. Heck, you're even teaching me some things. In spite of everything that's happened to you, you're coming to life."

Erin grinned, warmed from the inside out as she remembered her time with Mark only a few days earlier. "Do you think?"

"Yes, I do. All the more reason you need to tell him, soon."

Erin's heart contracted, then sunk like lead in her chest.

"You're right. I can't keep see-sawing like this. I'll tell him the next time I see him."

As she looked up at the beverages board and tried to decide what odd-tasting, infuriatingly caffeine-free tea to drink, she wondered if the next time she saw Mark might also be the last.

*****

That night Erin arrived home to find a parcel on her desk, pulled from the letter box earlier that day by her mother. She opened it and found a gift wrapped in tissue paper with a small card attached.

Dear Erin,

From both of us — we've talked, and we're both pretty sure it's a girl! A little set for your baby trousseau.

Love, Jo and Bianca

Erin smiled and opened the present, finding a little pink romper outfit with matching bunny rug.

"Ooooh, so cute!" The romper was a tiny, short-sleeved piece, clearly for a baby younger than three months, born in summer, as her child would be. *How thoughtful. And with all Jo is going through at the moment.*

She made a mental note to call them both and visit Jo some time when it wouldn't be too stressful for her. She had been discharged from hospital, but baby Jake was still there, and she was spending all her days with him.

Right then Judith appeared in Erin's doorway holding a small shopping bag.

"Mum! Look at this! Bianca and Jo sent it. Well, probably Bianca, seeing Jo's a bit busy with Jake at the moment."

Judith entered the room, put the bag down on the bed and took the blanket and romper from Erin. "Oh, that's beautiful. They both think it's a girl, I see." She gave them back and reached for the bag on the bed, handing it to Erin. "They're not the only ones."

Erin placed her hand inside the bag and pulled out a small carousel music box with three horses, all white and pink and covered in small pink diamante stones and intricate carvings of roses.

"Oh, Mum, it's beautiful! Thank you. You didn't have to."

"Of course I did! I want to. This is my grandchild you're talking about."

"Well, I love it!"

"It's not actually for you, my dear."

Erin laughed. "I know, but you know what I mean."

Judith reached out and turned it a few times and it began playing the *Nutcracker Suite*. "For the nursery," she said.

Erin eyed her mother. "Come on, Mum. What nursery?"

"Don't you worry, we'll sort something out," Judith said, an air of mock mystery in her voice.

Erin sat down at her desk and sighed. "This is really happening, isn't it?"

"Yes, it is. It's going to happen whether you're ready or not, so I thought we might start preparing," Judith said, sitting down on Erin's bed.

At that moment, a sharp pain in Erin's abdomen caused her to cry out and she bent over double. "Ow!"

Judith gasped. "Are you all right?" she said, immediately reacting and reaching out to support Erin.

Erin breathed for a second and the pain passed. "Yeah, I'm fine. It's gone now." She breathed in and out a few times. "Is that normal?"

"Cramping can be normal. All sorts of crazy things

happen to your body during pregnancy. Just keep an eye on it, and we'll get you to the doctor if need be."

Erin nodded. "Okay, I will." Her thoughts turned to the coming weekend.

"I'm seeing Mark on Saturday," she said. "I'm going to tell him about the baby."

Judith nodded in understanding. "That's good. He needs to know."

"Mum, I'm so nervous. What if he doesn't want to see me anymore?"

"Then he's not worthy of you, and you can move on with your life. But I don't think it's going to put him off."

"How do you know?"

"Apart from the fact that Mark appears to be a deeply faithful man with great character and integrity?"

"Mm hm?"

"He's quite obviously head over heels in love with you. That man would charge through a minefield, tossing explosives over his shoulders to get to you, if they stood in his way."

Erin laughed. "You only met him once. How could you tell that after only one meeting?"

"Easily enough. I've been around a while."

"Does this all come off as ridiculous to you?"

"I have to say, at first I didn't think it was wise for you to consider a new relationship right now. But no, it's not ridiculous at all. This is a wonderful blessing. See how the Lord is looking after you."

"Yes. Yes, so it would seem."

Chapter 12

Mark sat in the cathedral chapel before 12.15 pm Mass, turning his head to glance behind him, yet again, to see if Erin had arrived. He had been overjoyed yesterday when she had texted him asking that they meet up for Saturday Mass then spend some time together in the afternoon. He responded straight away and had been counting the hours till Saturday. It was still early, but she'd said she had something she wanted to talk to him about, and he couldn't wait to see her.

I wish she'd just let me pick her up instead of us meeting up like this. Then he remembered that it was her idea for them to arrive separately and that he was supposed to be giving her freedom and time to tell him when she was ready for a deeper relationship with him. Not that he wanted in any way to restrict her freedom, but he now found himself worrying about her, a feeling which perturbed him as he wasn't prone to worry.

Unable to shake the growing sense of unrest, he knelt down, focusing on the tabernacle. He closed his eyes and reminded himself of whose Presence he was in. Who better to take his concerns to?

My God, here I come before You once again. You have blessed me so abundantly. You have saved my life and lifted me from the miry clay. Thank You for Your mercy and love. I am Yours and everything good I possess You alone have blessed me with.

Thank You for Erin's presence in my life. Thank You for the time You gave me with her on Monday, for the delight she brings to my heart. If it be Your will, allow me to be for her everything that she is for me.

Lord, I see You working in Erin's life. But I'm afraid for her, as she still hasn't made the final steps back to You and Your Church. Help her complete her journey back to You. Don't allow her to be snatched away. Guide her through whatever obstacles still lie ahead.

Peace rose up out of a well deep in his soul, calming his unease. He took in a breath and let out a small sigh.

Thank You, Lord. Please help me to remember that without You I can't do anything. I can love and be loved only if Your love and peace and forgiveness is working in me.

A few more moments in silent reflection passed until he felt a hand on his arm. He opened his eyes and turned, finding Erin next to him. His heart gave a wondrous leap, and he grinned at her. She smiled back, whispered hello and knelt down beside him, making the Sign of the Cross and closing her eyes. *Oh, wow.* Was it just him, or did she become more beautiful every time he saw her?

At that moment the bell rang, and Nick appeared from the sacristy and entered the chapel to begin the Mass. The congregation recited the entrance antiphon as Nick ascended the steps to the sanctuary.

Mark leaned over towards Erin. "Would you like to meet Father Nick after Mass?" he whispered.

Erin turned her head, appearing slightly anxious. She raised her eyebrows. "Really?" she whispered back.

"Yeah, of course. We've spoken already. He can't wait to meet you."

*****

After Mass, Mark sat with Erin outside the sacristy in the main part of the cathedral waiting for Nick to emerge. Praying with Erin beside him during Mass filled him with a sense of completion, the same as when they'd prayed the Rosary together a few days earlier.

Joyful anticipation filled him at the chance to now introduce her to someone in his life, and his best friend, no less. People around them were praying so they sat together silently, but Erin seemed nervous, repeatedly biting her left thumbnail. Was that something she did when she was nervous? Mark hoped against hope he would have the opportunity to find out that and more about her in the coming months.

After a few minutes, the remaining parishioners left, leaving them alone in the church, and Nick came out of the sacristy, dressed in his black clericals, a broad smile on his face. Mark and Erin stood as Nick approached them.

"Hello, Erin," he said, putting out his hand to shake hers. "Good to meet you. Mark's told me about you. All good things, don't worry."

The concern on Erin's face dissolved immediately, transforming into a beautiful grin as she shook Nick's hand. "Lovely to meet you too, Father," she said. "I've been meaning to come and speak to you for a while now. I don't know if you remember but I saw you at Bianca's and Ryan's wedding a while back."

Nick nodded thoughtfully, as though recalling. "That's right, I do remember seeing you outside the church after the wedding. Are you friends with Bianca?"

"Yes, we went to school together," she said, turning then to Mark. "Mark told me you and he were in the seminary at the same time."

"Yep, we were," Nick said, nodding. "We all missed him when he left. He's smarter than the rest of us put together!"

Mark rolled his eyes. "Yeah, right."

"No, I'd believe that," Erin said, smiling in Mark's direction, causing his heart to double beat, yet again. Would he ever get enough of that gorgeous smile?

Mark listened as Erin and Nick conversed easily for a few more minutes before Nick had to excuse himself.

"Sorry, I would have loved to have grabbed a coffee with you both."

"No problem, Father," Erin said. "I was wondering

though, before you go, would you mind giving me a blessing?"

"Of course," he said. He extended his hand over Erin, and she bent her head. "May the blessing of Almighty God remain with you now and always," he prayed, then made the Sign of the Cross over her.

Mark watched as Erin lifted up her head and noticed there were tears in her eyes. "Thank you."

"My pleasure," Nick said and turned to Mark. "I'll catch you later, Mark."

"Yep, no worries, Nick." He would have quite a lot to talk to him about the next time they spoke.

Nick made his way back into the sacristy, and Mark and Erin headed out the back of the cathedral into a cold but pleasantly still and cloudless afternoon.

Mark could barely believe Erin had asked for a blessing. He was bursting to talk to her about it, but he resisted in case he came off as pushy and inquisitive. Perhaps she would talk to him without him asking. No matter. For the moment it was enough just to be with her.

He drew in a breath of air that was so clean and cold he could feel the outline of his lungs inside his chest as he inhaled. When he exhaled his breath formed a cloud as it came in contact with the air.

"Gee, when the winter arrives, it really hits you," he said, pulling his jacket a little tighter around him. "So what did you think of Father Nick? Not so scary talking to a priest, is it?"

"No, not at all," Erin said, a thoughtful expression on her face. "He's great. He really set me at ease."

Okay. Better not push further. "So, what do you want to do? Feel like getting something to eat?"

"Actually, could we go for a walk before lunch?" Erin appeared nervous and avoided eye contact as she spoke.

"Yeah, sure," he said. "This way?" They began strolling at a leisurely pace up Franklin Street, the tall trees that lined the quiet inner suburban street now standing bare in the early winter.

Erin walked next to him in silence for a minute or two and the euphoria that had filled him for much of the last hour began to subside. It occurred to him that whatever Erin wanted to talk about might not be good news.

Maybe she'd given it some thought and decided she didn't want a relationship, or worse, that she was ready but didn't want to be with him. *Oh no, I can't lose her now.* He took in another deep breath of fresh air to steel himself. *Remember, it's not your decision to make.*

Not a natural conversationalist, he immediately began racking his brains for something trivial and inoffensive to talk about, but thankfully Erin spoke up before he put his foot in his mouth.

"Thanks for this, Mark. I wanted to go somewhere where there weren't too many people around."

"No problem." *Not too many people around? Oh no, she wants to dump me in private to save me grief.* He put his hands in his pockets and began bracing himself for the rejection. *Don't say anything. Let her speak.*

Erin suddenly stopped in her tracks. He stopped also and gazed down at her. "I haven't been...completely transparent with you about my life up till now," she said, meeting his eyes, her face scrunching up slightly as though she were about to cry.

Concern instantly flooded his heart. Her expression betrayed such inner turmoil, he wanted nothing more than to hold her close and never let her go.

"What is it?" he said, daring to place his hands on her shoulders.

"Something that happened to me before I met you. I wanted to tell you before now. I almost did the other day, but I wasn't brave enough, and I'm sorry."

"Don't worry, Erin. Whatever it is, you can tell me." *What on earth is it?*

"See, the reason I wanted Father Nick to bless me was because I thought it might give me strength. I — "

Erin stopped dead, and her expression changed again. Her torment was replaced by something Mark found far more disturbing. The only way he could describe it was fear. Icy cold, unparalleled fear. Her face turned deathly pale, and she cried out.

"Ow!" She gasped and bent over, clutching her abdomen as she did.

"Erin! What's wrong?" he said, reaching out to support her.

"I'm okay," she said, trying to straighten herself. "I think — ah!" she cried out again.

Oh Lord, this isn't funny, what's the matter with her? "What's wrong? Tell me, you might need to get to a doctor."

She stood up, then winced and bent over again. She tried to right herself, grabbing on to him. He held her up, concerned only to get her to someone who could help her. There was nothing that could have prepared him for what came next.

"I'm pregnant. With Gareth's child," she said, with a strangled sob. "But I think I might be having a miscarriage."

*****

Pregnant? Miscarriage? For a second, he struggled to grasp what she was saying. The words tumbled around inside his head, colliding, bringing the devastating revelation sharply into focus and hitting him like a mallet between the eyes. In a split second of clarity, he remembered what Nick had said about a person returning to their faith when faced with life and death situations. The same way it had been with him. *This is it. She's been pregnant this whole time.*

But there was no chance for him to process anything further. She was clearly in pain and needed to get medical attention straight away. His car was close by, and Canberra Hospital couldn't be more than a ten-minute drive away.

"It's all right, Erin. Come on. I'm taking you to emergency. Are you able to walk? If you can get to the car, I can get you there pretty quickly."

Erin straightened herself and leaned on him for support. "Yes, I think so." She took a few steps then stopped. "I'm — I'm bleeding. It's heavy," she said and started to cry.

Oh Lord, please no. Hasn't she suffered enough already? "Erin, listen to me. I'm here, and I'll help you. Come on."

He supported her, walking her the hundred metres or so to the car and helped her into the front seat.

The short ride to the hospital passed in a blur. All the way he offered what feeble words of comfort he could as she cried and bled in the passenger seat of his car. In the moments in between, he struggled to come to terms with what was happening. All this while, the entire time he knew her, a tiny life had been silently forming inside her. And he'd had absolutely no idea.

And where was the father? Did that useless loser care about what he had done, abandoning the mother of his child when she needed him most? Was he even aware she was pregnant? Someone should tell him. He should be told that his own child might be dying.

A sudden rage mingled with a panic he didn't realise he was still capable of flared up in his gut. He gripped the steering wheel tighter as he swung into the hospital entrance.

Miraculously, there was a solitary empty parking spot right next to emergency. He pulled into it, thanking God as he did, and immediately got out to help Erin. He resisted the urge to gasp as Erin climbed out of the front seat. She had indeed been bleeding heavily and her face was an ashen grey. Panic seized him in his chest, and he wondered now if he should have called an ambulance instead of driving her to the hospital. He put one arm around her shoulders and another under her arm to support her.

"Come on. We're here now. Just a few more steps and we'll get you to a nurse."

Erin nodded weakly, her lip trembling and a small sob escaping her lips, from heartache or physical pain, Mark wasn't sure. In his mind, he was instantly transported back to the evening he sat with her in the café in Manuka a couple of months earlier. That same expression of grief returned to her now, tenfold. *Oh dear God, please don't let it be a miscarriage. Let her child be all right. Please spare her any more sorrow.*

They entered the emergency department through a large sliding door, and Erin went straight to the reception desk while Mark stood back enough to give her some space. He remembered that emergency treated patients in order of the severity of the complaint, but he still hoped they would attend to her quickly and not keep her waiting. Standing back, he cringed, noticing the back of her coat was covered in blood.

The nurse at the desk was a woman in her mid-fifties who looked like she'd seen her fair share of absolutely everything. She took one look at Erin and stood up immediately.

"Come straight through," she said, getting up from her station and leading Erin through to the triage area. Mark breathed a sigh of relief. At least now she was going to get the medical care she needed.

Erin turned and reached her hand out to Mark. "Would you come with me?" Her eyes pleaded with him. "I don't want to be by myself."

He took her hand, willing with all his heart that he could take the full burden of her pain and suffer in her place. "Of course I will."

Erin sat down in triage while Mark stood next to her. The nurse asked her several questions while taking her blood pressure. "Don't you worry, sweetie, we're going to take care of you," she said, picking up a phone. She gave Mark a sympathetic smile.

She thinks I'm the father. Why wouldn't she? That would be the logical conclusion; he was the one here with her. And from the expression on the nurse's face, she didn't think the outcome of this was going to be good.

Within a couple of minutes, a young nurse arrived with a wheelchair and helped Erin into it. She wheeled her out the back of the triage section and through a series of corridors to the emergency department, with Mark following behind.

The nurse took Erin to a cubicle equipped with a bed, a single armchair and some medical equipment.

"Is this your husband?" the nurse asked Erin, without acknowledging Mark. Erin shook her head.

"No, I'm not," Mark said. "I'm...a friend."

"Okay," she replied. "Would you mind, just for a minute?"

Mark stood back while the nurse drew a curtain around the area, leaving him on the other side. He wandered a little further down the emergency area to give Erin some extra privacy.

A few minutes later, the young nurse approached him. "Mark, is it?"

"Yes?"

"You can go and see Erin now. I've assessed her, and I'll be getting the doctor now for an examination."

"Thank you," he said. "Can you tell me, is she having a miscarriage?"

The young nurse looked at Mark sympathetically, a similar expression to the one he received from the nurse at reception. "I'll leave that to the doctor to confirm, but it does appear that way, yes. Go and see her. She needs someone with her right now."

"I will. Thanks again."

The nurse smiled and nodded and went off in search of an available doctor.

Mark went to the area where Erin was, the curtain still drawn around her bed. He stood there for a moment and made the Sign of the Cross, then pulled the curtain aside.

Erin was sitting up on the bed, dressed in a hospital gown. Her eyes were red and her face still pale.

He sat down in the armchair next to her. "How are you feeling?"

"The nurse gave me some paracetamol just now," she said, clearly trying to put on a brave face. "She said it will help with the pain a bit."

Mark nodded, at a loss for what he could say to console her. "Is there anyone you want here with you? I can call someone for you if you want me to."

"If you mean Gareth, no," she said, shaking her head. "He doesn't know. I didn't discover the pregnancy till after we broke up."

So he has no clue what's going on.

"I'll call my parents after I've seen the doctor. I don't want to talk to Mum till I have something to tell her. I've put her through enough already. She's been so good to me since I told her I was pregnant. And now —" Erin choked up again and started sobbing.

He reached out and took her hand in both of his.

"I've lost my baby, Mark. She's probably already dead," she said, squeezing his hand through her tears. "Oh, it's so painful!" She started groaning.

This is it. Mark's heart leapt up into his throat, and he prayed earnestly to God that she could stay strong through this ordeal.

A few moments later, Erin pulled her hand from his and lifted the sheet covering the lower part of her body. The nurse had placed a mat underneath her, and Mark could see that it was covered with blood. With her other hand, she reached down between her legs.

"Mark," she whispered, her voice shaking as she spoke. "Look."

In the palm of her hand, Erin held the lifeless, blood-covered body of a tiny, tiny human being. Mark didn't know how far along Erin was in her pregnancy, but he certainly wouldn't have guessed she was pregnant from her appearance so she couldn't be too far along. Which only made what he now saw all the more astonishing to him.

Erin's baby — a girl, Mark could see — lay there, her legs out straight, her arms folded across her body. Her skin transparent, ten perfectly formed fingers and ten perfectly formed toes on her minuscule hands and feet. Beautiful, perfect child. A child who, days or hours before, had been growing, moving and developing. Heart beating rapidly, fully alive.

Now, gone.

"Oh, Erin," he whispered, fighting back the urge to cry with her. "I am so, so sorry."

Mark looked on as Erin stared down at her dead infant, her face contorting, her jaw shaking. She let out a weakened sob right to the end of her breath. Then she sucked in a loud gulp of air and released a wail so mournful, so bereft, it struck fear into the very foundations of his soul.

*****

Mark exited the hospital through the same sliding door in the emergency department that he had walked through with Erin a couple of hours earlier. He found his car in the emergency carpark, a freshly printed parking ticket tucked under his windscreen wiper. Well, that was to be expected. He'd long overstayed the allowed time. Any other day he'd have been annoyed, but compared to what he'd been a part of this afternoon a parking infringement was barely a blip on the radar.

Numb and unable to face the thought of spending the afternoon alone in his empty house, he turned his back on the car and the parking ticket and started walking.

Mark glanced down at his watch as he settled into a brisk stroll. 3.30 pm. Really? Only mid-afternoon? Surely a hundred years had passed since midday Mass.

It might as well have done. The still-fresh image of Erin and her tiny baby had emblazoned itself into his memory and kept coming back to him again and again. A human soul — an entire universe — had been contained in that tiny body and had passed from the world today. A beautiful life God had chosen to call home before she had barely begun to live.

Pregnant. Erin was pregnant the whole time. And she was about to tell me, when this happened.

He peered up in the direction of the ten-storey hospital as he walked past it. She would be in one of the rooms up there now, but he didn't know which one, or on which floor. He had slipped out before the staff moved her from the emergency department. The baby miscarried intact and the placenta followed, but the doctor decided to keep her in overnight to monitor her.

Erin, Erin. That expression of total anguish on her face as she held her baby in her hand was like nothing he'd ever seen before. A look of complete desolation. And there was not one single thing he could do about it.

A voice is heard in Ramah, lamentation and bitter weeping.
Rachel is weeping for her children;
she refuses to be comforted for her children,
for they are not.

The words from Jeremiah now came, unbidden, into his thoughts. He knew while he had been with her, there was nothing he could say that would make any difference. When she let out that horrible cry, a couple of the nurses turned up at her bedside straight away. While they were taking care of her and dealing with the baby's remains, they asked him to contact her family. He had found Erin's phone in her bag and called Judith. She and Liam had been on the other side of town, and it had taken them a half hour to arrive, so he'd just sat with Erin while she cried quietly into the hospital pillow.

After Judith and Liam turned up, there didn't seem to be much need for him to be there. Judith had embraced her daughter, murmuring words of consolation and comfort, stroking her hair while Erin cried on her mother's shoulder. Mark had caught Liam's eye and raised a hand to indicate that he would go, and Liam had simply nodded. It seemed better to leave them to console her privately.

Mark continued walking down Yamba Drive for another ten minutes till the entrance of Woden Cemetery came up on his left. Without thinking, he turned the corner and began the walk down the tree-lined drive that led towards the burial ground.

The temperature dropped as the afternoon grew late, but Mark didn't try to brace himself against the cold. He made his way further into the grounds until he came upon a lawned section of burial plots.

It had been some years since he had been to a cemetery. He hadn't visited his dad's grave since leaving Newcastle, not even when he returned home to see his mother and sister. It no longer seemed as necessary as it had before returning to his faith. His father had been a God-fearing man, and Mark felt reassured in the knowledge that he would see him again, one day, in eternity. He felt his father's spirit close at certain times in his life, as though he wasn't truly so far away.

Now, thinking about his father, he spent some time walking amongst the small headstones embedded in the grass at his feet and reading the inscriptions in turn. Death did not discriminate, it seemed. This cemetery, like every other in the world, was filled with the very old, the very young, and all those aged somewhere in between.

Mark didn't understand — had never understood — why

his father was taken from them so suddenly. At a time when he, a young boy about to burgeon into manhood, had so desperately needed his influence. But over time, he had come to trust that God called his father home for His own perfect reasons, reasons Mark might learn some day in heaven. He had seen God's hand in his life, leading him in spite of all that had gone wrong for him. Or maybe it was *because* of all his mistakes that he had been open to seeing God's hand. He had made his peace with his father's death, in the light of God's love for his dad and also for himself.

My ways are not your ways. Those were the words the Lord had spoken. Mark believed the ultimate purpose of his life was to be with God in heaven one day. How long he spent on earth, and the manner of his death, was up to his Heavenly Father. He learned long ago to stop questioning God's actions. Sometimes He just called someone home.

Then, of course, sometimes He didn't. Sometimes someone else chose.

Natalie...

Despite the years since he had seen her, despite trying his best never to dwell overlong on her, the memory of what she'd done came now to him and engulfed him in anguish. Mark's head dropped as deep pain from the past — pain which, unlike other hardships in his life, he still had not entirely made peace with — began to crack open inside him. His throat began to contract as he found himself reliving that day, a day he wished had never happened. Nor what had come before it.

He remembered that Saturday afternoon in winter some years earlier, a day not unlike today, only not as cold. He turned the key in the door of their small flat after a session at the gym, opened the door and found Natalie sitting at their dining table. This surprised him as she hadn't been there when he'd left. Actually, she hadn't been around much at all recently. She'd been sulky for weeks, ever since their last argument about getting married. He felt a bit bad about putting her off yet again, but getting married didn't make any sense to him. What difference did it make anyway? Couldn't she just drop it? He was so tired of fighting with her about it.

"Hey, you're here," Mark said, dropping his gym bag by the kitchen bench and leaning over to kiss her cheek. "I thought you were out with your friends some place."

Natalie didn't move or make any effort to return the kiss or even look at him. "Sit down, Mark. I need to talk to you."

Mark frowned. "O...kay," he said, drawing the word out slowly and taking a seat at the table. "Hello to you too. What have I done this time?"

She turned her head and met his gaze. "It's not what you've done. It's what I'm doing."

Right at that moment Mark spied Natalie's suitcase standing in the corner, her handbag sitting on top of it. He turned and stared at her full in the face. "Going somewhere, Natalie? What crap are you pulling this time?"

Natalie's eyes flinched at his cutting tone, and he immediately regretted speaking so harshly to her. He expected her to come back with some sarcastic quip, something she'd become quite good at lately. But she didn't.

"I'm leaving," she said with a calm resolution in her voice that jolted him to attention. "I should've done it a long time ago, and I'm not putting it off a day longer."

"What? You can't be serious." Mark peered into her face and saw that she was, indeed, very serious. "I know we've been going through a rough patch, but we can talk about it."

"I've tried talking to you, again and again, and I'm finished with it. I've been finished with it for ages now. I'm just sorry I didn't have the guts to tell you before."

Mark's heart started beating faster as panic set in. He'd

never seen her like this before.

"Please, if this is about getting married, I suppose we can talk about it. I don't want you to leave. I love you, Nat. You know that."

Natalie laughed with a biting sarcasm and shook her head. "No, I don't know that. If it's true, you've got a funny way of showing it."

"Of course I love you. Don't do this. Please don't do this. Where will you go if you leave?"

Natalie paused and stared at him. "You have no idea, do you?"

Mark shook his head in genuine confusion. "No idea of what?"

"I've met someone else. I've been with him for a while now. I'm sorry I didn't tell you sooner, but that's where I'm going. After I leave here, I'm going to be with him."

Mark's jaw dropped open, but no words would come, only a stunned silence as he struggled to grasp what she'd just said.

"You don't need to look so surprised. You should have seen this coming." Natalie paused, then sighed. "But that isn't all. There's something else I need you to know."

She got up from the table and stepped into the kitchen. She opened a drawer, pulled out what appeared to be a small photograph and held it out to him.

Mark took the photo and glanced down at it. No, it wasn't a photo; it was one of those ultrasound pictures.

What?

He peered more closely at the image. Natalie's full name was printed along the top, along with some numbers that didn't make any sense to him. A small, bean-shaped figure was in the centre with the words "Six weeks" typed alongside.

This is an image of an unborn baby.

The date was printed along the top, underneath Natalie's name. 24 April. Two months ago. Natalie wasn't pregnant now, he was pretty sure of that. His head began pounding and a wave of dizziness came over him.

"What am I looking at here?" he asked, hoping against hope it wasn't what he knew it was.

"That was your child, Mark."

My child? Was? Mark inhaled sharply. "What do you mean *was*, Natalie? This image was from months ago. Did you lose the baby? What happened, damn it?" He stood abruptly, kicking the chair back behind him as he did.

"I had an abortion. At eight weeks."

"What?" The dizziness increased, and he felt a hard grip in his chest, like being punched from the inside. No, how could this be true? "Are you kidding me? You were pregnant? You were pregnant with our child, then you had him killed and you didn't tell me anything about it?"

"I didn't think you'd care, to be honest. I've been asking you for years if we could get married, and all you do is fob me off. I've told you again and again how important it is to me. I tried mentioning it again after I found out I was pregnant, and you just stonewalled me. I knew then I had to leave you. And I couldn't face bringing a child into the world with separated parents. That was the way I grew up, and it was hell. I'd never wish it on anyone. Especially my own child."

Mark's heart continued pounding in his chest, and his hands began to shake. How could his entire world be crumbling around him in only a few short seconds? *My God, what has she done?*

He crossed over to where she was standing and slammed the ultrasound image down on the bench with such force it made her jump. "By denying him or her a chance to grow up at all? How could you do that?" he said, his voice rising in volume and intensity with every word. "How could you think your being pregnant wouldn't be important to me? How could you make a decision like that without consulting me? How?"

Natalie regarded him with a pained expression. "I'm sorry, Mark, maybe I should have told you. But I couldn't figure out what else to do. You don't love me."

"For God's sake Nat, that's not true! I do love you. Why couldn't you tell me about this? Why? The baby was my child too!"

"I just couldn't. I truly am sorry. But I'm telling you now. I wanted you to know before I left."

Natalie touched him on the arm, stepping past him as she did and reached for her suitcase.

Mark swung around to face her, overcome by a surge of bitterness racing up from his gut and into his throat. "And how can I be sure the baby was even mine, if you've been off with some other bloke?"

"Why would you even ask me that? I loved you, Mark. I only ever wanted you. Nathan was a friend, he came with me to the clinic, and things developed after that. He was there for me."

"That isn't an excuse, and you bloody well know it."

"You're right. It isn't an excuse. But it's what happened." Natalie put her bag over her shoulder, extended the handle of her suitcase and wheeled it to the front door. "And, like it or not, you are partially responsible. That's why I needed to tell you. That's why you needed to know."

"Natalie, please."

"No. This is the way things are. I'm leaving, and I'm not coming back. I'm sorry." She opened the door and walked through, closing it behind her.

That was the last time he saw her. Six years had passed since that dreadful afternoon. But now, standing alone in the cold, quiet cemetery in the wake of Erin's miscarriage, he remembered it with such vividness it could have happened yesterday.

Six years. If Natalie had let their child live, he — or she — would be five years old now.

Was it a boy or a girl? Mark always thought maybe he'd

fathered a son. He had wondered so many times how things might have turned out if he'd taken better care of Natalie.

Oh, he knew the abortion wasn't his fault. He'd been over this with priests in the confessional many times before. He'd learned to put the guilt aside. But still, he couldn't help but wonder how different a path his life would have taken if he hadn't been so selfish.

Post-abortion syndrome was common, he knew that. Rarely was a woman not affected by having her own child disposed of, regardless of what had motivated her. He wondered now what Natalie's experience had been in the aftermath of ending their child's life. He had prayed for her. He prayed for her again now, and for all women who, for whatever reason, had chosen death for their children instead of life.

But people didn't talk as much about how fathers dealt with the sorrow when their children were taken from them.

Mark shivered and tipped his head back, staring up at the clear, darkening sky. There was only a few minutes of daylight left, and the frigid air seeped in through his less-than-adequate jacket, chilling him all the way through. He thrust his hands in his pockets and began making his way back to his car.

The last of the daylight was disappearing from the sky when he got back to the emergency department carpark. He pulled the parking ticket from under his wiper and got into the driver's seat. Just as he was about to toss the ticket on the passenger seat, he noticed the dark stain Erin's blood had left there, made visible by the light of a street lamp. His heart ached for her, upstairs now in the hospital, grieving the loss of her baby. It wasn't fair. Erin wanted to keep her child, and still she had lost her. It wasn't fair.

He thought also of the baby's father who didn't know — who might never know — his child had died.

Maybe it would be better for Gareth if it stayed that way.

Mark rested his hands on the steering wheel and leaned back in his seat. Then the reservoir of his grief finally burst open, and he sobbed longer and harder than he had ever done.

Chapter 13

Sunlight streamed in through the open window in Erin's room. She found herself sitting in a comfortable glider chair by the window that had not been there a few minutes ago, her feet up on an ottoman, rocking back and forth and relishing the warmth of the sun on her face and upper body.

Listening, she heard the sound of running down the hallway towards her room — someone small. She turned towards the door and saw a child, a little girl with fair hair, standing in the doorway. The girl smiled at her and skipped over to the window where Erin was sitting.

"Can I sit on your lap?" she asked, smiling up at her, confidence sparkling in her green eyes.

Erin nodded, wondering who the child could be. The little girl climbed up into her lap, wrapped her arms around Erin's neck and pressed a small, soft cheek alongside her face.

"I love you so much, Mummy," the child whispered.

Erin woke with a start. Rain fell steadily in the garden outside her window as it had been when she had fallen asleep on her bed sometime earlier, exhausted, fully clothed and without covering herself. She rubbed her eyes and sat herself up.

Three days had passed since being discharged from hospital. The ache in her abdomen from losing her baby had passed now, leaving in its wake a yawning, cavernous emptiness that had started in her womb and gradually began to seep through her entire being.

Empty? As if that word came close to describing what was left behind. The hope that had begun to colour her grey existence since Gareth's rejection had disappeared, replaced by a dejection she hadn't experienced before.

What purpose did she serve? What was she good for? She hadn't been able to hang on to her baby's father, or, in the end, her baby. A baby that, at first, she hadn't even wanted. Perhaps this was her fault. Perhaps she was being punished. The profound sense of inadequacy that flooded through her now made her wonder how her sad, pathetic existence in the universe could be justified.

She stared out at the winter rain soaking into the back garden and thought about the dream. The words spoken by the little girl echoed in her ears as clearly as though they had been spoken by a real, living person. Clearly, some function in the deep recesses of her mind was stepping in to try and ease the acute loneliness she felt for the child that had been taken from her. Conjuring up an image of what her baby might one day have looked like. Causing her to imagine holding her child, and being held by her. *My little one.*

The longing for her dead daughter was now so overwhelming she could breathe, taste and swallow it. She could still smell the little girl's hair, feel her breath against her face...

How could God be so cruel? He had abandoned her — this was the final blow. There was no way she could be anything for anyone. Not now. Not ever.

Erin lay back down on the pillow and was closing her eyes again when she heard a gentle knock at the door.

"Yes?"

Liam opened the bedroom door. "Only me," he said.

"Dad," Erin said listlessly, turning over to face him.

Liam opened the door a little further. "I didn't wake you, did I?"

"No. Why?"

"You have a visitor."

Erin clenched up inside, balking at the thought of having to talk to anyone. She shook her head.

"No, I don't want to talk to anyone right now. Please tell them to go away."

"It's Mark."

Mark? What is he doing here? Only days earlier she had worked up the nerve to tell him the truth when her baby had been expelled from her body right in front of him. She hadn't seen him since he slipped out of the hospital, right after her parents had come.

Gentleman that he was, he'd stayed with her till they arrived. But she supposed he had wanted to get as far away from her as possible, given the chance, and he did. She hadn't yet had the opportunity to process the heartbreak of losing both her child *and* her chance with Mark, or the fact that he'd rejected her at such a terrible moment.

Whatever the reason he had now decided to visit her, it didn't matter.

"I don't think I can talk to him."

Liam gazed at her steadily. "You don't have to talk to him if you don't want to. But are you sure? He's very worried about you."

Erin sat herself up on the bed. "You don't understand. He was there, he saw everything! It was so awful."

"I understand, my dearest," her father said, sitting himself down next to her on the bed. "It was awful for him too. He was the only one who was with you when you miscarried. I think it would be good for you both if you talk to him."

Erin cringed and let out a shaky breath. "Okay," she said.

Her father smiled at her and patted her hand, then got up and left the room, leaving the door ajar.

A minute later there was another knock at the partly opened door.

"Come in," she said, and she sat up a little straighter.

The door pushed open slowly, and Mark appeared, taking a tentative step into the room. He stood in the doorway and smiled at her, his expression kind and sincere, totally lacking in guile or false pity.

She found herself able to smile back, the tiniest bit.

"Hello," he said, taking another small step towards her.

"Hi."

"Thanks for letting me see you. I've been so worried about you."

Erin nodded but didn't respond.

"Mind if I pull up a seat?"

She shook her head and watched as he grabbed the chair from her desk and placed it next to her bed, sitting himself down beside her.

"How are you?"

"Physically, I'm healing, I suppose. But I've never been worse, Mark. Things weren't this bad for me even when my brother died."

"Of course. I know. I'm so sorry."

Erin nodded again, unable to dig within herself for a suitable response to his condolences.

"I didn't think I'd see you again."

Mark shook his head slightly, seemingly bewildered. "Why would you think that?"

Erin sighed. "I dunno. Because of what happened and how things were — what I kept from you. You didn't call me after you left the hospital."

"I'm so sorry. Please don't think for a second that I didn't want to be here with you. I wanted to give you some time to yourself before I came to see you again."

"I — I wasn't sure."

Mark shook his head again. "No, I've been going crazy staying away this long. But I didn't want to intrude on something so personal, when I wasn't involved from the beginning. I didn't think it'd be right to assume you would want me around so soon after what happened."

Of course. She should have realised that Mark would never let her down intentionally.

"Thank you. I appreciate you telling me that."

A pause fell in the conversation, and Mark stared down at his hands for a moment. When he lifted his eyes to meet hers, his face was calm and resolute.

"We never got to finish our conversation the other day," he said, leaning towards her a little.

"No, I suppose we didn't." *But what more can I say? You know now what I wanted to tell you. I can't be loved by you now. Can't you understand I've been reduced to nothing?*

Clearly oblivious to her state of mind, he continued. "I don't know if now is the best time to tell you any of this—"

"What is it?"

"You said that you hadn't been completely truthful about your life. Well, there are things I haven't told you too. But I want to tell you now."

Intrigued, Erin forgot her own sadness, in small part, for a second. "What is it?" she repeated.

"Something that happened with Natalie."

"Your ex-girlfriend?"

Mark nodded. "Remember I told you that she left me because she wanted to get married, and I kept telling her no?"

"Yes."

"That part is true, but there was more." Mark sighed and closed his eyes for a moment. "The day she left me she told me she'd been pregnant with my child. I'd had no idea. She showed me an ultrasound photo of the baby and then — then told me she'd had an abortion. At eight weeks."

Erin gasped. *Mark, a father?* This startling revelation caught her by surprise, the same as the day she'd discovered he hadn't always been the model Christian she'd first assumed him to be. *And the mother had an abortion without telling him?* "Oh, Mark, that's horrible. I'm so sorry."

He peered into her eyes, his face a mirror to her now,

reflecting her own sorrow. "I was shattered. A couple of minutes after breaking the news, she walked out. I suppose I've been dealing with it ever since. I felt so guilty for years."

"But it wasn't your fault she had an abortion. That was her own decision. She should have told you at the time that she was pregnant. It wasn't your fault."

Mark nodded. "Yes, I know." He leaned in closer towards her and took her hand in his. "Erin, I can't begin to understand what you went through, as a mother, losing your baby like that. But I wanted to tell you that I understand, at least a little bit, how it is when your unborn child dies."

"It sounds like you understand completely. Just one more thing we have in common, isn't it? We're both grieving the loss of our children." Erin gave his fingers a slight squeeze, relishing the feeling of his hand touching hers once again. "I can't imagine what it must have been like for you."

Mark gazed at her and smiled again. "See, how do you do that?"

"Do what?"

"Be so selfless when you're suffering so much? You forget yourself and think about other people. You don't realise what you've done for me. I didn't think I'd ever be able to fully deal with Natalie's abortion in this lifetime. But since meeting you, I've started to heal. I've found peace."

Erin said nothing. The surprising news that she'd made a positive impact on Mark's life should have made a deep impression on her, but her heart was too drained, too vulnerable to appreciate it. Death and all the emptiness it left in its wake were the only things prevailing in her heart. It had robbed her of too much of herself.

Mark continued to gaze at her with his unfailing steadfastness, only one of the many wonderful qualities he possessed that she had fallen in love with. But she had nothing left, and she knew it. Nothing left to give him or anyone.

"Erin, your pregnancy — had you not miscarried — wouldn't have changed anything. I understand why you didn't want to tell me sooner, but it still wouldn't have made any difference."

"I know. I didn't see it before, but I do now."

He didn't respond. A lull fell in the conversation, but he said nothing to fill it, seeming to be waiting for her to say something.

"Mark, before this happened, I was ready to — for us to take things further. But now..." her voice trailed off, unable to make herself complete the sentence. Mark nodded as she peered into his face.

"It's all right, I understand," he said.

"I can't be the woman you deserve. You need to go and find someone else. Someone who isn't me. Someone whole."

He shook his head. "Not possible. Knowing you has changed me. *I'm* whole *because* of you." He reached up with his other hand and held the side of her face. "I love you, Erin."

Hearing Mark speak those words to her, words she'd hoped so dearly he might say, tugged mercilessly at her heartstrings. Why now? When it was impossible for her to even stand on her own two feet? She raised her hand to her face and took his hand.

"No. You hardly know me. You can do better. I don't even share your faith."

"Yes, you do. You're just sad. You haven't lost your faith in God. You never did. He believes in you and so do I."

"Don't. You shouldn't waste your heart loving me. Please don't."

"Too late." Then he leaned towards her and kissed her.

For a moment Erin lost herself in Mark's love for her, forgetting what it was like to be exhausted and broken. When he pulled away, she saw tears forming in his eyes.

"Don't despair," he said and traced the Sign of the Cross on her forehead. "May the Lord bless you and keep you, may He cause His face to shine on you and be gracious to you, may He turn His countenance to you and give you peace." He quickly wiped his eyes then reached into a pocket inside his jacket and pulled out a small card. "Here, this is for you," he said, handing it to her. "It was given to me when I first came back to the faith, and I've kept it with me ever since. I want you to have it."

Erin took the card and glanced down at it, seeing the title of the prayer on the card.

Prayer of St Francis.

Lord, Make Me a Channel of Your Peace...

She opened her mouth to try to speak, willing herself to find something, anything, to say to him. But the lump forming in her throat made it impossible to speak.

He reached for her hand once again. "I'm here for you, always. Remember that. There won't be a day go by that I won't think about you and pray for you." With that he got up and started moving towards the door.

"Mark?"

He stopped and turned towards her, waiting for her to speak.

"I'm sorry."

"Don't be. You haven't done anything wrong." He smiled at her. "Just remember that I love you." He turned, walked through the door and closed it behind him, leaving her alone in her room.

Two months later

"....eighteen, nineteen, twenty! Ready or not, here I come!" Lily jumped out from where she was counting inside the cubby house and began racing around looking for her brother. Bruno was hiding behind Judith's pittosporum hedges, but he had one foot sticking out in plain view.

"Where are you, Bruno? I'm coming to get you!" At that moment she spied Bruno's shoe sticking out from under the hedge. "Found you!" she cried, leaping in after him.

"Oh!" Bruno yelled. "Not fair! You didn't look long enough!"

"I can't help it if you didn't hide properly. Right, Aunty Erin?"

Erin watched the children from her easy chair up on the deck. "Don't worry, Bruno. You can count now and find Lily. Maybe you'll find her even faster."

"Nuh, I'm bored," Bruno said, running up to her and climbing up into her lap. "When will Mummy and Daddy be home?"

"Soon, they won't be long now. They just went out to have a coffee together."

"How come Marie got to go and not us?" Lily asked, running up on the deck behind Bruno.

"Because Marie's still only tiny. Mummy feeds her so she needs to keep her close."

"Oh," Lily said, shrugging. "Hey, Bruno, wanna play tips till they come?"

"Yep!" Bruno slid down off Erin's lap and began racing around after Lily.

Yes, children, Mama won't be long now. Mothers long to be close to their little ones.

A biting wind blew from the south, and Erin shivered. The children had abandoned their warm jackets and jumpers in the course of their play but Erin, sitting still on the deck, felt the cold even in her wool cardigan. She got up and went inside through the back sliding door into the kitchen area to get a warmer coat.

Where did I leave it? Spying it on the back of one of the

dining table chairs, she grabbed it and was about to step outside again when she heard muffled voices coming from the living room. Turning, she noticed the door between the living room and kitchen was closed, something Judith almost never did.

Curious, she tiptoed over to the door and realised that Katrina and Emilio were already back. She placed her head up close to the door so she could listen to what they were saying.

"But, Mum, she looks terrible."

"I agree, but she *is* grieving. Her engagement ended, then she discovered she was pregnant. Then just when she was getting used to the idea of being a single mother, she lost the baby and things never got a chance to work out with Mark. She's had an awful year."

"Yes, yes. But is she eating? I almost died when I greeted her earlier. She's so skinny, it was like hugging a chicken wing."

Erin smiled a little at the reference. *A chicken wing?* She glanced down at her shoulders and arms and frowned. *I'm not that thin, am I?*

"We were thinking she could use a distraction." Emilio, with his accented English, joined the conversation.

"A distraction would be marvellous. Anything to help propel her out of the state she's in," Liam said.

"I have a suggestion that might help with that," Emilio said.

Erin backed away from the door and went outside again. *A distraction?* What would distract her from the knowledge her body was no longer swelling with life as the months continued to pass? She should have been twenty weeks by now. *Far along enough to feel the baby kick.* Erin wondered now what that might have been like. Tears stung her eyes, and she swallowed back a lump in her throat, determined not to cry again.

Let them talk about me. I guess they mean well. She

slipped on her coat and sat back down, resuming her watch over her niece and nephew.

A few minutes later, the sliding door opened behind her, and Katrina and Emilio stepped outside.

"Mummy, Daddy!" Lily and Bruno called out, racing towards them and leaping into their arms for hugs.

"Did you have a nice coffee with Daddy, Mama?" Lily asked.

"Oh yes, lovely, thank you, Lily." Katrina grabbed the hands of both the children and looked over at Erin. "Thanks for staying with them out here while they played. You didn't have to. You must be freezing!"

"No problem. I got warm just watching them."

"Hmm," Katrina said, rolling her eyes. "Listen, kids, come inside with me for a minute. Daddy wants to have a talk with Aunty Erin, okay?"

Katrina took the children inside while Emilio sat down alongside Erin.

"*Hola, cuñada*," he said, using the Spanish word for "sister-in-law" to address her.

"*Hola, cuñado*," she replied. "*Cómo estás?*"

Emilio laughed. "*Muy bien*, I'm okay, thanks. Your Spanish is very good."

"No, it isn't, and you know it," she said, swatting her hand in dismissal at her Mexican brother-in-law.

Emilio chuckled. "So, how's work?"

Work? Bland and pointless, just like everything else. "Fine. Just going through the motions."

"Hmm," he said, rubbing his hands together in the cold. "Want to take a break?"

Erin turned her head to look at Emilio. "A break? What do you mean?"

"How would you like to go away for a while? To Mexico?"

"What?" Erin said, incredulous. "Mexico?"

Emilio nodded decisively. "Yes, Mexico. We've all been

worried about you. Katrina and I spoke with my parents recently. My mother and father would be happy for you to stay with them in Querétaro. It would give you a rest from everything that's happened in your life. The city is really beautiful. It's summer there at the moment, and Querétaro is lovely in the summer. You'd love it."

"Emilio, that's awfully kind of you, but I don't know—"

"Come on, there's not much to think about. You arrange some leave, book a flight and pack a bag. The rest is taken care of. My parents will look after you while you're there."

Erin paused, allowing the idea to sit for a second. A trip to Mexico? Emilio's family were good people — she'd met them at his and Katrina's wedding and a couple of times since when they came to visit Australia and liked them. But travelling all that way?

A distraction. She shivered again in the cold. Yes, this might well be something that would distract her.

The truth was she was dying, day by day. She continued to put on a brave face in order to survive, but she knew she hadn't been the same since her miscarriage. She was shrivelling up more and more as time passed, but there seemed little for her to do other than allow her hollowed heart to consume her, bit by bit. The family was trying to throw her a lifeline.

Would getting away help? *Yes, it might.* Getting away — far away — might help her forget, just for a little while. Could she manage it, practically? Work owed her some recreation leave. And with little to spend her money on these days, she could afford the flight.

"Now that I think about it, some time out would be good. Are you sure your parents wouldn't mind me staying with them?"

"No, of course not. Things are rather quiet around their place these days. They're looking forward to you coming, actually."

"You told them I was coming?"

"Not exactly, but we were hoping we could twist your arm."

Erin smiled a little, then made a decision. "I think you've succeeded." She reached out and squeezed Emilio's arm. "Thank you so much. Please tell your parents thank you too."

"You can tell them yourself when you get there," he said, patting her hand.

Mexico. A rush of anticipation seized her inside, filling in some of the emptiness that had been eating away at her. "Is there anything you want me to bring back for you while I'm there?"

Emilio's face suddenly lit up. "If you could bring me back a jar of my mother's salsa, I'd be indebted to you for life!"

Chapter 14

Erin peered out the window as the plane banked and began its descent towards Mexico City. The sun had set an hour or two earlier, and she stared down into the darkness, the lights of the immense metropolis sprawling out beneath her in every direction as far as the eye could see.

She reached into her bag on the seat next to her for her travel documents. The entire row she sat in had been empty during the four-hour flight from Los Angeles to Mexico City, and she had been grateful for the extra space to stretch out and sleep a little. It had been over twenty-four hours since she first left Canberra, and it wasn't over yet. When she arrived in Mexico City, there would be a three-hour drive with Emilio's parents to Querétaro.

With passport and immigration forms in hand, Erin leaned her head back on the headrest and listened to the flight attendant's announcement, given first in Spanish, then English. It was astounding how the demographics on her journey had transformed once she'd disembarked from her Qantas flight in Los Angeles and made her way to the departure gate for the AeroMexico flight to Mexico City. At five foot six, Erin never considered herself tall. But in the departure lounge full of native Mexicans, her status in the world as a tall, white, monolingual English speaker became so obvious to her, she wondered why she'd never noticed before.

And now I'm about to get off a plane that's landing in Mexico. Mexico? Go figure. What an unexpected change in direction her life had taken in the three weeks since Emilio first suggested she take this trip. She thought by now she'd have stopped being surprised at life's unexpected twists and turns.

God has His hand on this journey, Judith had told her before she left. She thought about how her mother had held her a bit longer, a bit tighter than usual, right before she'd boarded the plane in Canberra. Judith had said little about her own feelings since the miscarriage, but Erin knew the whole event had caused her mother grief. The pain of losing her grandchild, of seeing her own child suffer, and renewed sorrow at the remembrance of losing her only son all those years ago. It was this knowledge that kept Erin from dismissing her mother out of hand, and what had compelled her to continue attending Sunday Mass with her parents. There was no weekday Mass attendance anymore, though.

Mark. Her thoughts now turned to him, the same as they did many times throughout the course of each day. She closed her eyes and immediately saw his smiling face. He had made no attempt to contact her since that day he'd come to see her, as she knew he wouldn't. As much as she missed him, the one thing she didn't regret was letting him go. *He can do better. So much better.*

A jolt went through the plane as it hit the tarmac. Erin opened her eyes and turned to peer out the window. *I'm here.* Her heart contracted slightly, and a wave of expectancy seized her from inside.

The plane taxied on the runway for some time then it took a further forty-five minutes to disembark and make her way through customs, immigration and baggage collection. Her head was spinning by the time she reached the arrivals gate, but she didn't have to search for Emilio's parents, Mercedes and Rodrigo Perez, who were waiting close to the gate when she stepped through.

Mercedes came towards her with a huge smile on her face, her arms extended. "Erin! You made it! It's so wonderful to see you again, *hijita*. How was your journey?" she said, enfolding her in an enormous hug.

Not missing Mercedes' reference to her as "daughter,"

Erin dropped her bag and hugged her back, instantly relaxing into the familiar arms enfolding her.

"It was long and tiring but uneventful. It's lovely to see you too. Thank you so much for having me."

"You must be exhausted. Don't worry, we'll take care of you from here," Mercedes replied, releasing her. "Here, Rodrigo, you take Erin's bags." Emilio's father greeted Erin with a kiss on her cheek and took her luggage.

"*Bienvenida*," he said with a charming grin that reminded her of Emilio. "Welcome to Mexico!"

Fifteen minutes later, they were on the road, Mercedes chatting away from the front while Rodrigo expertly navigated his way through Mexico City's intense traffic.

"So what do you think? A little bigger than Canberra, isn't it?" Mercedes asked.

"You're not wrong there," Erin said, staring out the car window at the staggering expanse of city lights, skyscrapers and highway interchanges. "I haven't been to a city quite this large before." The population of Mexico City and its surrounds was almost equal to the entire population of Australia, and Erin found it difficult to take in.

The freshness of the summer evening that penetrated the air was in stark contrast to the cold she had left behind in Australia and the stuffiness of the planes and airport terminals she'd been in for the last twenty-four hours. Erin allowed herself to relax into the back seat of the car and answered Mercedes' steady stream of questions about the family and her grandchildren.

As they progressed further into the city, Rodrigo spoke up. "See over there?" he said, pointing to the right of the car. "That street takes you right up to the Basilica of Our Lady of Guadalupe."

"It's huge — the most-visited Marian shrine in the world," Mercedes chimed in. "Ten million people each year. We'll take you for a visit there before you go back home."

Of course, Erin knew well the story of Mary, the Mother of God, appearing to Saint Juan Diego, a convert from the pagan Aztec religion, in the sixteenth century. The story went that an image of her had appeared miraculously on his cloak, or tilma, as it was called, and that the image survived to this day and was enshrined at the basilica.

She hadn't questioned the authenticity of the story as a child, and had given it little thought as an adult. The image of the Virgin of Guadalupe had been such a part of the landscape in her family home she barely noticed it anymore, despite the framed picture that still sat on the desk in her room.

"Um, all right," she replied. "Why not?" *Whatever*. She didn't want to appear rude, but a meaningful religious experience was the last thing she was interested in. Sighing, she reached over for her travel pillow.

"Try and doze for a while back there," Mercedes said from the front seat. "We won't be in Querétaro for a while yet."

"Thanks, Mercedes, I think I will."

Erin placed the pillow behind her head and closed her eyes. The whizzing traffic and the vast city outside her window faded away, and she fell instantly asleep.

*****

"So, how do you like Merci's *huevos rancheros*?" Rodrigo asked Erin while the three of them were having breakfast several days after her arrival.

Erin swallowed a mouthful of the fried egg and corn tortilla, along with a generous serving of Mercedes' salsa, and nodded with enthusiasm.

"It's delicious. I've never been much into Mexican food, but that changes from here on. Though I'm not sure I'll find it exactly like this in Australia."

"I did find corn tortillas in your supermarkets last time I

was there. That's a good start!" Mercedes said with a light-hearted laugh.

As Emilio predicted, Mexico had begun to have an effect on Erin, calming her senses and her soul. A week into her stay with the Pérezes, she found herself relaxing into the summer warmth and quite distracted by the vibrancy of a culture so different from her own.

Querétaro was indeed beautiful, and Emilio's mother and father were showing her the best of it. The first Sunday after she arrived, they had taken her down to the small, colonial centre of the city, established nearly five hundred years earlier. She spent a balmy afternoon meandering through the streets and squares, past museums and churches, restaurants and cafés. She marvelled at the life, vivacity and energy everywhere: mariachi bands playing vibrantly in the streets, vendors with enormous collections of coloured balloons and windmills in every conceivable shape and colour. The *colour* — there was so much colour. Even some of the walls of the old buildings were painted entirely in vivid blues or pinks or yellows. Purple and magenta bougainvillea flowers framed antique doorways. Potted flowers on small, second-storey window balconies were held in by iron barriers twisted into intricate designs. Somehow it was impossible for deep melancholy to take too great a hold of her here.

The streets right in the centre of the old city were narrow, and all one way for traffic as they had originally been designed for horse and carriage. Certain streets were so narrow they only accommodated pedestrians. On weekends, vendors with cart after cart of merchandise lined those alleyways, selling every imaginable item in every imaginable colour. Jewellery in jade and amber, Mexican silver — *plata Mexicana,* handwoven and embroidered placemats and table runners and bags and purses, woodwork and leatherwork.

Erin had strolled up and down in delight, browsing and selecting gifts and souvenirs for almost every person she could think of, simply as an excuse to take a little piece of everything home with her.

Finishing up her breakfast now, she thought of the stash of gifts upstairs in her room in the Perez's home and how fun it would be to give them away. *Thank goodness I brought an extra travel case with me.* Smiling to herself, she recalled Ingrid asking to bring her back a wide-brimmed sombrero. Hopefully she would be happy with the amber necklace Erin had chosen for her instead.

"We thought we'd take you to San Miguel de Allende today. It's about an hour's drive from here. It's beautiful — a World Heritage Site like Querétaro," Rodrigo said.

"Sounds wonderful," Erin responded. "Your hospitality has been amazing; I appreciate you taking time to show me everything."

"Our pleasure, *niña*," Mercedes said, taking Erin's plate. "You'll love it. I know it."

"Yes, I'm sure I will."

*****

The historic centre of San Miguel de Allende was every bit as deserving of its World Heritage listing as Querétaro, Erin decided after strolling through the picturesque streets with Mercedes some hours later. A feast for the eyes and ears, Erin soaked in the gorgeous colonial architecture, the sounds of the guitars and musicians singing serenades, the smells of the coffee and *maize* tortillas wafting from the stands of the street vendors.

They stood together in the entrance of a tiny shop hardly larger than a cupboard, carved out of the wall of some seventeenth-century building. Mercedes picked up a brightly coloured Mexican doll and held it up for Erin to see.

"Do you think Lily would like this, Erin?"

Erin eyed the doll, recalling Lily's much-loved collection

of dolls and teddy bears and smiled. "Yeah, I do. I think she'd absolutely love it."

"What about Bruno? What do you think he'd like?" Erin's eye fell on a creepy but colourfully painted mask of a skull and thought about Mr. Fossil Head. She hesitated. "Hmm, not sure. Why don't you just pick something you'd like for him?"

"Maybe you're right," Mercedes said, reaching for a spinning top. "Do you think he's too old for this?"

"I don't think so. He's only four. He's such a character. He could invent a whole game with that top."

"Yes, I know from my conversations with him on Skype. It's hard to keep his attention though. Technology is wonderful for helping to keep in touch, but it's not the same as having them close," Mercedes said, a hint of longing in her voice.

Poor Merci. Emilio was their only child, and Erin thought now about how hard it must be to endure separation not only from her son but also from his children. Emilio had met Katrina in Sydney for World Youth Day in 2008 and never really looked back after that. She supposed Merci lost him then, in a way, recalling how her brother-in-law never seemed to lose that look of lovestruck awe whenever he was in Katrina's presence. Her sister was so lucky to have him.

A memory of Mark regarding her with that same expression rose up in her mind. Her heart contracted and for the first time since her miscarriage, she questioned whether she had made the right decision in asking him to stay away. How many people in the world ached to have someone love them like that but never found anyone? Too many. She'd had that love right in front of her, yet she let it get away from her. Had pushed it away.

"Are you okay?" Merci said, placing down a turquoise-coloured shawl and peering at Erin. "Your face changed just now."

"It did? How?"

"Nothing bad. Good, actually. A little hopeful, a little happy."

That was just like Mark. Even a thought about him shone a bit of brightness into the world. Erin sighed.

Mercedes patted her arm and pointed in the direction of the cathedral, only fifty metres or so away from where they stood.

"Why don't you go and see inside the church for a minute? You haven't been inside any of the churches in Querétaro. You should see this one; it's beautiful. Take some quiet time. I'll meet you over there in a little while."

Erin glanced in the direction of the towering, neo-Gothic cathedral. *It can't hurt to have a quick peek inside.* "Okay, I will. I'll see you in a bit."

*****

With her heart beating a little faster than normal, Erin stepped in through the front doors of the Parroquia de San Miguel, stifling a small gasp as she did. The interior was in stark contrast to any church she'd ever been in at home. It was completely quiet, despite the many tourists wandering around inside. But what struck her was the intricate detail, the unapologetic beauty and richness of faith that was on display at every turn.

Desiring a closer look, she wandered further inside. Intricate designs were etched into the stone walls. Alcoves carved into the walls contained statues of saints surrounded by gold frames: Saint Thérèse of Lisieux, Saint Teresa of Jesus, Our Lady of Mount Carmel and many she'd forgotten the names of or didn't know. A statue of Saint Juan Diego, standing before Our Lady of Guadalupe, clasping his tilma filled with roses.

Beautiful, soft-lit chandeliers hanging from the ceiling cast light over the main and side altars, which were surrounded by numerous vases of flowers. The extraordinary attention to detail took Erin's breath away.

Erin sat down in one of the pews. In spite of herself, she reached for the pew in front of her and lowered herself into a kneeling position. The memory of how close she had come to rejoining her faith in those days before her miscarriage, of the peace she had experienced in the presence of God, came back to her now. Hot tears sprang up in her eyes, and she bent her head to hide them.

I'm sorry I haven't spoken with You lately, Lord. Even when I went to Mass with Mum and Dad, I didn't talk to You. I never did quite find my way back to You. I was almost there when my baby died. Why did You allow that to happen to me? Why did You abandon me?

Erin opened her eyes and a tear dropped onto her joined hands. An image of Jesus praying in the Garden of Olives suddenly presented itself to her, drops of blood rising from His veins and falling into the dirt in which He knelt.

A distant memory of something David once said came back to her, something he told her when he first became sick. She had been sitting with him in hospital while he was receiving one of his earlier doses of chemo. He'd been so uncomfortable. Clearly in pain, but making great efforts to hide it.

"Suffering is a mystery, Erin. But we have a God who entered our humanity and suffered with us. There is nothing you can go through that could be worse than what He went through for you. He is with you all the time. And when you cry, He cries with you."

"But I'm sure God will make you better, David. You'll see."

"Maybe. But if He doesn't, I'll still be your brother and your friend always. I'll never be too far away from you."

What an extraordinary young man he had been. Why hadn't she recalled this before? How many more memories of David had she buried away?

David. I miss you so much. There isn't anything in my life left un-ruined. I destroy everything I touch. Help me, big brother. I don't want to make any more mistakes.

Pausing in her prayer, she lifted her head and gazed towards the sanctuary.

Lord, did You truly cry with me when my daughter died?

Sensing, for the first time, a resounding *yes* to her question, the painful understanding of how proud and stubborn she had been started to sink into her soul. The many years she spent denying herself of the liberating grace of Confession; of the union with Jesus in Holy Communion, now seemed so foolish. It was hard to recall why she had even wanted to abandon her faith in the first place.

Can I really come back into the Church? Now? Help me where I am, right now, in this moment. I'm still so sad and afraid. I feel as though I'm starting to heal in this country, but what is it You want me to do here?

She quickly scanned the interior of the church. A mixture of tourists and people praying surrounded her, but Erin couldn't locate a priest anywhere amongst them.

A sense of peace descended on her, and she breathed in and exhaled, relaxing as she did. *Soon. Not now, but soon. It will be all right.*

Without another thought, she got up, genuflected and made her way out of the church. Stepping outside into the glorious summer afternoon, she looked around for Mercedes. As her eyes swept the square outside the church, an older woman, standing close to where she was, caught her attention. The woman had dropped her bag and was struggling to bend down to pick it up.

Seeing that no one close by was coming to the woman's assistance, Erin hurried over to her and reached down to pick up the bag and the few items that had fallen out of it.

"Here you go," Erin said, standing and handing the bag to the woman. The tiny woman, with a complexion somewhat darker than Emilio and his parents, appearing around sixty years old, straightened and peered up at Erin. She smiled perhaps the most beautiful grin Erin had ever seen on another human being.

"Ah, *mi espalda*," the woman said, rubbing her back. "*Muchas gracias.*"

"*De nada* — no trouble at all," Erin responded, hoping the woman was understanding her. "Sorry, ah, *perdon*. I don't speak Spanish — *no hablo español.*"

"Ah," the woman said again, nodding. "*Estados Unidos*?"

"No, Australia."

"Australia? Oh, *muy muy lejos.*"

Erin shrugged and shook her head, wishing Mercedes would show up to translate for her. Just at that moment, another, much younger woman, who bore a striking resemblance to the older woman came from the entrance of the church and joined them. *Mother and daughter? Must be.*

The older woman immediately turned to the younger and began speaking to her in rapid-fire Spanish. The younger woman then nodded and offered a grin equally as beautiful as her mother's and spoke to Erin in heavily accented but fluent English.

"My mother wanted to thank you for saving her back by helping with her bag. You're from Australia, are you?"

"Yes, I'm here visiting my brother-in-law's family," Erin responded, warming to the women instantly.

The young woman nodded again. "My mother was just saying that you've come a long way."

Erin smiled at the older woman. "Yes, it is a long way. The other side of the world, really."

"I'm Rosa Vázquez," the younger woman said. "And my mother is Ines."

"I'm Erin. It's lovely to meet you both. Are you from San Miguel Allende?"

"No, we're from Morelia. We're visitors to San Miguel, like you."

"Well, it's such a beautiful place. I've never been anywhere like it."

Rosa stopped to translate for Ines while Erin watched and tried to follow. Ines nodded and turned to Erin again, speaking Spanish and gesturing to the church behind her.

"My mother was wondering if you liked the Parroquia of San Miguel?"

Erin looked back up at the church, then turned back towards Ines and Rosa. "Oh, yes, it's magnificent. The Catholic churches in my city in Australia are completely different. Not as old, and most are nowhere near as beautiful. Have you been inside?"

Ines spoke again to her, relying on Rosa to go on translating.

"Many times," Rosa said. "My younger brother Miguel — my parents' only son — first told our family he wanted to become a priest here. He was young, only about fifteen. Miguel was named after the archangel, the same as this church, so it's special for us."

"Oh! Your son is a priest? You must be very proud of him," Erin said, thinking of Father Nick. "Is he here with you now?"

Ines's face dropped a little and her eyes began to tear. She shook her head and continued speaking directly to Erin.

"No, my brother died last year," Rosa said. "He was only twenty-nine."

"Oh, no," Erin replied, her heart contracting. "I'm so sorry."

Ines smiled through her tears and put her hand over Erin's. "*Gracias, niña.* He lived — *como se dice?* How you say? A good life," she said in even more accented English than her daughter.

Ines reached into her bag and pulled out a small wallet. "Here he is," she said, opening it and showing Erin a photo. Erin stared down at the picture of a young man dressed in a Roman collar and black soutane, smiling with the same grin she saw in his mother and sister. "This is Miguel."

"Miguel was a very holy priest," Rosa continued, pointing to the photo. "He was so kind. He loved everyone, and everyone loved him too. But he spoke out against the behaviour of the drug lords in our home state of Morelia. He preached conversion to them and urged them to stop the greed and murder and violence. They hated him for it. Then one Sunday after Mass, about a year ago, he was outside his church with us and some other parishioners. They drove by and shot him. He died there, outside the church."

Erin released an involuntary gasp. "Oh, how awful!" Erin struggled to find any words of consolation. Why did everyone she knew or met have so much death to deal with? "Were the killers caught?"

Rosa swallowed, clearly resisting the urge to cry. "No, not yet," she said. "It's a terrible problem here in Mexico. But we have forgiven anyway. We believe Miguel's death will bear good fruit for the drug problem here. He can do so much more for Mexico from heaven."

Erin stared at the sadness etched into Rosa's face. How could anyone have such acceptance and forgiveness in their heart after such a terrible loss? She placed her hand on Rosa's arm.

"I lost my brother too, years ago. He died of cancer, though, it wasn't violent or sudden. I understand what it's like to lose a much-loved member of the family."

"Thank you, Erin," Rosa said, and translated what Erin said for her mother.

"Ah, *pobre niña.*" Ines reached out and took Erin's hand in a gesture of consolation. "I was there with Miguel," she said in English. "I hold him as he die." She tapped her chest with her other hand. "I know, *un poco*, how it was for *La Virgen*. She hold Our Lord when He die."

Erin nodded in understanding, imagining the small statue of Michelangelo's Pieta in her parents' home, then thought of Ines holding her own bleeding son as he drew his final breath.

"I lost a child too," Erin said, her heart instantly rising into her throat at the memory of her baby lying in the palm of her hand. *Stop, Erin. Why are you telling this to two complete strangers? Don't compare your grief to theirs. It isn't the same.*

Ines shook her head and Erin waited while Rosa translated.

"*Qué? Cómo?*" Ines said.

Erin took a breath. "I miscarried my daughter a couple of months ago. I know it's not the same."

Ines nodded. "*No,* same, same," she said and released Erin's hand. She reached around her neck and took off a chain she was wearing, which Erin noticed held a medal of Our Lady of Guadalupe and a ring. Ines took the ring off the chain and handed it to Erin.

Erin took the ring and studied it closely. It was a silver rosary ring, with smooth silver notches for the Hail Marys and a small cross fashioned into it. Here and there the silver was stained darker as though something had been spilt on it.

She turned the ring over in her hand and studied it, then offered it back to Ines.

The woman shook her head and took Erin's hand, closing her fingers over the ring. Erin noticed Rosa's brow furrowing slightly, then relaxing, as Ines continued speaking in Spanish.

"My mother wants you to have this," Rosa said. "It was Miguel's. He was wearing it when he died. She says that Miguel wants you to have it."

Erin gasped again and shook her head. "I can't possibly take this. If your mother ever parts with this, it should be to you, Rosa."

Rosa shook her head. "No, if my mother says Miguel would like for you to have it, you can trust her. I have other things my brother had with him that day." Rosa picked up the ring from Erin's hand and gestured to the dark places on it. "This ring is a relic. The discolouration is Miguel's blood. My brother died for his faith in Jesus."

Stunned, Erin stood shaking her head, struck in no small measure by the profound significance of both the ring and the gesture Ines was making by offering it to her.

"But I only just met you! Why are you giving this to me?"

Ines spoke to Rosa, who listened and then translated for Erin.

"Mama says she doesn't argue with Miguel," she said, smiling. "He knows you've suffered loss, and you need consolation. We know what this is like. You need strength for the journey. It's okay, please accept this from my mother."

Not understanding what would compel Ines to give a total stranger the ring her son was wearing when he died, Erin simply stared into Ines's eyes, consoled by the ocean of acceptance and wisdom she found there. The older woman continued nodding and smiling, urging her to accept. Erin finally surrendered to her insistence.

"I don't know what to say," Erin said. She reached behind her neck and unfastened the silver chain she was wearing. She took off the pendant hanging from it, put it in her pocket then threaded Father Miguel's ring over the chain and refastened it around her neck. The presence of the ring close to her heart lifted a weight she didn't realise she had been carrying, and she felt herself glowing inside with gratitude towards the women for their generosity. "Thank you. Truly, with all my heart, thank you."

"*De nada, niña,*" Ines replied. "*Dime, cómo se llama? Tu bebé?*"

"My mother is asking what you named your daughter?"

The question took Erin by surprise. "Actually, I didn't name her," she replied.

"Why not?" Rosa asked.

"I don't know. I didn't think of it. I suppose it was all too painful at the time."

"You should," Rosa said, the expression on her face exuding sympathy. "Your daughter is real. She existed on earth for a while, and she lives in heaven now. You should give her a name."

Erin thought for a moment and made a decision. "Ines," she said. "I'd like to name her after your mother. And you. Ines Rosa."

"Ah, *niña*!" Ines said, understanding Erin's meaning. "*Gracias*."

"Yes, thank you, Erin. A little saint in heaven named after us," Rosa said, turning to her mother and translating.

A saint? My daughter is a saint?

Rosa hugged Erin. "We have to go. We need to take the bus back to Morelia, but we'll pray for you."

"I'll pray for you both too," Erin replied, knowing that she would. "Thank you so much."

"We meet you again," Ines said, pointing upwards. "*En el cielo*."

"Yes," Erin said, nodding in understanding. "If not on earth, then in heaven."

She watched as the mother and daughter walked away from the church grounds. They turned and waved as they approached a corner. Lifting her hand, Erin waved back and watched as they disappeared from her sight.

Chapter 15

The sun was just beginning to set as Mark exited his office that Friday evening and made his way to his car. He glanced down at his watch. *Almost 6.00 pm.* The days were getting longer this late into August though the cold temperatures lingered. Mass at the cathedral was almost over; he wouldn't make it today.

A deep sigh escaped him as he got in the car and drove out of the carpark. With the distraction of his job behind him for another day, he found himself once again remembering his last encounter with Erin.

The secret hope he initially cherished of Erin changing her mind about him — calling and saying she wanted to see him again, that she'd made a mistake — dwindled with each passing week. He remembered the expression on her face the day he had gone to visit her. The utter defeat. Perhaps he had underestimated what that kind of loss could do to a mother. The fact that she had loved the baby's father, and he had been absent — had not even known — no doubt made it worse for her.

That knowledge added considerably to his heartache. As much as it pained him not to be with her, he worried more about whether she would ever fully recover. He hoped and prayed that she would. The thought of Erin never being able to live fully again distressed him even more than the ever-growing probability that he would never see her again.

My Lord, I can't go on like this much longer. All I do is go to work and try not to think about Erin. I'm in limbo here. She rejected me. Why can't I just accept it and get on with it? I have to. Even if she does love me, she asked me to stay away. I need to forget. I have to. But it's so hard.

Help me let her go, to give her over to Your loving care.

Easier said than done. *I need a distraction.* He reached over to switch on the radio in the car but was interrupted by the sound of his phone ringing from the hands-free dock on the dashboard. He swiped the screen to answer it.

"Hello, Mark speaking,"

"Mark? G'day, it's Jared Wentworth,"

"Jared!" Mark replied, surprised to hear from his boss at his old job in Newcastle. "It's been quite a while. How are you?"

"Pretty good, thanks. You on the road?"

"Yeah, I'm just driving home. It's good to hear from you. What's been happening?"

"Quite a lot. The business is going well. We're expanding. The work keeps rolling in; we've got some major projects going ahead."

"That's terrific."

"It's kind of the reason I'm calling. You wouldn't be interested in having your old job back, would you?"

Stunned, Mark paused for a second. "You're offering me my job back?"

"Well, strictly speaking, it's not your old job. It's a step up. Much better pay than what you were on when you left. I know you're going great in Canberra, and you're exactly what this place needs while it's going through this growth period."

"Gee, Jared, I don't know what to say. This is quite a surprise."

"Well, you don't have to decide straight away. But does it sound like something you'd be interested in?"

"Honestly," Mark paused for a split second before continuing. "It could be. I'd have to get back to you."

"No problem, Mark. We won't have any difficulty finding someone if you turn it down, but you're my first choice."

"Thanks," Mark replied, flattered.

"No problem. Are you planning on visiting Newcastle anytime soon?"

"Actually, I was thinking of coming up this weekend. Maybe we could catch up?"

"Great. Give me a call when you get here. You still got my mobile number?"

"Yep, still got it."

"I'll talk to you soon, then."

"Sure thing. Thanks for the call, and for considering me for the position."

"No worries. Talk soon."

"Yes, talk soon."

Jared ended the call and Mark drove the rest of the way home, trying to ignore the weight of his heavy heart in his chest. *Maybe this is a sign from God. I think it's time to let her go.*

*****

"Are you excited to finally be here?" Merci asked Erin as they stood together in the enormous square outside the Shrine of Our Lady of Guadalupe in the middle of Mexico City.

"Sure." Erin swallowed and nodded, hoping she appeared calm and nonchalant. The square was full of pilgrims all making their way towards the basilica, many of them on their knees, something that struck Erin deeply. It had to be at least three hundred metres across the square to the opening of the Church.

Merci smiled and patted Erin on her shoulder but said nothing. In truth, Erin's fatigue from rising early and travelling the three-hour journey from Querétaro back to Mexico City seeped through her. It was her final day in Mexico, and they had all woken and travelled early so she could visit the basilica before her flight home later that afternoon.

But now, as they edged further and further towards the

basilica doors, surrounded by the near-palpable faith of the pilgrims all around her, she found herself gripped by mixed feelings of anticipation and apprehension. Like a magnet, she perceived her whole self being drawn towards the basilica. *Oh, Lord, I've been fighting you for so long. Have I finally reached the end of my resistance?* She grasped the ring Ines Vázquez had given her, still hanging from the chain around her neck.

Rodrigo guided her and Merci towards the entrance. He pointed through the large open doorways. "Look there, can you see? The tilma hanging over the main altar?"

Erin peered inside, her gaze immediately drawn towards a gold frame high up on the back wall of the huge building.

"Is that it?" she asked, pointing, unable to pull her eyes away.

"Yes, that's it," Merci said.

Erin strode ahead, irresistibly drawn to the image. Once inside, she had a clear view of the original image with which she was so familiar. Only it didn't look anything like in the reproductions she had seen in her home, in books and on the internet.

It *glowed*. Most especially the image of the beautiful lady glowed. With love. Pure, unadulterated love. A young woman. No one special in the eyes of the world. She called out to Erin, to everyone in the basilica, to everyone in the world: *Come. Let me show you the way to my Son.*

Erin's throat constricted as the gentle light emitting from the Virgin of Guadalupe shone into her soul and gently toppled the last of her defences. She placed her hand over her mouth to suppress a sob. Merci put a hand up to her shoulder.

"Sorry," she said, turning to Merci and Rodrigo. "I just wasn't expecting to feel like this."

"It's okay. Believe it or not, we've seen this happen before," Rodrigo said.

"Is it all right if we get closer?"

"Of course. This way."

They made their way to the very front of the basilica with the many other pilgrims and descended some steps at the left side that took them down behind the main altar. There, they found three travelators passing slowly along underneath the tilma, filled with people standing shoulder to shoulder, all staring up at the image of the radiant woman in the golden frame.

Closer, I have to get closer.

Edging her way forward, she stepped on to the travelator and leaned her head far back, staring upwards and aching for the moment when she would pass right underneath the image. Dizziness grabbed her, and she momentarily lost her balance, almost falling on someone standing next to her.

"*Cuidado, señorita!*" Erin turned for a moment to the middle-aged woman she'd bumped into who was shoving her upwards.

"Sorry, uh, *disculpe*," she replied, righting herself and grabbing onto the travelator railing.

"*Ándele pues*," the woman replied, who shook her head and then turned her attention back to the tilma, raising her phone to take a photo.

Unfazed by the woman's impatience, Erin's thoughts turned to her phone. *A photo. Good idea.* Just as she was reaching down inside her bag to find it, some invisible force drew her gaze upwards. The impatient woman next to her, the other visitors, the noise and chatter and the flashes from the phones and cameras all faded. The tilma appeared right over her head, but despite the fact she should be moving past it, she remained still, right underneath it.

What is this? Aware that something out of the ordinary was happening, Erin continued staring upwards, infused with the deepest peace.

You are the Mother of God. How could I have doubted you?

Erin waited for an answer, when, all in a moment, a change began to take place on the tilma. The image of the beautiful young woman began to dim, recede, almost as though she were taking a step back. Peering upwards with unblinking intensity, Erin watched as another change began to take place.

A light appeared over the abdomen of Our Lady of Guadalupe, a small, bean shape like that of an embryo. *She's pregnant!* The light shone dazzling and brilliant from the now-shadowed image of the woman, the Woman who stepped back in order to point Erin to her Son.

My Lord. Is that You?

No words came, but the light continued to shine, lighting the darkened spaces in her heart.

You were a baby. In the womb of Your Mother. Where is my baby?

She waited again for an audible response, but again, nothing.

Is she with you?

Joy entered Erin's soul, a shower of invisible grace permeating her being, and she knew, with unwavering certainty, that her child was indeed still alive. And safe. And happy.

Erin sighed. Tears welled up, and with them, release. *I know what I need to do. I will do it.*

The light from the womb of the Virgin of Guadalupe — the only true light that had ever been in the history of the world, it seemed to Erin now — continued to shine and shine and shine. Yesterday, today and for the rest of her days and all remaining days to be lived in the world. All the ages coming and passing and still, the Light would radiate.

How foolish I've been. So foolish.

A moment later, Erin found herself stepping off the end

of the travelator behind Mercedes and Rodrigo.

"Are you all right?" Mercedes said, peering into her face. "You seemed to disappear for a moment there. Would you like to go past again?"

Erin turned around to see the tilma high up on the back wall of the basilica, now returned to its previous appearance.

Without hesitating she turned straight back to Mercedes. "Do you think it's possible for me to talk to a priest?"

*****

The following moments passed in a surreal manner, as though she were walking through a dream. A priest seemed to materialise out of nowhere, a tall, middle-aged man with silver hair and a slightly receding hairline, dressed in Roman collar and black soutane.

Erin wasted no time in approaching him. "*Padre, perdon,*" she said, mumbling over her poorly enunciated Spanish. "*Tiene un momento? Habla ingles?*"

The priest smiled and put out his hand. "Hello, I'm Father Ruiz. And yes, I speak English," he replied. "How can I help you?"

Thank you, Lord! Erin shook his hand. Her heart leapt up into her throat and, for a moment, she wondered if she could speak the question she knew she had to ask.

"I was wondering if you could hear my confession?" she stammered, her voice breaking in the last three or four words.

Father Ruiz nodded and gestured to an empty pew where they stood at the back of the church. "Yes, of course."

*****

"God, the Father of mercies, through the death and resurrection of His Son has reconciled the world to Himself and sent the Holy Spirit among us for the forgiveness of sins; through the ministry of the Church may God give you pardon and peace, and I absolve you from your sins in the name of the Father and of the Son and of the Holy Spirit. Amen. The Lord has freed you from your sins. Go in peace."

Peace. That word took on a new meaning for her now, as she basked in the graces that came from making her first confession in many, many years. Tears ran down her face as she revelled in the wonderful sensation of renewal and release. That crazy jumble of chaos, noise and confusion that had been her heart's companion for so long, now gone.

"Thanks be to God," she prayed in response.

Father Ruiz removed the purple stole he wore while hearing her confession and rolled it up.

"Thank you so much, Father," Erin said, wiping her face with her hands. "Truly, I can't thank you enough."

Father Ruiz placed the stole in his pocket and smiled. "For me, this is one of the most rewarding parts of being a priest."

Erin nodded and sniffed again. "Well, I'm very glad I found you."

"God is in control. Our Lady planned for you to be here today."

Erin turned her head towards the direction of the altar and thought back to the experience beneath the tilma.

"Father, can I ask you about one more thing?"

"Of course."

"I hope you don't think I'm crazy, but I saw something while I was viewing the tilma." Erin related what she had seen as Father Ruiz listened.

When she finished speaking, she paused, fully expecting Father Ruiz to make some polite excuse and leave as quickly as his legs would carry him. Instead, he turned and gazed towards the tilma, clearly visible from where they sat.

"Did you know that very thing happened here at the basilica some years ago? Only it wasn't a private revelation like what you're telling me now. It was visible for everyone to see."

"No," Erin shook her head. "No, I had no idea."

Father Ruiz nodded. "Yes, it happened on the day abortion was legalised in Mexico City. Perhaps the Lord is telling you something."

Erin nodded tearfully, but didn't speak, thinking of Ines and her miscarriage.

Father Ruiz simply smiled at her. "This is an extraordinary revelation for you. A true moment of grace. A source of consolation from which you can draw strength for the journey."

Strength for the journey. Hadn't Ines Vázquez said something like that to her when she had given her Father Miguel's rosary ring?

"Yes, Father." Erin stood up. "Thank you, again." She turned behind her to see Rodrigo and Mercedes waiting patiently in a pew for her to finish. She glanced down at her watch.

"I really should go now. I have to be at the airport soon. I'm flying back home this afternoon."

Father Miguel stood also. "And where is home?"

"Canberra, in Australia."

"Really? I have a cousin in Canberra!"

"You're kidding! What a small world. Well, if ever you're visiting, I hope you'll look me up. My name is Erin Rafferty," she quickly grabbed a pen and notepad from her bag and wrote down her email address for him.

"Thank you, Erin. Perhaps we'll meet again one day."

"I hope so. Thank you once again, Father. I'll be praying for you."

"I'll keep you in prayer too."

*****

The light on the seatbelt sign finally turned off on the flight out of Mexico City, and Erin reached down to release her belt. Suddenly aware her shoulders were tensed up, she allowed them to relax, closed her eyes and sunk back into her seat.

I'm so happy now. Thank You, Lord, for pursuing me, for calling me back into Your Church. Thank you, Blessed Mother, for showing me Your Son.

Erin listened for a response but heard nothing. She smiled. She didn't need a spoken answer in return. It was enough to know the peace and joy from having offloaded the worst of herself to the Lord in Confession and received nothing but forgiveness in exchange.

It was such a shame I didn't have time to go to Mass. I can't wait to receive You in my soul again. Why was I so foolish, Lord? I don't know why I fought You for so long.

She felt herself beginning to drift and thought about how soon she could get to Mass once she got home. How she would be able to join her brothers and sisters in Christ in receiving Jesus' Body and Blood in Holy Communion. As she drifted further and further into sleep, she found herself in the side chapel in the cathedral back at home, Father Nick in the sanctuary saying Mass. Mark, standing next to her in their usual pew. She turned to see him. He was staring sideways at her, smiling. Her heart did a flip. How she'd missed him! It had been so long since she'd seen his lovely face.

Then he was gone. She now found herself back in the Basilica of Our Lady of Guadalupe. Pilgrims entering in every door, kneeling in the pews and the aisles. Priests at the altar praying the Mass. The image of the Lady of Guadalupe high above the altar. Erin's heart leapt. *Oh good, I can get close to her one more time.* She began making her way back towards the travelators behind the altar.

Then she stopped, her gaze distracted by three figures standing some distance ahead of her. A young man, with two children standing on either side of him, a boy and girl, holding his hands.

The pilgrims disappeared, and Erin found herself alone in the basilica. No, not alone. The young man and the two children were still there. She took a few steps towards them and stopped again.

"Who are you?" she called out, staring, trying to make out who they were. Why were they so familiar?

"Erin!" The young man called back, dropping the girl's hand and waving to her.

"David?" Erin tried to take a few more steps forward but found herself unable to move. "David? Is that you?"

The young man and the children walked closer towards her till they were only a few steps away, close enough for her to see their faces.

"David, it *is* you!"

"Hello, Erin."

"What are you doing here? I've missed you so much."

David smiled at her and then leaned down towards the little girl. "Say hello to your mother."

A little blond girl. Bright green eyes. A face that shone with a heavenly brightness.

"Hello, Mum," she said, in a sweet, flutey voice. The same voice of the little girl in the dream she had the day Mark came to see her. "I'm so happy about what you did today."

"Ines?"

The girl nodded. "Thank you for my beautiful name. I love it!" She laughed and peered up at David, reaching up to tug at his hand. "Tell her about Luke."

"Who?" Erin asked.

The little boy standing on David's other side took a step towards Erin. She peered into his little, smiling face. He appeared to be about five years old, with dark brown hair, dark eyes and a mischievous grin.

"Are you Luke?"

The boy just nodded. She continued to stare at him,

wondering why he looked so familiar to her. Till she finally realised that she was staring into Mark's eyes.

"Luke, are you Mark's son?"

The boy smiled at her.

Erin's heart throbbed as she turned her gaze from one child to the other.

"Ines, Luke," she said, and crouched down, reaching out her arms. The children rushed over to her and wrapped their small arms around her. She wrapped one arm around each of them in return and wished she could stay there, holding them forever.

After a moment, or perhaps an eternity, Ines spoke.

"I'm sorry, but we have to go now." She kissed Erin on the cheek, then released her and took Luke's hand.

They went back to David and began to withdraw, the gap widening between them and her.

"No. Don't go! Please don't leave me."

"Don't be afraid," she heard David say as he began to disappear from her sight. "We'll always be close to you."

"No, David."

"Erin. Don't be afraid."

"David."

"Don't be afraid."

*****

Some hours later, Erin sat in a departure lounge at LAX, minutes from boarding her flight to Australia. She pondered the dream she'd had on the flight from Mexico to Los Angeles, wondering how many strange, unexplainable experiences a person could have in one day.

The Lord had called her home, and she had said yes. Instead of rejecting Him again, she had said yes, and He was blessing her, consoling her in more ways than she could have thought possible.

That little boy. His was the face she had been dwelling on the most since waking in the middle of her flight over the American continent. David and her unborn daughter had spoken to her and reassured her, and her heart had been further consoled by their words and presence. But the little, silent boy captivated her no less, and she reflected on his face, startled by how vividly she could recall his appearance. Gripped by an instant resolve, she knew with absolute certainty what she needed to do. What she wanted desperately and what she knew now that God was giving His blessing to.

Pulling out her phone, she opened a new email and began typing on the screen.

To: Mark Ashcroft

Subject: It's me

Dearest Mark,

It's me. I don't know if you'll want to hear from me, and if you don't, I understand. But I just wanted to tell you I'm finally at a place where I can face how wrong I was the last time we spoke.

I'm so sorry I rejected you that day. You've no idea how sorry. I caused us both unnecessary heartache. If there was anything I could do to take it back, I would. Will you forgive me?

Is it too late for you and me? I hope not.

Forever,

Your Erin

PS. I never said it that day, but I love you too.

Chapter 16

That Sunday afternoon, Mark unlocked the door to his home and went inside. Throwing his backpack down on the entry floor, he went straight to the kitchen, pulled a beer out of the fridge and headed to the living room, flopping down on the closest armchair.

The time on his phone lit up as he dropped it on the coffee table. 3.00 pm. He'd been on the road since 7.30 am and the weariness was cutting into him. It had been barely a twenty-four-hour stay in Newcastle, and the rush trip back to his hometown had left his head spinning.

Just as he'd taken the first sip of his beer the phone rang, Nick's name lighting up the screen. He put the bottle down and picked up the phone.

"G'day Nick," he said, not attempting to mask his sullenness.

"Hi Mark, you back?"

"Yep, just got in the door now."

"How'd you go in Newcastle?"

Mark sighed. "Okay. Pretty good, in truth. I caught up with Mum and Hannah, and I met up with my old boss. They're keen to get me back on board. He's made me an amazing job offer."

"Hmm. And how do you feel about taking it?"

"Crap."

"That good, hey?"

Mark let out a sad laugh in response. "I don't know what to do. I'm just trying to do something."

"I know. I'm praying for you. Everything will be all right, you'll see."

"Thanks, Nick. I rely on your prayers so much."

"You've got them. You sound tired. I'll catch up with you soon."

"Yeah. Thanks."

"Bye."

Mark ended the call and tossed the phone on the seat next to him.

Lord, what do You want me to do? If You want me to take this job, why do I feel like I've had a ton of concrete dropped on me?

The phone on the table dinged again, this time with an incoming email.

"If this is something from work, I'm going to throw you out the window," he said out loud to his phone, glancing down at the screen.

1 New Message

Erin Rafferty

Mark's heart stopped for a few seconds then restarted with an almighty thump. His head reeled, and his fingers shook as he scrambled to unlock his screen and open the email.

Dearest Mark,

It's me. I don't know if you'll want to hear from me, and if you don't, I understand. But I wanted to tell you I'm finally at a place in my heart where I can face how wrong I was the last time we spoke.

I'm so sorry I rejected you that day. You've no idea how sorry. I caused us both unnecessary heartache. If there was anything I could do to take it back, I would. Will you forgive me?

Is it too late for you and me? With all my heart I hope not.

Forever,

Your Erin

PS. I never said it that day, but I love you too.

Tears filled Mark's eyes as he re-read the email, and he

laughed for sheer delight as they fell. His weariness and pounding head dissolved in a burst of euphoria. Barely able to contain himself, he hit the reply button and began to type.

My Beautiful Erin,

Of course it's not too late. It will never be too late. I loved you the first minute I met you and I still do. Nothing to forgive. Please don't ever think you did anything wrong by me. All I've wanted is for you to be happy — even if I couldn't make you happy. Every horrible minute I've been without you, I've offered to God for you. I've missed you more than I can say.

Would it be all right if I called you? Could I see you?

All my love,

Mark

Mark hit send and then waited. A few minutes later another message appeared.

Mark!

I can't believe it's you. I was so afraid you wouldn't want to talk to me. I'm so thrilled to hear from you! I've missed you too, very much.

God has used your prayers to great effect. I've healed. Thanks to Him I'm becoming whole again. I've come back to the land of the living. Thank you.

Nothing would make me happier than to see you, right now, if I could. I'm at Los Angeles airport about to board a plane back to Australia. Long story. I can't wait to tell you when I get back. I'll be back in Canberra by Tuesday morning. Mum and Dad will be picking me up from the airport around 10.00 am. Would you call me after that?

Love you.

Erin

Dearest Erin,

Of course I will. I'll be counting the minutes till then.

Los Angeles? You must have encountered something

amazing on the other side of the earth. You sound so peaceful, so happy. This truly is an answer to prayer. I can't wait to see you and hear about everything.

Love you always.

A few minutes later another email came through.

Mark,

I can't wait to see you again. Yes, I do have so much to tell you about what's happened over here.

I'm on the plane now, about to turn off devices. Pray for me. I'll be praying for you.

I'm praying again. Properly.

Mark hit reply once more.

You'll be in my prayers and my heart every minute of your journey and for all of my life.

Come back safely.

Mark pressed send and placed the phone down. He stayed sitting in the armchair but observed a lightness in his body, as though he'd suddenly been granted wings that were lifting him right off the ground and taking him heavenward. How could his life transform like this in only a few minutes?

Erin! She wanted to be with him again. He could barely wait to see her beautiful face again, to hold her close to his heart and never let her go.

The crucifix on the wall in his living room caught his eye in that moment. In one swift movement, he got up off the chair and knelt down to face the cross.

"Thank you, my Lord," he prayed aloud. "For granting the deepest desire of my heart — not only that of Erin reciprocating my love but for bringing her back to You. Thank You for answering my prayers more generously and graciously than I could have hoped for."

The phone alerted an incoming email one more time. Mark got up, reached for it and read.

Don't worry, I'll be fine. Nothing could keep me from coming back to you. I'll never let anything stand between you and me again.

Smiling like a fool, Mark reached into his pocket for his rosary beads and knelt again, an unparalleled happiness filtering through every fibre of his being. He made the Sign of the Cross and began the most sincere prayer of thanksgiving he'd ever offered in his life.

*****

"Is this from my *Abuelita* Mercedes or from you, Aunty Erin?" Bruno asked as Erin handed him the spinning top Mercedes had chosen for him in San Miguel de Allende.

"From your *Abuelita*," Erin said. "These maracas are from me."

"They're cool!" he said, shaking the colourfully painted maracas with glee. He wrapped his soft little arms around Erin's waist while still gripping them. "Thank you, Aunty Erin. When will Lily get her presents?"

"When she gets home from school, Bruno buddy," Katrina said, ruffling up his hair. "Grandma and Grandpa are in the living room with Marie — you go play in there for a little while, okay?"

"Yep!" Bruno said, and danced away with his unflagging energy, shaking his maracas as he went.

Katrina turned back to Erin. "When's he coming?"

"Soon. He messaged me almost as soon as I had phone coverage again."

Katrina laughed.

"What?" Erin asked.

"Nothing. You should see yourself. You're glowing. No one would guess you've been in and out of planes and airports for the last thirty hours."

Erin shook her head. "I'm not even tired. I just can't wait till he arrives here. We haven't seen each other in so long."

Katrina giggled again. "I'm so excited for you. You deserve some happiness."

"Thanks. I'm certainly not complaining!" Erin replied,

making no effort to hide her joy.

"I've got to say, Erin, you've come back a different girl. You must have had an amazing three weeks over there."

"I did, I really did," Erin said. "Thanks to you and Emilio."

Katrina waved a hand dismissively. "Thanks to the Lord."

"Yes, so true. Praise God."

Katrina peered apprehensively into Erin's face. "So you've reconverted? For real?"

Erin nodded. "Yep."

"What on earth happened to you over there?"

"I promise I'll tell you more about it when we get a chance," she paused as she thought of the night she'd first gone out with Mark, when he told her about his own conversion. "But I suppose I just stopped resisting."

Their conversation was interrupted by the ringing of the doorbell.

"Oh my gosh, that's him," she said, her heart flipping over in her chest. She smoothed her hair out. "How do I look?"

"Lovely. Mind you, I don't think it would matter if you were wearing a rubbish bin liner," Katrina said, heading for the living room door. "I think I'll make myself scarce. I'll talk to you later on."

Erin nodded, stepping into the hallway. "Yep, talk later."

With her excitement building, she stopped at the hall mirror and took a quick look at her appearance. Satisfied, she floated down the hallway to the front door, took a breath, and swung it open.

Mark stood there, holding a bouquet of orchids. His face — just as striking as she remembered — lit up when he saw her.

"Mark," she said, unable to believe it was him, a half sob crawling up her throat.

"Erin," he said, smiling at her so that her heart beat

faster. "It's you. It's really you."

Erin nodded, her eyes tearing up, then threw her arms around him.

Mark put his arms around her and held her to his heart, and for the first time in her life, she felt complete.

*****

"Is it just me, or has this afternoon been only a few seconds long?" Mark's arm tightened around Erin's shoulder, bringing her closer to him. They had spent a glorious afternoon wandering side by side through the grounds of Weston Park along the shores of Lake Burley Griffin.

Erin laughed and snuggled against his shoulder as they walked. "Well, my watch says we've been together four hours, but I think you might be right. The time has never gone faster for me."

"Me neither."

They strolled along a red gravel footpath close to the water, leading to a small footbridge stretching over a pond. A solitary black swan swam lazily on the water that flowed out into the lake. Erin sighed contentedly and peered up at the trees. The willows, the spotted gums with their long, leathery light green leaves and smooth white and grey deciduous bark, and many other eucalypts she didn't know the names of. She revelled in the beauty around them all the more because everything was more beautiful now that she had Mark.

"Let's stop here a moment," Erin said, taking Mark's hand and leading them to a bench overlooking a large grassed area where a mob of fifty or so kangaroos were grazing peacefully.

"Nice spot," Mark said, sitting down and putting his arm around her again.

Erin laughed. "I'm just so glad to be back home. To be back close to you. When I got to Los Angeles, I knew that I couldn't let another second pass without contacting you. I couldn't believe it when you responded so quickly."

"I couldn't believe it when I heard from you. I've never been so elated. There have been few times in my life that rivalled the moment I read your email."

Erin grinned up at him. He'd mentioned that at least five times that afternoon, and so had she, but it didn't matter. There was so much catching up for them to do, so much for them to learn about each other. So much time lost, and she didn't want to lose another second.

"I'm just so happy it wasn't too late."

Mark grinned back at her. "Tell me again about what happened to you at the basilica in Mexico City," he said.

Erin knew there were few people she could tell about that experience without sounding crazy. But she'd had no misgivings about telling Mark.

"I find it hard to explain beyond what I've already told you. It didn't seem to happen in the time I was on the travelator beneath the image. It seemed much longer, and yet, much shorter in a way. Like it was outside of time. I guess God chose to show me something with the eyes of my soul."

Mark shook his head. "What an extraordinary thing to happen to you."

"You believe me? You don't think I'm a bit, I don't know, *non compos mentis*?"

He chuckled. "No, I don't think that. I don't have any doubt what you experienced was one hundred per cent from the Lord. He's consoling you."

"Yes, it felt like that. Like a healing."

"We can't understand the way God works. But He doesn't waste anything. If He blessed you with this wonderful experience, you can be sure He had a good reason."

"Yes. I suppose so."

"I know so."

"There was something else too. A dream I had on the way

to Los Angeles. It was what compelled me to contact you as soon as I landed."

"Really? What was it about?"

Erin sat up straight and turned herself slightly towards him to face him properly.

"It was about my brother, David. And my daughter. And — *your* child too, I think."

Mark's eyebrows furrowed slightly, and the colour drained from his face.

"What?"

"I'm positive I dreamed about your child. A little boy. At least," Erin raised her hand and stroked his face. "At least, he *looked* like you."

Erin relayed her dream to him while Mark listened, his eyes filling. When she finished, he stared at her with wonder.

"That's — that's extraordinary, Erin. Just beautiful. Thank you for sharing that with me." He sighed deeply and closed his eyes for a moment.

"I'm sorry if it upset you."

"No, it didn't upset me. Not at all."

Erin squeezed his hand. "I just think the Lord is telling us everything is okay. We both need healing, you and me."

"Yes, we do." Mark paused for a moment. "A whole wonderful life is waiting for us after we die, isn't it?"

"Yes, I do believe there is."

"When I die and go to Heaven, I still want to be close to you."

"What do you mean?"

"I hope, when we both die, we can be together in heaven."

"What a beautiful thought. I hope that too." She turned towards him and studied his handsome face. "So I imagine that means you want to be with me forever, then?" she said, with a hint of teasing in her voice.

"You imagine that? You imagine right," he said and kissed her. The exhilaration of being so close to him again flooded her with such joy she wondered if she might dissolve.

"I wondered when you were going to do that again," she said when he ended the kiss.

"I was restraining myself. Resisting for the sake of — not placing us both in moral danger."

Erin smiled up at him, scarcely able to believe she had won the love of a man who treated her with such respect. "I understand, and I'm with you on that one. But you don't need to *over* resist."

She placed her head on Mark's shoulder. "I don't want to sin anymore either. I couldn't believe how wonderful it was going to Confession again. The priest I met was so kind to me."

"That was my prayer for you. I understand how it feels to make that first confession after so many years. I so wanted that for you. I wanted you to find peace."

A fresh breeze blew from over the water, and Erin shivered.

Mark reached with his free arm and took her hand. "I should be getting you home. It's getting colder."

"Mmm, it is. But it's still light. The days are getting longer." Mark stood and took her hand, helping her to her feet. She floated up off the bench into his arms again, feeling young and alive. "Thank you for taking the afternoon off work to spend with me."

"I would have resigned from my job if my boss had insisted on me staying."

Erin giggled. "Actually, could we do one more thing before you take me home?"

He held her back from himself to look at her.

"Of course. What is it?"

"Could we go to Mass together? At the cathedral? I haven't been to Holy Communion since, since —" she stopped, ashamed that she could no longer remember the last time she received Jesus in Holy Communion. "I don't even remember when it was, Mark."

Mark took her face in his hands and kissed her forehead. "It would be my privilege."

*****

Hours later, back in the kitchen at her parents' home, Erin filled the kettle and set it to boil. Fatigue from her journey finally started to bite into her, but she refused to succumb to it, desperate to hang on to the last few minutes of her delightful day.

Not only had she reunited with Mark, she had – even more importantly – been reunited with her God when she received Him in Communion from Father Nick during Mass that evening. The tears had rolled down her face as she approached the altar, and the peace that followed her reception of the Lord left every other experience in her life for dead. Finally, her soul was alive once again.

"I should go and let you get some sleep," Mark said, stepping up behind her and rubbing her shoulders. "Your parents have gone to sleep, and I'm sure they're trusting me not to stay too late here with you." He gently turned her around to face him.

"You're right," she said, wrapping her arms around his waist, not wanting to let him go. "My head is spinning, but I'm still on a high after Mass this evening. I can't understand why I ever gave up my faith in the first place."

"You were young and grieving. Don't beat yourself up about it now. Leave it in the past."

"Mm, best not to dwell on it," she said. "Are you sure you don't want a coffee before you go? Keep you awake on the road?"

"If I drink coffee now, I'll be awake until the sun rises tomorrow morning," Mark chuckled.

"Right, so not a nighttime coffee drinker. Still so much to learn about you," she said, giving him a hug. She paused for a second. "Are you sure you don't want to take that job in Newcastle?"

"Of course not. The only reason I checked it out in the

first place was because I was trying to let you go. I couldn't think of another way, other than escaping. Why do you ask?"

Erin pulled back a little so she could see his face. "It sounds like such a great opportunity. If you want to take it, I'd come with you."

"You'd do that?"

Erin nodded and stared into his brown eyes, losing herself in them. "I would."

Mark stared back at her and she waited, silent.

How can this be? We still hardly know each other. So how can I be so positive?

There was no doubt. There would be no coming back from this day, ever. She was his now and always would be. In her heart, she was his.

Ask me. If you ask me to marry you now, I'll say yes.

"Erin, I don't want you to give up being close to your family for me. I don't even want to go back to Newcastle. I could be anywhere; I don't care as long as I'm with you."

Erin nodded and waited for him to continue.

He took her hands and pulled her closer to him. "I'm going to do the right thing by you. I promise I won't do to you what Gareth did. None of it. Everything in my power that I can do to make you happy, you can be sure I'll do it."

"I know."

Mark brought her hand to his lips and kissed it. "We went to Mass together today. I can't tell you how much joy it gave me for us to go to Communion together."

"Me too."

"I'll go now. You sleep, and I promise we'll see each other again tomorrow."

"Okay," she said. "I just wish we didn't have to say goodnight."

"One day we won't."

That was enough for Erin, at least for the moment. It wouldn't be long now.

Chapter 17

Mark tapped his foot impatiently and checked his watch. Fifteen minutes late. He had a clear view towards the cathedral from where he sat at the outdoor table of some coffee shop in Manuka. There was no sign of him yet. Nick was rarely late, but Mark had to remind himself that since his ordination, Nick's time was no longer his own. Still, he found the waiting extra hard today.

"Bring you another coffee?" A young waitress had suddenly materialised next to him for the second time in a few minutes, a broad smile on her face.

"Sorry? Uh, no, I'm okay, thank you. Maybe in a minute. I'm still waiting for someone."

"Sure, let me know if you need anything."

"Thanks, appreciate it."

"My pleasure," the girl said, heading to a nearby table to serve another customer.

Mark picked up his phone to check for a text when Nick suddenly appeared at the table.

"G'day," he said, pulling out the seat on the opposite side of the table and sitting down. "Sorry I'm late."

"Nick, I didn't see you coming. You appeared out of nowhere."

"That waitress had your attention as I was coming across the road. Gee, the way she was looking at you. You've got a fan club there."

"I didn't notice."

"No, you never do."

Mark chuckled. "I'm more of a one-woman bloke."

"I know."

The young waitress appeared again almost on cue and took their order.

Mark waited for her to leave before continuing the conversation. "So, how've you been?"

"Good," Nick replied. "No complaints. How about you? How's Erin?"

"I'm fine. Erin's amazing. Everything's going great. Better than great. The last two months have been the best of my life."

"Nothing less than you deserve. So when am I going to be celebrating your wedding?"

"Funny you should ask." Mark paused for a second. "You don't think it would be too soon to ask her?"

Nick peered across the table at him for a second. "Do you think it's too soon?"

"Well, it does seem a little soon in one way, we've only been going out properly for eight weeks. But, no, I don't think it's too soon. At least, it doesn't feel that way."

"Right. And do you think Erin would think it's too soon?"

"Probably not. I'm pretty sure she's ready. In fact, I'm almost positive."

"What makes you say that?"

"I saw a marriage preparation book on her kitchen table when I was over last week. I don't think she meant for me to see it. I noticed she covered it over with a magazine." Mark thought back with tenderness to her efforts to conceal the book from him. "She's just so determined to do the right thing since her reconversion. She prays like an angel. She inspires me. I never imagined, when I first met her, that things could have turned out this way."

Nick continued to peer at him, a smile on his face.

Mark gulped. "She's everything I could wish for in a wife and, and...a mother for my children."

"Doesn't sound like you need my advice. What are you waiting for?"

"Nothing, I suppose."

"You're still worried about something. Tell me."

"I've never been engaged before."

"No, you've waited for the right one at the right time."

"Right." Mark paused.

"I sense a 'but.' But what?"

"Erin has."

"So?"

"And it ended in disaster for her. I don't want to disappoint her."

"You're not going to disappoint her. You're nothing like the other bloke."

"You're right. I'm not. She's more important to me than anything. But I'm still worried I'm going to disappoint her."

"Mark, stop worrying. You're overcomplicating this. You've finally found the one you've been looking for. Don't let her get away from you."

Mark half laughed and shook his head. "I don't plan to. I mean, I'm not going to. You've helped me set my mind at ease. As usual."

"No, I haven't."

"What do you mean?"

"You're still worried."

"Yes, I am. I just can't stand the thought of her being heartbroken again. I was with her when she was grieving over her engagement ending and when she had her miscarriage. What if I do something that causes her pain like that? Even if I didn't mean to?"

The waitress reappeared with two coffees and placed them down on the table. Mark smiled politely and waited again for her to move on. Nick took a sip of his drink then placed the cup down, a purposeful glint in his eye. It was an expression that Mark had learned over time meant no nonsense. Mark emptied a sugar sachet into his coffee and stirred it.

"You're trying too hard to be everything for her. You love her, and it's normal you'd feel that way. But it's dangerous. You're going to make mistakes. So is she. No relationship is perfect. You can both do your very best, but you can't be in control of everything. And you can't *be* everything. Only God can. Let Him do that. You're setting yourself up for failure if you don't."

Shocked, Mark pondered Nick's words for a second. Since he'd won Erin's heart, he'd been almost paralysed with concern about protecting her. It hadn't occurred to him that his concern could be a form of pride.

"I didn't really think about that before. But that's not all. I'm..." Mark stared down into his cup, losing his thoughts in a swirl of black coffee.

"Natalie?"

Mark nodded. "Ever been terrified of your own actions? Or lack of? Or what you might potentially be capable of?"

"Yep, I have. Every day, actually. It's a blessing. Not the terror, but the awareness of our weakness, and that only God can bring good out of evil. God works with weakness; He chooses the weak and makes them strong. We only have to be willing to listen to and obey His voice. It's because you're aware of your weakness that you're concerned, and it's to your credit. But God created you both, let Him do some of the work."

Mark relaxed all of a sudden, as though lightened of a load he hadn't realised he was carrying. He smiled. "You mean I'm not God? And all this time I thought I was."

"Sorry to disappoint you."

"I feel better. Thanks."

Nick picked up his cup again. "That's what I'm here for."

"So, if all goes to plan, and she does say yes, do you think you could take us through marriage prep?"

"Mate, I thought you'd never ask."

*****

"Isn't the springtime beautiful?" Erin said to Ingrid as they walked out of their office for their lunch break. The large wisteria that grew in the front of the building was in full flower, and Erin reached out to touch one of its lacy lilac blooms. She breathed in deeply. "Isn't that gorgeous?"

Ingrid sneezed. "Oh, yeah, it's bloody fantastic." She sneezed again. "Oh, man, I hate the spring."

Erin laughed. "Sorry. I mean it's wonderful except for the hay fever." She reached into her bag and handed Ingrid a tissue. "Why don't you take an antihistamine?"

"Come on; let's get away from these wretched flowers," Ingrid replied, ignoring her question. "Let's just walk. I feel like walking today."

"Okay."

They walked for a few minutes through the leafy inner-south suburb, settling into a brisk stroll together. "Feeling better?" Erin asked.

"Yeah, a bit, thanks," Ingrid said. "So, tell me, do you think he's going to ask you soon?"

"I'm hoping so," Erin said with a grin. She had been grinning so much lately. "We haven't exactly discussed the possibility outright yet, though he's hinted a few times. I think he'd like to come out and discuss it openly. Funny, I'm not sure why he won't. I think maybe he's worried about rushing me because we've only been going out a couple of months. I've done my best to drop a few hints to let him know I'm ready. I even left a marriage prep book on the kitchen table for him to find." She laughed to herself. "I suppose we're still learning about each other."

"Aaah," Ingrid said, a play-mock tone in her voice, her signature humour returning as they moved further away from the offending wisteria plant. "Love. So sweet. Gee, I wish I was in love."

Erin glanced sideways at Ingrid, refusing to take the bait. "Lucky thing you are, then."

"Oh yes, I am," she said. "How could I forget that?"

Erin laughed. "You're a crack-up, Ingrid. That's why I love you."

"Of course you do," Ingrid said as they approached a set

of traffic lights at Wentworth Avenue. "Let's cross here and go down to the lake."

Ingrid pressed the pedestrian crossing button. "So, let's say he does propose soon. You're not, you know, worried about being engaged again?" Ingrid asked while they waited.

Erin shook her head firmly. "No, I'm not. Not at all. Mark is nothing like Gareth. Our whole relationship is completely different from what I had with Gareth."

"Do you think it's the religion thing?"

Erin cringed a little inside. She knew how Ingrid was thinking. She used to be the same, so far had she distanced herself from the faith of her youth. *But not anymore.*

"Yes, for certain. Our faith is the most crucial part of our lives individually and what drew us together. I don't think our relationship would be what it is if we both didn't love God more than we love each other."

"And the relationship's going okay without, you know, the other thing?"

"If by the other thing you mean sex, then yes, the relationship is going fine!" Erin laughed, genuinely amused.

"I don't get it. You guys have been going out for two months. You're madly in love. Aren't you tempted?"

"Well, we do our best to stay out of situations that might lead us in that direction. The desire for each other is there, of course. But we're choosing not to indulge it till the right time."

"Still weird. How can you do that?"

"Because we've stuffed up on that exact thing before and we're committed to not doing it again. That's exactly what went wrong with Gareth. Sex is a language. We were telling each other with our bodies that we were married already. But we weren't. I'm finally understanding why marriage vows, declared in front of God and witnesses, are so important. You say it. Then you follow with the act of joining yourselves. God spoke the world into existence. Then it was."

"Hmm. You continue to enlighten me," Ingrid said, a note of thoughtfulness in her tone. "Well, I hope he doesn't keep you waiting much longer."

"Thanks. I don't think he will."

The pedestrian light turned green. They crossed to the other side and headed towards the lake. Ingrid sneezed again.

"For heaven's sake, Ingrid," Erin said, reaching into her bag for another tissue. "Why don't you just take something? You always take antihistamines for your hay fever."

"I can't."

"What do you mean you can't?"

Erin turned sideways and studied Ingrid closely as they walked. She stopped dead. "You're not."

Ingrid stopped too and stared back, a sheepish expression on her face. "Yep."

Erin shook her head in disbelief as she stared at Ingrid, pausing for only a moment before throwing her arms around her neck and squealing in delight.

"This is incredible! How far along are you?" She pulled back from Ingrid but held onto her shoulders. "How did this happen?"

"What do you mean how did it happen? Well, it's like this. When a guy and a girl get together..."

"Oh, stop it," Erin said, rolling her eyes. "You know what I mean. Nothing's worked before now."

"Well, after you got talking about all the natural family planning stuff, I started to research it a bit myself. I found out about this thing called NaPro Technology. You heard of that?"

"As a matter of fact, I have."

Ingrid nodded. "Yeah, well. We checked it out and got into it. Non-invasive and a fraction of the cost of IVF. What can I say? It worked. I'm still a little stunned myself."

Erin hugged Ingrid again. "Well, I'm absolutely thrilled for you and Jim. How far along are you?"

"About twelve weeks."

"Why didn't you tell me sooner?"

"Partly because we were worried about miscarriage, but also because — you know, it was because — "

"Because *I've* had a miscarriage?"

Ingrid lowered her head and hesitated before responding. "Yeah, I wasn't sure how you'd react. I didn't want to upset you. Sorry, I wanted to tell you before now."

"Ingrid, you've waited so long for this. How could I be anything but thrilled for you?"

"Thank you. I can't tell you how I appreciate you saying that. It's kind of crazy though, isn't it? Only a short while ago you and I were in this same conversation, but the roles were reversed."

"Life can change just that quickly," Erin replied. "And it does. All the time."

"Never take anything for granted, eh?"

"Yep, nothing. But I believe each day is a gift, no matter what it brings."

*****

Erin sat staring at her laptop late one Saturday afternoon. Bright sunlight streamed in through her bedroom window and she got up and lowered the blinds, so they sat only a few centimetres from the bottom of the window. She sat back down again and switched on a small fan on her desk. It was only mid-November, but a run of warmer-than-average days seemed to announce summer had arrived early. It didn't bother Erin. The onset of summer always made her happy and never more so than this year.

This had been the year of her freedom. Not from suffering, no. There was no such thing as a pain-free life. She was coming to terms with that. Whether it was the pain of coming out of a bad relationship, or losing a brother, or a first child, there would always be difficulties. Life was hard and would continue to be.

But this was the year she finally realised there was nothing that could rob her of her joy unless she permitted it. The deep peace and joy she daily perceived permeating her was in itself proof enough that God could draw enormous good from even the most awful of circumstances. She was convinced of that now. God had waged such a long battle for her heart.

Ah fondest, blindest, weakest,
I am He Whom thou seekest!
Thou dravest love from thee, who dravest Me.

Those final lines from Francis Thompson's poem "The Hound of Heaven" entered her mind now. Mark had recited them to her as they sat on the deck outside on a beautiful spring afternoon a couple of weeks earlier. Holding her hand and gazing right into and through her with those magnetic eyes of his.

"This is one of the things that makes our relationship so remarkable. The Lord chased us both down. He went to so much trouble to do it, and now he's brought us together." It was true.

Mark. My Mark.

She felt her face flushing. It was that afternoon on the deck that had led her to staring at an empty document on her screen. Erin was no Francis Thompson, but she loved to write poetry. It had been so many years since she had written anything, but she was determined to write something for Mark to give to him as a Christmas present. At the rate she was going, it would take her that long to come up with anything. Beautiful poems from the heart didn't come as easily as writing advertising copy. Or, at least, not today.

Distracted, she found herself thinking back to the ring she had seen in a boutique jewellery store earlier that day.

Despite her conviction that she never again wanted another engagement ring, her time with Mark had begun wearing down her resistance and she'd begun looking in shop windows whenever she passed.

She'd seen the solitaire diamond a few times, but only once with Mark. She was fairly certain he'd seen her looking at it, and she hadn't made any efforts to hide the fact. They'd been discussing marriage a little more openly lately. It was kind of like they were engaged already, only that the actual proposal was missing. *One minor detail.*

She shook herself, then glanced at the time in the corner of the screen and snapped the laptop closed. Her heart did a giant flip at the thought of Mark arriving in a couple of hours. They'd spent the morning together, but he'd needed to work in the afternoon and promised they'd spend the evening together. Time to get ready. Nothing but her most gorgeous.

The new, green summer dress that matched her eyes hung by the mirror, a selection she'd made earlier that day. She got up and pulled the dress down and held it up to herself. *Yep, this is the one.*

Her mobile phone rang. She dropped the dress on her bed and lunged for the phone, lighting up inside when she saw the name on the screen.

"Hello, you," she said, grinning into the phone. "I was just thinking about you. But then, I'm always thinking about you."

She heard Mark chuckle. "I've been thinking about you too, all afternoon pretty much."

"That's no good," she teased. "How did you get any work done?"

"Don't worry about that. You still want to see me this evening?"

"Hmm, not sure. Let me check my diary...yep, looks like I'm free."

"Good. I'll see you soon then."

"I'd better see you soon. I love you."

There was a pause, and she heard Mark swallow before he continued.

"I love you too, Erin."

*****

Later that evening, Erin sat in the now-thoroughly familiar passenger seat of Mark's car. The interior was tidy and smelled clean, as usual. She turned towards him in her seat as they sped down Pialligo Avenue, once again thrilled by the sheer joy she experienced in his presence.

"So, where are we going this evening?"

Mark smiled but shook his head firmly. "I've already got something planned, but I thought we could make a detour first."

"A detour? Where?"

"Have you ever been to Mount Ainslie Lookout at sunset?"

A tingle ran up Erin's spine. "I've been to the lookout before but not for a long time. And not at sunset."

"Me neither. Let's check it out together." He took her hand in his, holding it for a moment.

"All right," she said, raising his hand to her lips and kissing it. "Here, you'd better have your hand back before you drive us off the road."

"You're right. Having you next to me is enough of a distraction as it is," he said, caressing her fingers quickly before taking the wheel again.

Anticipation grew in Erin's heart as they arrived at the base of Mount Ainslie and began the short ascent in the car to the lookout. Though little more than a hill by most of the world's standards, the views out over the city from the lookout at night were beautiful, and Erin could barely wait to see it with Mark.

They arrived at the top within a few minutes, and Mark parked the car. It was warm; the light at the end of the day remained, but there were no other cars or people within sight.

"I can't believe no one else is here on such a nice evening," Erin said as Mark opened the car door for her and took her hand, something he always did and which she loved him for.

"You might have me to blame for that."

"What?"

"Well, not me, exactly. I sent my guardian angel ahead and asked him to clear the area for us."

Erin laughed and stared at him in disbelief. "Your prayers are clearly very powerful! Your angel certainly did what you asked him."

Mark took her hand, and they strolled up the few steps that led to the lookout over the city. The sun was just starting to sink beneath the horizon, and they stood together in silence, watching the sky turn vibrant shades of pink and orange.

God's painting in the sky. She thought of one of little Bruno's phrases and silently thanked God for the gift of His creation and the joy of witnessing it with Mark. She linked her arm through his and leaned her head against his shoulder.

"Erin, I want to ask you something."

Oh my. This is it.

"Yes?"

Mark turned Erin towards him, so they were facing each other. He took her hands in his.

"Erin. I love you, and I prefer you to my life itself. For the present life is nothing, and my most ardent dream is to spend it with you in such a way that we may be assured of not being separated in the life reserved for us. I place your love above all things, and nothing would be more bitter or painful to me than to be of a different mind than you."

"Saint John Chrysostom," Erin said, remembering the

quote from her recent study of the Catechism.

"Yes," he said, smiling down at her. "They're the words Saint John Chrysostom said young husbands should say to their wives. We're not married, but I want us to be. Will you marry me, Erin?"

Raw emotion caused Erin to begin laughing and crying at the same time. "Yes. Yes, of course I will. I'm already married to you in my heart. I have been for months."

Mark's face broke into an enormous grin. He said nothing, but reached into his pocket and pulled out a ring. Not the one she'd seen earlier that day, but it was no cause for disappointment. The diamond was considerably larger, and it was surrounded by smaller stones set around the larger diamond and in the band. He reached for her left hand and placed it on her ring finger. The fit was perfect.

"Mark, it's magnificent. It's like it was made for me."

"It was. And I asked your mum for your ring size so you wouldn't need to have it refitted. You won't have to part with it for a moment. Like you won't have to part with me. This ring isn't like the last one you had. I promise you."

"I know. Thank you so much. I love it."

"I love you," he replied, then took her face in his hands and kissed her.

Chapter 18

"Mark? Did you hear what I said?"

"Hmm?"

Erin Rafferty, the most beautiful girl in the world, the one who had agreed to be his wife, smiled up at him, apparently amused. "You're staring straight at me, but I get the impression you haven't heard a word I've been saying."

"Sorry," he said, leaning down and kissing her on the forehead. "You're right. Problem is I find it difficult to concentrate on all these wedding details when all I can think about is how lovely you are."

Erin grinned back, reaching her hand up and caressing the side of his face. "You're so sweet."

She sighed and placed her phone with its lunatic wedding planner app on the coffee table in his living room.

"Honestly, Erin, I'm happy as long as you are. You should organise whatever you want."

"Okay. But I want you to be happy with what we do too. This is our wedding."

"All I care about is marrying you. The rest is just details."

"Truthfully, that's all I care about too. But I still want it to be beautiful."

"Of course you do. I do too. I'm sorry. I should be more interested. What were you asking me about?"

Erin giggled. "Nothing. Don't worry about it. We can talk about it later."

She leaned back in the armchair and put her head on his shoulder.

Mark put his arm around her and kissed the top of her head. Her hair smelled heavenly and he felt her relax against him.

The potential danger of the situation at hand revealed itself sharply to him, and he shifted a little in his seat. Being alone with her in his quiet townhouse invited a world of temptation that he realised was more difficult for him to resist than her.

"Erin, I hate to say anything, but would you mind if we headed over to your place? Are your parents at home?"

Erin sat up straighter and turned to face him. "Yeah, I think they are." She reached down and took his hand. "Don't worry. Just a few more months and there won't be a need for a chaperone anymore."

"I don't ever want you to feel used again. I want to prove my future faithfulness in our marriage by demonstrating my faithfulness to you before marriage."

"I don't doubt you. I want the same for you too. I'm sorry, it was my idea to come over here. I really love the layout of this house. I can't wait to move in with you. Not that I won't make a few changes once we're living together." She stood, reached over to one of his bookcases and ran her finger along one of the shelves. "Yuck. Starting with a weekly dusting!"

Mark chuckled. "Sorry. I do get the duster out occasionally."

"Yeah, well there might be a few more changes in store for this room, and maybe, you know, every other room as well." Her eyes lit up as they darted around his living room.

Mark quietly delighted in her joy. A physical ache rose up in his chest at the thought that there were still some months ahead before they could share their lives, and he silently made an offering of the pain to God for the good of their marriage. He got up and crossed the room to where Erin was and turned her towards him, putting his arms around her.

She put her arms up around his neck. "You know, you should have a Christmas tree up in here. At least some tinsel or something. It's only three weeks till Christmas."

"I have a nativity scene, but I don't normally put it out till right before Christmas."

"It's the Second Sunday of Advent already. Come on, let's get it set up."

Mark went into his room to retrieve his nativity set from the back of his wardrobe and brought it to Erin.

She placed it on a low-standing bookcase and arranged the figures. "There," she said, kissing a tiny figurine of the Child Jesus and handing it to Mark. "You keep him somewhere safe. We'll come here on Christmas Eve together and place him in the manger."

"All right," he said, kissing the Child and placing him in his shirt pocket. "Do you think he'd mind being in my pocket for the moment?"

"No, I don't think so! He'll be close to your heart, right where I like to be too. Only mind you don't lose him."

"I won't."

"And think, this time next year, we'll be preparing for Christmas here together. And who knows," Erin said, taking both his hands in hers and linking their fingers together. "We might even have a baby on the way by then, God willing."

"That would be more than I could even dare to hope for."

"Well, dare to hope. Pray for it. I am. A child in the first year of our marriage would be the greatest gift God could give us, and that we could give to each other."

"We'll pray for it together."

*****

That evening Mark reached over and switched off the computer on his desk at work. It was late and the office was dark and quiet. After leaving Erin's place earlier, he'd come to work in an attempt to avoid the glumness of his lonely bachelor pad.

Saying goodnight was undoubtedly the hardest part of

engagement, and he found some distraction by being productive in his career. Since winning Erin, he'd had increased motivation to achieve in his job anyway. It wasn't hard. Nothing was difficult since being with her. He smiled to himself and thought for the millionth time how he must be the luckiest guy in the world.

He picked up his wallet and keys, switched off the lamp over his drafting table and allowed his mind to relax. The office was closing down for two weeks over Christmas, and he was enjoying planning out what they would do together over the Christmas holiday period. A trip to Newcastle was definitely on the list. Erin hadn't yet met his mother, though they'd called her when they'd got engaged. He couldn't wait for her to meet Erin.

Yawning, he headed to the front of the office and set the alarm before letting himself out the door. He pulled out his phone and checked the time. 11.30 pm. A bit late for a nighttime call to Erin. Instead, he opened up a new text message:

Leaving the office now, beautiful. Hope you're sleeping, but wanted you to see this when you wake up. I can't wait to marry you. Counting down the days. I love you.

He hit send, slipped the phone back in his pocket and pushed through the door to the internal stairs. He skipped down the first set and turned at the landing to take the second flight, the same as he did every day.

What happened next wasn't a result of being tired. And he didn't catch his foot on the bannister or trip on something left lying on the step. The fall simply happened. One moment he was stable and upright. The next, his feet had collided beneath him, and he was tumbling headlong down the stairs.

It was the speed with which he fell that surprised him. No sooner had he stumbled than he had fallen the entire length of the staircase, with barely an opportunity to try and right himself or control the manner in which he landed. He had hardly a chance to process what was happening when the back of his head hit the concrete floor at the bottom of the stairwell with a tremendous smack, and the world became a blur.

*****

Pain. Unspeakable pain. Pressure in his head that made it feel like it was about to explode.

Phone. Where was his....what was the thing he was reaching for? What was the word?

Mark tried to open his eyes. A tremendous weight pressed down on his face, or perhaps it was from the inside, preventing his eyelids from obeying his will. He struggled again and managed to open them, the scene in the stairwell swaying and swimming in front of him.

Someone was with him. A man, standing close, leaning over him. The torture in his head magnified as he worked to make his eyes focus on the face in front of him. A familiar face. A face he hadn't seen for many, many years.

"Dad?"

The man smiled down at him. Then the pain in Mark's head split through his skull, and he felt himself fading.

Erin. Please, Lord. I don't want to leave her alone.

After that everything in the world came to a halt, and he slid beneath a wave of blackness.

*****

Lights from the neighbours' back porch shone around the edges of the blinds in Erin's bedroom. Ordinarily the light didn't keep her awake. Most times she was able to drift back to sleep if she woke during the night, but tonight sleep eluded her. Wide awake, she'd taken to prayer, as she always did now in any and all spare moments.

With Father Miguel Vázquez's rosary ring between her fingers, she finished praying the final decade of the Sorrowful Mysteries.

Glory be to the Father and to the Son and to the Holy Spirit....

At that moment, her mobile phone rang, making her jump. She reached out and snatched it up from her bedside table in alarm. Who on earth would be calling her at three o'clock in the morning?

Not recognising the number, she swiped quickly to answer.

"Hello?"

"Is this Erin Rafferty?" A soft-toned but unfamiliar female voice filled her ear.

"Yes, it is," said Erin, sitting herself up in bed and switching on her bedside lamp. "Who's calling?"

"My name's Beth Miller. I'm a nurse at the Canberra Hospital. Are you a relation of Mark Ashcroft?"

Erin's heart performed a double thump, and her mouth went dry.

"Yes. I'm Mark's fiancée. What's this about? Is he okay?"

"I'm so sorry to be informing you of this, but I'm afraid your fiancé had been involved in an accident."

The sound of those words, spoken by a stranger in the middle of the night, hit Erin with all the force of a deadly blow and her body slumped back against her bedhead.

"What?" she half sobbed, her voice catching in her throat. "Was it a car accident? Is he all right? Is he dead?"

"No, it wasn't a car accident. A security guard found him unconscious at the bottom of a staircase in an office building in the city. He's been brought to hospital and undergone surgery. He's in intensive care now."

"Intensive care?" The simultaneous news that he was alive but seriously injured created an explosion of relief, anguish and unanswered questions. "What was the surgery? Is he okay now? What happened to him?"

"It seems he just fell. The police attended, and they're not completely ruling out someone else being involved, but they think that to be unlikely." The nurse's gentle tone was doing nothing to alleviate Erin's distress, but she waited for her to finish. "He's suffered an acute subdural hematoma."

"What's a subdural hematoma?"

"A bleeding on the brain. Doctors performed a craniotomy to relieve the pressure."

"So will he be all right now?"

"The surgery was successful, but he's in a coma, and he needs assistance with breathing. If you come in, the doctor can explain more."

Assistance breathing? *Oh no.*

Sick dread began seeping into her, as though she were a sea vessel rapidly taking on water.

"Are you still there, Erin?"

"Yes, yes, I am. I'm coming. I'll be there soon."

"Of course. ICU is on the fourth floor. The lifts are behind reception. I'll be on duty till 7.00 am. My name's Beth."

Erin hung up, and the phone slipped from her hand onto the bed beside her. The room started to spin.

"No. No, this can't be happening," she said out loud, her voice breaking into a sob.

Her Mark. How did this happen? He'd sent her a text message only a few hours ago.

Father Miguel's rosary ring lay on her doona next to her phone, and she picked it up again. Slipping it over her thumb, she clasped her hands together and bent her head over them.

Oh, my Lord. Why have You allowed this to happen to him?

First David, then Ines. Not Mark. Please not Mark. She held the ring tight, desperately trying to throw off the thought that he would die.

No, please, no. Please don't take him away from me.

Chapter 19

Up and down. Erin sat close by Mark and watched as his chest rose and fell in the rhythm of his breathing. He lay stretched out on the hospital bed, eyes shut, breathing tubes inserted in his mouth. His head had been shaved during the operation that relieved the bleeding, leaving a large, horseshoe-shaped incision, heavily stitched, in the side of his head.

Erin shuddered and suppressed yet another sob. Doctor Tran, a young Vietnamese doctor, had given her all the details she needed. She had been sensitive and kind but hadn't minced words.

Mark was in a post-operative coma. Time had lapsed between when he fell and when they'd been able to operate. While the pressure was relieved, it was unclear how much damage there was to Mark's brain, or if he'd be able to function on his own. All they could do was wait. The following days would be critical.

Oh, dear God. Why?

She reached out and took his hand, his fingers cool and unresponsive. "I'm here," she whispered into his ear. "I love you and I'm here."

His chest continued to rise and fall, the breathing apparatus working for him, keeping him alive.

"Erin?" A voice behind her made her turn around. Judith stood there, staring at Mark.

"Mum. I can't believe you're still here."

Erin had woken her after the phone call from the nurse, and her mother had driven her to the hospital. When they arrived, the staff hadn't allowed Judith into the ICU. *Immediate family only,* the doctors had said. They had found Erin's number in his phone listed as next of kin.

That made her immediate family.

"I thought you would have gone home by now. How long have we been here? I haven't been watching the time."

"A couple of hours," Judith said, placing her hand on Erin's shoulder. "The sun will be coming up soon. I've been praying the Rosary in the waiting room. How is he?"

Erin's throat contracted, and she tried again to suppress a sob. "He's not good. He's —"

"Shh," Judith pointed to Mark and took Erin's elbow. "Come over here."

She led Erin a little further from Mark's bed close to the ICU front desk and sat her down. "Tell me."

"It's bad," Erin said, crying. "They think his brain is damaged. They can't tell too much at this stage, but it's not good. They just have to wait now."

Judith said nothing but drew Erin in, holding her while she cried.

"He might die. I don't know what I'll do if he dies. I don't want to go through my life without him."

"I know."

Erin cried silently for a moment longer, then let out a shaky sigh. She wiped her eyes. "I'm thinking about myself. I should be thinking about him."

"You are. You're thinking about the life you have planned together."

"Mark wouldn't let that get in the way of what God has planned for his life. If he's here now, it's because God allowed it. He'd accept that. He accepts all the good and all the difficulties of life with such joy. And he's taught me to do the same."

She glanced over towards his unconscious form a short distance from where she sat. "Mark's not afraid to die. If it's his time now, he'd be happy."

"Excuse me, Erin?" Beth Miller, the nurse who had phoned Erin earlier in the night, approached her and Judith.

"Yes?"

"Here are Mark's belongings. They were on him when he was brought to hospital." She handed Erin a small bag.

"Thank you."

"My shift is finished now, but I'll be on again tonight."

"I'll see you again soon, then."

Beth smiled at Erin. "We're doing our best for him."

"Yes, I know. Thank you."

Erin emptied the items out of the bag on to her lap. Mark's phone, wallet, keys and the small figure of the Infant Jesus he had placed in his shirt pocket only hours ago.

"What's going to happen, Mum?"

"I don't know. But don't give up yet. Pray for healing."

"I will. And I want him to live, but his life isn't mine. I need to be prepared to let him go."

*****

The next few days passed like a strange, vague dream for Erin. She went through the motions of doing what needed to be done.

The excruciating call to Mark's mother, Rhonda, and his sister, Hannah. They came immediately, and Erin put them up in Mark's house. Work fell off the radar. She explained the situation to them, fully expecting them to let her go, but they didn't. Management gave her indefinite leave without pay and told her they'd hire a temp to fill her position till she was able to return.

Messages came through in abundance, and close friends called or came to see her at the hospital. Ingrid, Bianca, Jo. Flowers and cards arrived at the hospital for Mark. Father Nick came each day, praying over him and dispensing the blessings of the Church. Through it all, she barely left his side.

"Erin?" She felt a hand on her shoulder.

"Huh, what?" Erin turned her head, unaware of the time

of day or where she was.

"Erin, darling, you nodded off."

"Rhonda." Her head was resting on Mark's hospital bed by his hand. She sat up and sank back in the armchair next to the bed. "I didn't remember where I was just now."

"You're exhausted. Here, I brought you a coffee."

"Thanks," Erin said, taking the warm cardboard cup from Rhonda. "Where's Hannah?"

"She went back to Mark's place to get some sleep. She'll be back a little later on."

"Okay." Erin sipped from the cup and watched as Rhonda sat down on the other side of Mark's bed. "How do you think he's doing?"

"I don't know."

"He's still unconscious. It's been three days."

Rhonda didn't respond but looked at her son.

"I'm so sorry you're going through this. He's your only son."

"I'm sorry for what *you're* going through. I can't imagine what a torment it's been for you."

Erin shook her head. "Of course you can. You went through this with your own husband."

"True. It's different when it's your child, though."

"It's worse."

Rhonda nodded and wiped her eyes.

The shared tears of the last few days had formed a bond between the two women, the type of bond formed only by deep crisis. Erin had come to see her as a mother.

"He's very much like his father. I'm astonished at just how much he's turned out like him."

"Your husband must have been a wonderful man, then."

"He was. He was good to me and to the children. I never understood his faith, though. It didn't matter much to me, after he died. I didn't encourage them to keep practising. But somehow the children rediscovered it. Even Hannah has been more amenable to her faith lately. Mark has been helping her a lot."

"I know."

"He's been happier these last months than I've ever known him to be. Meeting you is the best thing that ever happened to him."

"He's the best thing that's ever happened to me."

Erin stared at Mark's face for a moment, then lay her head down alongside his arm. Her eyes began to close again.

"Why don't you go home for a little while, Erin?" Rhonda said. "Try to sleep a bit."

"No, I can't. What if something happens?"

"Then I'll call you straight away. I've had more sleep than you. Go and rest. You need it."

"You're probably right. I can barely think straight."

"You'll be able to cope better if you rest."

"All right, I suppose I should."

Erin reached for Mark's hand and gently kissed it. "I'll be back soon, I promise," she whispered.

*****

A wall of mid-afternoon heat hit Erin as she exited the hospital and made her way to her car. Summer had arrived with a vengeance, and all the forecasts were predicting a hot Christmas, or so she had heard the nursing staff say. It didn't seem to matter to them that the love of her life lay there with his life hanging in the balance.

Why would it? They didn't know him like she did. They didn't love him like she did.

There was no way she could go home straight away. She had to make a stop off first.

Fifteen minutes later, she stepped inside the chapel at the cathedral. She genuflected, made the Sign of the Cross and sat down in a pew close to the tabernacle. It was only slightly cooler inside the chapel, and the warmth of the day compounded Erin's fatigue. The red light next to the tabernacle flickered in the empty chapel. Her eyes began to fill with tears, and she leaned her head on the pew in front of her.

"Why, Lord? Why? Why are you putting us through so much?" she whispered.

She waited for an answer in the stillness of her soul but heard nothing. "I'm trying to be brave. I'm trying to trust you. But I'm slipping. How will I survive if he dies, or never wakes up? I can't believe You'd allow this to happen. We were so happy. Why are You doing this to me? Why?"

The last few words she spoke came up and out her throat in a distressed yelp. Exhaustion and anguish blocked all her inhibitions, and she continued crying out. "I've done everything you expected of me. I came back. I'm obeying your laws. Mark did too. Did I do something wrong? Are You abandoning me again?"

No. I could never abandon you. I'm here.

The sound of the sacristy door creaking on the other side of the cathedral told Erin she wasn't alone. Quickly wiping her face, she attempted to compose herself as she heard footsteps coming in her direction.

Turning, she looked up to see Father Nick standing in the aisle next to her, concern on his face. "Erin, I was just on my way to visit Mark at the hospital. Are you okay?"

Erin shook her head. "No, I'm not. I'm not!"

Nick's expression softened, and he sat down in the pew next to her. "Of course you're not. And you're exhausted. Have you had any sleep at all?"

"Rhonda told me to go home and try and rest but I can't. I can't understand why this is happening. I thought I had it together. That my faith would sustain me. But this is too much. It's too much. Why is He testing me like this? What have I done wrong?"

Nick sat by patiently and let her cry for a moment before

speaking. "You haven't done anything wrong. You've done everything right."

"Then why is He allowing this to happen?"

Nick sighed and paused before he spoke. "The Lord has seen fit to grant you some extraordinary sufferings. Both of you. What I know is He calls on his dearest friends to share in his greatest sufferings. And God can draw great good from even the worst and hardest of situations."

"I can't do it. I want to throw it all away. Throw my faith back at him."

"You're tired and worried and heartbroken. Lean into Him. He hasn't left you or Mark. He's sustained you this far, and He will continue to sustain you. You can't do this, or anything else, in your own strength. You don't have to. *He* will be your strength."

Memories from the previous months suddenly came flowing effortlessly into her mind. The many times she had experienced God's unmistakable presence and how peace had followed.

Peace, now, made its way back into her heart. She studied Father Nick's face and saw sadness written there too.

"I realise this is so hard for you as well. You and Mark are such good friends."

Nick nodded. "He's one of the best friends I've ever had."

"Me too. He's my dearest friend in the world. His unconditional friendship was what won me over in the first place, I think."

"You've been blessed. I haven't encountered many relationships like yours and Smark's. Nothing and no one can ever take that away from you. It belongs to you and him and always will, no matter what happens to Mark or to you."

"Father Nick, do you think you could hear my confession before you go?"

"Of course."

*****

In the days that followed, Mark continued on life support. He showed no improvement or any sign that he might be able to survive on his own. Still, Erin waited by his side, his mother and sister also close by. The three women drew strength from one another, and Erin had lengthy chats with Hannah, whose faith appeared to be burgeoning in the wake of Mark's accident. She accompanied Erin to the occasional weekday Mass and Erin drew inspiration from watching the faith of another grow in front of her. It was as though she was witnessing a miracle.

It seemed strange to her that life carried on around her — much of it good — despite her own life being put sharply on hold. Christmas preparations continued everywhere. Then, in the middle of the third week of Advent, Bianca went into labour three weeks early. Unlike with Jo, the labour and birth went well, and Erin left Mark briefly to see Bianca and her baby.

Despite all that was happening to her, she rejoiced with her friend. Life continued to have joyful moments even when tragedy struck, though Bianca's baby brought with it the painful reminder that Ines would have been due soon as well, had she lived. Erin kept the visit short, using Mark as her excuse for getting away from the maternity ward.

After visiting Bianca, she got into the lift alone and leaned against the wall. The lift doors were just closing when someone's hand appeared and opened the doors again. Erin gasped quietly when she saw the person entering the lift with her.

"Gareth!"

Gareth saw her at that same moment and stopped still, gawking, appearing stunned. His fair hair was ruffled, his eyes were drawn and the black tee shirt he wore looked as though he'd slept in it, and for more than one night. He reminded Erin of the kangaroo she'd dazzled in her headlights and almost hit a few nights earlier. The lift doors closed on him, and he jumped out of the way and inside the lift with Erin.

"Erin!" he said awkwardly. "What a surprise. How — how are you? Are you visiting someone?"

Erin ignored the first question. "Yes, what a surprise! Um, yes, I've been visiting Bianca. She's just had a baby."

"Bianca! I did hear that she and Ryan were expecting a baby. Haven't been in contact much with either of them lately. Was it a boy or a girl?"

"A boy. They named him Matthew."

"Nice name."

"Were you — visiting someone?"

Gareth lowered his head. "Um, yeah, I was."

Erin didn't enquire further. Still processing the shock of seeing Gareth so unexpectedly, the lift bell sounded, and the doors opened at the lower level.

He stood back for Erin and she stepped out of the lift with him following behind. Anxious to get away, she searched for a way to escape back upstairs to the ICU without taking the lift.

But Gareth didn't appear to be in a hurry. "Erin, are you doing anything right now? Do you have time for a coffee?"

She peered into his face, which appeared uncomfortable and slightly chastened, an expression she never recalled seeing on him before.

"I suppose so."

"I promise I won't take up too much of your time."

"It's all right. There's a café here on the ground level. We can go there."

Several minutes later, she found herself sitting opposite him in the hospital coffee shop. A waitress appeared with an Earl Grey tea for her and a long black for him, a combination they'd had together countless times in the past. The familiarity of the situation made Erin uncomfortable. She took a sip from her tea, anxious to get away from him and back to Mark.

"I'm so grateful I bumped into you," Gareth said. "It's bothered me for months the way we — ended things."

Erin nodded. "I should apologise. There was no excuse for treating you like that."

Gareth regarded her across the table with a strained expression. "Of course there was an excuse. I deserved so much worse."

"Still, I'm sorry for slapping you."

"I'm sorry for betraying you."

Erin exhaled and placed her hands on the table on either side of her teacup. "You didn't really betray me, you know. Not in the strict sense. We weren't married. We never had a claim on each other. You were free to go and find someone else."

"I sneaked around behind your back. There was a promise there — we were engaged. I lied to you. I should have been honest with you from the start."

"It's okay, Gareth. I forgive you."

"I'm glad you forgive me. Thank you. But it still wasn't okay."

"Thank you for apologising. Let's leave it in the past, now. In spite of it all, I think everything worked out for the best."

"Yeah, I suppose it did."

Erin observed Gareth from across the table. The tone in his voice made her doubt that he meant what he said, but she decided not to probe further. "So, who were you visiting?"

"Michelle."

"What's wrong with her?"

"She's six months pregnant, and it's been complicated. High risk. She's been in and out of hospital for a few months now. It's been very rough on her."

Michelle's pregnant? Oh Lord, should I tell him I was too?

"I'm sorry to hear that. I hope she and the baby are all right."

"I think they will be. But this will probably be her only child. I can't see her going through this again."

"Not the type?"

"You could say that. She's not you."

"Was it planned?"

Gareth rolled his eyes and laughed with incredulity. "Shit, no. You know what I'm like. Could you have imagined me signing up for this? It's been nothing but stress and hormones and drama since I moved in with her. It's like I'm being punished for what I did to you."

"Come on, Gareth. You're not being punished. Surely it can't be as bad as all that."

"It's not. I just wasn't prepared for it. I guess I need to grow up."

"Yes, I wouldn't disagree with that."

"You know, I wondered a lot about how you got on after we broke up. That last time we were together haunted me. I worried about you."

Erin drew in a breath and paused. What should she say? That he'd had good cause to be? That Michelle wasn't the only woman he'd gotten pregnant this year?

Perhaps it was time he knew. She hadn't sought Gareth out. God had put him in her path. It was time to tell him.

"I had a hard time after I left you that night. I missed you. But that wasn't all. About a month later I — I found out I was pregnant."

The colour immediately drained from Gareth's face. "You were pregnant? With our child?"

Erin nodded. "Yes. It happened the night of Bianca's and Ryan's wedding, I think."

Gareth paused and seemed to be struggling for

something to say. "What happened? I mean, what did you do?"

"I had a miscarriage at about thirteen weeks. Here, actually. A little girl."

"Oh, Erin. I can't believe it. Why didn't you tell me? I could have done something; been there for you in some way. I'm so useless."

"I didn't want to contact you. I couldn't bear to tell you. I was crushed and so angry at you. But I should have told you before now. Our baby didn't live, but you were her father."

"I'm so sorry." Gareth's shoulders slumped, and he hung his head. "I can't believe you were pregnant with my child. And I wasn't there for you."

"I had my family. Bianca and Jo were there for me too. And Ingrid. And —"

"And?"

"And Mark."

"Mark?"

"I met him shortly after you and I broke up."

"What's he like?"

"He's the most wonderful person I've ever met. He really changed things for me. It was like God sent him along to me at my lowest point. I began practising my faith again because of him. He saved me."

"Wow." Gareth leaned back in his chair and stared at her. "Well, he's clearly a better man than me. I can't believe I turned into the guy who fathered children with two different women in the one year."

"Gareth, you can be a better man. You have someone now who needs you. There's a baby coming who needs a father. These are precious gifts, not punishments. You can make it work. But you *do* need to grow up. Michelle and your baby are relying on you to pull yourself together."

Gareth rubbed his forehead with the heel of his hand.

"You're right. I know you're right. I've always been self-focused, too self-focused." He stared soberly across the table at her. "So, you could tell the baby was a little girl?"

"Yes. I held her in my hand. She was perfect."

"A daughter. Unbelievable."

Erin nodded. "You might think it sounds silly, but I dreamed about her. She has green eyes like me and your fair hair."

Gareth continued to stare at her, and his eyes began to tear up. "Thank you for telling me. It's a lot to take in; it'll take a long time for me to process it. But I'm glad you've told me now."

"I'm glad I had a chance to tell you."

"So you're going back to Mass?"

Erin nodded. "And Confession too."

"There *is* something different about you now. I noticed it as soon as I stepped into the lift and saw you. You've changed somehow. In a good way. I mean, you look amazing. Beautiful, actually."

"Thanks."

"I'm so pleased you've found someone else." He looked at her engagement ring on her left hand as she put down her teacup.

"Woah, that's not the one I gave you. I guess congratulations are in order. When are you getting married?"

At that point, Erin's resolve to stay cool and detached began to crumble. "We were planning for April, straight after Easter but —"

"But what?"

Erin gave Gareth a brief outline of Mark's accident and his condition, and Gareth listened with an expression of horror on his face. "My God, Erin, you've been through so much. I'm so sorry. I really hope he recovers soon."

"There's nothing I want more, but the longer he stays unconscious, the less likely that seems. More people than not die from this type of injury."

Erin began to cry, and Gareth reached across the table and took her hand.

"I don't know how you're coping as well as you are. You're doing wonderfully."

"I'm at peace about his future, no matter what it is. But it's just that I'll miss him so much if he dies."

"Of course you will. But don't give up yet."

"I haven't. But I *am* accepting God's will in our lives."

"It can't be God's will for you to be heartbroken."

"God allows so many things we don't understand. But I've realised it doesn't mean that He's left us alone. And if God takes him now, I know I'll see him again one day in heaven."

Gareth stared at her, a look of wonder on his face. "You've changed. You're not the same person you used to be."

"Probably not."

"Mark deserves you. I never did. I was never good enough for you. I can see that now. What I did to you was horrible, and you didn't deserve it, but it got you away from me. That was a good thing."

She sniffed and Gareth handed her a paper serviette. She took it from him and dabbed at her eyes with it.

"Don't go thinking things like that about yourself. Things happened the way they happened. We can't take it back. You have a new path ahead of you, and so do I."

"I wish I'd been there for you. I wish I'd seen our daughter."

Erin patted the top of Gareth's hand, which was still holding hers. "Talk to her. I know you don't have much time for God or heaven or saints. But talk to her. She's alive. She loves you."

"Maybe I will."

Later, when she was back with Mark in the intensive care

ward, she sat close to him and told him what had happened.

"You would be proud of me, I think," she said, gently stroking the side of his face with the back of her fingers. "I wasn't bitter or angry towards him. I just told him about the baby, about Ines. I wasn't overwhelmed. I was completely together. And I didn't just act it. I felt it. The only time I cried was when I told him about you. "

Mark's face remained still, unanimated, his eyes firmly closed. Hair had begun growing again on his head where it had been shaved off for surgery. His skin lacked its usual colour, and he had stubble growing on his handsome face, something she had never seen on him before. His appearance seemed so wrong. It was all so wrong.

She reached down for his hand and brought it to her face, kissing it. "I wish I knew if you could hear me, my love. Please don't leave me. Please wake up."

But the only response she got was the rhythmic hiss and click of the equipment that was keeping Mark alive.

Chapter 20

"Are you sure? Are you absolutely sure nothing more can be done for him?"

Only two days remained till Christmas, and Erin glanced at Rhonda from across Mark's hospital bed, standing by her unconscious son, imploring, pleading with the surgeon to somehow make it all better.

Erin stood alongside the young doctor who had been caring diligently for Mark and accepted her diagnosis. She longed with all she had in her for it not to be true, but she knew the doctor was right.

Mark's condition had worsened. Complications after the surgery had left him with an infection, and scans had shown significant brain injury. The hope of him ever recovering or functioning on his own had dwindled to almost nothing.

"I'm sorry. We truly have done everything for him. If there was anything more we could do, we would."

Rhonda nodded and began to cry, while Hannah stood alongside her, gripping her mother's arm, her lip quivering, but refusing to submit to the tears.

"The decision lies with you as his family, of course," Doctor Tran said.

At that point Hannah spoke up. "I don't think there's any disagreement between us. Mark wouldn't want this. Would he, Erin?"

Erin reached instinctively for Mark's hand and squeezed his fingers. "No. No, he wouldn't."

"Honestly, I rarely see a decision like this made so calmly. This is one of the worst things we have to do as doctors. I've been very touched by how you've all handled Mark's injury."

"We know you've done everything you can," Erin said, her heart faltering inside her. "Would it be all right — could we each have some time with him, alone, before the equipment is switched off?"

"Of course. There's no need to rush," Doctor Tran said, placing her hand on Erin's shoulder.

"And Father Nick Bentley too," Hannah added. "He's my brother's good friend, and we'd like him to give Mark the last Sacrament."

Doctor Tran nodded. "We won't do anything until we receive consent from you, Erin."

"How long will it take? Once support is removed?" Erin asked.

"No one can say. A few minutes or hours. Possibly a few days."

Erin simply nodded, the huge rock that had just settled inside her chest cavity crushing the last of her strength and will power.

"Take some time now. I'll come back later," Doctor Tran said, giving Erin one last pat on her shoulder.

Erin sat down on the bedside chair that had almost become an extension of her own body and lay her head beside Mark on his sick bed.

"I'll go and call Father Nick," Hannah said, sniffing and turning to her mother. "I'll just be in the waiting area."

Rhonda nodded and stroked Mark's forehead, leaning over to kiss him. She whispered some words Erin couldn't make out, lingering over his forehead for a moment before she stood up.

"I'm going to leave you with Mark for a little while, Erin. Give you some time."

Erin lifted her head. "No, you don't have to do that."

"It's all right, my dear. You were planning on spending a lifetime together. No one would begrudge you a few minutes alone now. I'll be with Hannah for a while."

"Okay," Erin whispered and let Rhonda leave. She picked

up Mark's hand in hers and carefully stroked his forehead with her other hand.

"I suppose we won't be needing that silly wedding planner app now, will we?" she said, remembering how his eyes changed the last time she'd used it. But they didn't glaze over with boredom. They focused wholly on her. All Mark had done since they first met was love her.

"Mark, I never imagined anyone could love me as much as you have. And I know you'll go on loving me. It would be selfish and callous to be anything but grateful to you." At that moment her voice cracked, and the ocean of tears inside her that she had yet to cry rose up and started spilling out of her. "But I'm just going to miss you so much!"

She placed her head once again by his face and sobbed quietly on his pillow. After a few minutes, she lifted her head and wiped her eyes with the back of her hand.

"I have a surprise for you." Erin reached down into her bag and pulled out a piece of folded paper. "It's a poem I wrote for you. You remember I told you I used to write poetry? I haven't written one for years. It was going to be a present for Christmas. You might not be with me on Christmas Day, so I'm going to read it to you now."

Three
When heart cries out to Heart,
And mind seeks Truth and Light,
Then Truth, Love will impart,
And soul escapes the night.
Yet from His love we turned,
Shunned all He has to give,
Defeat, our hearts have learned:
We fight, we lose, but live!
My love He gave to you,
And yours He gave to me,
The world saw us as Two,
But with His Love, we're Three.

And though my heart will bleed,
Will break, when you are gone,
Death's scourge will not impede,
Our hearts remaining One.
For live or die, I hold,
Forever we'll be Three,
Joined by that Love untold,
Into eternity.

"I believe that. I know you'll always be with me." Erin folded the paper and tucked it in Mark's hand. "I hope you liked the poem. It was a little rushed. But I had to finish it before, before—" her voice caught, and she paused before attempting once again to complete her sentence.

It was no use. She leaned over and kissed Mark's face and the tears streamed from her eyes like a torrent. She surrendered to the grief and allowed the tempest to consume her.

*****

"Life support switched off at 7.35 pm." Dr Tran marked something on a clipboard, then reached out and turned a switch off on Mark's equipment. Erin sat close to Mark and kept her eyes on him. She watched his face, pale and peaceful. His chest, rising and falling beneath the hospital sheet. Rising, falling. Rising, falling. A pause. Rising, falling.

Then, no more. Erin waited.

"Is that it?" she whispered to Doctor Tran. "Is he gone?"

The doctor nodded.

"No," Erin said, gripping Mark's hand. "I'm not ready for you to die. Please, Mark. Don't leave me. Please don't. Just wake up. It's easy — you can do it. Please."

Dizziness. Erin fell back in her chair. "Please, Mark," she whispered. "I can't go on without you." The sound of her voice faded in her ears.

Erin opened her eyes with a start. "Mark," she gasped and lurched forward. "Mark?"

"Erin," Rhonda said. "You were dreaming. Are you okay?"

Erin blinked and peered around the semi-dark, quiet hospital room that Mark had been moved to, the only lighting coming from the nurses' station outside. Then she turned to see Mark, his chest still rising and falling. *He's still here. Oh, thank God.*

"What time is it?"

"It's 11.30."

"It's been four hours since they took him off support. I dreamed he'd died already."

"Not yet."

"Where's Hannah gone?"

"For a walk. I don't think she wants to be here when it happens."

"I don't want to be away from him when it does. I'm going to stay with him to the end."

"I'll go and find her. I'd like to check on her. I'll be back, all right?"

Erin watched Rhonda leave the room and settled herself as close to Mark's face as she could get. Up and down, his chest continued to rise and fall. How much longer? Erin watched, anguish fluttering within her chest, dreading that inevitable moment when the rising and falling ceased forever. She didn't want to be away from him for a single breath.

A buzzing sound coming from her bag on the floor at her feet distracted her. She pulled it out, blinking as she tried to make out the message on the bright screen. It was from Judith. She was at the hospital.

Erin caressed Mark's face, now free of breathing equipment. "I'll just be a minute," she said, and gently kissed his lips.

Out past the nurses' station, Erin found Judith sitting quietly, rosary beads in her hand.

"Mum, what are you doing?" Erin approached her

mother and sat down beside her. "You should be at home."

"I wanted to stay here till it's, you know, final. I want to be here for you when he's gone."

"Thank you," she said sighing, her voice barely above a whisper. "But it might be a little while yet."

"I want to be here for you, sweetheart."

"You have been. You've been my tower of strength. But I promise I'll call you once it's over. Rhonda and Hannah are here. We'll stay together until you're able to come and get me. Please go home. I don't like the thought of you sitting in a hospital corridor here when you could be home with Dad."

Judith looked at Erin. "Truly, honey, it's fine. I'll stay for a bit longer. I want to pray here for him, and for you. But I'll go home if I need to. You get back to him now."

"Yes, I will."

Erin left Judith and went straight back to Mark through the quiet, nighttime hush of hospital. As she approached his room, she noticed a soft light that hadn't been there when she left a minute earlier. She entered the room, expecting to see a nurse, or Rhonda, or Hannah. Instead she found a man, dressed in black clericals holding open a breviary and praying quietly. Erin sat down next to Mark, but the priest didn't acknowledge her.

Who was he? And what was he doing here? Nursing staff didn't allow just anyone to walk in, and certainly not at this time of night. *Perhaps they let him through because he's a priest.* Still, she thought it strange that she didn't notice him pass her when she was speaking with Judith.

"Excuse me, Father?" Erin said tentatively, taking Mark's hand. "I haven't met you. I'm Erin. Are you a friend of Mark's?"

The young priest closed his breviary and smiled at Erin. "Yes, I'm a friend of Mark's," he said in accented English, offering no further explanation as to who he was. He turned to Mark and traced the Sign of the Cross on his forehead. Then he stared across the hospital bed and straight into Erin's eyes. "Everything is going to be all right."

"Thank you, Father. But I don't expect he'll be with us many more hours."

The priest simply smiled at her. "Pray. The Holy Family will soon arrive in Bethlehem. And the Son of God, the Light of Life, will enter the world. Welcome Him into your heart. This isn't your time for sorrow."

Erin stared back at him, wondering suddenly at the familiarity of his face. Had she met him before? She was about to ask his name when she heard a voice calling her.

"Just a moment, Father," she said and left the room, walking down to the nurses' station, approaching the nurse on duty who was sitting behind the desk, noting something in a chart.

"Excuse me, was someone out here asking for me?"

"No, no one's been here except for the lady you were talking to just now."

"Really?" She could have sworn she heard her name being called. Perhaps exhaustion was catching up with her. "I'm sorry, but there *has* been someone else here this evening. What about the priest who is in with Mark right now? I was wondering if he mentioned his name when he came in."

The nurse stared doubtfully at Erin, frowning. "No. Like I said, no one's come in or out of Mark's room this evening except for family."

"No. A young priest is in his room, right now. Hispanic, I think. Maybe Spanish. He's a friend of Mark's. I was just speaking with him."

The nurse continued to stare at Erin as though she was speaking with a confused toddler.

"I'm telling you no one has been past this desk this evening except for you and the family."

"But he's in with him right now. I'll go and get him." Erin turned and went back to Mark's room.

The priest had gone.

No. No, that couldn't be. Where could he have gone? The only exit was past the nurses' station, and she'd just been there. She hadn't seen him leave.

She sat down again and placed her hand on Mark's chest. Up and down. He continued to breathe.

Everything will be all right. That's what the young priest had just told her. Who was he? Why did he look so familiar?

The memory of her visit to San Miguel de Allende came back to her suddenly. Ines and Rosa Vázquez. The photo of Father Miguel. That photo. She closed her eyes and strived to recall his face.

They were the same person.

The man in the photo Ines Vázquez had shown her of her son and the priest in Mark's hospital room.

They were the same person.

Erin's heart thumped irregularly in her chest. *This is not your time for sorrow.*

Where had that light come from? It wasn't from a light source in the room.

That was it. The young priest had brought the light with him. And he left it behind. It no longer shone in the room, but it was there in her heart.

Erin reached around her neck and took Father Miguel's rosary ring from the chain. Why hadn't she thought to do this before?

She kissed it, then took Mark's hand and put it on his index finger. Then she took the card with the prayer of Saint Francis that he had given her months before and placed it on his chest, and the figurine of the Baby Jesus and placed it in his hand, closing his fingers around it.

"It's almost Christmas Eve, my love," she said, bringing her face close to his. "And you and I are going to place the

Infant Jesus in the manger. Together."

*****

Darkness. Total darkness. But no fear. Only peace.
Why was it so dark?
Walk on.
Mark took a step forward. Then another.
Walk on.
"But I can't see." He took another step, then another and another. As he walked the darkness began to lift. It became lighter and lighter till he was surrounded by grey, like a fog. He walked on, seeing nothing, meeting no one.
"Hello?" he called out. "Is anyone there?"
Footsteps. Someone was walking next to him. "Is someone there? Who is it?"
The light — wherever it was coming from — became stronger and the grey surrounding him turned into a soft glow. Mark turned and saw a man walking alongside him. A priest.
"Hello, Father," he said simply.
"Hello, Mark." The priest smiled at him, his face radiating an ethereal brightness.
"Have I met you before, Father? Do I know you?"
"No, but I know you."
"Where am I?" He struggled to think of the last thing that happened to him. Something that would help him understand where he was.
There had been pain. And helplessness. A fall? "Did I die, Father? I'm dead, right?"
The priest smiled again and laughed. He placed his hand on Mark's shoulder, and he could feel it — a warm, firm grip. "No, my friend, you aren't dead."
"Where are we?"
The priest turned from Mark and pointed ahead through the soft glow that surrounded them.
Mark peered out in front of him. A short distance from

where he stood, he saw a stone. The stone was hollowed out at the top, with straw placed in it. But there was something else inside the hollowed stone besides straw. Or rather, Someone. Stepping a little closer he saw it was a baby. Wrapped tightly, sleeping. Cold. Small. Defenceless.

He turned back to the young priest. "No. I'm not worthy."

"You weren't worthy to receive Him, Body, Blood, Soul and Divinity in Holy Communion either. But he invited you, and so you went, again and again. Go and kneel, like the Magi did. Pray and worship."

Mark turned back towards the baby, and this time he saw a man and a woman also kneeling by the stone manger. He had never seen the man before but knew him from the many silent conversations they'd had together. Knew his great strength and honour and wisdom. And the Woman! How well he knew her. How many times he'd honoured her unique place in the history of salvation. Her sacrifice and her love.

Approaching the scene, he knelt down and bowed his head. "Lord, I am not worthy," he said over and over in his mind. Then his mind quietened. The peace in his soul magnified and his entire being became filled and overflowing with life and warm light. He became aware of just how high a price had been paid for his soul.

He remained kneeling, not knowing for how long, or whether time even existed for him anymore. Perhaps forever could pass him by, and he would just stay here. Praising his God for what He had done. *Yes. That is as it should be.*

Then he felt the priest's hand on his shoulder again.

"It's time to go, Mark."

Mark lifted his head and found himself alone with the priest. He stood up. "Go where?"

"Back to live your life. This is not your time. The Lord

still has work for you to do."

"I thought my earthly life had ended."

The priest shook his head. "No. The Lord wants you to continue as His witness in the world, to be a channel through which His peace may flow."

"Who are you, Father?"

The priest said nothing but prayed silently, placing his hands on Mark's head and blessing him. Peace continued to permeate his entire being. He closed his eyes.

A voice began speaking, somewhere. Familiar. Close. The dearest voice. What was she saying?

"....Holy Mary, Mother of God, pray for us sinners, now and at the hour of our death. Amen."

Erin?

More sounds. Another voice, also familiar. Hannah? Also, praying. Praying with Erin.

Breathing. He could feel himself breathing. His lungs taking in air, exhaling it slowly.

I'm alive.

Mark opened his eyes.

Epilogue

Erin reached out a hand to feel for droplets of rain and peered up at the sky. Dark clouds had been gathering for more than an hour and now threatened to empty themselves on the earth. It had been a dry spring, and she welcomed the rain.

"Michael! Time to come in now! Come on, we can watch the rain from the window."

"Okay!"

Erin watched her exuberant four-year-old clamber down from the trampoline in his Superman cape and race past her into the kitchen.

"Mmm! What's that yummy smell?"

"Anzac biscuits," Erin said, ushering him inside. "Would you like one?"

"Yes, yes, yes! And some milk too?"

"Already waiting for you on the table, Mikey-man."

"Goody. Thank you."

"My pleasure, sweetness."

Erin put a biscuit on a small blue plate decorated with trains and placed it in front of him at the table. They sat together and watched through the window as the rain began pouring down on the garden.

"Sit close to me, Mama. Is your back hurting? Your tummy is getting bigger now."

Erin pulled her chair closer to her dark-haired, dark-eyed child. "That's very thoughtful of you. What a lovely thing to be concerned for me."

"Oh, yes, I'm very thoughtful."

Erin laughed. "I'm all right. My back doesn't hurt too much. But my tummy is getting bigger now, isn't it?"

"Mm hm," the child said through a mouthful of biscuit

crumbs. "Is the baby a boy or a girl?"

"I'm not sure. But I think perhaps a girl. Would you like a little sister?"

Michael nodded enthusiastically. "Yep. Will she play trains with me?"

Erin laughed again. "I don't know. She might be more interested in dolls and tea sets, like I was. But I'm sure Dad will always play trains with you."

"When's he coming home?"

"I think he'll be here soon."

At that moment, they heard the sound of the front door opening. Michael jumped down from the table. "He's home!" he yelled exuberantly and ran to meet his father.

"Mikey!" Mark appeared in the doorway of the kitchen and scooped up his excited child.

Erin's heart gave a leap, the same as it did every time he came home. After five years of marriage, she still rejoiced in being reunited with him, even after a short absence. She grinned in delight as she watched him with their son.

Mark grinned back, winking at her. "Goodness, it's really coming down out there," he said, placing Michael down and taking off his jacket.

"Yes, we're watching the rain and eating Anzac bikkies."

"Mmm, sounds nice. Have you been a good boy for Mum?"

"Oh, yes," he said, jumping excitedly around his father. "Will you play trains with me now?"

"Woah, buddy," Erin said. "Give your daddy a few minutes to get himself in the door, now."

"Okay. And we should pray first. Pray with me, Dad."

Michael took Mark by the hand to a small table in the corner that held a crucifix, a small statue of Our Lady of Guadalupe, the poem she'd written for Mark after his injury and a card with the Prayer of Saint Francis, "Make Me a Channel of Your Peace." Erin joined them by the little home altar. Mark reached out and took her hand.

Michael clumsily made the Sign of the Cross, joined his hands and closed his eyes.

"Dear Jesus, thank you for bringing my dad home safely today and for making him well when he was sick so long ago. Thank you, Father Miguel, for looking after me and my mum and my dad and my new baby sister who isn't born yet. I hope I can be a saint in heaven one day. Amen."

Erin listened to the heartfelt prayer of her innocent child and became overwhelmed by a desire to clasp him in her arms and never let him go. "What a beautiful prayer, my darling boy!"

"Yes, a wonderful prayer, Michael David. Good boy," Mark said, tousling the child's hair. "You go and get your trains out, and I'll come play with you in a minute."

"All right!" Michael darted out of sight.

Erin turned to face Mark. "So, how did your appointment go?"

Mark smiled down at her and gathered her into his arms. "Terrific. Same as last time. My case continues to baffle the doctors. I'm going fine, though they still can't explain why."

"It doesn't baffle me. I knew that you would wake up. After I saw him standing over you, I knew that you would. But I still wasn't prepared for the unspeakable joy I experienced when you opened your eyes. It was like having you come back from the dead."

"I know. Those moments before I blacked out after I fell, I thought I was going to leave you. That was the worst part."

They stood quietly for a moment, listening to the rain, Erin privately reliving the days following Mark's accident.

"I got in touch with the Bishop of Morelia in Mexico, with Emilio's help, like you suggested," Mark said, stroking her hair. "I told them what happened to us, and I just got an email back from them. Apparently, this isn't the only unexplained incident associated with Father Miguel."

Erin pulled back so she could see Mark's face. "You're kidding! How incredible."

Mark nodded. "They'll probably want to talk to us more about what happened to me. Perhaps his cause for canonisation will be introduced."

Erin felt tears stinging in her eyes. "That would be unbelievable."

"Aren't you glad we named our son after him?"

"Well, I'd be glad either way, my love. If only we could name the next one after him too." She placed her hand on her protruding tummy. "Perhaps God had some greater plan when He allowed your accident to happen. When we trust, God can cause great good to flow out of our sufferings."

"Yes, He can, and He does," Mark said, placing his hand on her stomach beside hers.

"Father Nick taught me that."

"It does sound like something he'd say."

Erin smiled. "Yes. In his homily, the first day I went back to Mass. The day I met you. He said if we allow Jesus in, He'll work His marvels in our lives and the lives of others."

"That has to be true. You certainly worked a marvel in mine," Mark said, drawing her close to him again. "Your love is a gift for which I'll be eternally grateful."

"I'm grateful for your love too, and would still be even if you'd died then," she said, wrapping her arms around him. "Because the thing is, before I met you, I always thought my faith had imprisoned me. It wasn't till He stripped me of my pride and sent you along that I was able to see what accepting His love and His will means."

"And what's that?"

"Freedom. True freedom. And peace, peace that doesn't waver in the face of hardship. Who could have guessed I would have peace in the face of you dying? Still, there it was. And now I'll never doubt again."

"Why is that?"

"Because there never was a need to. I know now that I can do all things through Him who strengthens me."

Acknowledgements

To Our Lord God and Our Blessed Mother: I wrote this for you. Thank you for inspiring me and assisting me with my writing during the very quiet late nights and early mornings as I sat huddled over my laptop. You helped the words to come. I was never alone.

To my dear husband Pablo, the only person I was brave enough to show the story to before pitching it to Full Quiver Publishing. You are so brilliant: your good opinion was worth a hundred and gave me the courage to proceed. Thank you for encouraging me to keep writing when I thought I should give up.

To my wonderful children, Daniel, Benjamin and Gabriela. You are all so prayerful and unique and funny and clever. You'll never know how much you inspired me during the writing of this novel. I hope you all read it in a few years' time and draw something from it.

To all my dear family members and friends, many of whom are the wonderful priests who've made such a difference in my life. Thank you, each and every one of you, for your prayers, love, support and friendship. You all know who you are.

In a special way, I would like to thank Monsignor Frank Leo, Jr. for allowing me to use your words of wisdom and guidance to form the main gist of Father Nick's homily in the early part of the story, which ultimately ended up inspiring the novel's title.

To Ellen Gable Hrkach, and James Hrkach, a truly remarkable team. Thank you, James, for the wonderful cover design! And thank you so much, Ellen, for taking my story on board and publishing me. It is beyond an honour for me to be part of your extraordinary ministry of sharing the Church's teaching through storytelling.

About the Author

Born and raised in Australia's capital, Canberra, Veronica published her first work at age eleven when a Christmas poem she wrote was printed in the local newspaper.

Growing up, her two main focuses were her Catholic faith and music. After tireless efforts in these endeavours, Veronica is now resigned to being a deeply flawed, though fairly devout Catholic, and a less-than-mediocre pianist.

She married her husband in 2005 and lived with him in his native Mexico for three years till they moved back to Canberra. After returning to Australia, Veronica ran her own one-woman resume and copywriting business for a few years till she decided she'd rather write fiction instead. This novel is the fruit of this labour.

Veronica and her husband Pablo have three beautiful children. She is a full-time homeschooling mum who enjoys reading and photography, hearing about her kids' adventures in Minecraft, and spending some quiet time with her husband, preferably when they're both awake.

Published by
Full Quiver Publishing
PO Box 244
Pakenham Ontario K0A2X0
www.fullquiverpublishing.com